Ascension of Peary

bh alsop

Randall & Whitcomb Publishing

Burlington, St. Johnsbury, Westmore

Ascension of Peary

© 2015 Barbara H Alsop

Cover Art: © 2015 Sarah J. Waldock
Editor: Katrina Robinson
Formatting by Wild Seas Formatting.

Dedication

To the members of the Burlington Writers Workshop for the aid they have given me in developing my craft, such as it is; to Alexey, for many long talks on philosophy and inanity; to Quinne Darkover for countless hours spent discussing, brainstorming, reading, and otherwise pushing me to produce this story in a readable form; and to Ann, for putting up with me through thick and thin as only a friend can do.

Part 1

Home Again

1

I thought I would go wandering, though my fate intervened. My mother always said there had to be more to the world than our little village, and there was rumor of a city if I were to take the high road out. My father died years ago when he and some of the men tried to build a tower of stone, which they hoped to use as a lookout to observe the roads to the north and south of us and warn of any dangers. When the men raised a course of stones, the tower tilted and crushed them all, twenty-three men between the ages of twenty-two and fifty-nine. Only five men in the village remained alive, four grandfers and Olly Bright, the biggest fool anyone would be likely to meet. Olly always had pretensions of running us, and when he became the only able bodied man left, he certainly tried. The old ladies put such a fright into him that he never did more than take his equipment to all the fields of all the ladies in town and plow them for free, or for an occasional home cooked meal.

I was the first of the kinder to reach adulthood after the tragedy, and my mother had said that when I was grown she would make me an explorer to go out and find any thing that could help our town. Privately she told me I was to get far away and stay away because the old ladies had plans for the boys and girls of the town. I loved my mam and would walk to the ends of the earth for her, and it appeared that it was just what she wanted. I was loath to leave the comfortable valley where we lived, for it was green and the soil rich, the water clean, and the air bright. The surrounding mountains protected us from whatever was out there and we had only the high road to the north and the low road to the south. But I did have the itinerant spirit in me, so I was torn between staying in the valley and venturing to the outside. The latter won out at about the time my mam had hoped I would go.

And so, one spring day, I kissed and hugged Mam and she ruffled my close-cropped hair. I was tall and lean, with broad shoulders and long legs, and could be taken for a young lad, and so we hoped I would make my way in relative safety. Mam packed provisions, clothes, a bedroll, a flint, and small utensils with which I could feed myself. She packed cheese, dried meat and fruit, and something she called waybread, which she said would last longer on the road. I picked up the small axe that I had used, since Da died, to bring in wood for the stove, and I slung it through a strap of the pack Mam had made. As ready as I could be, I headed out across our field into the forest. We had decided it was best no one knew my plans, but I doubted Mam could keep the secret long. The old ladies had their ways.

The way through the forest was familiar both from my childhood play and my occasional forays earlier this spring so I'd know the way to the north road. I was confident, if a bit flustered, to be on my way. During my walks I had never seen anyone in this part of the forest, but I was alert to anything out of the ordinary that could delay my departure. I heard many birds and small creatures aloft and under foot throughout the woods. The trees were mature, and their leaves nearly full, though still the bright green of early growth. Only the occasional fir showed the darker green that would be common in a few weeks.

The birds suddenly stilled, and so did I. I slipped into a bushy growth; through its branches I could observe much of the surroundings. I listened for the birds but they did not resume their songs. Instead to my right and about fifty feet away, all the birds suddenly fluttered from a copse I had not previously noticed. I remained still, thankful that my clothing and my hair were similar to the growth around me and would likely keep me hidden. If I hunkered down, I could see better through the foliage. I kept my feet on the ground and did not sit completely, as I wanted to be able to move quickly at necessity.

I heard a low, quiet voice from the direction of the copse, though I was too far away to understand any words. The voice slowly increased in volume until words came into focus. They weren't words I knew, but they were strangely familiar. As the voice got louder, I recognized it belonged to Amerlie, the only old one I'd ever gotten any sense out of. The sound increased until she was almost yelling, and then it ended with her calling my name: "Peary Heathrow." I felt compelled to move but resisted. As the compulsion increased, I got more unwilling to move. My feet grew roots to prevent any reaction, and my arms held my body so it wouldn't betray me.

Amerlie strode out of the copse, not nearly as bent or as withered as she'd always appeared in town. I heard her say, "Where is that damn girl? I was sure she would be here by now." She raised her stick, the one she leaned on in town, and murmured, seeming to speak directly to it. She placed it on the ground and it began to move. It seemed to pull her in my direction though I didn't for a minute believe this was possible. I thought she was trying to trick me, so I sat still. For a moment, I thought I was safe, and then my left calf began to shake. It began to cramp. I had been in this stooped position for too long and my legs were about to betray me.

I heard her laugh. "Come out, Peary, that bush was never meant to be your haven. Did your mam not tell you about me? That, I suppose, is not surprising. I told her in your early days that you would come with me, a vagabond over the whole world. She undoubtedly has forgotten, but you have the mark."

I had no idea what she was talking about, and no intention of revealing myself, if my left calf could just be brought into line. Imagine my startlement when I saw Amerlie's face one foot away from me, at my eye level. She leaned over, using her stick for balance, and poked her bony finger through the branches and at my nose. She laughed, and it was not quite the horrifying cackle I expected. There was warmth to it as it faded to chuckles.

She grabbed my arm and yanked me out of the bush, cramping legs and all. I was astonished at her strength. She pulled so hard that we both landed on the ground, and she broke into gales of laughter. I tried to shush her, but she said, "Oh, don't be silly, girl, I sent the others to the south road."

She got to her feet and pulled me up too. She took my pack, opened it, and put various items into it—a comb, a number of vials, a hat and other things I didn't recognize—though I couldn't see where she got them. The first few objects seemed to come from pockets; then she pulled them out of her hair, her bodice and the air. She put so many things into the pack it should have burst, but when she handed it back, it weighed less than it had before.

"I'll teach you all these tricks, but now is not the time. We must be out of the valley before the sun leaves the sky. Once we are past the barrier, they will not be able to find us."

I looked at her in disbelief. "What's going on here? I'm just trying to find a city or someplace where I can get help for the valley."

"No, you're not and don't ever say anything so ridiculous again. Don't try to speak about things of which you are ignorant. And you are ignorant, and it is my unfortunate task to teach you."

"But I finished school already. What more do I have to learn?" I was exasperated by her insistence.

"Oh, I could kill your mother. How hard would it have been for her to tell you a little about it? No, she had to leave it to me. Listen,

I'll tell you everything if you can just get us out of this valley as quickly as possible. And don't worry about me. The stick is purely for self-protection."

I shook my head, and told her she could follow me if she wanted to, but there was no way I would traipse around the world with a little old lady hanging on me. She harrumphed, saying no more. I walked through the woods with Amerlie behind and underfoot, complaining that I could have found an easier route. We scrambled up one last slope, which was covered with deadfall and leaves from the prior fall and winter, but from the top we could see the short distance to the road as it led into the forest.

2

Amerlie held my arm to prevent me from walking to the road. She sniffed the air, and brought her other hand, finger pointed, to the side of her nose. She stood like that for what felt like several minutes, and then she pulled me down into cover, settling beside me. Leaning over she whispered in my ear, "There is a watch."

I looked at her, eyes wide, and whispered, "Where?"

She held her finger up, pointing; I moved around so I could sight along it. I saw a blue jay sitting in a tree about a hundred feet away from the road on the other side. I must have snorted, as she shushed me insistently.

"That, my child, is the familiar of Margot. He has watched you frequently for the past several months. Have you never noticed?"

I had to think about it, and then realized I had frequently seen the jay in the woods while figuring my way out of the valley. Amerlie saw the look on my face and nodded. "He knows where you plan to go. Give me a few minutes to work on something."

I sat quietly, bemused and feeling that it was out of my hands. My surprise was overwhelming as I saw myself get up, and head toward the road. The "me" I watched had hair a little longer than mine, and she frequently tossed it out of her eyes. She walked to the edge of the valley, looked out at whatever was there, and then turned around and began to walk back down the road toward the village. She was out of my sight for only moments when the blue jay flew after her.

Amerlie grabbed my hand and pulled me toward the road, which we reached quickly. She pushed and pulled me out of the valley, not even giving me a chance to look back one more time at my home. As we stepped over the edge and started down the hill on the other side, there was a heavy fog obscuring the valley, though we had come through no fog.

I stumbled after Amerlie who appeared to have the energy of a five-year old. I looked at her back in wonder; she seemed to grow taller, and her wild white hair calmed and colored to a reddish brown. As her body straightened, her attire reshaped itself into a beautiful black dress that bloomed around her legs. I rubbed my eyes as if doing so would change the vision. Her feet were now shod in black leather walking shoes, and her stick had turned into a cane with an ivory handle. I didn't recognize the style of her dress, for it didn't have the bodice I was familiar with; instead she wore a dark black vest covering a white shirt with a scarf made of a fine material knotted around her throat.

"Amerlie, what's happening? Who are you? Why have you changed so much?" My consternation must have moved her to answer.

"Peary, you are a very important person in this world, and you have been hidden for most of your life to protect you. The men of the village had to die because several of them were asking unfortunate questions, especially those who had been beyond the valley for any length of time. They speculated about the cause of the fog barrier, as well as about who was being protected. The superstitious old fools were saying the rest of the world was going to die and that they were being saved. Enough believed it that they began to behave badly."

"You killed my da?" I nearly cried at the thought of that tremendous loss of life. I stopped and stared at her, wondering if I should go home to Mam. I certainly wanted nothing to do with anyone who'd been responsible for Da's death. She turned and walked back, eyes piercing and brow furrowed.

"It was necessary to keep you safe. It was of paramount importance. I have been your guardian since your birth. The woman you called "mam" has loved you as if you were her own child—in a way that thrilled me, for it meant you grew up knowing your worth, and I don't have to break as many bad habits as I'd feared. We only have a week to get you ready. We'll get on a train at Riverside, and we should be in Springfield by Thursday."

"Train...Riverside...Thursday. I don't understand what you're saying and I don't know these words. How can this be happening? Why didn't Mam tell me?"

"You'll know all the answers in the first five leagues on the train. A train is a big metal carriage that runs on steel tracks and can carry us quite quickly where we need to go."

"How is she not my mother? Who is my mother? And why was I not raised by my mother?" Everything she told me was so strange that I didn't know what to think or how to react. I was scared, with nowhere to turn.

"Oh, I knew you'd be asking me that as soon as I said anything! Better to get it told before we come to civilization."

"What do you mean by *that*?"

"Oh, Peary, the world is much larger than you were led to believe and you have a big role to play in it. Your mother was a very powerful woman in the society we are about to enter, and her title can only pass to a female offspring. She had two sons and bore a daughter only as she was dying¬—from a poison that should have killed you too. It was only through your father's quick thought, and my and my sisters' skills, that we were able to save you. We hid you away so you could grow strong."

"I have a father and two brothers?" I choked up. Could it be true?

"You did the last I heard, though I haven't checked in the last six months and anything could have happened since then. We'll acquire horses shortly and move through a few small towns before we get to Riverside. I should be able to learn quite a bit before we catch the train."

"Horses? I don't know how to ride a horse."

Her look nearly burned me.

I wasn't quite sure I believed what Amerlie had told me. I'd never had reason to doubt her before, but this pretty, red-haired lady was not the Amerlie I knew. She went pensive on me, and I didn't want to interrupt her thoughts, since presumably she was thinking of a way to keep me safe, assuming she was being truthful. I almost laughed at the innocence with which Mam and I had planned my foray out of the valley. It appeared we'd been sadly misinformed about what the world was like.

3

Over the next few hours, I learned my name was not Peary Heathrow, it was Periwinkle von Winthrop-Ransom, and I was due to be the next Duchess of the Duchy of Winthrop. In fact, I had apparently been that since minutes after my birth. My father had been acting as regent in my absence and a glamour suggesting I was being educated far away from home had been laid on the land. The people didn't expect me to return until shortly before my eighteenth birthday when I would be able to take my title.

Of course, it took poor Amerlie a fair amount of time to get this much information into my head. I didn't know what a duchess was, or a duchy for that matter. I didn't know we were part of an empire covering most of the earth—which, I discovered, was a globe. Amerlie tried a spell known to be finicky to impart as much knowledge as possible into my poor spinning head. The spell lived up to its reputation, and I found I knew a lot of interesting facts and theories, but not many that would be useful if I were to take over my duchy from my father. For example, I could calculate the area within any enclosure after making no more than two or three measurements. I could convert any currency into any other currency by using a spell that I could trigger by pulling on my left little finger. I knew we were a magical society but there were people trying to find mechanical answers to our problems. I thought that could prove useful, but Amerlie said it would have been the first thing I'd have learned anyway, since one of my brothers was a proponent of the mechanical, while the other had minor magical abilities. I hoped some of this abstruse information might come in handy at a time when I didn't know what to say or do.

By the time we reached Riverside, I could do a few small spells, like setting someone on fire (an accident), or growing my hair. Amerlie required the latter spell, since my father wouldn't easily believe who I was if I walked in dressed like a boy with very short hair. My hair fell slightly below my shoulders. I wore a vibrant blue skirt cut much like Amerlie's, but with a very frilly light blue blouse. I did however obtain a lovely cape matching the skirt and a dashing hat. I could quite bear to be spoiled if clothes like this were to be my lot in life. Amerlie snorted. She knew, if I did not, I would not be allowed to wear my favorite trousers in my new position. Amerlie bought us tickets for the train and bought me a booklet about the styles and houses of the nobility.

When the train started to move, pulling us out of Riverside, it was all I could do not to scream at the movement of the vehicle. Amerlie gave me a stern look, and I settled down.

"How is my father supposed to recognize me? I mean he hasn't seen me since I was a little thing." At that moment, I would have done anything to distract myself from the ride.

"You're marked. You have a birthmark on the bottom of your left foot the exact size and shape as one your mother had. When the true heir is born to the duchy, she is known by the birthmark. You were conceived because neither of your brothers had the birthmark. There was no way to know whether you would be the true heir until your birth, though the person or persons who attacked your mother clearly hoped that *you* would die from the poison. Your mother's last pronouncement was that your father would stand regent until one of their children either had the birthmark or gave birth to a child bearing the birthmark. When you were born, it was present and perfect. Your father feared for your safety and sent you away."

"Has he heard anything about me? Does he know we're coming? And where's this birthmark? I don't know of any birthmark." I guess I still wasn't convinced.

"It's on the sole of your left foot. You never noticed it? And your father has received reports over the years concerning your progress, although he hasn't been delighted with your tomboy ways."

"My what?"

"It's not considered proper for a duchess to climb trees or play conkers with the boys in the schoolyard. Nor should she play tag with every ruffian child who dares her. You had a wild youth, and I suspect your father thinks you will have no self-control—and plenty of desire for adventure."

"He's bound to be disappointed, isn't he?" I must have looked a little woebegone until I heard her answer.

"You are beautiful and bright. If he is disappointed in you, then I am disappointed in him."

I smiled and leaned back against the seat. I felt much better when Amerlie said that.

4

The train ride was an adventure though it didn't last long enough. Not that I could have seen more of the train or sampled any additional delights, as I would soon be locked away into a world of duty and boredom. Diplomacy was a skill I would have to learn, as well as dancing, fencing, and "riding out to the hunt," whatever that meant. I was also supposed to learn to sew and knit, though I wondered how that could be possible. If I were the lady in charge, I thought, I would choose what I'd do. Amerlie smiled and said my mother had said the same thing at my age. I was already quite anxious when the conductor told us there were three more stops before we would arrive in Springfield.

"Too soon you will feel the heavy yoke you put on your shoulders by returning to your home."

"You made it sound as if I had no choice!"

"You have no choice if you are to honor your mother's wishes. You have no choice if you are unwilling to let your father and your brothers run roughshod over your inheritance and your people. You have every choice if you think only of yourself, but that is what your brothers are doing, and perhaps your father also." She was so serious that it scared me.

"Surely the people, my people, are better off without a lame-brained under-trained duchess."

"I will give you one, not both, of those descriptions. You're not lame-brained, though you are rather under trained but that can be rectified when I bring you to your father. Speaking of which, we should go over proper forms of address before your credentials are verified."

"You mean I can't throw myself into his arms and call him Da?" I asked, playfully.

"Enough. We have work to do."

The closing days of the journey were no different than the opening ones, and I feared, the rest of the days of my life. Learning and practicing, rules and tendencies to avoid, ways to work with people I never would have found in the village I thought of as home. I asked if anything could be done for the woman I knew as Mam. If she could be brought to Springfield to live in comfort.

"Do you think she would be comfortable in the high society of which you'll be a part? Wouldn't she rather stay in the village she has known her whole life with the friends she has always had?"

"I don't think she's ever liked anyone in town except perhaps you. I think the other older ladies scared her witless."

"Perhaps you're right. It's certainly something to think about. I don't know that she'd want to be a lady-in-waiting to you, but she might be content with spending breakfast with you and having you read to her in the evening. I know she's always liked that."

"Did she? I always thought she just put up with me as a noise in the house other than the wind or wild animals. It's funny the things you don't realize another person might find important or pleasant."

Our conversation continued in a desultory manner as the leagues passed beneath the metal wheels. A teacart came around, and Amerlie got a pot for the two of us to share, along with crumpets and chocolate biscuits. It was, she indicated, a way to ensure we weren't peckish when we reached the family seat. As we finished our refreshments, the conductor walked down the car, calling that Duchess's Springfield was the next and last stop. All would be required to disembark.

5

The terminus was an elegant building, at least to me. It was made of red stone and had a beautiful peaked roof that flowed down in four directions. The building was square, with train tracks running on either side of it, and featured colorful coats of arms on its façade. I couldn't keep from staring. Amerlie grabbed my arm and led me away.

"This is nothing compared to what you are about to see, my lady, so come with me. Put your cloak and hat on; they're essential for your presentation. And don't scuff your feet."

"These shoes are dreadfully uncomfortable. I won't wear them when I'm in charge. And I'll wear pants, too."

Amerlie merely shook her head and waved at a carriage that appeared to be for hire. "Please take us to the regent, if you would."

"The regent is off at a hunt, marm, and I dunno when he'll be back." The thin man with wispy gray hair bowed slightly at Amerlie.

"Where does he live now?"

"Oh'm, he's at the duchess's house these days, marm."

"Please take us there, and I expect you to wait for me to discharge you."

"Ayup, marm." He pulled at his forelock and climbed into his seat.

The ride was a bit rough over the cobblestones though no worse than that horrible train. I looked around, seeing what a marvelous place I had come to, and Amerlie told me not to be so obvious about it. There was a hill with a large white castle on the top. I turned to Amerlie in puzzlement.

"Who lives in that castle? I thought the duchess was in charge here. Where's her house?"

Amerlie smiled and said, "The castle *is* the duchess's house, my lady. You will see it soon enough."

I couldn't keep my eyes still. The road was wide with shops on either side. Above the stores were offices of various types; here a seamstress, there a man at law, and farther on was an inn that looked quite prosperous. Side streets irregularly branched off, with small saddleries and dressmakers cheek by jowl with purveyors of gems and jewelry.

The people were as fascinating as the places, all shapes and sizes of both sexes in dress as varied as seemed possible. Here were women in pants and men in aprons, there were women with bustled dresses and men in service uniforms, of which there were many. They ranged from those like the conductor's; to bright-white beribboned; to olive green with patches; to little maids' uniforms, all black underneath and frilly-white on top.

Amerlie finally forced me to look forward and take on as serene a demeanor as possible. It was not an easy task. Our carriage was forced to the side, not once but twice, by young men intent on racing horses and creating potential disaster at every turn. Amerlie ahemed at one young man in particular, but she wouldn't tell me who he was. According to her, I'd find out soon enough.

The road ran around the hill, and subtle as the change was, the stores appeared to be more prosperous, the jewelry in better taste, the meat available in the market of much better quality. With a final turn around the hill, we came to the upper crust's area of the city. Huge houses with magnificent gardens and high fences competed for elegance, class, and alliance with the duchy's royalty. Amerlie murmured the names of the various houses, indicating which were on my side and which were not. There were rather more of the latter than I cared to think on.

Finally the carriage drew up to large, golden, closed gates. A number of soldiers walked the top of the wall that surrounded the castle. A small door within one of the gates was pushed open and a short, wiry man came to Amerlie's side of the carriage. Amerlie murmured softly to the man who then yelled for his brethren to open the gate. The driver chucked at his horse and we padded softly into the courtyard in front of the great doors to the hall.

Amerlie alit and held the door for me. I nearly fell out of the cart, having never been in one before whether in a dress or otherwise attired. That dress was determined to do me in, but Amerlie waved her arm, as if to swat a fly, and the dress fell free allowing me to retain a modicum of dignity. Amerlie nudged me in front of her to walk up the castle's steps. I glided up them as easily as I ice-skated on Windless Lake in the valley. Amerlie later told me she'd had to stifle a smile. I reached the top, and Amerlie stepped ahead of me to speak with the intricately dressed guard in a whisper. He opened the door and bowed me inside.

We entered side by side, and I wanted to believe she was supporting me. I had no clue what investment she had in my success, but I felt she knew something, or many things, she had thus far kept from me. I walked beside her, head held high, down the long hall toward double golden doors which had massive images in relief sculpted on their panels. Pillars lined the corridor, holding an arching ceiling. Pedestals were placed between the pillars, a few with flowers, but more with busts—mainly women. There were several portraits, too, but the light was dim, so that their subjects weren't clear. The pedestals appeared to be made of marble, a substance I had only seen in the ritual box that Margot, the oldest of the old ladies in my village, owned.

Two guards in ornate dress stood at the golden doors, staring straight ahead and standing still, as we got closer. It felt eerie to me, but Amerlie acted as if it were normal, and I took my cue from her. When we finally approached the doors, we paused and it was hard not to say something.

One of the guards finally stepped over to open his door, and a skeleton of a man emerged, "Madam Amerlie, I believe you are aware of your pending death sentence to be carried out upon your apprehension for kidnapping the child. These guards will take you into custody immediately."

"NO!" I said. "I won't have it." They'd take her over my dead body.

Amerlie tried to shush me, but I would not desist. "I will be heard. Do I have to take my left shoe off to prove to you who I am?"

"Sylvester, what's all the fuss about? Who's at the door?" The voice coming from within the room was a little shaky, but whether from age or illness was not clear. I stormed into the room. An older man sat in a gilt chair beside a throne-like monstrosity, his head in his hand, his elbow propped on the arm of his chair. He stood when he saw me, and demanded, "How dare you? Who are you?"

"Would you like to see the sole of my left foot? Father?"

"Amerlie, get in here!" he yelled.

I was surprised at his assumption that Amerlie was here.

"Where did you hide her? I want answers, and I want them now."

Amerlie calmly replied, "You can hardly expect me to tell you anything with a death sentence over my head."

"Why should I believe this is my daughter? Why shouldn't I suspect you of nefarious deeds? Bringing some other girl if my daughter died of that damn poison. You owe me answers and I will have them."

"Excuse me," I said. "Don't I get any say in this matter? Don't you want to look at the damn mark on my damn foot? You've seen it before. You saw it when I was born. It had a slight peculiarity. Can you name it?" How dare he put a death sentence on Amerlie?

Amerlie sighed and looked away.

"You couldn't fake that, could you, Amerlie? Were you going to let me rant on and make a fool of myself?"

"She's your daughter, my lord. I told you I would bring her back with no evidence of the dreadful flaw she acquired from the poisoning. I told you it would be a long time to ensure she was no longer affected by the toxin. I only saw proof of that two weeks ago, and we began our journey to return here that very day."

"What are you saying, Amerlie? How did I change?"

The regent answered instead. "My child, you inherited from your mother a link with this place, a feeling of rightness that you should be here. It was what I always hoped would awaken within you, so that, even if Amerlie had deserted you, that connection would bring you back to your home."

"Amerlie?" I asked.

"He's right, Peary, as long as you were content in that village, the poison still had a hold on you. You needed to feel an overwhelming urge to leave the valley before I could be sure the evil within you was gone. Your mam came to me the night before you left, saying you were antsy, eager to be wandering. She told me you wouldn't make it through the next day before it took you. That was why she had your pack ready when you came down to breakfast that day. And why I had to send the other biddies to the south road. They could not see how you looked when you left."

"I don't understand."

"Let me guess," said the man who was, apparently, my father. "Your eyes were a deeper blue, your hair was wild and your face was flushed as if with too much sun."

"How do you know?" I was confused again.

"Because your mother had a similar appearance once when we were traveling in another part of the land. Her mother had died unexpectedly, and she'd immediately felt the need to come home. It is, more than the mark, proof that you are the heir to this ugly piece of furniture."

"Then you *are* my father."

He rose and came to me, held me by the shoulders and looked into my eyes, and then he embraced me in the biggest hug I had ever felt. He whispered in my ear that he had never stopped loving me, and that he'd been terrified that when I finally showed up, I would be a fraud. I pulled away and sat on the monstrosity to pull off my left boot. I held my foot up so he could see my map of the duchy on the bottom of my foot, with the bright-red star at exactly the center of Duchess's Springfield. He sat in his gilt chair and rubbed my foot lovingly. I felt peaceful for the first time in months. I was home.

6

The first thing I did was to talk my da out of killing Amerlie. It wasn't as hard as I thought it would be. He realized she had kept a good eye on me for a long time under horrendous circumstances. For almost eighteen years, she'd had to act like a shriveled old lady without a whole lot of magical ability. Her new role, as my magical tutor, would keep her busy for a time, but she seemed happy to be back in the real world again.

The next big event was meeting my two older brothers. I could tell Da didn't want to influence my opinion of my siblings, but there was clearly something he wasn't saying. I wondered if this was something I could do, sense when someone was being less than fully honest with me.

I met my brother, Henry, at dinner the first night of my arrival. By this time, I had settled in to the main suite and knew all about the secret passageways leading to parts of the castle. Earlier that day, a maid had come with two seamstresses right after lunch, and they poked and prodded me, measured, and held various cloths up against my face and hair. I had no say at all in what they made, though I tried to get them to make something in a brighter blue. One of the seamstresses told me I would have more say in my clothing when I reached my eighteenth birthday and had a little more experience in society. Amerlie had gotten to them, obviously, and told them royal blue would not do. Instead they built a beautiful, if young looking, empire waist dress of a golden silk with the merest hint of green. It brought out the blue in my eyes. I didn't know what they'd done to my hair, but it had grown at least five inches since I'd left the valley.

I went to the dining hall with Amerlie by my side. She looked spectacular in a brushed rose dress with a brocade print. I thought I looked quite washed out next to her, but she said that she felt she looked raucous next to me. We laughed together and walked arm in arm into the dining hall.

Sylvester led me to the head of the table, while Da sat at the foot. Amerlie was seated next to Da, and I felt deserted. A sneering fop sat to my right, and he introduced himself as my brother, Henry.

He indicated that he thought I was a bumpkin who would need all the help he could give me. I turned to my other side and met Lord MacAlpine, an older man with gray hair and a stunning white mustache. During our conversation, I learned that he was an old friend of my mother's and saw her in me. I begged for him to tell me more, and he obliged, leaving me free to eat a good portion of the magnificent food in front of us. I managed to stay occupied with Lord MacAlpine for the majority of the feast, which allowed my older brother to stew in his own juices. I felt a little petty about Henry until my father winked at me and lifted a glass in my direction.

As the main course was taken away, my brother rose to make a toast. I gritted my teeth for I was sure I would be insulted.

"Here's to the return of my delightful baby sister, who has grown into such a swan to grace this court. May her ruling be as magnanimous as she has been to me this evening." The guests rose and lifted their glasses to what they thought was a poignant toast, but both Amerlie and my Da caught the deep dig beneath my brother's words.

After the meal, we all moved to the drawing room, where the artificial, forced intimacy of the dinner table gave way to the ability to roam for ever-greener pastures. Lord MacAlpine put my hand in the crook of his arm, patted it, and said that he would introduce me to all the old guard who had waited so long for this moment. I went happily with him as Amerlie tackled Henry, and steered him toward my da.

I met a number of people whose names I wouldn't remember the following day, but that was one of Amerlie's tasks. They were all quite jolly and lightheaded by the thought that the monstrosity would again be occupied. I was careful not to call the throne by my pet name in front of them. They were reverent about the hallowed throne, which they persisted in calling it. When I queried why it was called a throne when there was an overlord, they laughed. The overlord hadn't been here in years, which was just as well because the emperor would not be pleased to learn of an heir who was missing for almost eighteen years. One of the people Lord MacAlpine introduced me to was the head of the exchequer, and I made a point to tell him I would like an early appointment. I was stunned by his response, as was Lord MacAlpine.

"Oh, don't you worry your pretty little head about the numbers. I report to Henry and we have everything in order."

"I assure you, I am not worrying my head. Do you need an order?"

"Well, shouldn't your brother be there at the meeting?" He was surprisingly condescending.

"I'm sure my father's advice will suffice. Tomorrow at ten in the morning? Bring all your books and accounts for the last five years. That will do for starters. Goodnight, Mr. Pusivey You may want to leave early to ensure you're properly organized for our morning meeting."

I walked away, again accompanied by Lord MacAlpine. I turned to him curious about his reaction to my handling of Pusivey. But Lord MacAlpine was chortling and waving two of his special friends over. He excitedly told them how I had ordered the exchequer to come with all his papers for the past *five* years! They all congratulated me on taking the reins so quickly and establishing who was in charge.

I had to admit I wasn't technically in charge yet, not for about three months. They scoffed it off, saying that my father had waited long enough to get someone he trusted to handle the affairs of the state.

"Doesn't he trust Henry?" I asked as innocently as I dared. They wasted no time in telling me about my brother's dissolute life and sneaky misuse of funds obtained from the exchequer. They seemed to think this wasn't news to me, and I wasn't about to disabuse them of that belief. I had much to talk with my father about and hoped he too was an early riser. I doubted my self-indulgent brother would rise so early.

The evening continued and I met older friends of my mother who were clearly cheered by my arrival. Da and Amerlie spent most of the evening together, mending fences, I suspected. I was still taken aback by Amerlie's true age and appearance, and Da seemed to be enjoying himself.

I corralled Da and Amerlie to discuss what had tweaked my suspicion, as well as what to expect in the morning. Neither was surprised when I reported the comment by the head of the exchequer, and Da agreed it looked suspicious that Pusivey had tried so hard to keep me from the financial records. Da asked Amerlie and me to join him in his suite for breakfast and we agreed.

As I headed off to bed, I noticed one of the guards walking behind me. He stepped ahead of me as I came to my door.

"Let me check first, my lady. People do strange things when strange things happen." He entered the room, which was well lit, and a maid came out of the bedroom, fussing with her buttons.

"What are you doing here, Wilfie? You'll get in trouble, boyo!"

she said. Then she jumped when she saw me by the door. "My lady!" she cried.

I dashed by her to the bedroom in time to see a panel closing by the head of my bed. I grabbed an unlit lamp off the dresser and threw it at the panel, hoping to jam it from closing. My aim was as good as it had been in the valley.

Wilfie ran to the panel and applied a little pressure; a mechanism engaged and it slid open again. He grabbed a lamp to pursue the individual who was in the passageway, and looked up in time to yell, "Watch out!"

I ducked and the vase that the maid had hoped to bash me with fell harmlessly out of her hand to the floor just as a second guard arrived and grabbed her.

"Go!" I yelled at Wilfie and he was through the panel in a trice. The second guard had the maid firmly in hand and hollered for support. Within seconds two more guards arrived from different ends of the hall. A loud whistle sounded throughout the tower, or at least, it seemed so loud to my ears.

Needless to say, because of this incident, I didn't get to bed as early as I would have liked. Amerlie and I were moved into my father's suite. It meant I wouldn't get lost trying to find his rooms in the morning, which was of minimal comfort.

T

When I awoke in the strange bed in the morning, I had to think for a moment to remember where I was. The events of the prior evening came hurtling to the forefront of my mind and propelled me from the bed. I must have made a noise because the maid who I'd met in my own bedroom earlier the prior day appeared at my door, asking if all was well.

"I am eating breakfast with my father this morning, and I don't know whether I have the appropriate attire for such an event."

She curtseyed and said, "My lady, there are clothes for you in the dressing room, and I would be happy to assist you."

"What's your name?" If she was to be my maid, the least I could do was to know that.

"Daisy, my lady."

"Well, Daisy, let's go to the dressing room. Lead on!"

The dressing room was, if possible, even bigger than the bedroom. It held a clothes press, enough mirrors for a dozen seventeen-year-old girls, and a separate staff who tried to send Daisy away. I wouldn't have it!

"Excuse me," I said, trying to keep calm, "but this is my maid and I want her to stay. You do know who I am?"

The two dressing-room maids sullenly bowed their heads but didn't curtsey.

"Leave this room and do not return to it until I have gone back to my own suite. Am I understood?"

One of the maids curtseyed and said, "Yes, my lady."

The other glared at her and said, "You can't do that. I'm Henry's maid when he's here and he won't allow it!"

Daisy gasped.

Without expecting much, I called out, "Wilfie?"

Moments later, I heard a couple of people enter my bedroom and come into the dressing room. One was Wilfie and I didn't recognize the other.

"Wilfie, I want this woman detained for suspected treason." I felt oddly in control. I don't know how I came to say this, but it seemed right.

"Yes, my lady." He took the woman roughly by the arm and left with her and his companion.

I then turned my attention to the remaining maid. "What do you have to say for yourself? You knew who I was the moment I walked into the room."

"Excuse me, my lady, but she told me if I didn't ignore you, she would make me pay worse'n she ever has before. An' Sir Henry lets her do anything she wants. I'm so sorry, my lady." She began to cry. "It's so wonderful having you back!" I turned to Daisy and asked her to take care of the maid. I would call for Sylvester; we would get this straightened out.

I returned to the bedroom and noticed a robe of sorts hanging over the chair. I put it on; it was clearly made for me. Then I rang the bell I had seen near the door in hope that it would bring a servant. After several minutes, just as I was about to pull the bell a second time, a knock came at the door.

"It's Sylvester, mum."

I asked him to enter but I wasn't prepared for his disheveled appearance. His fine black coat was coated in grime and what surely must be rust and I notice a tear in one sleeve. The look on my face must have prompted him to explain.

"I'm afraid I have very bad news for you, my lady. I had planned to get cleaned up before I reported to you. Ought you to sit down to hear what I have to tell you?"

I sat on the edge of the chair, and said, "Well? What's the news?"

"The head of the exchequer is dead and all of his papers have been destroyed or damaged beyond hope of repair."

"No!" I jumped from the chair, my hands clutching my head. "What have you found out about it?"

"My lady, I came as soon as I had received and confirmed the news. I must go back now to learn more. If you could get dressed and come to the crown room, you'll hear it as soon as I."

I nodded and returned to the dressing room, where Daisy had calmed the other maid. "I must dress quickly. There is bad news of a political nature and I need to go to my father. Could you help me dress? We'll work out the other issues as soon as I am done. My dear," I said turning to the second maid, "you must tell me your name, since I can't call you 'other maid' and I want you to stay as my dressing room head maid."

"Oh, thank you, my lady. I'm Alyssa, and the light blue gown will work splendidly for a council of the high about political doings." She bustled off, taking Daisy with her, into a vast closet off the dressing room. They returned expeditiously with a gown and unmentionables, shoes and stockings, and what I guessed to be a makeup kit.

Daisy helped me undress while Alyssa produced the unmentionables. When that stage was done, I laughed at the expressions on their faces.

"What is wrong, you two! You both look astonished, or is it horrified, at something!"

"Ah, my lady," Daisy said, "you are beautiful, and this dress will do you up proper, make no mistake."

It was Alyssa's turn to be horrified. "Daisy! You can't say such a thing to the Duchess!"

I laughed, "Why ever not? While we can't be open friends, I see no reason not to be friends in my own rooms."

They pulled the lovely dress over my head. It was made of a light-blue fabric of a type not seen in my valley, with little buds picked out all over, cap sleeves and an empire waist. They sat me in a chair, and Alyssa worked on my face while Daisy tried to bring order to my hair.

In a matter of minutes, they had me in front of a mirror hoping for my approval and showing me how to stand so I could also see my back in a mirror across the way. My old mam would never have recognized me. My hair was pulled, somehow confined, in the back by the most beautiful thing I had ever seen. Daisy slapped my hand away when I tried to touch it.

"I'll show you one like it, but please don't mess up what I worked so hard to put right."

I acquiesced and said I would look upon my return, but at that point my main priority was to find the crown room. Alyssa nodded and led me to the door where there were now two guards. She whispered to one, who flushed and then bowed at me.

"My lady, I will show you to the crown room. Your father doesn't wish you wandering alone at this time, since it's clear, he says, that someone is up to no good, and we can't lose you as soon as we've found you, my lady."

He steered me through hallways I thought I'd begun to figure out until we came to a level I hadn't yet seen. We approached a door that had a gilt crown in its top panel. The guard knocked and then opened the door.

8

The room was somber, with walls of dark wood at the bottom and above painted a bluish gray. Shelves along one wall held books and several scrolls that looked as if they might be maps. My father and Sylvester were seated on one side of a large, square table in the center of the room. On the other side of the table sat an obviously belligerent man.

Sylvester saw me first and said, "My lady, thank you for your speed."

My father chimed in, "This fool may listen to you if he won't listen to me!"

The man turned a chilly eye on me, and I surmised my father was incorrect in his analysis. "Perhaps if you would tell me who this fellow is, I could have a few words with him."

"He is the second-in-command at the exchequer," my father said, "and he's reluctant to allow anyone not directly employed by the exchequer into the offices where his superior was found early this morning, deceased."

"His name?"

"My name is Lapsitarie and I will not be talked about in the third person."

"Oh?" I said. "Do you owe *me* no courtesy?"

"I haven't a clue who you are, young lady. A witch brought you here so you could be just about anybody, as far as I'm concerned."

I called for my guard, who entered a little suspiciously. I asked if there was somewhere we could put this intemperate man to cool off a little. He suggested something he called "the closet," and my father laughed at the suggestion. Even Sylvester was trying to avoid smiling, while our target said, "You wouldn't dare!" I accepted my guard's suggestion, and indicated for the man to be brought back before me prior to the noontime meal. Lapsitarie was unceremoniously bundled out of the room, crying for forgiveness as he went.

It seemed that the closet in question was a new method for human waste disposal, and depending on the mood of the guard when they got there, Lapsitarie could be put in either the upper or the lower chamber. The latter, I gathered was the worse of the two. In one, only the smell was offensive, in the other it both reeked and was nearly impossible to avoid coming in contact with the material there.

"Will you come to breakfast now, my dear? I'm sure Cook is quite angry with us for these delays!" Upon my assent, Da placed my hand in the crook of his elbow and we walked side by side to the small dining room in his suite. My wonderful guard had apparently alerted the kitchen as we arrived only slightly in advance of hot food.

We sat at the small table beside the floor-to-ceiling windows where we had a lovely view of the city and the lands beyond. Only a moment or two after we were seated, Sylvester came in to announce Amerlie's arrival. She followed him in, and my father sprung up to greet her and helped her sit where we would all benefit from the lovely view. We filled her in as we ate.

"Da, why was the second-in-command so against telling us what he knows?"

"Likely he was involved in whatever was going on. Why? What have you heard?"

I shared the tale of the maid who had relied so much on Henry that she wouldn't curtsey to me. "She wouldn't use any honorific, I was only 'you'. I got mad and pulled rank on her. She's being held for treason."

Amerlie said, "It appears Henry was fully intent on treason. If he was so comfortable with the thought of ruling, he *would* let a maid act that way, wouldn't he?"

"He must have been very upset when I walked through the door and was welcomed with open arms by the only one who could firmly identify me." I tried to feel sorry for him to no avail.

"But how he thought he, as a man, was going to rule in this duchy, I have no idea. He has been difficult since he was about eight years old. I wonder if one of his tutors ever mentioned the right of the firstborn to him. There are only five or six states where the firstborn succeeds no matter the gender. Most of the states are ruled either by male or female, and they are about evenly divided in number." Da was pensive as he said this.

Amerlie said, "About two hundred years ago a group of men decided it was shameful to be ruled by a woman. Or so they said. It was widely speculated at the time that they were more after the lady in question's coffers than her power, since her principality was a very wealthy one. My foremothers performed a study that was quite surprising. They looked at all the duchies and principalities that had women leaders by right, and compared them with those with male rulers.

"The results were fascinating, and I expect they would hold true today. Regions run by women were almost fifty percent more productive than their male-ruled counterparts. Then, they looked at the lands that abide by the firstborn rule, and found they were closer in productivity to the women-ruled states. They concluded that the level of disputes in the male-regulated states was much higher than in either of the other two groups. Any thoughts?"

I was stunned by this revelation. Having known nothing about this duchy or my place in it before arriving, I found I absorbed knowledge at a much higher level than I had in the valley. I knew manners of speech and control of emotions that were well beyond what I had learned with Mam. When I mentioned this, Da and Amerlie smiled.

"This is further evidence that the poison is gone from your system," Amerlie said. "The person you are meant to be is pulling herself out of the abyss. When you sense her, a little bit of her merges with you. This is why you know how to behave with unruly servants."

"I understand the poison didn't affect Periwinkle the way it did my wife, but I don't know why."

"Our best understanding is that the poison had two properties. The first suppressed magical ability and we are fairly certain we can identify that part of the poison. We have known of it for centuries. We have used a form of it, pramip, when highly gifted magic users are having a difficult accession of their magic. It lowers the magical impulse so that the new witch or wizard survives the transition.

"We think the other property of the poison was triggered by the attempt to use magic because the prior duchess didn't deteriorate when she slept—only when she was awake. Something you will find out, Peary, is once you have learned magic, you'll be constantly on the cusp of using it. The little things you do now aren't significant enough to cause this to happen, but you'll see what I mean."

"You mean it was her constant attempt to heal herself that killed her?" Da asked. The anguish on his face brought tears to my eyes.

Amerlie too looked grief stricken. "Isobel was my best friend growing up. Her mother allowed my presence because I could keep her under control. When I wasn't here, she would unintentionally fire off bolts of lightning and spears of energy at the most inopportune moments. My presence calmed her down enough that she could have better control over magic. The first time you kissed her, Robin, my presence in the background saved your life."

"Oh, I'd forgotten that nickname. You and she were the only ones to still use it as I grew older. When Henry was in his teens, he used it as a way to hurt me. He would taunt me, using that name or, worse, Robbie, knowing I could never beat him in a fair fight, and he never fought fair. I kept him close to make it harder for him to plot against me, but if the exchequer is any example, I obviously didn't keep him close enough."

"Perhaps it was the only plot he tried, and he continued to pursue it because he could," I said. "He doesn't strike me as a man of powerful intellect or of charismatic charm."

"That's because you're immune to it. His primary magic is an overwhelming charisma. It's why he's something of a leader, and something more of a lover. If you felt it every time you were near the castle, or where he was hunting, you'd understand how intrusive it was. Our only means of sanity was to walk great distances at night, tiring ourselves out, in hopes of sleeping past ten o'clock in the morning, with breakfast at noon. It meant several hours that would have involved being affected by broadcasts from Henry were now carried out peacefully, at least within a community of women in this state." Amerlie's face reddened as she spoke, her hands clenched at her side.

Robin spoke, "I wish you had told me. I had influence on him when he was young—"

Amerlie cut him off. "No, don't believe it. He had a good tutor who told him to appear cowed to you. It was another effort to lull you into complacency and I wasn't here to protect you. None of the others who remained here were strong enough to help as I could have, but I had to take the stronger ones with me to protect the duchess."

"I don't blame you for that, Amerlie, because she was more important than I. I'm sorry I doubted you so much as to put out a death warrant on you."

"I knew about it as soon as you did. My sisters still in the duchy proper could get news to me. They begged me to bring her back, even if she wasn't ready, and the old biddies I took with me intended to keep her for themselves, so they could return in a wave of glory after the 'men' had torn the place up. Neither of these situations was your vision or mine. I brought her back when she was well and ready." Amerlie took a deep breath. "Now we must look to today's crises."

9

Shortly thereafter, Sylvester came in with the news that Henry couldn't be found in Duchess's Springfield or any of the near surrounding towns, villages and farms. That put one concern to rest at least momentarily.

But I broke the peace. "Has anyone mapped the tunnels and passageways throughout the castle? I'm just surprised that creep and the maid knew about them."

"Not so surprising," said Da. "Your brothers explored every inch of them they could when they were younger, and I'm sure Henry told those two exactly how to get to your room."

"Who and where is my other brother?"

Sylvester replied, and until then, I hadn't been aware that he was still in the room, "He was found about three this morning in a drunken stupor at one of his favorite watering holes. We've traced his movements for the night and the only time he's unaccounted for is between about eleven p.m. and one a.m. Unfortunately, that's the time we believe Henry left the city. He isn't completely in the clear, although reports from the bar he was at until eleven place him even drunker than he was when our guards found him."

"If he's still out, I may be able to read him," Amerlie said. "At least his intentions, if not his memory or thoughts. Those always get messed up by alcohol, and he's been drinking a lot lately."

Sylvester ushered Amerlie out, and Da turned to me. "I don't want you to worry about this, darling. We have good people on our side, and when you come into your full strength on your birthday, you'll be unstoppable."

"What's his name? The drunk one?"

"He's Chresterley. We call him Chres."

"When will I get to meet him?"

"When he's sober and recovered—and not before!"

We then discussed what to do with the rest of the day. I thought there might be a wizened old guy at the exchequer who was still loyal enough to walk us through what we needed to recover the information. Da thought the idea was a brilliant and said he had a good candidate to find that guy. He rang the bell and asked for

Willery to be found.

Willery arrived about five minutes later, and I almost laughed. His sheep like curls of off white on top of a sheep like face ensured that I'd always think of him as Woolery. He even had a smear of black ink on his nose that contributed to the overall effect. I managed to keep an interested, if stern, look on my face, thanks in large measure to my attempts to deceive Mam in the valley. When Da explained to Willery what we needed, he was delighted.

"I know just the man; the rectifier."

"Who's the rectifier?" My father and I were almost a chorus.

"His name is Dandifer. He's as old as the hills, but the head couldn't fire him because he was given a lifetime appointment by the late duchess. He's the one who rectifies the accounts and I *know* he keeps copies of all he's done."

Da yelled for the guards, ordering them to find and protect Dandifer at all costs, and to recover his files if possible. If Henry and his cronies really had planned this scheme with great precision, we might already be too late.

"If he's got the wind up, he may go into hiding," Willery said. "And I got a good idea where!" Before we could respond, he was gone.

"Is it always like this?" I asked. "We send people off to do all the digging and we just sit here and wait?"

"We could go through Henry's rooms. He's never as careful as he thinks, and I know where he has a few hidey-holes for things he wants to keep safe, and not tramp over the countryside with. Shall we? Or do you want another cup of coffee?"

After we finished our coffee, we headed off to Henry's rooms, the obligatory two guards behind us. When we arrived there, we saw two guards Da didn't recognize standing at the door. Da and I continued to walk by, speaking casually to each other, acting as if nothing was up. We turned at the next corner and waited for our guards to do so as well. When they didn't, we looked down the hall and saw they were engaged with and losing to the strange guards. Da yelled at me to stay where I was and ran toward the combat, pulling two knives out of his boots.

I followed, wondering what I could do, and suddenly I realized I could do only one thing. I pointed at the bigger of the two strangers, and *pushed*. He flew through the air, crashing head first into a stone pillar and falling, motionless, to the ground.

The other stranger was taken down quickly once the odds had changed. My father stared at me, and our two guards wouldn't even look my way.

"How did you do that? You shouldn't have that power until you're eighteen," Da said.

"I don't know. I felt it coming out my finger so I pointed it at him. I have no idea how I did it, and I certainly can't control it."

He looked angry somehow, but I didn't understand why. When Amerlie joined us, though, he calmed down pretty quickly.

When she saw what I had done, she came and put her arms around me. When I struggled a little, she whispered that I had killed him. I stood still for a moment and then started bawling. It was a funny thing, how I could feel so mature one moment, and like a little girl the next. I was definitely the latter then. I had never killed anything bigger than a rabbit for our dinner in the valley. To kill a human being, no matter how evil, was something I didn't think I had the right to do.

10

After the mess had been cleared and our guards were established at the door, we went into Henry's suite, Amerlie first because she feared booby traps. She found two in the entryway and disabled them quickly. She pulled out the evidence of the spells: in one case herbs and a smelly rat skin, in the other a stringy mass that was turned in on itself with feathers and beads at strategic places. Based on the evidence, Da was happy to let her continue on point. They moved on to the inner rooms, but something held me in place. I sensed something evil and finally guessed that I was standing on top of it. I got down on my knees and pulled the carpet back, revealing a tiny trap door. I immediately realized I would be better off with Amerlie by my side and called for her.

She came into the room, and yelled, "Don't touch that!"

"I have no intention of touching it! That's why I called you," I said but she paid no attention. Her eyes were on one thing only.

She called my father and told us both to get out.

I headed for the door, but Da stayed by Amerlie's side until I came back, grabbed his hand and pulled. We waited outside behind a pillar. I had never been so nervous. That trap had felt so much worse than either of the prior ones. Suddenly we felt the castle rock, the stones vibrate. After a few seconds, it stopped but I was already running back to Amerlie. At first I couldn't see her, but then she stepped out from a closet, and showed me the string she had attached to the trap door and used to pull it open.

Da rang a bell and asked one of his captains to survey the damage to ensure everyone was all right. He didn't seem sure there was any point in trying to go further into the rooms today, but Amerlie was adamant that they continue.

"With this level of defense, I'm sure he left something here—perhaps something he needed to keep here if his plan is to work. We now know he has a black-magic user in his group...unless he's using black magic himself."

"What if anything did you learn from Chres?" I asked.

She looked at me for a minute and then said, "He doesn't know which side he is on. He loves his da, he's scared of Henry, and he thinks you're a myth."

I started laughing when I heard the last. "We can disabuse him of *that* belief, don't you think?"

We continued our search, and I noticed a place on the wall that didn't look right.

Da came over to look and laughed. "I showed him how to make a keeper when he was five and wanted to keep Chres out of his things."

Amerlie came over and looked at the keeper. She ran her hand over it two or three times and looked puzzled. "My reading shows it's empty, but I can sense something in there. Would he expect you to search personally, Robin?"

"I doubt it. He thinks I'm still under his charisma somehow, and I have certainly led him to believe that I don't suspect him of anything, when in fact I suspect him of everything."

Amerlie told us to step back as far as we could from the keeper. She found an old fishing pole in the closet and used it to trigger the keeper. The fissure opened to a round hole. Da took a lamp from the table and walked toward it, but Amerlie put her arm in front of him, taking the lamp and approaching the hole herself. She reached in and pulled out a sheaf of papers. After rifling through them for a moment, she gasped.

Da was at her side within a second. He took the documents from her hands and looked at what had caused her to react. "Oh, damn!" he said.

"Please, one of you, tell me."

Da hesitated before saying, "We may have evidence of an attempt to assassinate the emperor. Take over the biggest female-based units, of which we're one. Put the dauphin on the throne and have an edict calling for the repudiation of female rule. My own son. I-I, can't believe it."

"Da, what if it's a trap? What if he left that here so you'd get caught with it? We have to protect you above anyone!"

"No, sweetheart, you're the one."

"By the time all this comes to fruition, I should be fully awoken, right? Then it's you we have to worry about, since I'll be able to protect myself."

We were interrupted by the guard's reappearance with a report on the castle's integrity. "None of the foundation is damaged, my lord. There are a few places that may need shoring and I have people working on it. The only person hurt was a scullery girl who had boiling water poured all over her when she went to pick up a dish for washing. I sent the healers down and they said it shouldn't be a problem. A few paintings fell off the walls in a number of places, but that's it. Any other damage must be within the apartments themselves. I suspect we'll be hearing from those parties in the next day or two."

"Any news on Dandifer?"

"Only that he's been seen by a lot of people downtown—the guards found him in a bar and were trying to collect a fine that he had failed to pay. He refused and went back outside to find much of his stuff had been stolen."

It was a common bait and switch. The guards were in on it, Amerlie told me, and it was a sad state of affairs. It would change under my hand, and quickly.

II

We returned to Da's sitting room to evaluate the documents. The first was a letter from someone calling himself "Liberator" to someone called "In Waiting." It gave information about the emperor's itinerary for several months including a stop in Duchess's Springfield. It provided exact details of the route the emperor would take, and the stops that would have to be made. And all the marked positions were in areas controlled by women.

"Why is he only going to places ruled by women?"

"My question exactly," chimed in Amerlie.

Da's knowledge of the land was deemed to be encyclopedic. He rattled off the names of the female-ruled districts, and they were all on the list. Only two male-ruled districts were being visited and they were firstborn districts. He was not going to any male-ruled land where to rule, one must be a male.

"Do you think," Da said to Amerlie, "he's planning to change the rules and looking for our advice, or is the emperor coming to change the way we've existed for as long as records exist?"

"He can't change the way a magical succession works, and ours is certainly one of those. His magic doesn't allow him to tamper with the magic that establishes a land's rule. Of course, less than half of the lands have a magical succession and most of the male successions don't."

Other documents proved to be interesting. After reading and commenting on the things we found, we now knew there were four leaders of the conspiracy and the goal was to turn the empire into a male-dominated society. There was even a hint that the dauphin was involved, or at least on board with the plans. He would help them when he succeeded his father. The empire itself was a firstborn system, and the dauphin was the eldest child, though all his siblings were princesses.

"If the emperor finds out the dauphin is involved, maybe he'll disown him and we'll get an empress!" I was so excited at the prospect I momentarily forgot the seriousness of the issue.

After we had gone through each of the documents several times, we decided on a council of war. The goal was to figure out how to save the emperor and me, how to catch the conspirators, and how to notify the female rulers of the possibility of violence within their borders and directed against them.

"My biggest concern is who we can trust," Da said. "I would never have expected Henry to go so far. I thought he was just a thief, living high on his sister's money. If I can't see it in my own son, how will I see it elsewhere?"

Amerlie had a solution. "One of the witches in this city is a truth-teller of significant repute. I can contact her if you like."

"How do we know she's trustworthy?" I asked, genuinely unsure.

Amerlie smiled at me. "I've known Derona since childhood, and we've worked together a lot over the years. She's the only one outside your father and the witches in the valley who knew about our plan to keep you safe there. She's the one who passed messages on to your father, although he didn't know it. If you'd like I can have her come by this afternoon and meet with us."

When we both agreed, Amerlie went into a trance-like state for a few minutes.

"She's available, and she has wonderful news. There's a new seer among us, and she'll bring her around with her. They should be here around three this afternoon."

I asked about the seer, curious to learn more.

"The seer's name is Melalee. She's only sixteen, but she has the soul of an ancient."

"Age doesn't seem to be an issue in magic, does it?" Da asked.

"Only when it's an inherited grant, like with Peary."

"How young can a witch be?" I asked in surprise.

"The youngest I've known was six years old. She had a very special ability; she could see ghosts and communicate with them. As she grew older, she developed other talents, but she never lost her communication spells.

"When she was twenty-two years old, she was killed by an irate survivor who didn't like what she was reporting from his dead father. He smashed her head with the ale jug he was carrying. She never regained consciousness. The witches nearby managed to get the assailant, and he was tried for murder."

We paused to think on that short life and were taken out of our musings by the arrival of Sylvester. He had come to report on the search of the secret passages, and he had interesting news.

"Henry had an entrance into the back passages from his room which was fairly recently constructed. I found the builder who worked on it, and he was told it was to allow Henry a faster route to his father should anything go wrong. The poor man was worried he'd done something wrong, but I assured him he was fine.

"Henry also had a map, which we found in the passages, in Chres' childhood writing; so it was something from way back, and doesn't indicate Chres was involved in this at all."

Da said, "That doesn't surprise me. Chres was a wonder at maps of places he'd only seen once. Henry was not graced with that talent. In fact, Henry couldn't draw at all."

"Was there any other news, Sylvester?" I asked.

"We heard from Willery—Dandifer has been found. He's slightly the worse for wear. Apparently he had a run-in with the guards. He says he didn't touch the corpse for it was obvious the head was gone, but he ran out to 'get extra courage,' as he put it.

"The guards have sent out a very large party to retrieve him and Willery, and if everything goes well, they should be here in an hour or two."

"That's really good news, Sylvester," Da said. "You've earned your keep once again!" He chuckled at the offended look on Sylvester's face.

We were just finishing enjoying sandwiches and tea when Sylvester informed us that Willery and Dandifer had arrived and were in the kitchens being fed a much heartier meal than we'd had. Since Dandifer had a large number of documents with him (There were documents!), it was decided that we'd meet in the library so we could spread out the papers more easily.

We finished up and headed for the library, anxious to see what we had. Of course, then we had to wait for over half an hour for the two men to arrive. But it was worth the wait.

Sylvester showed Willery and Dandifer, a large, stooped, old man, into the library. They both hastily removed their hats and bowed first to my father, who shook his head, indicating that they should go elsewhere. Willery got it, grabbed Dandifer (who was bobbing up and down to my father) and pulled him until he looked my way. A lovely little smile graced his face, as he once again bobbed up and down. Willery looked pained as he bowed.

"You can stop bowing now," I laughed. "Have a seat and we'll get started."

A servant came in carrying a small chest, which he placed beside Dandifer. Without looking up, Dandifer turned and opened the box. He pulled out a stack of papers that looked like ledger sheets. He glanced at us and smiled again. "I made a clean copy of all the accounts because he occasionally wanted to check something after wine was spilled or whatever." His voice was low and soft.

Da asked, "He?"

"Oh, you know, Pusivey, the head. He thought I was simple and could only copy cleanly. I did a little more than he expected though. I first noticed something strange over ten years ago, and it turned out Pusivey was being bribed. That went on for about five years and I didn't know what to do. Then suddenly the money was going to someone else, and it was hard to figure out since it was going to different places. But it was the same amount each month as before. Here, I'll show you." He got up and rifled through the papers, pulled out three, and laid them in front of us.

The first page was incomprehensible with its multiple columns and tiny numbers randomly in various places on the page. I was soon to find the numbers weren't random.

Dandifer pulled out a long thin piece of wood with a pointed end. He leaned over the table and used the stick to point out certain items. "In all of these over here, the amount entered as owed was about ten percent over what the bill stated. When you look over here," he pointed to another series of numbers, "this is what we paid to the vendor, and next to it is the difference, but that part never gets summed. Look at the bottom line." He was getting excited and waving his pointer a little. We saw what he pointed at. In spite of the numbers in the higher rows, they had never been added to the box next to what was actually paid.

Da slapped his brow and said, "And I thought he was being a brilliant negotiator, saving nearly ten percent on all our bills. I complimented him on his abilities. What a fool I was."

"No, sir," said Dandifer. "Look at where the page folds. You wouldn't have seen any of the entries above, see. There was nothing there for you to see. How could you know? Only I knew, and he'm thinks I'm simple. Ha!" He laughed heartily. He looked very pleased with himself, and Willery grinned as if he'd won a tournament or something.

"Can you show where this money went?" Da asked. It started Dandifer laughing again.

"Why, certainly, sir. A ledger isn't balanced 'til every dime is accounted for. Here, let me show you where I found these missing pieces." He again started pointing at numbers that were sums of the numbers we'd seen earlier, but they were on different lines of the page and represented payments made to someone else. On the first three ledger sheets, we could see the money went to "Cilipher," which Dandifer thought was an alias, since there wasn't any evidence of an individual with that name in any of the invoices. The name had changed once in the first five years he had known about this situation. He couldn't remember the name used prior to Cilipher.

Then he showed us another change that occurred about five years ago. Again he produced three sheets, showed us the same points, and noted that the amount of the theft had gone up to closer to twelve percent. Dandifer then pointed to the name that received the money: Peregrin.

"Don't you think that's a little close to Periwinkle? Peri 'winkled'—or she grinned." And Dandifer laughed again. "He was trying to point the finger at his little sister, who wasn't even in town!"

"When did you figure this out?" Amerlie asked.

"Why, I never had a thought on it till our duchess returned! And then I knew immediately. Oh, it was glorious." He grinned and his eyes twinkled. "The reason I had the documents with me was because I was getting prepared to bring 'em to you. My request for an appointment was received yesterday, and young Willery came this morning to warn me that I might get my chance today. Course, he couldn't find me where I shoulda been, but he knew where I'd be. I weren't staying in a building with a dead body, no, sir!"

"Did the later payments ever go to anyone but Peregrin?" I asked.

"There was one funny one, where the person who usually picked it up didn't appear. A day later, a man came and said he was picking up for Peregrin. But Pusivey wouldn't give it to him unless there was advance notice, and only Peregrin knew how to do that. This happened about four months ago, and Pusivey was nervous from then on. I guess he had good reason, poor sod."

Amerlie pounced. "Did you see this fellow?"

"I saw him, right enough. I was in Pusivey's office bringing up the week's books, and this man comes in, looking peculiar. He had a very red face, like he was hot, but he had on about five layers of clothes—and this is when it was hot outside. He musta been hot. His pants looked like they had seen better days, with the cuffs all frayed and the knees sticking out, and they looked too big for him. He had dark hair, and looked like he'd missed a shave or two, and he had the longest, skinniest nose I've ever seen."

"Would you recognize him if you saw him again?" I asked.

"Only if he was dressed up funny, 'cause otherwise I wouldn't have looked at him twice."

Da said, "I'm worried you may still be at risk. You should stay in the castle for the next few days, and you must be in the family wing because it is harder to sneak in there. Willery, can you arrange that?"

"Of course, my lord. Come with me, Dandifer, and we'll set you up."

When they were out of earshot, the three of us looked at each other and talked eagerly.

"I don't think the evidence convinces me it was Henry," Da said. "I know someone had taken over the blackmail operation, but it would help to know who began it in the first place."

Amerlie chided him, "You're looking for anything to make your son look less culpable, but remember the traps and the secrets we learned in his room this morning. If he wasn't involved in the money heist, where was he getting his money? He certainly has been acting as if he has a steady source of income, more than you would've likely given him."

"He gave me no reason to love or protect him last night," I said. "His words were hurtful, that toast was a joke, and he wanted me to let him ramble on for the whole meal. It was wonderful to have Lord MacAlpine next to me to let me escape.

"I'll stay out of the money argument. I have too little knowledge of the world to be able to comment other than superficially. I don't like him, and I don't want that to color my thoughts."

Da looked unhappy at my declaration.

"Please don't think I take any delight in this," Amerlie added. "I remember Henry when he was five. He was so generous and nice with his younger brother, and so sweet with adults."

"Ahem, my lord, your other visitors are here." Sylvester seemed to know he had interrupted Amerlie and was not the least apologetic about it.

13

Sylvester led Derona and Melalee into the room. Derona was a middle-aged woman, slightly frumpy, with salt and pepper hair. Melalee was a shy and washed out girl, with dirty blond hair, sad eyes, and a simple shift that did nothing for her appearance.

Smiling, Amerlie walked over to them and said, "How wonderful to see you again, Derona. It's been far too long!" She hugged the older witch for a few moments. The friendship was clearly mutual. Amerlie then turned to Melalee and said, "Do come in and sit down, you look so tired. I'm sure your main talent is responsible for your fatigue." She led the two witches to the couch and indicated they should sit down.

Before sitting, both turned to Da and me and curtseyed. Amerlie blushed at the error she'd made. She told them I was the Lady Peary until my eighteenth birthday, and my father was Lord Robert, and then she apologized to us both.

Da turned to Sylvester, and signaled for tea. Then he spoke to the witches. "Welcome and thank you both for coming. We have something of a difficulty right now, and you both have skills that would help us greatly. Did Amerlie fill you in?"

Derona replied, "I only know there appears to be a question about loyalty after a murder in the city. Is that the problem?"

"I'm afraid that is only a small part of the problem." He then went on to describe my encounter with Henry's maid, the problems with spells in Henry's room, and the problem at the exchequer, which may have had something to do with the murder.

"My fear is that my son was part of a conspiracy and there is no way to know who in the castle has taken his side. It would be easy to convince us of loyalty, but we wouldn't know—couldn't know—if we were making the right decision. Your assistance would be invaluable, especially if you could do it under cover. But since I don't know how your magic works, I may be completely off track." Da looked at Derona as he paced before the windows.

She replied softly, "My talent takes two forms, and one is suited to under cover work. It is, however, the more fallible side of my art. I can read someone much better by touching their bare skin. For instance, I know you told me what you believe to be the truth just now. The best I can ever say with the touch is I'll have absolute certainty you're saying what you consider to be the absolute truth.

"Well, someone may say completely truthfully that they know nothing about an incident. With proper questioning, the person can remember things that establish that he does in fact know something about the incident, but he doesn't realize he knows it. It's by no means a precise magic, though with the contact, I can come much closer to knowing if an individual is unaware of something or if he's really without knowledge."

"What if the individual swore to tell the truth before you read him?" I asked.

"Then I could tell quite easily, without even touching the person, whether that person told the truth as he knew it."

Da asked, "Do you know whether we are all the people we say we are?"

"Oh, yes, I knew it as soon as I walked in the door. I could tell from your auras you were honorable and honest people."

Amerlie then addressed Melalee, "Are you able to see anything here? Or do you need a special setting to have visions?"

"I have no control over when the visions come, and sometimes I don't ever know the people in the visions. But now, I can make sense of at least one. I have seen you, Amerlie, and haven't known it was you. I have seen Lady Peary also, and she's been in your company. You're traveling together in the late summer, and your clothes suggest you're hiding who you are."

"Couldn't this have already happened?"

"Not unless my Lady Peary has recently cut her hair."

Amerlie and I looked at each other. We both knew my hair had never been longer than it was presently.

"Is there no one with us? " I asked, uneasy for a reason I couldn't name.

My da looked troubled also.

"No one else in any of the outdoor visions I've had of the two of you, my lady."

Amerlie pressed her, "How many of these visions have you had?"

"I saw you come out of the valley through the fog. I saw my lady in a bright blue skirt with a matching cape and hat. I saw the two of you with his lordship in the room with the traps. And I saw what the traps did. That scared me enough to tell Derona, and she recognized you, Amerlie, from my description. That's why she suggested I come with her this afternoon. She thought I might figure out more about the visions here."

"Do you know where they were when you saw them in the late summer?" Da asked.

"No, for it was a forest and it had nothing distinctive in what I saw. I've seen the young lady invested as duchess, but there's family strife involved. I couldn't tell the source of the conflict, but I know it wasn't a difficulty between you and your father."

As I was about to ask another question, we heard a gentle knock on the door, and Sylvester entered. He announced to my father that Chres was here and requesting to see his sister.

I spoke up, "Now would be a good time for Derona to try to read a family member. Do let him in, Sylvester, but please tell him we're entertaining one of Amerlie's old friends and her daughter."

"Very good, my lady."

My father laughed and said, "I've clearly spawned a politician with tricks up her sleeve!"

In a matter of moments, the door was again opened and Sylvester announced, "Chresterley to visit, my lady." He backed out, winking at me. I rose to my feet and reached out my hands to Chres. He hesitated briefly and then came to take my hands and kiss them both.

"Is it really you? I haven't seen you since I was three years old, and you don't look at all like you did then!"

I leaned over to him and kissed his cheek. To my surprise, he blushed.

"Please let me reintroduce you to Amerlie, and this is her friend Derona and her daughter Melalee. Now come sit by me and tell me your whole life," I said, "I want to know you!"

"I'm just shocked that you've come and brought Amerlie back with you! I remember Amerlie as a tough taskmaster, keeping Henry and me in line and educating us in the ways of the world.

"And I'm doubly glad you're back, because it means I won't have to get married as soon as I was being told."

The conversation became general, and we moved around the room. I managed to get a private moment with Derona and she assured me that my brother was devoted to me. She felt he was anxious about something and he didn't know if he should to tell me about it. If I were gentle with him, she said, he might open up.

I saw Chres talking quietly with Da, and I worked my way towards them without being obvious. I was stopped briefly by Melalee who told me she had seen me with Chres in another vision but hadn't realized it. In the vision, Chres seemed to be saving me from something. He looked panicked as he pulled me back from either a pit or a body of water and she couldn't be sure which. She thought I should be friends with Chres because he was important in my future.

When I finally reached Da and Chres, they were discussing Henry. Chres looked at me as if he didn't like talking about Henry in front of me.

I put my arm on his shoulder. "I'm very happy to have you as a brother."

He smiled a very crooked smile, and I saw Da gleam at that. It turned out Chres had been asked to join a plan of Henry's, and he had declined. As a result, Henry sent nightmares to Chres, and he had started drinking to put himself into a stupor so that Henry couldn't get in.

I asked, "How could you tell it was Henry? I don't know much about sent dreams, though I suppose I should learn about them, huh?"

"They all started with that nasty little laugh he has," Chres replied. "Sometimes it's like there's a storyteller, and that guy is always Henry. The storyteller says I murdered our mother, and poisoned you too. That's why you had to go away, to get away from me because I was a danger to you. And I'd started believing it in the dream, as he'd show me all the ways I could have given our mother the poison. Occasionally I'd argue that I'd been too young when she died, and he'd tell me that I wasn't his brother; I was a demon." Chres was shaking by this time, and I hugged him harder.

He went on, "In every dream, he'd tell me he could kill Da in a way that made it look as if I did it. Sometimes, awake, we'd be just sitting around in one of the drawing rooms here in the castle. He would give me more drink, but there'd be something in it that would make my mind go funny. Then he'd show me something he said I did while under the influence the night before. It was always evil. Once he showed me a murdered child and said he'd had to haul me off the child, but couldn't do it in time. Then he'd say I was just practicing to kill Da." Chres was nearly in tears, and he looked longingly at a carafe of wine on the sideboard.

I said, "I'd rather hear your story without the alcohol. I know it'll hurt you more, but it'll also allow me to believe you and not worry about what you learned in dreams."

Da added his voice. "I have no difficulty believing that Henry did these things. But I know he's gone now, at least for a time. I don't think he dares to come back, especially if he knows we found the hidden documents in his rooms. He'll know something has happened when he hears that we're all still alive even though one of his traps was triggered."

Amerlie, who had approached quietly during this discussion, said, "There was black magic in more than one of the traps he set. That tells me all I need to know to confirm what he was doing to you, Chres. If you want, I can give you a tonic tonight that will help you sleep and act as a barrier to his intrusion. He'll sense it as drunkenness but it'll actually be peaceful and restoring sleep. What do you think?"

By then I was holding his hand, and I squeezed it. "I know from experience Amerlie can make miraculous tonics. She got me through a couple of really tough times with her treatments. Go on, Chres, give it a try. If it doesn't work, you can get drunk then."

He grudgingly agreed, though he longed for drink, and said he could meet Amerlie wherever she wanted.

Da interrupted, "Well, if you'll spend the evening with us, have dinner with us, you should be in the same place as us at the time the tonic is needed." Chres's smile was a little weak.

I saw Derona trying to catch my eye. She was slowly shaking her head as if to say "no." I nodded her way.

Derona stood up and said, "It's time Melalee and I were heading off. We have a few errands to run before dinner. It was so delightful to see you again, Amerlie, and we can't thank you enough for introducing us to the duchess and her father." She and Melalee curtseyed to us both, and Amerlie walked them out.

Sylvester came in, asking after dinner plans. Could it be set up in Da's sitting room, at the breakfast table? Sylvester indicated it could and that he'd better go make sure it was ready.

14

We had all assembled in Da's sitting room to see the table pulled several feet from the window, with the angle of the table pointing toward the window. There were two seats kitty-corner to the window and two who could see out the window at an angle. Da and Amerlie took the seats with their backs to the window, while Chres and I sat facing the window. We chatted lightly with laughter as we awaited the first course.

Chres crowed in delight that the appetizer was a shrimp salad confection. I quickly applauded his speech as I had my first shrimp salad ever. It was delicious and called for a toast. We had a light wine as the aperitif, and then red wine with the service of deer from Da's hunt yesterday morning. There was only one glass with each, but Chres didn't seem troubled by it. There was a light dessert but no wine with it, to my relief. Chres didn't need another glass and I didn't want it getting in the way of Amerlie's tonic.

Amerlie left for a short time after dinner while we moved to the couches in the sitting room. Chres and I sat cozily together, speaking quietly while Da lit his pipe. I often wondered if the smell of it was so comforting because I was remembering the few days I spent in this house as an infant. Amerlie, I was sure, would say it was a ridiculous thought.

When Amerlie returned, she had a flask with her potion in it. Chres looked warily at it, but seemed surprised that he was willing to take it.

"I want us each to drink the tonic tonight. When Henry finds he can't enter Chres's mind, he might try for one of ours. It's unlikely, but better safe than sorry," Amerlie said. We watched as she poured a little of the potion into four glasses. There wasn't much in each glass but Amerlie seemed sure it would work for all of us. "We won't drink until just when we are ready to depart to our rooms. Chres, Sylvester has made up a room for you here, because it's possible this is the last place Henry will look for you. If you start having a Henry dream, I want you to say to yourself, over and over if necessary, "Wake Up' as loudly as you can. It's an old but tried and true way to wake from externally imposed dreams."

Da said, "I'd rather not take it. I want to see if he dares come to me. I have my doubts he's strong enough to enter my mind without my permission. He's never been able to best me when the odds are fair in a purely mental way."

"Da, don't forget he has a black-magic user in his camp," I said. "*He* might not be able to get you but the black wizard could. That's probably how he got to Chres before, allowed the black wizard to piggyback on his signal to him—and he could do it to you."

"I'd like to get a chance to tell my oldest child what I think of him."

Amerlie settled it by saying, "None of us is strong enough to take him tonight. We've had a long day with the expenditure of much emotional energy over this problem and also in searching for the person who invaded Peary's room last night."

Chres exploded, "What? Peary was attacked? How? Weren't you all watching her?"

"Hush, it was nothing." I said, then explained the whole story to him, downplaying anything that might make him nervous or upset. He seemed to accept that it was not a major issue, but was visibly saddened to hear that one of his childhood maps allowed the aggression against me. I told him I thought the map was beautiful and wanted to keep it. He smiled, saying he had no objection to my taking all of his maps.

When Da and Amerlie saw the state Chres was in, they decided perhaps it ought to be an early night for all of us. Amerlie gave each of us a glass of her concoction. I looked at it a little uneasily because I remembered her tonics tasted either very good, or very bad. There was no way to tell, so I just tipped the glass up and drank. Over the edge of the glass I watched Chres; it appeared he was at best sipping the tonic. I raised my eyebrows to Amerlie, and she too looked at him.

She said, "Chres, stop playing with your tonic. Drink it down like your father and sister." She started walking toward him and that was all the impetus he needed; he swallowed the remaining fluid in one gulp.

The greenish tint to his face suggested he had let the tonic spend too much time on his tongue. Chres said, "I feel a little queasy."

Amerlie had a spell for that and she settled him down easily. He now had no excuse to spit it out, and he knew we knew. He sighed and said he thought he was ready for bed. Da and Amerlie were ready to escort him to his room for the night, and his eyelids were drooping even before he left the sitting room. Mine were also heavy and Wilfie was there to take me to my room in this section of the castle.

15

When I awoke the following morning, I felt as refreshed as I had ever felt since Mam's husband died with the other men. I found I couldn't call him Da, as I did when he was alive, for now I had my real Da and the connection was so much stronger and more complete.

Apparently I wasn't the only one who felt reinvigorated arising from the depths of sleep. Chres was practically bouncing out of the house that morning, but we made him come back for breakfast. Looking at any of us, one would have thought we had partied all night, as we had such obvious satisfaction about our time together. We gathered one by one in the sitting room, which had again been set up for a meal for four.

When Da went to look out the window, I screamed at him to get down. As he began to duck in and away from the window, an arrow flew through the opening, missing him by inches and sticking into the chair he would shortly occupy. I don't know how I knew he was in danger, but the need to cry out was intense. I called for Wilfie who appeared immediately. He recognized it. It came from the hunters of Henry's group, according to the fletching.

I showed him the apparent trajectory and from where I thought the arrow had come. He walked to the window and stared brazenly in the direction I'd shown.

"There's a number of men running in the direction toward where the archer must be! It looks like they're chasing a tall thin man I've never seen." Wilfie said.

Then the man came around a corner, still visible to us but for only a moment, when he disappeared. His pursuit came around the corner and slowed to a stop, confused and looking around. Wilfie whistled sharply and they looked up. He cupped his hands around his mouth and roared, "He disappeared. Poof!" They seemed to understand, shrugged, and went back to their stations.

"Can't we just arrest everybody who uses these arrows?" Chres wondered.

"No, because only one person with those arrows has the right address. He is our wanted man. He must be gone for us to protect the duchess. If you find him, kill him." Amerlie was very stern of a sudden.

Da looked at us and said, "Oh, my children, I hoped this would never come in your time, that one of our family could so thoroughly betray the rest of us. You know he must act quickly since he must succeed before Peary is eighteen. Then she'll be too strong for him and the black-magic wielders he's with."

Amerlie began to pace the room. She muttered to herself, "Should I go down there or is it too late to sense a trail? If he's the black one, I won't be able to. Oh, what shall I do?"

I went to her and shook her a little. She stumbled and looked at me, smiled weakly, and said, "I'm sorry I wasn't faster. He may be the last link we'll have. But there was black magic involved again, and I can't tell if he used it or if there is a wizard here helping him."

"Why would there have to be one here? Can't the one on the other end grab him back on a timed run?" I had no idea if there was another wizard involved.

"Someone on the other side wouldn't know he was nearly captured here. There would have had to be someone here for him to escape as easily as he did."

"Then we haven't lost the lead," I said. "We know we're looking for a black wizard here, and it can be done surreptitiously. We're in charge on this side, and we can say we're just trying to get an accurate count of true wizards in the area, because of new fraudulent claims or something."

"Now that's something I haven't heard of before but it could work. What do you two think?" she said, turning toward the two men. They looked up from their perusal of the ground below, with lost expressions on their faces.

I repeated what I had said for their sake, and we waited for one of them to reply. Finally, Chres said, "It's bloody brilliant!"

Da wasn't so sure. "I've always had a strong relationship with the wizarding community around here, and I wouldn't like for them to feel put out by this inquiry."

"Surely they'd be interested if they knew there was a chance Peary would be killed if they didn't cooperate." Amerlie was almost begging him.

Chres added, "It's three against one, even if the one is the regent."

Da laughed. "I can't fight two women and my remaining son!"

16

We called for guards to accompany us down to the area below as if we simply wanted a breather from the troubles of the day. We walked quickly down the stairs and out the nearest portico, finding ourselves in the plaza where the archer had tried to take out the regent. As we walked to the area where we believed the arrow to have been shot, we were met by a number of students along with a sprinkling of professors. The students all wanted to report what they'd seen.

Amerlie approached a group of students and asked if they knew anything about what had just happened, and whether they'd felt black magic. One of the younger boys said the focus against black magic is the thing everybody thinks about when something out of the ordinary happens. He didn't think it meant black magic just because someone could fire an arrow and then disappear, because that ought to be a spell anyone could learn with enough practice.

Amerlie laughed and told the students to look around and try the walls, the windows, anything they could think of. "Do you know what you're looking for?"

One bright lad said, "A black wizard will be awfully strong and will feel strange."

"Wouldn't that include our new duchess? Her magic is strange to you and she's pretty powerful, even before her eighteenth birthday."

"No way! Can we meet her?"

"Maybe if you find the black wizard...."

The students grumbled but began to look carefully around the area, both on and above ground. One young student indicated he had found a strange trace. Amerlie rushed over to sense it and agreed it was odd although the likely culprit was the man who had disappeared around the corner.

She suggested he try following it; he could figure out which way to go by how strong or weak the trace was. He quickly noticed that the trace wasn't along the path the shooter had taken. Amerlie and he followed it to a culvert under one of the towers that took rainwater out of the town.

Amerlie called for us to join them and then she became quiet, summoning local witches to help in the search. She found one named Mariamne who lived near where this culvert emptied. Amerlie asked her to go toward it cautiously, hiding her magic, and acting like a bread woman. This was a ruse the witch had used before, and she was reasonably confident her fresh baked bread would contribute to her disguise.

The guards who had been protecting us decided that four of them should go down the culvert. To their knowledge, the culvert had a magical mesh across the bottom that wouldn't allow anyone with ill intent to pass through. The mesh was capable of detaching from the wall and capturing anyone with bad intent. The guards included two who were magical shields and they would take the forward position in case the mage they were seeking was still free and prepared to fire on them.

As we hurried around toward the postern gate, I asked Amerlie what a magical shield was in a person. She said, "Most magical shields are born, not made. A magical event triggers the magical shields and they suddenly realize that they must go and help the people in danger. When arriving at the scene, they can't be harmed by any of the more powerful wizards, as they seem to have a personal shield that can expand to help a large number of people at one time. The army has sought out magical shields trying to convince them to enter war on the side of those against the magic users. But shields are themselves magical creatures and do not respond to pleas."

"So we're sending two to protect the rest of us by destroying the magic user. Right?" the young student who'd found the trace asked.

"Absolutely. Who's your tutor?"

"Derona, and she's great!"

"I didn't know she had returned to teaching."

"She said she came back because the demons have arisen again, and our only hope against them is to have more and better warriors. And solidarity."

"Definitely the latter! What level are you?"

"I'm still only a lower rank since I have trouble with the more mundane knowledge. But Derona gave me a board game and I'm getting good enough at it to start strategy again."

"Would the game happen be to chess, or dragons and soldiers?"

"She calls it chess, and names the figurines accordingly. And she's whizzbang at it."

"You wouldn't by any chance be Mikal, would you?"

"How'd you know that?"

"Derona and I have been good friends since long before you were a glint in your daddy's eye. She has her eyes on you as a major player in the future. In another year, we can start determining where your strengths lie...or do you already know?"

"I think I'm an historian, by nature. I like to know who we were and where we came from. I'd like to see more use of history because I'm sure there were great spells we've lost and talents that have disappeared because we weren't paying attention."

"You're a treasure, my boy, and when you're ready, assuming we're still a matrilineal society, you will be a boon to the new duchess and her government."

"Why wouldn't we be a matrilineal society? I mean, isn't it the magic of the place that makes us so?"

"That's certainly true, and most likely the reason we shall succeed in the coming conflict. But there's a group of people, men predominately, that say there is no reason for the weaker sex to be in power."

"Man, are they crazy? We know in school that matrilineal societies are much more successful than patrilineal societies. Why would we want to change?"

17

On the far side of the culvert, Mariamne went out with her fresh-baked bread in a basket. She was walking toward the culvert as a short cut around the base of the hill to the postern gate. She heard a loud boom coming from the direction of the big pipe. She looked curiously in that direction as anyone would who'd heard such a noise. She looked a little afraid as one might be. Then she hurried away without running. Haste was the watchword. Then she heard a loud clang, and looked back to see the grille blown off the end of the culvert, and a wild looking man came out. She didn't recognize the man, but her terror now was real, and she stumbled away as quickly as she could. But she wasn't fast enough, as she heard the speedy blast that bowled her over. Crying mind to mind to Amerlie, showing her the picture of the man, she breathed her last.

18

Amerlie gasped, and clutched at the boy and me. She was trembling and looked faint. I held her as well as I could, and guards moved forward to help me lower her to the ground. I chafed her hands in an attempt to bring warmth back into them without much luck. Finally she lifted her head up and told us Mariamne was dead. The black wizard had blown out the gate, taking her with him. Amerlie formed in her mind the image translated to her by Mariamne. I couldn't bear to see it, the horrible face of the wizard, the hate he bore her and us.

I put my hand around Mikal's shoulder as he was still several inches shorter than I. He leaned against me for a few minutes. He looked shocked at the image sent from the dying woman. "I've seen him before," he said. "He's been dressed like someone at court or from the upper town. I'd know him if I saw him again."

Amerlie pulled herself up and looked at Mikal. "Where did you see him, Mikal? Was it near the palace?"

"He's been here since yesterday. Or at least that's when I first saw him. He drank at the Pig and Whistle. I saw him with Sir Henry on a number of times throughout the day. You must know that the Pig and Whistle was one of Sir Henry's favorite drinking places." Mikal appeared almost drugged in his delivery, as if he were fighting for every word. As I watched, he slid from under my arm to the ground unconscious. Amerlie rushed to his side, and fell to her knees as I had done, and between us we brought him around.

One of the schoolteachers, Belvedere by name, came over to see what had happened to his student. When he heard that the boy had seen the black magician, he asked Amerlie to show him. He, too, recognized the man, and thought he might be able to put a name to him.

"Mikal's right; he has frequented the Pig and Whistle, but he's also visited the Collegium occasionally over the last month or two. I don't know whom he was visiting there, but surely that can be discovered fairly quickly. I know Mikal and I are not the people this man came to see. I'm afraid we have someone in the Collegium who is involved in a way with black magic." He sighed before finishing, "But we'll help you in any way we can."

"Thank you for your help in this, Professor," I said. "I ensure you and Mikal will be given full immunity and whatever magical protection we can supply."

"My lady, I didn't recognize you at first. We're delighted to have you home and are looking forward to your investiture."

Mikal stuttered, "Are y-y-you the d-d-duchess?"

"I will be in under three months. And you'll be there too." The look on his face was priceless, and encouraged me more than it had any right to do.

I went over to Amerlie and put my arms around her. She had lost a friend to a fiend, and I could do nothing to comfort her other than to be present.

Within moments, two guards came back to report there wasn't enough left of Mariamne to do more than scrape a little for an urn. An overseer was on his way to get what was possible into a proper receptacle for a service.

My party, including the professor and the boy, returned slowly to the castle.

19

The next morning, we visited the Collegium, Amerlie, Mikal, Belvedere and I. We intended to question the gate guards, the dean, the chaplain and anyone else our initial inquiries sent us to. Our first stop was the gatekeeper who we assumed let him in. This was an awkward encounter, since the gatekeeper was old, and apparently hard of hearing.

Belvedere took the lead. "Tom, Tom, can you hear me?"

"Ya don't need to yell, I'm not deef."

"Were you working here two days ago?"

"What? Speak up, yer mumblin'."

This went on for several minutes until it was finally determined Tom had worked each of the last fourteen days, and he was peeved about it.

"Did you see a strange tall man with wild black hair and beady eyes?"

"Ya mean Professor Meildy?"

"I said a strange man!"

"He be strange."

"I mean a visitor who you didn't know."

"Lots of 'em. Ya want the tall one with the half bald head or the tall one that smelled peculiar or the tall one that wanted to see Professor Rasmus?"

"What about the tall one to see Rasmus?"

"Sent him away for Rasmus on leave this year."

"I'm looking for someone who came back a few times over a period of a couple of weeks."

"That be the smelly one."

"Who did he want to see?"

"He want ta use the libry. Professor Smedley say it okay."

"Did Smedley know the man?"

"Don't think so. Knew someone in common I think."

"Is Smedley in now?"

"Likely."

We set off to find out exactly what "likely" meant. Belvedere knew where Smedley was likely to be if in Collegium, and led us in that direction. He said, "Smedley is the head of the Arcane Magic Department and he could be up to anything—perfectly innocently—since he believes everyone is innately good. He lives in a dream world where evil never treads."

Amerlie and I looked at each other and nodded. We had a common mind on pompous men who had no idea how the world ran. We were prepared for the worst.

Silly us.

We entered a hall with the word "Science" carved on its lintel. There was a large auditorium on the first floor, partially dug into the ground so that all in attendance might see. It was empty. We climbed broad stairs to the second floor where we saw long corridors with doors on either side. None of the doors we could see had a sign or number by which to identify it.

Belvedere led us to the first cross hallway and turned left. In this corridor, there was only one door on the right and two on the left. He led us to the door on the right and rapped his knuckles against it quite sharply.

After a few moments, he was preparing to knock again when we heard a muttering from inside. The door was flung open, revealing a very small person in a suit of gray velvet. "What do you want?"

"Is Smedley in?" Belvedere asked.

"Oh, it's the master you're after, eh? Well, he's gone to town, and I could have spared you the trouble of coming up here if you'd believed that little twit down in the gatehouse." He cackled.

"I swear I would look through the fields and the byway of this town, if I were your master, to find another who could laugh as sweetly as you. You are lying as at least three of us can tell. Where's his office?"

"He uses several, but he has a favorite one, across the hall."

"Which of the doors?"

"Must I do all the work for you?"

Belvedere turned to look at the two doors, and then went to the right one to knock. A woman came to the door and identified herself as Mrs. Smedley and could she help us in any way?

Belvedere looked her up and down and said, "I don't believe you're Mrs. Smedley."

Since Amerlie and I agreed with Belvedere, we were anxious to hear her response.

"How dare you! I've worked for Mr. Smedley for over fifteen years and I never missed a day of work until we were married and took a honeymoon. Since he wasn't working either, I didn't think it counted."

"I've worked at the Collegium for twenty years myself," said Belvedere, "and all the married professors bring their wives to a number of functions each year. He has never brought you, and has maintained as recently as three months ago that he would never marry, since it would weaken his magic."

"Oh, that's an old joke of his. I don't do parties and he says it to protect me."

"Why don't you have a talk with these two friends of mine, Amerlie and Peary? I'll be back in a few minutes after I've taken this young man where he needs to go. Then we'll talk about Smedley." She agreed, and Belvedere and Mikal went off down the hall.

20

Amerlie and I entered the room. It was an appalling mess. There were signs of a little cleaning in one corner, and the woman led us there to sit at the one clean table. There was nothing on the table to indicate it had been in use before we knocked on the door.

"Tell me, ma'am," I said, "who does the cleaning around here? It looks as if this room has somehow lost its turn in the rota."

"Oh, we wives take turns and I've been trying to get away from my work to do my turn, but you know how it is when you're really excited by your real work."

"Oh," said Amerlie, "what is your real work?"

"I can't be telling," she said, with a look that I guessed was trying to be coy. "People steal each other's work so much I just keep it close to the chest."

At that moment, the door opened and Belvedere and Mikal entered. The look of repressed excitement on Mikal's face told me all I needed to know.

"Well, ma'am," said Belvedere, "I checked with Amory and he tells me his best friend doesn't even have a cleaning woman, let alone a wife. So would you mind telling me who you really are?"

The woman in front of me started changing into something else, and I couldn't tell what. Amerlie pushed me behind her, and Belvedere did the same to Mikal. Once the transformation had ended standing before us was a monster. At moments like these, I wished I'd stayed with Mam back in the valley.

The creature was over six feet tall and had four arms and two legs. Its head was roughly the shape of a skull, and completely black, like the rest of its visible skin, which was quite a lot. A loincloth was all that covered the creature's lower half, and a black fur was pulled across its chest. I had no idea if it was male or female, and I didn't suppose it mattered much.

"I should have guessed a demon!" said Amerlie. "You're in league with that black wizard, so he was more active than I thought. Are you here to keep watch over Smedley, or have you already killed him, planning to take over for him?"

I noticed Belvedere and Mikal were moving so the demon was

the center of an equilateral triangle. Oh, that was one of the things I learned from that teaching spell! I didn't know if I could contribute, but I felt very much like I had when I *pushed* the strange guard. I figured I'd stay where I was and lull the beast into believing me harmless. I wasn't prepared for what it did next.

It reached over, although I couldn't see what was doing the reaching, and then I was immobilized, being drawn closer to it. I didn't like the feeling; whatever potential for magic I had at that moment was boiling out.

Each of my companions was weaving a spell to protect me. I hoped that I wouldn't hurt them when I exploded. And then I did whatever my body was trying to do, and freed myself from the demon's hold. In the process I'd apparently burned it as a horrendous stink filled the room. Amerlie and Belvedere threw massive spells at the demon and it fell to the ground, smoking from every place smoke could come from.

Amerlie went to the demon, and enveloped it in a casement of some sort. I could see it but didn't understand it. She spoke to the demon, "You'll stay in this tomb without sustenance or care until you tell us about the plan you're a part of. You must also tell us if Smedley is alive and where he is. If he's in the custody of your conspirators, you will not be released until he is returned intact and alive. Do you understand?"

"You don't stand a chance." the demon replied, in a scratchy, deep voice. "Your way of life will die. I am immortal. Do you think I care if you hold me for a year or two?"

"Try forever! You've attacked the ruler of this duchy. Do you honestly believe they'll ever forgive you? Unless you beat us completely, you'll stay where you are *forever*. And if we figure out a way to kill you, don't be surprised to wake up and find yourself dead."

I laughed at that last statement and then paused, "Amerlie, I just felt something from him. He turned his attention to me."

"That, my dear, is part of your magic. You're a little ahead of where you should be. When you're invested, you will know if there are other demons in your domain. Your protective magic applies not only to kin, it applies to all your people."

Belvedere said, "But he's not giving us information, and our magic can't reach him any more than he can reach us. It's a dead issue."

"Not exactly," I said, reaching toward the box, and wiggling my fingers. The demon howled. "Are you willing to tell us where

Smedley is now?"

"Smedley is ... at the ... culvert ... stuck in the wall."

"In the culvert wall or the wall above the culvert?"

"Culvert."

"Is he alive?"

"Should be."

"That should be a task for the Collegium, surely," said Amerlie. Belvedere agreed and headed off to find the appropriate authority to start the recovery process. Amerlie invited Mikal back to the castle for an information session since he may have seen or heard things she or I had missed.

We left the room with the case and its unsavory content following as if on a leash from Amerlie's left hand. Mikal stayed on the outside of the case, to Amerlie's left, to ensure no one touched it on the way to the castle. I was on Amerlie's right side trying to be as observant as possible. Unfortunately I was so unfamiliar with the sights that I was almost useless in my viewing of the crowds and the buildings.

Amerlie was murmuring a running commentary as we walked along, in part, I'm sure, trying to teach me. I tried to follow her swiftly changing gaze, but more often than not I missed what she indicated. I was overloaded with new sights and emotions. When I voiced this, she said we should hurry.

By the time we got to the castle, I had to walk with my eyes closed and my hand on Amerlie's arm. Even so I felt buffeted by the noise and the smells from cooking food, but also from perfumes and unwashed bodies. When Amerlie said we were approaching the gate, I prepared to open my eyes. This would be a nice, calm scene for me to take in. But she warned, "No!"

"Why?" I asked, my voice sounding odd to my ears.

"There are soldiers gathering from three or four different directions, and their uniforms are different colors. The way they move in and around each other creates a mosaic that will likely hurt your eyes again."

"What's happening to me?"

"You're coming into your powers a little early. It will go away after a good night's sleep. Your brain is changing as the powers awaken and it upsets your senses. They get back to working order if you just don't overdo it."

I heard her talking to Mikal but it sounded as if she were on the other side of the courtyard.

I felt myself being lifted and let out a small yell. A male voice I didn't recognize said, "It's just me, my lady. I'm helping to get you into the castle. Amerlie's right ahead of us with the creature and Mikal has gone ahead to notify the staff. In case you don't recognize my voice, I'm Wilfie."

"Oh, Wilfie, thank you. I owe you so much."

"Hush, my lady, just relax."

21

The next time I became aware, it was early morning and I was in my bed. Daisy entered with a tea service and muffins, and I was hungry enough to eat every crumb. I took a bath, was dressed by my maids, and headed to the dining room to see who was awake for breakfast.

The sitting room was set up for breakfast but the food was just coming in when I arrived. Da was at the window, his shoulders hunched and his head moving in denial.

"Da? I'm fine, you know."

He turned suddenly and rushed to hug me. I hugged him back as hard as I could. It felt as if I were home as I had never felt in the valley. He held me back so he could look at me, and his eyes bulged once he saw the grin on my face.

"If that was the only price I have to pay to come into my inheritance, I'm a very lucky girl."

"Your brother Henry very nearly died when he came in to the little magic he has. I was worried because you had so much more coming in to you, but I should have realized that you're your mother's daughter."

"Amerlie said I'd be fine with a night's sleep, and I've never felt better. I'm sorry I worried you."

We smiled and sat down at the table. I poured tea for him and myself as Amerlie and Mikal entered the room. I was delighted to see them both since I supposed they too were worried.

"Are you fine today?" Amerlie asked, and I nodded in reply.

Sylvester came in with a tray of eggs, bacon and fried potatoes. He served me first, then Da, Amerlie and finally Mikal. I found the precedence interesting since I would have assumed Amerlie had significant status. Then I realized that, in spite of my acquisition of magic, Da was still the regent and would be for another two months.

Da asked Amerlie, "Have you found out anything more about our new guest?"

"I called on one of the women in the Collegium who's made a particular study of demons, and she says she suspects he's Iblis. He's very high in the order of demons—it's surprising to have him so intimately involved in this plot."

"Can I force him to acknowledge that he is Iblis? Does he have to respond to his name?" I asked.

"His name will require a response but we don't know what he considers his true name. He's also known as Shaitan, or what we would call the Devil. As long as you know all three, you should be able to get him to respond. Then we can get real information from him. Maybe even names."

"Where is he now?" I asked.

"He's in a part of the castle only someone with magic can access. It's a specially built room with no door. No one outside of a few trusted advisors knows where it is," said Da.

"Does that mean I'm a trusted advisor?" Mikal wondered.

"It does indeed," I said. "You're going to be very important when I take over."

Da and Amerlie smiled.

We finished our breakfast with no more business, just a casual discussion regarding why the soldiers were all here, and who they represented in their various uniforms. It was a standard muster that was done every year at about this time for joint training. It had been going on, according to Mikal, for over a thousand years.

As we prepared to leave, I asked, "Is there anyone else who we should take, like from the Collegium?"

Amerlie indicated we would pick up Belvedere on the way.

22

We ended up outside the "cell" in a hallway between two storage bays. Da gave the history that a little space had been taken from each bay to make room for a small cell. The curving of the wall made it difficult to judge if any space had been taken from either. Amerlie prepared to bring me, Belvedere and Mikal through as Da reached into an invisible alcove where he pulled out a small chalice. Wielding it, he went through the wall.

Amerlie had made an artificial light in the room. Mikal was on the far side of the clear box that held the demon. Belvedere went to the corner opposite Mikal, while Amerlie and Da took the remaining corners.

I went to the side of the box, and looked at my quarry. He was awake and glaring at me. I reached in as I had before, squeezing his internal organs, or such as he had, and said, "Iblis. Shaitan. Devil. You are mine."

He writhed and tried to pull away but my hold was firm. Lights reflected off his dark skin and his eyes, caused by the power he was releasing in his effort to beat me.

"Iblis, Shaitan, Devil. Stop!"

He went still.

"You will talk with me. You will answer my questions truthfully. Do you understand?"

He glared, but nodded.

"Are you acting under the orders of anyone but me?"

"Not now."

"Before I said your name, were you working under anyone's orders?"

"Yes."

"Whose?"

"I cannot say."

"You *will* say."

"I've been barred from ever saying his name."

"Iblis, Shaitan. Devil. You are no longer barred."

He struggled then. His face contorted to the extent that a skull could twist. He moaned and writhed as I prepared to make another order.

But then he spoke. "I was bound to Gabrille Montrade."

I looked at Da and then Amerlie who both looked shocked. When I raised a questioning eyebrow to Belvedere, he told me Montrade was the emperor's chief wizard.

23

"Iblis. Shaitan. Devil. For what reason were you in the service of Gabrille Montrade?"

He again struggled, but said, "To assist in a plot. A plot to kill the emperor."

"Iblis. Shaitan. Devil. Tell me all you know about this plot."

"I was to meet with Sir Henry and take him to Wallameer to meet with the conspirators. I didn't find Sir Henry, but I saw one of the other conspirators take a shot at the regent."

"Who took that shot?"

"Prince Briaint of Wallameer."

Da murmured something, as Mikal gasped.

"Who else is involved in this plan?"

"Representatives of five principalities, one state and two duchies, other than those I've mentioned."

The interrogation went for several hours before I became too exhausted to continue. By that time, we knew the names of all the conspirators—at least all those known to the demon, but we couldn't be sure that there wasn't more to this scheme, or more people involved.

We reconvened in my father's study to discuss our options. One thing we knew for sure was that Henry, supposedly part of the conspiracy, wasn't where he was supposed to be at any of the three times set for his rendezvous with the demon.

Da pulled out a map to see if the demon had the relative positions and routes of the plot correct. He thought at least one part of the plan seemed unlikely unless there was either another part of the conspiracy, or a magic user of greater strength than Iblis had reported.

The map showed the various states that were implicated in the plot, Wallameer, Pengliton, Aflingham, Roprosoni, Marsettleroo, Wicklebot, Nostromana, Authenato, and Harrington. They formed an arc around one of the empire's most successful duchies, Middleland, a matrilineal society that had been stable for as long as anyone knew, and according to Da, it was a wonderful place to live. He would know as he'd been born there.

"Shall we go back to Iblis and ask what role, if any, Middleland had to play in this plot?" I asked.

Da shook his head. "It'll be better to send someone undercover into Middleland to see if anything is amiss. If something seems off, then approaching and warning the duchess, an old friend of your mother's, might be in order."

"Could I not go to visit her, with Amerlie as my maid? Or would it be better if I dressed up as a boy again and Amerlie could be a slightly older woman?"

"You were dressed as a boy?"

We explained the escape more fully to him, so he'd understand I could pull it off. Amerlie pointed out that my magic would likely help in making me look and sound more masculine. That rather surprised me, and I said I'd have to think about it. Da was finally convinced I could masquerade as a man when I grew a mustache before his eyes and spoke in a voice deeper than his.

"I don't want you to go officially. There'd be too many people who would know of it and would be able to plan ill doings. No, you'll be much safer disguised. But this is only to get information, and be back quickly, understand?"

"No one other than Henry would even have a chance at recognizing us," said Amerlie.

"I'm serious," Da said. "Peary's too important to allow her to travel so unprotected and so far from her own duchy. Given that she just arrived here days ago, her people may wonder where she's off to now, and whether her return can be guaranteed. Plus, I personally am reluctant to let my long lost daughter out of my sight for any longer than necessary. Have I made myself clear?"

Amerlie and I nodded and went off to prepare for our journey.

24

Amerlie, looking several years older, and "Percy," her son, got on the train to Markerburg. The capital city of Middleland seemed like a good place to start. I didn't like the name I'd be going by, but it made sense in that it wouldn't be hard for me to act naturally when I was called that. This train was quite a bit fancier than the one we had taken to Springfield with separate cabins with doors to keep a level of privacy. We quickly secured one for us but left the door open as if for air.

A number of middle-aged gentlemen stopped to flirt with Amerlie, and I could sense in each his intentions. Only one was truly dishonorable, and I pretended to get sick as he was beginning to advance toward my "mother." It was effective and efficient. After he left and we were sure he was out of hearing, we giggled at his artlessness.

We were pleasantly surprised when an older gentleman stopped to make our acquaintance. My sense of him was that he was honorable in general, but there was something obstructing him or weighing on his mind. I didn't know if Amerlie sensed this as well but I rose to give him respect. I gave him my seat next to Amerlie and moved to the seats across the carriage from them.

I watched patiently as they did their courtesies and nodded at the gentleman who identified himself as Lord Featherworthy of Middleland. He asked whether this was to be our first trip to his country, and Amerlie gushed in a way that struck me as humorous. There was nothing of consequence in their mild flirtation, but the emotions in the man struck me as false in some sense. I was pondering this as he suddenly made a move to grab Amerlie. As he did, he changed into a man with dark wavy hair and deep black eyes. His back was at an angle to me and I struck him over the head with my "mother's" walking stick.

The man crumpled to the floor pulling Amerlie on top of him as his grip did not release. I smacked his hand with the stick and two fingers fell off, but no blood flowed. I whacked again and the hand disconnected at the wrist. Amerlie got off him and pulled me toward the door. Before I followed, I hammered the creature on the head, which dented but did not break. I picked up our two bags as we hurried out. We saw an attendant and called on him to show us another space where we could have privacy. He looked over my shoulder, but only saw the man on the ground, his back toward the door.

We moved to a different carriage and a cabin within it, and shut the door.

"I read him and he seemed only a little suspect when he came in. He got more questionable as the conversation went on. I never thought he would change like that. What was he?"

"I have no idea. I've never seen a creature that can be cut like that and not bleed. I'll contact my sisters and see if any of them understand this creature. We must be a lot more careful in the future and I want to check that there really is a Lord Featherworthy of Middleland." She went into a trance state, and I knew enough to leave her be. I wanted to be able to follow what she did, but was afraid my learning had not yet risen to that level.

She came out of the trance to tell me what she had discovered. "There really is a Lord Featherworthy of Middleland, but he's been bedridden for years and one of my sisters watches over him. There is little known about the beast that attacked us. These creatures have been seen over the last four or so years but not frequently. This is only the eighth to be discovered, and they are thought to come from Nostromana. That duchy has been using magic for some time to create odd effects. I suspect they appear so far apart in time because they are difficult to make. How they knew who we are and where we're going is troubling since so few people were in the know. There will be protection for our changing images when two of my sisters join the train at the next stop."

"You mean, we're changing our plan?"

"I believe it's necessary now, don't you?"

"How do we know he wasn't just running amok?"

"They seem to be controlled from a distant place, and the emotions you feel are those of their director. At least that is the current working hypothesis. After all, that *thing* didn't have any emotions for you to sense!" We considered possible disguises and we reduced Amerlie's age to closer to mine. Amerlie altered my face a little, and we became a young husband and wife.

When the two witches joined us, they were carrying a slightly more appropriate outfit for Amerlie as a new wife, and they added their magic to Amerlie's to reinforce our new look.

25

As we entered our hotel room, Amerlie sighed and relaxed a little of the hold she had on our disguises. I looked more feminine and she looked older, but only to the point she could resurrect the correct looks if there were a knock on the door. We'd have to do a little shopping because the clothes fit for a widow were a trifle hard to change into clothes of a newlywed, and the new outfit would only survive so long. We had plenty of the local coin to be able to shop well. We planned to ask the owner in the common room if there was a competent clothes mistress in the area.

Having gotten directions to such a one, we sallied out into a bustling street. Carriages flowed in each direction, stopping often for a vague pedestrian who slid into the carriages' lane. We nodded to those we passed, and they to us, always a smile on their faces. It didn't seem to matter about the relative stations in life for they smiled at us much as they smiled at the poor beggars on the side of the road.

We came to the place recommended by the clerk and looked in the window to see what we could see.

"Oh my," said Amerlie. "Look at that pretty muslin they have. It would make a lovely dress, don't you think, dear?" She squeezed my arm as she spoke.

I deepened my voice, carrying on with the charade, and replied, "If you must have it, my dear, then we must go in."

We entered to see a large front room with bolts of fabric and mannequins dressed in fine designs to tempt us. We wondered, conversing quietly with each other, whether there was anything inimical in the shop. Neither of us sensed anything and so we settled in to explore the options. When we stood in front of one wonderful design in a flowery silk for a few extra minutes, a woman walked up to us smiling.

"Have you seen something you like? I'd be happy to show it to you in a different fabric. It's amazing how it changes character that way." When we agreed, she went to the back of the store and brought forth a plain muslin dress that looked so different from the silk I cried out.

"So the sir is acquainted with feminine clothing?"

"It's new to me since I married my beloved wife," I said, quickly recovering. "I watch and learn. And this is certainly educational."

Amerlie spoke, "I can afford to get the same design in both kinds of fabric, for they hang completely differently." We went on to look at other fabrics and picked two: one silk and one muslin. The order was placed and the woman took the mannequin and the two fabrics to the back of the store.

After more looking, Amerlie ordered two more dresses and was pleased to discover the first two were already complete. We were told we could come back in an hour to pick up the other two.

We wandered up the street, looking in shops and stalls, finding the place friendly and strangely comfortable. I wondered aloud whether it was because this was another matriarchal society.

"It's that and because it's been so strong for so long. I believe we ought to walk in that direction," Amerlie said, pointing at a street sign posted on a wall at the top of the first floor that indicated "Simples, Spells, and Charms."

I followed her along the narrow path onto the side street, which was almost blocked by the various carts and tables on the main road. After we got through the bottleneck, we found ourselves in a quiet little cul-de-sac, shops lining the road on both sides, some looking quite prosperous. Amerlie appeared to be looking for a particular establishment, and suddenly pulled me toward a small, cozy shop.

Upon entering, I heard her cry out, "Rosamund!" as she threw herself into the other woman's arms. I realized then how we would find the news in Markerburg. The two women were whispering to each other but I couldn't hear what they were saying. I stood back and waited, a little frustrated at being left out.

"Both of you, come back and have some tea! I want to meet the young man who could talk my friend into marriage!" Rosamund said. She walked to the door, turned a "Closed" sign to the street, and barred the door. Then she pulled us to the back of the shop and up the stairs to her private rooms. As I entered the kitchen, I saw Rosamund and Amerlie murmuring a spell together.

When they were done, Amerlie said, "There have been strange folk about and some have magic. There's no reason to assume we are the target, but caution is never wasted."

Rosamund curtseyed and said, "I never thought I would have the fugitive duchess in my rooms!"

"Oh, I'm not a fugitive, am I?"

"Don't be silly, dear, you've come in from your hideaway as Amerlie tells me, but the world has been agog at your disappearance, especially at such an early age."

"I had nothing to do with it." I was a little miffed at being treated like a child. My abilities were growing every day, and it was all I could do not to scream with frustration at being not allowed to really *do* anything.

Amerlie shushed me and led me to a comfortable chair to sit. "We've put up a good shield that looks like we're simply sitting and having tea. We appear to be talking softly about Rosamund's business and our ability to supply herbs for her balms. It is, in fact, a business meeting between two old acquaintances but now it's safe to talk."

Rosamund said, "The town is quite concerned by the number of strange men who have been arriving, most by themselves, for the past few months. Do you know anything about it?"

"I'm afraid we do," said Amerlie and she told Rosamund the whole story, leaving out only Henry's involvement.

Rosamund looked stunned by the news. "This is peculiar. Where would men get such funny thoughts? Why would they believe they have the right to rule just because they're stronger?"

I said, "I suppose brothers who are passed over for their sisters might wonder why they weren't good enough to rule. We do have three completely different kinds of governments in this area, and my brother Chres told me there are places with no ruler at all. They actually pick their leaders for a short period of time and then they choose another ruler." I shook my head. "It sounds quite odd."

Rosamund said, "I've heard tales but never thought there was any truth in them."

"Chres said the tutor when he had as a child was supposed to have come from such a place, but I don't know anything about that. It certainly wasn't anything I learned at my little school in the valley."

Our conversation continued for a while until Rosamund indicated it was time for supper, and she would be happy to entertain us. Amerlie went with her to prepare the food since neither thought it was an appropriate task for me to do. I wondered if this was because of my disguise or my new station in life, and then I began to worry that I was being coddled. My offers to help were rebuffed. I settled back into the chair and picked up a small book from the table next to it. I could hear them speaking in the kitchen, but couldn't make out what they said, so I became determined to amuse myself with the book with the strange title *The Scarlet*

Bower.

The book was full of stories, I discovered, but these stories contained recipes and magical instructions. I wondered why Rosamund had left such a book just lying about, since magic was supposed to be secret and unavailable to the non-magical. But presumably, she had few visitors to her private rooms, and they were already familiar with the magical life. My nose was buried in the second tale by the time I was called to dinner. I carried the book with me into the dining room.

"Have you been reading that? Do you like it?" Rosamund asked.

I told her I'd made it through the first story, and had started the second.

She laughed. "You didn't try to do what the story told you, I guess."

"How can you tell?"

"You still have all your hair, and you're still clothed." Rosamund roared with laughter while Amerlie took the book and opened to the first story.

"Rosamund, where did you get this horrible book? It was supposed to have been destroyed!"

"It's a collector's item, and I'm holding it for a client. One who is fully aware of the silly games the author played in that book."

"I don't understand. You mean that first spell won't make you powerful?" I asked.

"No, it sets off a mildly powerful blast that blows off your clothes and tears out your hair. The author was expelled from three magical academies because he wouldn't follow rules, and played with dangerous ideas."

Amerlie said, "You left it on the table on purpose!"

"Of course I did." Rosamund grinned at us. "I slid it there when we all walked in. I wanted to see what the duchess did with it. Seems she's as sensible as her mother was."

We laughed and settled in, tea at our sides. Amerlie wanted to know if there was a way to get a message to the Duchess of Middleland about the conspiracy afoot at her door.

Rosamund said, "I have a few contacts in the castle, although we witches are not currently in good favor. Her daughter tried to invoke her magic early, apparently on a dare from one of the more lively demoiselles of the court. The Duchess Madory believes the youngster couldn't have gotten so close without assistance, and we aren't allowed to make our denials."

"I don't want to disclose Peary if I can avoid it, but it may be our only hope."

"Is it possible for you to get a message to the regent requesting an introduction for Peary? Perhaps we'll need a subterfuge to get her into the castle, or maybe the heir will want to invite this lovely young couple to tea or a soiree."

"I can get a message to the regent easily enough, but it must be in a code he will know. I need to think on this before I act." Amerlie turned to me. "What do you think, Peary?"

"Did you know I can talk to Da from here? Or did I forget to tell you? I've talked with him every night before going to sleep. So I can set it up tonight, and he can do whatever he has to do through diplomatic channels. But I'd like to move more quickly if these strangers have made themselves known."

We talked about the need for haste, and decided I should try to contact my father as soon as could be. At that time, it was likely he was still at dinner, so we played card games, and Rosamund offered to read my Tarot for fun. Amerlie was reluctant fearing some great truth about me would emerge, but Rosamund tut-tutted. She pulled a worn set of cards out of her desk and spread them across the table.

"Peary, I want you to concentrate on an issue you want resolved. Is it creative?"

"I don't want to do this," I said. "With the magic in this room, I'm likely to put a compulsion on me I don't want." Amerlie took a deep breath when I said this.

"My goodness, you are a serious young lady, aren't you?"

"You should know," Amerlie said, "her magic came in a little early."

Rosamund said, "I'm so sorry, Peary, I wouldn't have suggested it if I knew. You're perfectly right—a mundane use of the cards should be avoided by those with new magic. Many regular people use it as a parlor game, but they cannot affect forces as we can."

"I think I can probably reach my da by now, if I can have a quiet place to try," I said.

Rosamund said, "Amerlie and I can go make dessert; would we give you enough time?"

I nodded and slipped into a trance-like state. Before they were out of the room, my da had already responded.

<Peary, are you okay? It's early for you to be contacting me.>

<Da, we've met with a friend of Amerlie's here. We need to find

76

a way to get me invited to visit with Duchess Madory. Things are already starting to happen. Strange men have come to the city.>

<It's started?>

<I think so. I need to see her personally and privately to explain the conspiracy and the evidence of its activities in this city. Can you help?>

<I can get word to her that Amerlie has a very special package that must be opened privately. Would that work?>

<Oh, Da, that's brilliant! Does she know Amerlie?>

<She's the only other leader I told about what happened to you, and about your being guarded by Amerlie. She should make the connection.>

<When can you do this? And how will she be able to get in touch with us?>

<Let me see what I can do. Can you reach me in about three hours?>

<Of course. You're the best!>

<I love you, my little one.>

I slumped back in my chair. It was still hard work maintaining the connection since Da had only a minimal amount of magical talents.

Amerlie poked her head around the kitchen door and saw me. "You couldn't reach him?"

"I did. I'm just resting because it takes so much out of me. I have to contact him again in a few hours because he may have already worked things out by then."

With the good news shared, Rosamund came into the dining room carrying a dish that smelled wonderful and fruity. It was a lovely apple cobbler, with cinnamon and other spices made it delicious.

After eating dessert, Amerlie and I made our thanks and left for the hotel. Amerlie thought I could take a nap and she would rouse me in time to contact my da. A nap sounded wonderful to me about then.

26

The next day, we were summoned to an audience at the castle that was generally held once a month for people visiting Markerburg. According to our landlord, the castle had that morning inquired of the inns on this street if they had foreigners among their guests. This had happened before, so he was not surprised at our summons.

"You will find our duchess quite a breath of fresh air, especially if you have visited any of our near neighbors," he said.

"I know nothing of the politics of this area. We simply came for our honeymoon, having heard of the culture and beauty of your city. Could you tell us more?" I asked.

He harrumphed before saying, "I don't normally talk politics with my guests, but I suppose I should tell you a little so you don't make any mistakes this afternoon." He went on to tell us the kind of government in each of the surrounding states. "Some of these places are actually saying the matriarchal states are outdated and should be modernized. Haven't a clue about their reasoning, but we're all quite content with our duchess. She's a fine woman with a good head on her shoulders, and business is great, so I have no cause to listen to this carping by our neighbors. Just because their business is ailing is no reason to attack us. Fair to say, I think, we have enlightened government here, and proud of it!"

"And well you should be," said Amerlie. "Why this is just as fine a place as Duchess's Springfield in our own country. Not that we go there very often, but it is a rare treat. Like being here, I might say."

We congratulated each other on our good fortune to be in Markerburg and went into the dining room for lunch. I had pointed out to the landlord that the common room was not quite the place for my delicate wife. As he walked away after seating us, Amerlie and I had to stifle our giggles.

We engaged in loving small talk when approached by others, but spent the rest of the time plotting our course with the duchess this afternoon. Amerlie was convinced there would be a way to meet with her alone. I wasn't so confident.

"What if we can only meet with her in the presence of guards or advisors? We have no way of knowing if they'd be with us or against us," I said.

"We have to assume your father's message was clear and comprehensive. If it was sent by one of his mages, it undoubtedly carried the full weight of the need for privacy. Have faith, my dear," she added as our waitress drew near.

We finished our lunch and decided to walk around town and see the sights before our audience with the duchess. We asked our landlord which way we should walk and what we might look out for. He obliged by showing us the way to the main square, where there was an open-air market, a library for the public, and the courts of law, which were considered to be the ugliest buildings in the empire.

Taking our cue, we went in the direction of the main square, named Davidio Square after the current Duchess' maternal grandfather. I asked, "What is the nature of the mark on the heir here?"

"It's unknown, just as yours is unknown to all but the intimates of your family."

"But surely Henry will divulge it to his friends, won't he?"

"I'm sure he would if he could. But the nature of the magic that names the true heir constrains all other potential heirs from speaking of it. He cannot write it, nor divulge it in mind-to-mind communication. In fact, if someone tried to force it from him, he would die by the magic before disclosing the information. We must also not lose sight of the fact he left Springfield before Iblis arrived to take him to the conspirators. He may have already parted ways from the conspiracy, though how we could possibly verify it is beyond me."

"Maybe he left early only to give us hope he had left. Maybe he is still in the thick of it and working on a part of the plan unknown to any of the other conspirators."

"You think too uncharitably, my dear. We must hope for the best though we fear the worst."

We reached the market and browsed many of the booths. A few held some trinkets of interest, one of which was a spelled item Amerlie and I felt from two booths away. We meandered over to that booth as nonchalantly as possible and perused the items for sale. I caught a quick thought from the seller before he slammed shields down in his mind. We were targets for this man! I warned Amerlie mind to mind, and we shut our own shields down in less time than it took to tell this.

The merchant pretended to be surprised that we were looking

at his humble wares.

"I really like this ring, dear, don't you?" asked Amerlie of a hideous piece that might look good on an ogre.

"I don't think it quite reflects your eyes, my sweet, and you know how much I like that. I don't think it is suitable for you."

Amerlie pouted prettily and said, "You said you would buy me something."

"I think we can find better elsewhere. I see nothing here that appeals to me," I replied.

The merchant said, "Oh please, madam, sir, there are a few nice baubles among the drab. Here, look at this." He pointed to a sparkling trunk, small enough to be used as a jewelry case. It was crusted with metal and crystal gems. It smelled clean, but I couldn't reach out with my magical senses with my mind barricaded. I thought if one of use could reach for it, that would give the other time to do a quick read. I gambled and reached for the box, the merchant's eyes following my every move.

Amerlie said, "Oh, no, my dear, I don't need such a box. Remember the one Aunt Robin gave me so recently."

I pulled my hand back with something like regret. I turned to the disappointed merchant, and said, "If my lady doesn't want it, I'm afraid we have no use for it. So sorry to have taken your time." I put my arm under Amerlie's hand and turned her away.

The merchant made one last attempt to make a sale. "I can reduce the price!"

We walked away, her hand in my arm, dropping our shields to hear him cursing us and passing his failure to someone ahead. I saw Rosamund across the circle and pointed her out to Amerlie.

"My dear, isn't that the wonderful herb lady we met yesterday?"

"Oh, yes, my love, do let's go and talk to her."

In that way, we didn't follow the natural path along the outside of the market and hoped we could sneak by the next trap. Amerlie sent a mental shout to Rosamund, who stopped and looked around her, seemingly at the market but actually locating us. She went back to look a little more at the table she had just visited. When we arrived she was involved in a vigorous conversation with the merchant regarding where a particular ring came from.

The merchant was awkward in his response: "Madam, that is a ring left with me on consignment. The owner is aware it's here and is hoping for a quick sale. It's why the owner didn't go to a regular jewelry shop where the sale could take years."

"Then you should have no difficulty in telling me the name of the owner, so I can negotiate directly with him or her," Rosamund said, inspecting the ring. "I see there is a family crest on it, and I'm sure you can tell me to whom that crest belongs."

"It's not a common one, madam, and I'm not at liberty to say."

"You say it's not common and yet I see it on the shoulder of every guardsman or soldier who works for the duchess. I see it on the front of the castle and in the halls, on the china and silverware. Would you care to explain that?" She asked, angrily.

The merchant's face went pure white, and he backed away from the table. I had seen a guard and waved at him. The merchant tried to hide at first, but the guard was fast approaching, so he sprinted toward the gate to the lower town. The guard cut him off and grabbed the merchant by the scruff of his neck, pushing him back to the table.

Rosamund said, "I was trying to get information about where he found this ring, and he became concerned—acted quite suspiciously. You saw his flight." She indicated the jewelry in question. "And this is the ring."

"That's the duchess's missing ring!" the guard exclaimed. "We've been searching for weeks!"

I said, "Note the different quality of his other wares. He couldn't have seriously thought it wouldn't be discovered." I tried to keep my voice deep but there were a few squawks. "The man is either a scoundrel or part of a larger conspiracy."

The guard asked our names, and we told him. His was Herokio. Amerlie also advised him we needed to go back to the hotel and prepare ourselves for the duchess's tea party.

"Ah, no, you're fine for it, and I really must bring you with me to the castle as witnesses. I don't want this man arguing that I planted it on him! It will do you no harm to meet the duchess before the tea. You'll have a leg up in the acquaintance over the other foreigners." He chuckled softly and led the way.

Rosamund and Amerlie linked arms, and I followed behind. They talked softly, and I knew they were planning to use this event as the basis for a private meeting with the duchess. I was not as convinced as they, but harbored them no ill will for the thinking of it.

27

The castle was larger than mine by a good amount, but it was not as classically beautiful as it had acquired several towers and appendages apparently over the years. According to the guard, many members of the court had apartments within the castle, and it was more than his job was worth to take us anywhere near the apartments of the hoity-toity.

We went in the main gate, and up the main steps, much as we had done in Springfield. Herokio, conferred with the two guards at the front door for a few minutes. One of the guards entered the castle while the other helped ensure the obedience of the prisoner.

A moment later, the majordomo walked out to greet us. He was a tall man with rusty hair and a pleasant smile. Herokio advanced, showing him our find in the market. He looked at me strangely, before immediately having the way cleared and ushering us into the main hall and leading us further into the castle. We followed him with alacrity. This wouldn't to be a typical guided tour. He moved swiftly toward a central room and opened the door after signaling us to wait. He returned in a moment and waved us in. That we were in the audience hall left no doubt in my mind. It was much like mine was but on a larger scale. The duchess looked tiny given how far away she was.

Her voice, however, was not.

"Go away, Smithery, go away. I'll meet with these heroes in private." She also ordered the guards in the room to step outside for the duration of the meeting. One tried to protest but was quickly brought into line.

She asked us to approach her throne, and we did. There were a number of chairs available, but I bowed first before assaying any of them. Each curtseyed or bowed as was appropriate.

"One of you should not be making obeisance. Speak up, which is the fugitive Duchess?"

"I am, madam," as Amerlie lowered the illusion she had cast on me.

"Why, you're a mere chit of a girl. What can you possibly tell me?" She looked at me with wonder.

"I can tell you of the conspiracy afoot to deprive you of your rule, me of mine, and the emperor of his. And I can show evidence that your neighbors are ready to rise against you and how they've been smuggling men into the city. But first, if I may, we should deal with this miscreant and send him to the appropriate hole."

"And what has this scoundrel done?" she asked.

Herokio approached with the ring and placed it in her hand. She immediately recoiled and tried to shake it off, but was unsuccessful. I jumped to her side and pulled the ring from her hand. The duchess was wan of face, and having difficulty breathing. I called for Amerlie, and she was with there immediately. She knelt and placed both hands on either side of the duchess's head. Within minutes, the duchess was fine, but the ring was not. After examining the ring, Rosamund had found that the jewel in the ring wasn't in the right place for magical use; instead, it was in a negative orientation to the observer.

"The ring has been tampered with, the stone moved just enough to carry a spell, which is still present, and," I looked at the duchess, "is only triggered by you, my lady."

"We should keep it far from the heir as its scope may be larger, but the succession ceremony can now be performed," said Rosamund.

The duchess looked closely at Rosamund and said, "You were one of those who led my daughter astray. I've banned you from my castle."

"I did *not* lead your daughter astray. I saved her at every chance I could, from the machinations of others. And if you listen now to the Duchess of Winthrop, you may have a better idea of who these wrongdoers are."

The duchess turned to Amerlie, who pointed my way. She said, "I don't understand."

As Amerlie unwove more of the illusion, I said, "I *am* the heir to the Duchy of Winthrop. We knew we were being followed, so we disguised ourselves as you now see."

"I do see," she said, though she looked startled. "What's the state of your magic, then, since you're still two months shy of ascension?"

"I'm fully awakened." I replied. "And if your heir shows signs of awakening, then it's proof there's inordinate danger here, in this duchy."

"That's what your father intimated, but I declare it's fools' play. Your brother has believed himself capable of high scheming, and some fools have come along with him—no doubt to get his wealth."

"I wish I could believe you, but my father couldn't have told you everything. First, my brother fled my duchy the night I returned to claim my birthright—and after a failed attempt to do me harm. Second, we found a hidey-hole in his room, hidden behind wards of black magic, containing documents establishing the existence of a conspiracy to place the dauphin on the throne and to revert all states and duchies to patrilineal rule. Third—"

"Oh it was just a game, I'm sure."

"Excuse me, madam," I said firmly, "there's a third point. Amerlie and I captured a demon that was part of a scheme to assassinate my father. We have him thoroughly constrained, and he has divulged the name of his master." I paused before adding, "Gabrille Montrade."

Duchess Madory stepped back, clutching her throat. "It can't be," she whispered.

"I can't be certain my magic was sufficient to break him, but I have reason to believe it was, since he is imprisoned in a glass case, inside a stone tomb, at the foundation of our castle. The tomb has no doors, and the detained one doesn't know which walls have doors and which have solid rock. It is more than his life is worth to gamble under those odds, particularly since he acknowledges that no more than a sliver of stone can be opened. He must wait for my, or my heir's, return."

"Surely you don't believe a demon who would reveal his master's name."

"If you had seen what I had to go through to get him to talk at all, you would understand why the information is trustworthy. What convinced us that we had to make contact today is perhaps more disturbing. I'll let the others tell it, since they understand it more than I."

"If you will allow me to speak," Rosamund started, and with a nod from the duchess, she continued, "there have been men in town from other places. They have tried to ascertain all the magic workers in the area, and their intent is bad."

"There was a merchant in the square who tried very hard to make one of us take a small jewelry chest," Amerlie said. "When we didn't take it, he signaled to someone farther up the marketplace. Being cautious, we decided to walk directly across the square to where Rosamund stood. There was an outcry from behind us." Amerlie nodded back to Rosamund.

"These strange men have been coming singly in greater

numbers. They seem to have no use for work, but nothing to sell either. They disappear into the town, but no one knows where they go. A number have magic, but the majority don't. One of the magical ones hung outside my shop for almost a week, scaring away business." Rosamund sounded more serious than I'd heard her so far. "Oh, the people know about these men and they steer clear of them."

Madory, wringing her hands, looked each of us in the eye by turn. She reached out and I went to her. Placing her hand on my forearm, she whispered, "Do you believe this?"

"With all my heart, I do." I trembled as I said it.

"I want advice from my own mage, if you don't mind, but I would like you there to make sure I don't misstate anything. Are you willing?"

"What about the tea with the other visitors?" Amerlie asked. "Ought we to do that at least, first?"

"I think you can be excused from the tea, but I cannot. I'd like you to meet with my daughter. If what Peary says is true, then my daughter is also on the verge of acquiring her powers, if she has not already."

28

After we had been escorted to the sitting room and were left alone, we decided I would do the talking at the beginning while the other two would try to ascertain the state of her magical maturation.

"She probably won't remember me," said Rosamund. "We only met once when she was first feeling the strain of the change."

Before either of us could comment, the door opened and a girl who could have been my twin walked into the room. She stopped and stared at me. The girl looking at me could have been the same one I saw in the mirror on my first full day in Springfield. It took me a moment to remember that I still looked vaguely male. I tried my best to return to my normal looks, but was unnerved by the way she was staring at me.

"Who are you?" she asked. "I thought I was going to meet Periwinkle, and maybe a witch or two. Who are YOU?"

Rosamund walked to the girl and tried to soothe her, but she yanked her arm away and strode over, stopping a few inches in front of me.

"I'm Periwinkle," I said quickly. "Please compose yourself. I'm as shocked as you by this similarity. Rosamund, why didn't you tell me?" As I turned to look at Rosamund, I felt the other's hand slap me across the right cheek. I reached out with—what?—my magic, and grabbed her hand. "Don't try that again. My rank is higher than yours for the time being, and I will have you punished," I said, then softened my voice. "What's your name?"

She hissed at me trying to pull away, but I held her with a freezing spell. When she looked as if she were about to scream, I filled the spell in around her mouth.

"I wish one of you would help me! I do agree with her in one respect, why are we identical? Amerlie, talk to us."

"You are thrice cousins. Your fathers were brothers, and your mothers were first cousins on both sides. I suspect when we have you both dressed and made up properly like the young ladies you are, the resemblance won't be as great as you now think." Amerlie did not look as if she believed her last statement.

"Her name is Nenory," Rosamund said. "She was born on the same day and at the same time you were. After her birth, she showed signs of being poisoned as you were. The birthmark on her right foot is of Middleland, and on her left foot that of your country—without the addition you are said to have."

Nenory and I gazed at each other in wonder. I released her, and Amerlie stepped forward to help her as she looked faint. We were both led to a couch and sat on it side by side. I could feel my disguise sliding off my face.

Amerlie and Rosamund stood a few feet in front of us, staring and comparing.

"Peary's hair is quite a bit lighter than Nenory's." Amerlie remarked. "Of course, it could be because Peary has lived an outdoors life while in exile. Note how Peary's skin is slightly darker, and her face looks older. That could be the outdoor life, her complete accession of magic, or the number of traumas she has had compared to Nenory."

"I'd say the likely culprit is the harder life. I think though their hair color is naturally different. We can't expect them to be totally identical. This isn't a case where we could exchange one look-alike for the other. They are equally high in the succession for both duchies, even though Peary is a little closer to sitting than Nenory. I doubt there's any use we can make of the remarkable resemblance." Rosamund seemed disappointed with her conclusion, almost disgruntled with our wasting of the similarities.

I butted in. "I can think of a very good use we can put this to. Heaven forbid, that I could have a thought before the two of you. Can you not imagine a time when it would be useful to have the heir sitting in the formal dining room, while at the same time meeting a conspirator who wants to recruit her? Come on, you two have been at this much longer than I. Surely you can see the many ways this could be useful. Assuming we'd go along with it."

"Oh, we'll go along, shan't we?" Nenory awoke to the possibilities, and I reminded her that she had led a sheltered life. The idea of adventure didn't yet mean danger and discomfort to her the way it did to me. We smiled at each other tentatively: I was unsure of her ability to conspire with us.

There was silence in the room. I thought perhaps Amerlie and Rosamund were communing silently, but didn't think so, judging from the looks on their faces. Rosamund bit her lower lip, her head cocked to one side. Amerlie had moved over to a window and was leaning against the wainscoting beside it, her head lowered. Nenory peered at me as if she expected that I'd come to take her on a magic carpet ride.

29

A great hue and cry sounded from the corridors near our hideaway. Explosions, swords shrieking against metal, men's voices rising and suddenly ceasing. The two witches immediately came to attention and interposed themselves between Nenory and me, and the door.

A moment later, our two guards opened the door. One of them yelled, "Get down!" and they exited as quickly as they had come.

A *frisson* of magic flowed across my arms as I dropped to the floor behind a couch. Nenory huddled beside me, frozen in fear.

I whispered to her, "How much magic have you acquired?" Looking at her face, I knew her mother had died. The flushed cheeks, bright eyes, and curling hair all replicated the change through which I had gone a few short weeks earlier.

"Amerlie, Rosamund, the duchess is dead," I said softly.

Nenory began to cry quietly; Rosamund came to her side, and Amerlie gestured for me to join her. Watching the door, we knew it was a matter of time before the assailants made it to our floor. I looked around the room, seeking the entrance to a back corridor or a secret passageway. Nothing was obvious, but I stood, to Amerlie's hissed warning, and walked to the sideboard in a back corner where the light was dim even though it was broad daylight. In a few moments, I spotted a strange black lever at the bottom of the back lower shelf, and I pulled it.

Very slowly, the wall moved sideways, revealing a back passageway with no light. I hissed at the two witches, and Amerlie arose to help Rosamund carry Nenory; they preceded me into the tunnel. I stepped through and saw the handle connected to the lever on the other side. I pulled it and the wall moved softly back in place. I realized there was a bit of light in the passageway, shining through a spy hole, and wanted to look through it. The main door to the sitting room was bulging inward. Shaking, I sent it a strengthening charm before turning and following the others to the lower levels of the castle.

We walked for a few minutes, but there was no indication the insurrectionists had found the door. Looking back, I saw no flame of light as if the door to the back passages had not been found by the interloper. It was just as well since we'd made no attempt to hide our flight.

As we approached the hall where the council assembled, we saw through another spy hole that we wouldn't be pursued in the passageway. The few council members present were tied to their chairs, and a soldier of evil mien stood over them, taunting their vaunted superiority. I couldn't see if there was another soldier in the room because the hole was so small. Amerlie nudged me; she held a little device with a free-floating arrow on top. She had me blow gently on the machine and I was surprised at the joyful tune that played.

This was, according to Amerlie, a way to ascertain if there was an unseen person in the room. The light tune indicated there was an unseen supporter in the room who was free to move about.

"Had the free person been a foe, we would have heard dirge-like music. Now we just need to see who this person is before we barge in and make fools of ourselves," she said.

"Are the ones tied up on our side?" I whispered, and Rosamund came to take a look.

Nenory was sitting on the floor with her back to the wall, looking devastated. As Rosamund took her place at the spy hole, I sat next to Nenory hoping I could get her motivated.

"Don't you want to get back at the folks who have done this to you and your mother? You have a lot to offer, you know. I can feel the magic growing in you from across the room."

"I feel lost, and I can't believe this is happening. Did you know this was going to happen? Did you warn her? My mother?"

"That's why we came, and, yes, we warned her...but we never expected something to happen so soon. Please, come over and help us. You know more about the council people than we do. You could help so much!"

She stirred, and then stood up. Her shoulders drooped and her face was woeful, but she came anyway. I felt proud of her and this was something I needed to analyze in calmer times.

Rosamund stepped aside so Nenory could peer through the spy hole. When she put her eye to the hole, Nenory gave a brief start and then turned to us in surprise. "If those two are in there, then the likely third is Samony, my mother's wizard."

Rosamund protested, "Your mother didn't have a wizard!"

"That's what she wants...wanted everyone to think. Samony can maintain a fake skin that prevents others from sensing his magical abilities. He's been with us since my dad died, and everyone has just thought he was Mother's lover." She wrinkled her nose at this. "Dad arranged for him to be with us when he knew he was dying. Your father must have known him too since they were all childhood friends together."

Rosamund and Amerlie looked as stunned as I at this revelation. I thought it strange Da hadn't at least mentioned this before I left. I was determined to contact him that night to confirm this odd tale.

We all jerked when we heard a loud voice coming from the room.

Amerlie put her eye to the spyhole and softly reported what she saw. "The soldier is yelling at the person we can't see. He's walking out of sight in the direction we sensed the other person, and he's raising his hand as if to strike. Oh! " She put a hand to her mouth. "He just came stumbling back into view with a knife in his throat! Nenory, come look, is that Samony?"

"Yes, oh, yes! Can we go in and see him? Please?"

"Let's see how it plays out first," Rosamund said. "Is he untying the others?"

Amerlie returned to her post at the hole, and said, "Yes, he's freeing the others and they're all talking at once. Give me a minute to sort it out." She looked anxious, and then said, "There's one man he's not sure about. It's the one at the end of the table. Nenory, come tell me who that is."

Nenory returned to the spyhole and peered in. "I think that's Alleman; he's the head of the exchequer. My mother was worried he wasn't ethical. Samony is really yelling at him, now!"

Amerlie returned to the spyhole and watched for several minutes. "Oh! He knows we're here!"

We all perked up at that.

"How?" asked Nenory.

"Well, he's clearly a wizard! He was looking at the man right in front of us, and his gaze continued up until he was staring at the spyhole. He pretended to be thinking, but his acknowledgement was clear. I'm not sure if he knows who is here, but I suspect he'll find out in a few minutes. He's giving tasks to the men and sending them on their way." Amerlie paused, seeming to hold her breath. "Here he comes."

We all watched the wall with bated breath. A section of the wall moved silently to one side, and Samony entered the tunnel. The look on his face turned to wonder when he saw me standing next to Nenory. I suspected the darker skin and lines on my face allowed him to kneel before the appropriate heir. I realized I didn't know the practice in Middleland when a duchess expires before her heir's eighteenth birthday.

"I'm delighted to find you safe, my lady, although I know only one of your companions. Would you be so kind as to introduce me to the two I don't know?" There was excitement in his voice.

Nenory pulled herself to her full height, taking on an aura that had been foreign to her less than an hour earlier. Like me, she had filled out somehow with her magical awakening.

"This is my cousin Peary from Winthrop, where she will become the duchess on our birthday. With her is the witch Amerlie, who has been Peary's guide all her life. They came with warnings about this assault and they know why it happened. Will you speak with them?"

"Of course, my lady. As you know, you cannot rule until your eighteenth birthday. It's only two months, but during that time, there will be a regent. And I am reluctant to tell you the regent will be Lord Hollyroux."

Nenory cried out in horror. Her hands clutched to her face, she turned to me in supplication. "Can you stay for two months? I can't bear him alone. He'll try to force me to marry him!"

Samony laughed and said, "You need not fear him, my lady. I can control him as much as is necessary—as I've done for years."

"Then you haven't done such a good job," Nenory snapped. "He's accosted me on several occasions and it's only with the help of my guards I've turned him away!"

"And who ensured your guards were nearby on each and every occasion? It was the simple way to protect you without revealing magic at work. And it led him to believe you weren't beyond his reach, which is what allowed us to keep *him* in check. Now we must find another ruse to hold him off for two months. The first we can accomplish with mourning, but the second will prove challenging. We need to bring many to your side to help protect you."

I jumped in, "Aren't you forgetting there is an attack going on *as we speak*? Hadn't we better deal with that before we start worrying about this Lord Holyroux?"

Samony furrowed his brow, surprised that I dared to confront him; he was about to respond when Amerlie spoke.

"This is the duchess in all but ascension of Winthrop. You will treat her with appropriate respect or you will hear about it. She is much further along in her acquiring her full character than Nenory is, and she is a force to be reckoned with. She may even be stronger than you, given what I've seen over the past few weeks. Don't make assumptions based on your experiences here."

"I apologize for my apparent lack of respect, Lady Periwinkle. I had not forgotten the assault on the castle, but I have heard from the coven. They're on scene and several of my fellow wizards have also arrived. I believe we will find the assault all wrapped up by the time we enter the audience hall. And we'll need to do that so the world can acknowledge that the heir survives. This is of paramount importance. It's fine for you to look a little disheveled, and in fact it might help. Will you come with me?"

"I won't go without Peary, Rosamund and Amerlie," she replied. We all smiled as beatifically as possible.

"But Lady Periwinkle is in trousers!" he protested.

"We can go by my room and find her something appropriate to wear. But she'll be by my side when I walk into that audience hall. And she'll be by my side every time I have to meet Hollyroux. Is that clear?"

I had to interrupt. "My dear cousin, I cannot promise to stay with you until our birthday. I have my own ascension to get to. We can stay for maybe a month to straighten out what we can and to destroy as much of this conspiracy as possible, but then Amerlie and I must return home."

"You won't stay with me longer?"

"I think it highly unlikely that I will need to. Didn't we discuss a situation where it would be good for us to be in two places at once? I can see an opportunity for the total embarrassment of Hollyroux, and the duchy's total support in removing him. That we can accomplish before we leave."

Amerlie expressed shock at my suggestion. "How can you promise such a thing?"

But Samony had a smile on his face. "That's a plot I would happily assist!"

We headed off to Nenory's suite to find a dress for me to wear. Samony walked with a funny expression on his face, but then I noticed that both Amerlie and Rosamund had similar expressions.

Apparently, these gifted people could not communicate with each other and walk at the same time without showing some difficulty.

30

We entered the audience hall, Nenory leading, with me right behind her. Samony followed while the two witches made themselves scarce in the crowd. Hollyroux was there, speaking loudly about his role now that the duchess and heir were dead. A round of titters began as more and more people saw our entrance. Hollyroux's face reddened with the giggling, and he began to roar at the audience until one of his aides pointed at us.

"My sweetness, you live!" he called.

"I expect you to address me correctly now, Lord Hollyroux. I'm no longer a child. I've been forced to grow up rather suddenly, and you were nowhere to be seen."

"My lady, your forgiveness, of course. I¬—"

"No, sir, you do not have my forgiveness. You must ask for it like anyone else. It's not granted as a matter of course. Am I making myself clear?" She looked at Holyroux through narrowed eyes.

"My lady, I meant no disrespect. May I ask the reason for this hostility?" His whining plea fell on deaf ears.

"I am merely placing the correct distance between us, a distance you have frequently breeched in the past, I will not tolerate it. And you shouldn't have behaved so licentiously before. Are we in agreement as to your acceptable behavior in the future? We need only deal with each other for the next two months before I ascend to my rightful seat. Can we not do so cordially, if distantly?"

The crowd was again tittering, causing the blush to return to Hollyroux's cheeks. I patted Nenory on the back as inconspicuously as possible, and she pulled herself to an even straighter posture, feeling my support. Out of the corner of my eye, I saw Samony gesture quickly in Hollyroux's direction.

Hollyroux knelt to Nenory, bowing his head, and said, "Do not send me from your side, my lady. I want only to dwell in your glory. You have little need for a regent as you have clearly already begun the access of your birthright. I want only to be there if you need a friendly bit of advice or a shoulder to cry on."

"I have both of those in my dear cousin, Periwinkle, heir to the duchy of Winthrop. She will stay with me for the month of mourning I intend to enter for my dear mother. I will ask you to limit your dealings with me for at least that period as I rely on family to get me through."

Nenory then walked to the center of the hall in front of the throne. Her throne wasn't nearly as ugly as mine, and I felt a momentary stab of jealousy. But then I compared my father to Hollyroux, and I knew I'd gotten the better deal.

Nenory spoke loudly enough for all in the hall to hear. "I am sorry you had to lose your duchess at such an early age. There will be a time that we can mourn her properly but the fight today shows that we must work to contain this uprising first. If there's this much unhappiness in our land, we must find a way to redress it. Fighting is never the answer, and I intend to work with my people to resolve this amicably if possible. I am coming into my magic already and should be able to stand for you and protect you within the next day. I will keep you in my thoughts as I hope you will keep me in yours." She nodded to the crowd, which began hollering and clapping in approval. She turned and we began the solemn exit.

31

We settled into the sitting room, thankful that there had been no damage to this room at least, and the wizards and witches were going around making repairs. We felt worn out, but the energy flowing through Nenory was visible in an aura around her. She recovered first and ordered that dinner be sent up and a table set for the four of us.

"Did I do okay?" she asked.

"Don't you think these two would be all over you if you didn't?" I replied lazily. "You hoping for praise? I never got any." Amerlie did not deign to reply. "It's supposed to build character or something."

Rosamund sat up and looked around as if she didn't know where she was. "Is food coming?" She had no sooner spoken than a knock at the door indicated that something was afoot.

Our guard swung the door open and said, "The table has arrived and the food is right behind." He let in the footmen, and within minutes, we were seated and investigating the chafing dishes before us. There was no conversation for several minutes as we loaded our plates and began to eat. The majordomo came in with wine, though neither Nenory nor I was much interested. I sought a fruit juice and Nenory agreed. A pitcher was quickly forthcoming.

Amerlie began, "Now that our preliminary foray into insanity is over, what ought we to do next? Can we find out if all the strangers noticed in the past several months have now been accounted for?"

"I can certainly contact my sisters to ascertain what they know. Samony should be able to do the same with the wizards although they appear to have been unaware of the undesirables' arrival." Rosamund sniffed at their failure.

"Is Samony likely to join us this evening?" I asked.

Nenory shrugged. "He always spent his evenings below stairs in the past to try to figure out any gossip of a dangerous nature. He would come up to my mother in the later part of the evening to report. I have no idea what he intends to do now," she paused, thinking, "and I wonder if he even thinks he should stay here. This isn't his original home, and I always thought his loyalty to my mother was personal, not professional."

"Perhaps," I said, "we ought to summon him. Is there anyway to determine where he is now?" I addressed the latter question to Amerlie and Rosamund. When it appeared they were ignoring me, I harrumphed and made a comment about incivility. That got a response.

"My lady," Amerlie said, "I took your question as rhetorical. You are by far the strongest one here at this table. Ought you not to find out for yourself?"

"What a charming thought! And it would be so easy if anyone had ever bothered to teach me how to seek a person, rather than telling me repeatedly that I would have plenty of time to learn it once I ascend my throne." I glared at Amerlie, who at least deigned to look a little embarrassed, with reddening cheeks and the biting of her lower lip.

"I'd love to learn how to seek a person," Nenory opined. "I'm just so excited to have gotten my magic and I'd love to know how to *use* it!"

I grinned.

Rosamund decided to calm the waters. "It's a rather simple skill, but one frequently used for frivolous reasons. As a result, it's usually reserved for the more senior practitioners. However, in light of your nearing majority and your positions as rulers in your own lands, it's probably a skill you both should know." Having sufficiently justified it to herself, she took Nenory's hands and took a deep breath.

I looked to Amerlie who appeared to be woolgathering and who declined to look at me.

"You're going to allow Nenory to be taught and not lift a hand for me?" I asked with some ire.

"Only one of you needs the skill tonight. I thought we might wait until the morning when you're less irritable, my lady. You have now gotten into high dudgeon twice this meal, and I believe you are tired after the excitement of today."

"I'm not a child, no matter how much you'd like to treat me as one. If you persist in these follies regarding my behavior or my readiness, you may find yourself supplanted in a few scant months when I ascend. I'm perfectly capable of making such decisions if I feel you are holding me back. Do *not*, I pray you, take me for a fool."

"I wouldn't think of it, my lady. If you insist, I'll teach you tonight. I only thought it might be easier in the morning." With that, she reached out for my hands and I grudgingly placed them in hers.

I haven't previously explained how the teaching of skills occurs.

It begins with the passing of information mind to mind of the nature of the skill. Because skills arise from different areas of the brain, teaching through the link is the easiest and best way to transmit the lesson. Once acquired, practice is necessary to deepen the knowledge acquired. Indeed, it is only with practice that a skill becomes second nature.

When Amerlie entered my mind, she was needlessly rushed and a little harsh. This I hadn't experienced from her before, and I wondered at her reluctance to teach me. But then my mind was wholly enrapt in what she was conveying, and I lost the sense of discomfort I had initially felt. The task was simple and required no great concentration or ability to acquire it.

However, when Amerlie's guard dropped a little, I saw what concerned her. She was contemplating a romantic entanglement with my father. I gave no sign that I'd intercepted this thought, although I understood her concern that I might seek her and find her in a compromising position.

When we separated, I caught her peering at me determinedly. I, in a fit of youthful hijinks, stuck my tongue out at her.

Nenory apparently caught it for she screamed with laughter at the two of us. "You are as bad as two old ladies fighting out the last of their days!" she chortled.

Rosamund took a sterner path. "You must stop this frivolity and practice. If you are to find Samony, it will be a difficult task. He is known to blur his signal in order to hide his whereabouts from nosy snoopers. It will tax your skills and strength, so I suggest you begin. The first one to find him, wins!"

Nenory closed her eyes and dropped her head to her chest. I also closed my eyes though I remained upright and stern in my demeanor. I felt my way out of the room and down the corridor to the stairs, traveling only in my mind. I realized I wasn't bound by the reality of stone walls and magnificent staircases, and allowed my sense to drop through the floors, sending out tendrils of seeking at each level as I went down. I didn't have a good sense of Samony, having not spent much attention on him earlier in the day. But I soon figured out what those without magical ability looked like, and I could set my search pattern to ignore all of those so configured.

I suddenly struck gold and cried out. "I think I've found him. At least I've found someone with quite a bit of power and he doesn't appear to be under guard."

Nenory asked, "Is he on the second sub-basement?"

I realized I had no idea where he was in relation to us. I hadn't counted the floors as I floated through. But in widening my scope of sight, I noticed I was at the level of the main kitchen, with a few people other than the dishwashers still working. I knew the source I had felt was somewhere on this floor.

"I'm in the kitchen, and he appears to be on this floor," I reported.

"That's the second sub-basement and I too think he's on that floor. Can you tell which way?" Nenory asked.

I stopped talking out loud, and instead found an inner way to connect with my cousin. We smoothly melded our searches together, and discovered we sought in slightly different ways. When we combined our paths, our joint mind raced down a corridor to a storeroom in the back, and we flew through the door. There we found Samony lying insensate on the floor. His head looked misshapen and there was blood on the floor. I don't know how I did it, but I wrenched myself, body and all, to his side. I felt Nenory fall away.

I stumbled a little at the sudden feeling of my feet and body. I knelt beside the fallen man and felt for the injury to his head. The skull was broken and there appeared to be swelling in the brain. I reached with a sense similar to the seeker sense and felt the damage in his brain. This new sense began to draw the swelling from the tissue though I wasn't sure how. I don't know where the dampness went, but it dissipated from his tissue. Then I felt for the edges of the broken bone. Luckily none of the bone had entered his brain, and the large pieces fit back together as easily as a child's jigsaw puzzle.

A wave of dizziness crashed over me. I'd done all I could do and felt myself slipping away. I heard a groan from Samony as the last thing before I went out.

When I was next aware. Amerlie was beside me, holding my hands and pouring strength into me.

"You ridiculous child! You nearly killed yourself. How did you get down here? What did you do when you touched Samony? Oh, you silly, silly girl." She threw her arms around me, nearly sobbing in relief.

Samony struggled to sit up. "She saved my life. I was losing all my power trying to stanch the swelling, but my mind was out of countenance. I could feel what was wrong but didn't have the ability or strength to address it. Then I felt a soothing warmth reducing the swelling. The same feeling then pulled the bones together and began to mend them. I felt her falter, just as I was regaining consciousness. She'd done enough though how I don't know."

"She's so young and inexperienced, and yet already so far beyond me that I don't know what to do," Amerlie said, shaking her head. "She's stronger than her mother ever was although her talents tend toward healing rather than lightning like her mother's. They were seeking you together, and suddenly her body disappeared. Nenory's stayed where it was, so we had no idea what was happening. Nenory returned to her body and started crying, so it took us a time to find you."

"I'm as well as can be expected after being coshed over the head with an andiron from the kitchen fire. It's as though a master healer and ten apprentices had worked on me."

I feebly asked, "Do you know who did it?"

"It was one of three, and the most likely is your older brother. If he did not, then it was that brat from Wallameer, Briaint."

"He took that shot at my da," I exclaimed. "He's here? And with Henry?"

"There were three and they were disguised by magic. That was all I could tell at first although that alone is suggestive enough of a plot. I picked at their disguises until I could sense what lay underneath, not the face but the character. The two I was sure of were Henry and Briaint. I've had run-ins with them in the past. The third was too wily and kept putting up more layers after I peeled away a few. He's the primary wizard amongst them, and should be easy to deduce when I get together with my brethren."

"You should know we caught a demon in Springfield. After a fair amount of pressure, he divulged his master to be Gabrille Montrade. Is there any chance the third man was he?" I held my breath in anticipation.

"He was certainly talented enough to be Montrade, but why would he partake in these infantile games?"

Amerlie interjected, "This is not the time or place for these conversations. We must go somewhere safe and secure. We'll tell you more then." She helped Samony to his feet, and then put her arm around me. I wasn't at all reluctant to accept the support, and Samony appeared to be moving well for a man near death only a few moments earlier. We went back to the sitting room where we had dined.

32

"Now you must tell me why the emperor's magus would be here and not by the emperor's side. I cannot believe that this is so." Samony was enjoying a glass of white wine, leaning back in a comfortable chair near the fire. I left it to Amerlie to tell him about both Henry's and Montrade's perfidy. Samony was as reluctant as Madory had been to believe the tale, but was convinced to see reason in light of the attack.

He tried to take over the planning but was quickly disabused of that notion. He wasn't prepared for the strength of will exhibited by the two seventeen-year-olds in the room. I took a little satisfaction in his discomfiture. He seemed totally unaware he was in a matriarchy. It was only later that I learned he had been Madory's lover and had guided her rather thoroughly as he apparently expected to do with us.

"Someone must go to the emperor to begin laying the ground work for his entry into this battle. I think it ought to be me since I am the strongest of us and I am much further advanced than Nenory," I said. "She's needed in her duchy to hold firm against the patriarchal invasion. My father is still my regent and has Winthrop in good and safe hands. If Amerlie wants to come with me, I see no objection to that, but we must remain few to maintain our maneuverability. Any objections?" I had every intention of going alone if possible although I expected quite an outcry from the adults in the room.

"I must ask Samony to stay with me as he gives me strength on the male side I cannot otherwise procure. I also need him and Rosamund to protect me from the advances of my regent for the next two months. If I knew of a way to impeach him, I would." Nenory looked pleased with her speech.

"Would it make sense to take Hollyroux with me for a short while, perhaps on an embassy to somewhere on our way? We could ensure his departure from your capital and lose him along the way," I offered.

"You two sound as though you think you're already in charge, but you aren't," said Rosamund. "None of your current plans make any sense, and there is no way, Peary, you are going to the emperor."

"And you're going to stop me how?"

"Actually, I think Peary has shown her leadership skills," said Amerlie. "It makes sense to try to reach the emperor when his wizard is away playing with his little friends. And the emperor is moving toward us, isn't he? He's supposed to be in Winthrop for Peary's ascension. Why shouldn't she ride out to meet her overlord and bring him to her own rite?"

"There's much to be said for this plan," said Samony. "But it's late, and it's been a busy and frightful day. We'd all do well to retire for the evening and meet for breakfast to see to the details of the plan."

Nenory said, "You're all welcome to the duchess's dining parlor for your breakfast. It's one of the most secure places in the palace, and the food is much better than the general fare from the kitchen. Only the stars of the week are allowed to cook for the parlor!"

Upon a general agreement to dine shortly after dawn, we went our several ways, Amerlie and I already discussing how to tempt Hollyroux away. We didn't go straight to bed though we had been assigned adjacent rooms in the royal wing. Instead we went to our sitting room to continue the planning.

"Do we know how far the emperor has come to date?" I asked.

Amerlie sat at a table with writing paper and pulled out a quill and ink. I moved to the other side of the table and sat. She quickly drew a diagram I vaguely recognized as the outline of our continent. I had only learned of it in the few short days in Springfield. I had thought there was land forever on either side, but Amerlie had shown it was not so. On her diagram she picked out Springfield, Markerburg, the known rebel states, and a dotted line to show the Emperor's intended route. From the drawing, it looked as if we could cut across most of Middleland and hope to intersect the emperor's route more than thirty leagues from Springfield.

We were in agreement. When I asked if there was unrest elsewhere in Middleland. Amerlie quickly shaded in about a quarter of Middleland, which was only slightly athwart of our projected trek.

"Wouldn't that be a fine place to send Hollyroux?" I asked with a smirk. "He would only briefly be directly behind us, undoubtedly recruiting our foes. Whether because he is stupid or unaware, I'm not sure."

Amerlie nodded her head and grinned. "He could be appointed the ambassador of good will toward the unclean masses and allowed to raise men into a standing army. Not that any are likely to follow such a slob. Oh, he's a horrible man." We both laughed.

"Are you really going to support me in going to the emperor?"

"Why wouldn't you believe it?"

"Isn't it a bit audacious?"

"That's why I love it." The corner of her mouth curled up. "Your brother and Montrade will never expect you to jump that way, nor to be in the company of the baleful Hollyroux. We'll make it look like we're part of his entourage when *we'll* be the ones in charge. Before he even reaches the rebels, we'll split off."

"You're on! This could have amusing aspects to it." I was enchanted with the plan. I doubted I'd be able to sleep. But the traumas of the day had worn me out more than I realized and sleep came easily.

33

I had nothing against wearing dresses on high occasions, but it was nice to get back into a pair of pants. Nenory and Samony were shocked by my attire but were soon enticed away from their alarm by the marvelous food that had been prepared for us.

"We think we have a plan for the first part of our trip," Amerlie told the others. "We can travel as part of Hollyroux's embassy to the rebels in Abenathis. Nenory, you'll make sure medals will be had for the one who can bring the Abenathians back into the fold, Nenory. And it should solve your problem with him for at least some time, probably long enough for your ascension to be performed."

Nenory smiled broadly at this news. "I have plenty of other people to advise me as I learn my way. But, Peary, you'll miss so much in doing this."

"Not at all, I'm an incoming duchess riding out to meet my emperor who is coming for my ascension. We've passed the news on to Da, who's happy to have me moving away from Markerburg. He thinks I'll be very safe with the emperor if Montrade is away."

We buckled down to eat the exquisite meal prepared for us. I noticed that Samony watched each of us in turn, as if he were trying to read us. I could sense he was trying to access my thoughts, so I built a wall against intrusion right below my surface thoughts, which I turned to the cuisine. I didn't trust Samony too much since I suspected he held secret patriarchal thoughts. Glancing at Amerlie, I guessed we were thinking the same thing, given the sour look on her face as she glanced at him.

After the meal, we returned to the parlor we'd been using the previous day, with the purpose of summoning Hollyroux to advise him of the honor we were doing him. We awaited his arrival, having sent a footman for him from the dining room. After several minutes, we began almost as one to show signs of nervousness.

Finally, Samony went to the door to inquire if the guards knew what was holding up Hollyroux's appearance. He came back none the wiser. He began to pace and then got a thoughtful look on his face. He went to the window and looked down into the square.

"Here he is, coming across the courtyard from the direction of the Triniston Tower. If he has been to see the troops, it will be interesting to see if they are going to join him. Or is there a particular officer he may have been with?"

Rosamund responded, "He's been known to spend hours watching the men practice. He is, I suppose, ashamed of his obesity, and would like to learn exercises he can do to improve his physical and mental acumen. A hopeless case, I assure you."

Samony shushed us as he heard the heavy man coming down the hallway. There was a loud and angry discussion outside the door, and then the guard opened it.

"You have a visitor, my lady—"

"Get out of my way, you buffoon. Don't you know that I'm the regent?" Hollyroux shoved his way past the guard.

Nenory stood, and glared at Hollyroux. "You may be the regent, but you are here at my command. You *will* be still and keep your thoughts to yourself!" Then turning to the guard, "Thank you for your insistence on proper protocol. I won't allow him to make the same mistake twice." She then returned to her seat and ignored him completely.

I stood and gushed at Hollyroux. "Oh, sir, thank you for agreeing to let me and my associate come with you on your trip. It'll be an honor to ride with one such as you, especially on this difficult embassy."

Hollyroux, looking perplexed, turned to Nenory. "Of what is she speaking, my lady? I know nothing of this."

"I thought you came in response to my message," Nenory replied. "Did the footman not tell you of the signal honor we are giving you? Perhaps he meant to keep it to himself. I'll have a word with him later."

"My lady, I don't understand. I'm your regent and I must help you through these trying times."

"Nonsense. Did I not tell you I would be in mourning for a month? During that time, I'd hoped you would perform the important task I've assigned you. If you don't think you're able, I'm sure many others would like the opportunity to gain titles and wealth in support of my realm."

"My lady, I'm at your beck and call. Assign me whatever task it was in your heart and mind to do, I beg of you!"

"If you insist, though I am uncomfortable with your apparent indifference. I need a very skilled diplomat and negotiator to visit Abenathis and treat with the separatists there. I expect him to acquire, over the course of this embassy, a fighting force unparalleled in our nation. The recent assault against my mother and myself cannot be repeated."

"My lady, I am indeed the man you seek. I'm talented at the art of negotiation in politics and other topics, and I can undoubtedly effect the reconciliation you desire. I'll begin to gather a train to accompany me as quickly as possible. This is clearly an urgent matter."

"You will take my cousin and her servant to the border of Abenathis and the Emperor's Way. She should be given ten or more days' worth of provisions in awaiting the emperor's arrival for her investiture. You will supply her and her maid with horses, and at least one pack mule. If the area is as dangerous as I have heard, you're to name a bodyguard among your most trustworthy deputies to ensure my cousin makes it to her rendezvous with the emperor. Am I clear?"

"Oh, yes, my lady. The Duchess of Winthrop will be guarded like the Crown Jewels." He looked me up and down before saying, "Does she intend to wear pants on this journey?"

"Perhaps you ought to ask her. I certainly don't know."

"When would you like me to leave, my lady?"

"Why, as soon as possible. I should have thought the urgency was obvious after yesterday."

"I shall be off then, to make my preparations. We should be able to leave within the week, my lady."

"The week? I shall have to find someone more industrious than that!"

Samony stepped forward. "If I may, my lady, I believe I can assist the regent such that he'll be able to leave by midday tomorrow. Will that suffice?"

"Oh, come, Samony, surely you can make it first light tomorrow! I am mindful of the faith my late mother had in your prodigious skills."

Samony bowed and took Hollyroux by the elbow to lead him away. Hollyroux pulled his arm out of Samony's grasp and turned back to Nenory. "My lady, I—"

"Oh, no need to say more, my dear Hollyroux. I knew I could rely on you." Nenory smiled at her regent, in all ways seeming to approve of him. She then turned to Rosamund to begin another conversation. Hollyroux had no alternative to leaving with Samony.

After they had left the room, we held our laughter as long as we could, afraid Hollyroux would hear us if he chanced to return.

34

First light the following morning saw us in the courtyard with a large number of troops and horses as well as carts filled with war equipment and supplies for our trip. Hollyroux was nowhere to be seen, but Amerlie and I were present and accounted for, with Samony hurrying to make final adjustments to the plans. As our horses were brought to us, Samony turned and looked toward the castle. Two footmen were pushing Hollyroux out the door while he was still buttoning his coat, his hair and trousers in disarray.

"Ah," said Samony, as he walked toward the ambassador. "I see you've made it in good time, my lord."

"This is outrageous!" Hollyroux shouted. "I was still in my bed when I was rousted out by these uncouth louts. I wasn't given time to bathe or eat and was hustled into my clothing without the assistance of my valet. It cannot be borne!" He whined, as if he might expire from the indignity.

"Did I not make it clear to you last night that I would expect you here at dawn?" Samony replied.

"And didn't I tell you then that I was in charge of this embassy and we would leave only when I was ready?" Hollyroux blustered.

"And here you are, ready to go," replied the wizard.

"I am *not* ready to go, sir. I have not eaten, and I have not taken my leave of my duchess."

A voice came from the audience balcony above. "I'm so glad to see you arrived and ready to go and in such fine voice, my regent!" Nenory called down. "Do send Samony back when you depart. I must applaud him for equipping you so quickly and so well. I am well pleased with this diplomatic foray."

"Thank you, my lady," Hollyroux responded a bit desperately. "We go to defend your honor and your rule."

Samony brought over his horse and held the horse's head as Hollyroux attempted to mount. He was finally assisted by two of his soldiers who came at his difficulties. They returned to their mounts and fell in behind the regent. Amerlie and I took our positions behind the two soldiers, and we were quickly followed by the remaining mounted men. I couldn't see whether the carts followed immediately since my view was blocked by the number of riders behind me.

I waved at my cousin and saw her brilliant smile at the departure of her least favorite courtier. I smiled back, and we both laughed. Samony appeared at her side and also waved. Amerlie whispered that Hollyroux was turning toward us, so I returned my gaze to the front of the line. I composed my face to appropriate serenity and raised my eyes in time to see Hollyroux stand in his stirrups in an attempt to bow to Nenory. I was lucky enough to see him fall off his horse and hear him land in the mud left over from the storm the night before. The two soldiers who had helped him onto his horse before alit and picked him out of the mire. He was unwilling to get on the horse again, and the horse seemed pleased with that eventuality.

A rather ornate carriage drew up next to Hollyroux, and two footmen came to his rescue. The two soldiers were reluctant to let their boss be co-opted by such pantywaists and again pushed him onto the horse, which promptly bolted, leaving him once more in the muck. The horse disappeared into the early morning mist, and was only retrieved days later by the saddle master to the duchess.

The effeminate footmen were then allowed to place Hollyroux into the carriage and he yanked the shades closed. I didn't see him again until we were settling into a camp built completely by the footmen. It was another day before I realized the guards were helping the footmen keep Hollyroux out of trouble by consigning him to his tent at all times the company was not moving. Meals were taken to his tent, as was bath water, and any other service he might demand.

35

The trip was the nicer for Hollyroux's ineptitude. He couldn't corral me to ask about my father or his intentions. He couldn't question me about my plans for the trip, including after we separated. In all, Amerlie and I were pleased with the situation, although it was fraught with complications.

When we entered Abenathis, we were not prepared to deal immediately with the rebels. But they were there in full force.

Amerlie and I slipped away for a while since we didn't want to be caught if there were any difficulties. We found a place behind decorative bushes to hide and watch what was going on. One of the soldiers had gone to Hollyroux's carriage to try to roust him, a task that must have been the more difficult because of the amount of alcohol he'd consumed at lunch.

Eventually he made an appearance, only mildly disheveled, and wearing the sash of an ambassador from the duchess. He was greeted by an oily brigand who was less than thrilled with his noble token.

"My good sir, I'm an ambassador to your people from our noble and gracious duchess. Have the courtesy to show me the respect you'd give the duchess." Hollyroux's statement did not have the effect he desired as the brigand spit in his direction.

"You're not wanted here. We've got men in charge here like they should be. You're a sucker, working for a woman. She's got no right to rule those bigger and stronger."

"Whatever are you talking about? We're the richest state in the empire. We became that way with women leading us. You're crazy. And anyway, the magic in this duchy runs through the women. How do you expect to run a place instead of magical women?"

"There ain't no such thing as a magical woman. They got no right to be the rulers of our land. They just got all you guys snookered and we intend to do something about it. So if you want us to listen to you, you better start singing a new song, 'cause we ain't having *any* of what you're selling."

Hollyroux looked around, I suspect for us. We had no intention of saving him, but Amerlie was concerned by what the rebel had said. She thought the time had come to show some magic although I strongly disagreed. We had another job to handle and couldn't take the time to deal with illiterate, uneducated men. I was reasonably satisfied the soldiers Hollyroux had brought would be able to handle the insurrection.

One of the soldiers we had dealt with on the journey sidled over in front of our bush. "My lady, can we do nothing to prove that the duchess *is* magical?"

"We can have you declare that the duchess will send a sign when certain words are uttered," Amerlie replied.

I objected, "Can we get Hollyroux to play along or is he too under the weather from his lunchtime drink?"

Our soldier said, "I can cry out the words, if you can do the magic."

He and Amerlie worked out their respective roles, although I had no idea what Amerlie intended.

Suddenly, the soldier arose and ran toward the rebels. "The duchess said you would not believe, you've been lied to by outside people. She said she would send a sign when certain words were spoken."

Hollyroux tried to interrupt him, but another soldier quickly took him away.

"Repent, you men, and no harm will come to you. Deny the duchess and you will burn!" At that exact moment, lightning struck the rebel who had addressed Hollyroux.

"Does anyone else deny the power of the duchess?" he yelled, and a murmur of discontent rose among the crowd. A second lightning bolt flew into the crowd, downing five men. The remainder fled in an unruly mass.

Hollyroux got away from his handler and ran toward us. "You usurped my power! I will have you both put in chains to be taken back to Markerburg on a charge of treason, and I will rule on your fate as regent. You've gone too far. My lady sent no such instructions."

"Oh, but she did, you know," I said. "After you went off with Samony to arrange the trip, the duchess and I had a lengthy talk about what might need to be done if the rebels spouted such nonsense. That's why Amerlie and I ran to hide, so none of the rebels would be able to claim an evil witch had done these things. She would have told you herself had you not been so late on the day of departure."

One of the soldiers behind him snickered, and soon most of

them were laughing loudly.

Hollyroux turned red at the scorn in the men's laughter. "You do not treat me with the respect I am owed. I am an ambassador of the duchess!"

"And I am the duchess's cousin and heir and a duchess in my own right. Shall we talk about who is entitled to respect?"

Amerlie stepped forward and laid a hand on Hollyroux's arm. Somehow she pacified him.

His choler decreased, the flush in his cheeks faded, and he nodded in my direction. "I'm sorry, my lady, as I wasn't appropriately respectful in my address to you." It was the prettiest speech I had ever heard Hollyroux given.

"I'm sure you were caught up in the furor of protecting the honor of your duchess, and I wouldn't have it any other way," I said.

At that, a group of soldiers returned with most of the escaping rebels. I stepped back to allow Hollyroux to take over.

"Did I not tell you that your duchess was a powerful wielder of magic? Do you question now why I'm here to bring you back to the fold? Your duchess is generous to a fault, and will grant forgiveness to all who ask for it. If you feel that you haven't shared fairly in the wealth of our duchy, I am prepared to take your grievances to the duchess. I am prepared to advocate with her on your behalf. Come, gentlemen, tell me what you want. Tell me your woes and I'll do what I can to resolve them."

An older man stepped forward and tugged at his hairs. "Your worship, we didn't know the lady could do such things, nor at such a distance. We didn't know that we could be heard by such as you." He continued to prattle as Amerlie and I again slipped away.

36

We met with the provisioner to discuss what could be spared for our march to the emperor. The provisioner reminded us we were to get a competent escort, and said he'd selected the group.

Within an hour, we were ready to go. There were several hours of daylight left, and we were eager to be away from the scene of the turmoil. The provisioner had found a local boy who would assist us in finding the fastest and safest route. Our escorts arrived and we wasted no time in getting our horses moving out from the area.

The leader of the escort was our friend from the lightning strikes. He introduced himself at Honorious, son of Welting. He wanted us to call him Orus, which was what his younger brother had been able to manage many years ago, and which had stuck. He was as appreciative of leaving Hollyroux as were we and the rest of the crew. We could finally move at a reasonable rate of speed, with only brief breaks during the ride to walk the horses and to answer calls of nature.

The local boy, Roddy, was very familiar with the borderlands and knew where other rebels might be lurking. We had to take a number of detours to avoid watering holes, and hovels that were clearly in use. By the time the sun was lowering in the sky, Roddy had led us to an area slightly elevated from the surrounding land. It had trees and undergrowth surrounding a central clearing.

"If'n you have sentries, you can see anyone coming near. They can't hide from the folk on the heights. This is where me and Grandma stay when we's coming back from the border."

"Roddy, what do you and your grandma do at the border?" Amerlie asked.

"We'm can sell our milk for more on t'other side of the border. They'm don't got much pasture over there. Their cows be skinny and barren most the time. When we got a young bull that's not yet growed his horns, we sometimes sell him to them for food we'm can't get here."

"Do you know the people we are likely to meet?"

"Most of 'em won't pay you no mind if you be riding with soldiers. Even alone, you probably okay, with the young lady acting like a man."

Amerlie's eyebrows rose at this remark.

As we set up camp for the night, Orus sent out sentries to keep watch while there was still light to see. The one assigned cooking duties came to see what we might like. He looked as hoary and wizened as any man I'd ever seen, but he had a ready laugh and was delighted to be away from the cavalcade.

That night, we didn't put up tents, which might be visible from lower ground and ate a cold meal to avoid any telltale smoke.

With dried meat, cheese, and bread for dinner, we sat in companionable silence. The area was quiet, and we did nothing to disturb the night. It wasn't long before I indicated my desire to sleep. Amerlie agreed it was time for all to get rest, especially since a number of them would have to relieve the current guards.

I slid into my bedroll, noticing Amerlie was close by my side. "Do you think we'll get out of rebel territory tomorrow? And get across the border?" I whispered.

"It's likely that we'll get beyond the reach of the current scruffy crew, but it's unclear if they're all aligned. If it's all part of Montrade's plan, then any future rebels can be expected to be very similar. But if the locals are doing their own planning, clearing one group won't help with the next. Get a good night's sleep because tomorrow will be busy."

I watched Orus as he made rounds of the camp. He leaned over the shoulder of one of the guards and he must have said something, for the guard shook with silent laughter. He continued his slow peregrination around the camp, and returned to settle several feet from Amerlie and me. But he neither lay down nor tried to sleep. He sat with his sword lying on his crossed legs as if he were prepared to guard Amerlie and me with his life.

The next time I was aware, the sun was peeking over the horizon, and the sky graded from light blue in the east through all the blues into blackest night in the west. I turned to Amerlie and saw her looking at me with a slight grimace on her face. Within seconds the scowl turned into a smile, but I had seen and wondered what it meant.

"Did you sleep well?" she asked me, and I answered in the affirmative.

As I began to rise, she reached out and grabbed my arm.

"Montrade passed in the night. I had to conceal us all, and he didn't discover this party. He was laughing with his companions about 'the idiot Hollyroux and his entourage.' I'm afraid our companion is about to or already has walked into trouble left by our friend. We shouldn't be too far behind Montrade for he may win the emperor's favor with his bald lies."

"Are the others awake? Can we get going now?"

"They're packing up as we speak. I let them start knowing you would awaken shortly."

The horses were being saddled as we joined the guards, several of whom smiled and nodded at us. This was a marked change from the early days of the venture. Whether it was the absence of Hollyroux or the proximity of the border that made them happy, it was a welcome change.

One of the men handed out chunks of bread after we mounted. Munching away, we headed to the border.

31

There was no real trouble through the morning, although our outlying scouts reported movement by the rebel forces toward the border north of where we were headed. This put them further away from the emperor's progression. It was one more thing we'd have to pass on to him as a problem in his future. It was, in fact, likely they were an ambush party, and they might have had more current knowledge of the emperor's progress than we had.

"Amerlie, is there anything we can do magically to determine their objective? Like reading their minds or something."

"No, but we might be able to impede them if we have a good enough map. Orus, what sort of map of the region they're in might we have? And is there someone in the group who knows the terrain well?"

"We have the maps and we have two soldiers as well as our guide. Let me go get them." He moved off quickly to arrange a conference.

We barely had time to breathe before he returned with two parchment rolls under his arm as well as two men and Roddy in tow. He rolled out one of the maps and indicated approximately where we were. Looking at the map, I saw no real impediment between our current position and the border about ten leagues away. It would be an easy ride and we would be over the border by noon if our sabotage didn't take much time.

Orus then indicated the probable site of the rebels paralleling us to the north.

Amerlie chuckled at the sight of a small brook a few leagues ahead of that locus. "I'll be able to flood that brook long before they reach it. Look at this spring up here, and this horrid little pond here. Together they'll flood the brook, making it two or three times its normal depth and spreading across the valley. We can best judge this if we know exactly where they are. I don't suppose you know someone in that rebel group?"

"Yes'm, ma'am, you sure do. That prince from Winthrop is there, and so's that other prince, Brain or whatever, from some other place," Roddy said.

I looked at Amerlie in astonishment, "Henry here?"

"Briaint too. We'll definitely be able to read them. Let's start with that, then, as it'll tell us how much time we have to spill the waters." Amerlie led me further away from the soldiers, whispering, "You're the better contact for Henry, much stronger than I would be against him or Briaint. I'll guide you, but the final assault will have to be yours. You need to be really subtle to make sure he doesn't feel the touch. I don't know how strong he is, but we should act as if he's powerful. It's only logical."

"I agree, but you're going to have to guide me all the way in."

"Probably not," she laughed. "You'll get it figured out quickly. It's not hard to do."

We sat on the ground and settled into a minor trance. I began to feel outside my body, a skill Amerlie had been teaching me in odd moments since we'd left Markerburg. I touched her outside self gently and she showed me weird gossamer stuff that flowed around the part of me outside my body.

I heard her voice. <This is your family aura. You'll find something similar coming from Henry. Not as full, and a slightly darker color, both because he is male. You have such a full aura because you're the head of the family in all but title now. We'll move to the rebel base now.>

<How?>

<Follow me.>

I couldn't see how she moved, and she had to come back for me. <You must *want* to come with me. It's a movement of will. Will yourself to that tree.> She pointed to a tree in the middle of the field below us. I tried to will myself to the tree and ended up half a league beyond it.

Amerlie laughed as she came next to me. <You'll have to learn subtlety. If you try that near Henry, you'll go straight through him, leaving him shivering. He may not know why, but there's a chance he might.>

With a few more moves on my part, I finally got the feel for what impetus would produce how much movement. I was able to turn around quickly and calmly, dart from side to side, and stop in an instant. The training was fun, as Amerlie sent me non-vocal commands that I had to learn to decipher quickly, and before long, we were heading at great speed toward the spot where we expected to find the rebels.

Once we arrived at the place we'd targeted, we were surprised to find no sign of the rebels. We agreed to go in opposite directions for a few moments to see if we could find them. I went east toward the stream and Amerlie went west back in the direction from which we'd come. I saw no sign of them before the stream, and it showed no signs of having been crossed. I headed back to Amerlie, looking for signs all the way.

I didn't see her before I ran into the rebels, who were fighting amongst themselves about which way to go. A number wanted to come straight at us, while others wanted to go on to block the emperor. I quartered the area, looking for Amerlie, when I caught a glimpse of her struggling with something on the far side of the field where the rebels had camped for the night.

I was at her side instantaneously and saw the horror she was fighting. It looked like a black fog, but human faces kept rising to the surface, a few I could almost recognize.

<What can I do to help?>

<You have to get what's inside the fog.>

I leaned into the fog, keeping my face clear of it, and reaching to the full extent of my arms. I felt something but it was squirming so quickly I couldn't get a good hold. I focused on freezing the fog, and it began to slow. I then could get both hands around *something* and I pulled. Amerlie was quickly at my side, helping me free whatever it was in my grip. Suddenly the thing flew out of the murk, which rapidly dissipated.

Our spectral forms were holding my brother Henry, whose usually neatly coiffed hair was standing up all over, his shirt in shreds, both feet bare and his trousers ripped in a number of places.

"Thank you, thank you, thank you," he muttered with a wild look in his eyes that showed no comprehension of who we were or even where.

Amerlie slid her hands across his forehead and down over his eyes, closing them. Her spectral form wavered and then solidified as she brought her body to her.

"Go, get Orus and the rest of the men. We can take these rebels now because they're terrified of what they've seen. Ride hard, it may not last." Before she had finished, I was flashing into my body back at the camp.

"Orus!" I called, but he was already there. "We must ride with all haste to the rebels. We have a fine catch for you to return with!"

The horses were already saddled and ready in preparation for our return, and the men rose into saddles as Roddy brought me my horse. I shouted instructions as I climbed onto the horse and the men were headed out at a canter before I was ready to move.

38

We arrived in time to see Amerlie herding the rebels into a circle, the unconscious Henry across the saddle of a horse she'd captured. Some were catcalling at her while others sullenly pushed the others into order. They all looked up at the sound of our hooves. Our soldiers whooped and hollered and the rebels quieted immediately. As we rode up, Henry began to stir.

Orus took command of the prisoners while Amerlie and I attended to my brother. He began to recognize us, and he seemed relieved. I stiffened thinking he would try to con us.

He smiled weakly. "I've been terribly wrong," he said, and I didn't believe a word. "There's a demon abroad on Montrade's side, and I'll have none of it. This conspiracy was simply a fake to allow Montrade to take the crown. He had no interest in raising men to all thrones. In fact, he wants to keep the matriarchies since they'll form the heart of his empire. He left us after Markerburg and told us that he'd be in touch. We followed his trail this far and then that thing attacked us."

"Where's Briaint?" Amerlie asked anxiously.

"That thing got him first, I was trying to stop it when it pulled me in too. The men ran, but obviously didn't get far."

"They were arguing which way to go. Either after us or over the stream to the border to await the emperor." I looked critically at my brother and found nothing to love or evoke pity.

Amerlie said, "Orus, I'd like you to take the enemy combatants back to Markerburg along a path you deem most appropriate for safely getting your charges to the duchess. Can I have faith in you?"

"Oh, yes ma'am, I know these ways better than you can imagine. And what I don't know, Roddy is sure to set me straight." Roddy smiled at the compliment, and nodded his head.

"Ma'am, what do we do with the lordling?" Orus asked.

I looked to Amerlie for the answer, but she deferred to me.

"In the best of circumstances, I would send him back to my father for appropriate discipline, but I doubt he can handle Henry, once his terror dissipates. Must we take him with us? What if his partner in crime is there? Or both of them with this demon at work?"

"If it pleases you, ma'am, I would be happy to take him on."

"He has magic," warned Amerlie. "So how will you guard him?"

Orus merely waved at a pile of heavy iron chains. Henry blanched at the sight. His breathing became labored as if the thought of the chains unmanned him. I was puzzled for I felt nothing inimical in the chains, nor did I feel weakened by their proximity.

Amerlie quickly cleared up my confusion. "Iron only affects males with magic. It weakens their magic but does no harm to the men. Most men don't believe this because they never realize how much magic they use simply to maintain their looks. They're as ill informed as they are incompetent in using their magic. You and I can touch iron because there is nothing in our magic that iron can use. We're not belligerent or grasping in the way that men are. We have our own faults but they are not encouraged by iron." Amerlie looked a little smug.

I watched as my brother was bound in chains, swearing disconsolately as each link touched his skin. His torn shirt and ragged pants did nothing to protect him from the burning iron. I surmised that the pain sufficiently distracted him so he could no longer call on his art.

Amerlie and I took our leave of our guardians. Orus was considerate enough to give us the mule for our luggage and supplies. He kept only one of the rebel's horses, driving the others away with a slap on the rump of the sole stallion, a horse I recognized as belonging to my brother.

Henry was lashed to the back of a nag, so his opportunity for escape was minimized. He glared at me, as if expecting me to flinch. I merely winked at him, to his clear distaste. As we reached the top of a hill toward the border, I looked back to see the little troop moving slowly, to accommodate the prisoners who were on foot, into the woods we had avoided on our way east.

39

We came across the border well before noon, and took only another fifteen minutes to make it to the road upon which the emperor's progression would travel. Heading south, we passed a number of farms, and inquired at one if the emperor had reached this area. The housewife told us the emperor was indeed residing at her ladyship's manor not five leagues farther down the road. We thanked her before heading off to meet the man we hoped to save.

We could see the manor from across several fields for it stood high on a hill, quite large by comparison to anything else we'd passed. I was surprised not to see a bustling town nearby and expressed as much to my companion.

"This is her country retreat, if I recall correctly. The rumor has always been that she buys nothing locally, and instead ships everything in from outside, not even using her locals at her mansion. She doesn't support her people and is said to consort with men not of her class."

"Amerlie, are you spreading gossip? I never would've thought you'd succumb to it."

We neared the gate and found it locked, with an empty sentry post next to it. I "halloed" loudly but got no response. I looked to Amerlie, and got a nod in return so I repeated my hail.

A man came clanking down the road on the other side of the fence. He was heavily armored and looked unhappy at the interruption. While he was still several feet away, he barked, "What do you want?"

"We're wanderers from Winthrop, and knew we would be away from home during the emperor's progress through Springfield. We thought we might see him here on our way out of town." Amerlie smiled at the guard as if there was nothing irregular about her request.

"I can't let you in without there be a guard to watch and I'm alone today. I—"

I quieted him by pushing my card through the gate. "I have no problem waiting, my friend. It is my wife's simple hope that we be allowed to avail ourselves of this opportunity. We'll wait here for your response, and please don't feel you have to run in this heat."

The guard replied, "Thank you, sir, we don't see much kindness around here. I'll be back as soon as possible."

When he was far enough away, I asked, "What do you know about this Lady Oghamry? I mean, this is the most unwelcoming place I've come to since I left the valley. What's it called?"

"She's famous for her support of Briaint, and there may even have been an affair there." Amerlie paused. "She won't want to hear he's been eaten by a demon. She's also a little uncouth if the stories about her are even half true. According to rumor, she lives a wild life, and has the table manners of a hog. I've never seen her eat, and I hope I never have to. This lovely place is called the Castle of the Pocari."

"Do we know where she stands, politically? Does she support her compatriot women?" I questioned. "And who's Pocari and why is this considered a castle?" I was curious to see such a person.

"She's been seen in the company of several of the rebel group, so I think we should assume she's opposed to His Serene Highness and yourself." Amerlie explained with a shrug. "The Pocari are an ancient race that was defeated a century before Maximillian's great-grandfather started building this empire."

"Will she keep us from seeing the emperor?"

"I don't think even she would dare keep a message from the emperor. And our message was given to an imperial guard who knows what he must do. Now we can only hope Nenory has done her job."

"You don't like her, do you?"

"What makes you say that?"

"Your tone of voice and the way your eyes rolled at me when I asked that question."

"Unlike you, she hasn't had the advantage of going through experiences that teach maturity. A coddled life with a doting mother who loved her but suspected her daughter didn't actually have it in her to rule, at least according to Rosamund."

"I should think her competence in handling Hollyroux would somewhat raise her in your esteem, yes?"

"She did an acceptable job at that, but it shouldn't have taxed her in the least." Amerlie said with a huff. "Where is that damned guard?"

"Perhaps it taxed her because she was abused by the man as a child. You must have felt it as strongly as I did. Her disgust and fear of the man were blatant and totally in keeping with his groping of her when she was young. And, besides, her memories came to the fore when she looked at him."

"You saw her memories? That's unheard of!" Amerlie exclaimed with widened eyes. "Normally we can only hear surface thoughts, yet you sensed memories and emotions. There really is an extraordinary bond between you.... Maybe it's because she has both birthmarks."

"You realize that, if I die, she becomes the Duchess of Winthrop too."

The expression on Amerlie's face was as confused as she probably felt on the inside, for while she showed a clear smile, her eyebrows were knitted and her forehead lined. I watched to see which emotion won, and at first, I was pleased to see her smile win. But then she pointed behind me, and I saw the guard coming toward us with a royal factotum.

"My dears, I'm Pietro. You must come in. His Excellency would love to meet you. He's asked me to see if you'll have tea with him after a short time so you can refresh yourselves."

"That sounds lovely, sir. I *am* in need of dust removal," Amerlie said and fluttered her eyelashes.

I almost laughed. The man returned her regard with something akin to adoration, and I felt I had to step in, "If we're going, 'twould be best to go now." The hint was not lost on the guard although the servant appeared to be oblivious to what was going on around him. The guard came forward and opened the gate. We pulled our horses and the mule through it, while Amerlie continued to tease the servant.

We had arrived at the current residence of the Emperor of Andirony, Maximillian IV, and we were about to enter stage right.

PART 2

The Emperor's Progression

40

The emperor was not a happy man. He'd been on this progression for four months already and he was tired from the endless politicking and social whirl. It was late at night but the day had been so hectic and nerve jangling that he knew he wouldn't sleep.

"Festino! Festino! Can you get me something to drink that will settle me down?"

"Sire?"

"You choose."

He went back to pacing. This Castle of the Pocari was old and drafty, welcome on a warm summer day. His formal coat lay on an overstuffed chair next to the window; the desk opposite it was strewn with papers. The room was large and poorly lit with tall candelabras at two of the four corners. A large chandelier that might have been enough to provide light was left unlit, bereft of candles. These economies had been taken by the duchess even with the prospect of an imperial progression.

His sources told him there was plenty of money in Pocari; the stinginess of this duchess arose from simple greed. Not content with her third-place standing on the Parade of Merit, she was intent on catching Winthrop and Middleland, the second and first respectively on the list ahead of her. He was disgusted by her behavior and had called her on it. She feigned not to understand. It added to his current discomfort. He sighed as Festino appeared with his drink.

"Sire, you must stop pacing. Let me get your dresser to help you prepare for bed. I'll put your tea on the bedside table, shall I?"

"No, Festino, stop fussing. Put the tea on the desk. I'll drink it as I cope with this paperwork. Thank you."

Festino put the tray on the table, pushing aside papers to make way for it. He took the cover off the plate of sweet and savory tartlets he had brought to tempt his employer.

"I said, don't fuss, Festino. Go, go, find some other use for yourself."

Festino turned, bowed slightly to the emperor, and slipped from the room.

The emperor renewed his pacing. One of his primary worries

was Montrade's absence. He had gone off again without explanation as he'd done several times during the progression. Previously, Montrade's returns had been so timely that he'd immediately been thrown into work of an urgent nature, so there was never the opportunity to question him.

The emperor sat down briefly to drink his tea, sorting papers until he again came upon Robert's letter, dated one week earlier. Surprised anew at the language about Duchess Periwinkle, he wondered how a regent could let his charge go wandering about the world so close to the ascension. Robert should know better. What if the emperor arrived for the ascension and the one ascending didn't appear? When they had known each other before, Robert had not been the type to lose an heir.

The tea began to work its magic and his mind slowed down. He had no intention of calling for his dresser. He was perfectly capable of removing his own clothes, once he got the fancy knot out of his cravat. After struggling with the damned thing for a few minutes, he was ready to call for Pietro when the knot fell apart in his hands. Laughing quietly, he finished undressing and crawled into bed. With one last call for Festino to douse the candles, he slipped into sleep.

***

Festino hurried downstairs to the servants' area after snuffing the candles. He wanted to meet with Rogebon before Rojo went to bed. Their nightly meeting was important to Festino, though whether Rojo felt the same way was another question entirely. Festino took everything Rojo said with a gram of salt since the former wasn't sure of the latter's honesty. Rojo was only one of the several staff members Festino consulted, and it was always pleasant when Rojo's claims were confirmed by someone else.

***

The emperor had meant to talk with Festino when he came to put out the candles, but he was already asleep. His dreams contained people he'd met with earlier that day. In the moments following their dream-meeting, each was dead within five minutes. He would rouse slightly at each unpleasant death, and finally he woke with a start.

The last person in his dream was someone he hadn't met that day, or any day. He couldn't determine who she was or where she came from, but she fascinated him. She was young and beautiful, and thankfully, he didn't watch her die in his dream.

There was a hint of dawn in the east, and the emperor decided to rise. With the dreams he had been having, any sleep he did get wouldn't be restful. He heard someone coming down the hallway to his room, and looked at the door with interest.

Festino rushed in, then stopped when he saw his emperor out of bed. "Sire, terrible news! We've just heard there was an attack on the castle in Markerburg. The Duchess of Middleland is dead!"

The emperor stood absolutely still. "How sure are you about this information? Where did it come from?"

"Montrade—he returned with the news."

"Send him to me immediately. No excuses."

"Shouldn't you dress first, sire? I'll send in your dresser, shall I?"

"Oh, damn, yes. You get Montrade here!"

***

The emperor was well dressed and sitting in an armchair when Montrade entered the room. The emperor's face was still, his lips loose, his shoulders down. His eyes glinted in the candlelight, reflecting the yellow and blue flame.

Montrade briefly bowed his head and said, "Sire, I need to tell you what has happened in your most powerful state. You won't believe that—"

The emperor had only cleared his throat, but the effect on Montrade was galvanizing. His eyes darted around the room, his hands clenched, his shoulders drooped and his back curved forward.

The emperor said, "I'm not sure when it happened, but I've noticed you've stopped giving me the respect due to my position. A slight nod, a quick 'sire,' and you're my equal in some way. Have you noticed that?"

"My lord, sire, I've had no intention of placing myself at your august level. If I've been inappropriate, please tell me—school me. I'm sorry to say that my fear for your safety has made me too bold."

"Tell me what you've come here to say. We'll deal with the other afterward."

"Sire, if I may, I've been gone on a period of espionage on your behalf. I snuck into Markerburg with no one the wiser, and discovered much. There's an active rebellion in Middleland comprised of men who feel they've been submissive for too long. One district is in active revolt, and they sent men to Markerburg to assassinate Duchess Madory. They were successful, sire. The streets run with blood."

"Who is the leader of this rebellion? Who entered Markerburg with that heinous goal?"

"I've been unable to name the leader. He has a deep shroud of secrecy around him. The assassin was unknown."

"Is he a Middleland man?"

"I don't know, sire, I haven't been able to get close enough to find out. The protective circle around him is too tight."

"How did you learn of Madory's assassination?"

"I was there, sire, I saw her die with my own two eyes." His eyes were wide as he told his tale.

"And you did nothing to stop it?" The emperor arched an eyebrow.

"It was over before I could act. I was so stunned I misjudged the energy it would take to stop the assassin and I killed him."

"Oh? Could you read him after he died?"

"I'm no necromancer, Your Highness. I have neither the desire nor the skill to acquire those talents. You know this, sire."

"Up to now, you've proven yourself a tremendously powerful wizard. You've boasted how much you can do. Why is this act beyond that boast?" He paused for a minute, scrutinizing the man before him. "You can bed any woman by controlling her mind at will. Why did you need to kill the assassin?"

"Sire, I beg you, listen to me; I was in shock, like any other man. She was a brave and true leader and her state contributed more than any other state."

"I'm aware of the unique value of that picture-perfect state. I'm aware it had a vibrant and active duchess leading it," the emperor said, then narrowed his eyes at Montrade. "You've failed me. Your avowed state of shock is inconsistent with the man I've known for nearly twenty years. It's an unacceptable response for the man I expect to guard my life. Would you go into shock and leave me to die as well? I suggest you go and meditate on whether this story is one with which you can live."

"My liege, I don't know what to say. I'm afraid you're mistaken. It wasn't my role—"

"I've heard enough. You know what I wish you to do. I suggest you do it." He raised his hand to his majordomo, indicating for the door to be opened.

Montrade's face suffused with blood. He stood up straight, squared his shoulders, and raised his arm, his right hand beginning to glow. Before he could speak, he was struck from behind by the guard who'd entered when the majordomo opened the door. Montrade slumped to the ground, the glow about his right hand fading quickly.

"Place him in the special prison cell. Call for assistance. He *must* be imprisoned before he awakens."

"Yes, sire."

A

Once Montrade had been carried from the room, the emperor called for Alcorn's presence. When Alcorn arrived, the emperor quickly filled him in on the situation.

"Montrade is only slightly stronger than I, Your Highness. I can seal the cell. Should I go now, sire?"

"You'd better. Return when it's done."

As Alcorn raced to the prison area, he wondered if he'd finally be made the first wizard of the land. He had difficulty believing that Montrade fell over such a simple mistake. Why hadn't he acted? He certainly had the ability.

Upon arrival, he saw four guards trying to hold the cell door shut. He began chanting the closure spell, his arms reaching toward the door. The door closed as clicks of locks latching ran up and down the edge of the door.

"Alcorn, I'll kill you!" Montrade yelled.

"I assume you'll confirm the threat," Alcorn said to the four guards who nodded. The guards returned to their posts while Alcorn wended his way back to the emperor, dodging maids who tried to flirt with him.

Alcorn was readmitted to the emperor's room and reported the scene in the dungeon. "How do we know her prison will hold someone of Montrade's abilities?"

"Don't you trust Lady Oghamry? Tut, tut. Though I must confess she's shown us precious little of the hospitality we've come to expect!"

"Sire, I'm mainly concerned that the Duchess Madory's death isn't the only plot afoot."

"You're right, of course, but I'm not sure how we go about finding the rest of the conspiracy when our captive is the least likely to talk."

"My liege, I doubt we'll find anything within his rooms. Unless it's concealed by magic, and even so, I doubt it would be anything significant."

"Too true. We must think of a way to determine what their ultimate goal might be."

"I think we must assume, sire, *you* are that goal."

They both paused to think on that unsavory conclusion when Festino entered with a note on a tray. The emperor took it, noting the direction: "To the Most August Emperor, Maximillian IV of Andirony and its constituent states."

"Someone is being most formal," he said as he opened the note, handing the envelope to Alcorn. "Why, it's from Madory's daughter who styles herself the Duchess Nenory, although I believe in that she is a little premature. She writes that the heir of Winthrop is on her way to see me. She's disguised as a man and in the company of a witch, who's disguised as her wife. Most irregular, but Nenory seems to think they have cogent information about the subject we were just discussing." The emperor stopped and put his finger to his chin. "Yes, indeed, most irregular."

Shortly thereafter, a young couple from Winthrop wished to give the emperor their greetings, as they'd be away from Winthrop at the time of his visit. The emperor indicated that he would see them— "given that they've come so far," he added.

42

The emperor waited in his dayroom for the witch and the duchess. The door opened and his valet approached the couple standing in the hallway. The witch whispered something to the valet, which the emperor couldn't hear. The one he assumed to be the duchess asked for a private meeting.

This "man" spoke, making his request, and then started coughing. It appeared to be a real cough and not a stratagem. The witch put her arm around the man and took the opportunity of pretended solicitude to look around the room at the others in the room.

The emperor told the servants they could leave.

The man began to lose his integrity, and hair grew as legs shrank. As the shape of the face changed, the emperor watched the face of the woman from his dream appear. He thought she looked a little older than in his dream, although he surmised she had aged during her terrible journey. Her hair now fell below her shoulders in an appealing curl.

The emperor approached her and lifted her from her bowing position by gently pulling up on her arm.

She looked into his face and said, "My liege, I am at your service."

"You are Periwinkle, Robert's daughter?"

"I am, sire."

"What the dickens was he doing, allowing you to gallivant all over the country? He must have lost his mind!"

"No, no, sire, it was the only way we could get the documents to you. The only safe way."

"What documents? Alcorn, find out from the other one what this is all about. I want tea brought in, and I want it now!"

Alcorn turned to Amerlie and they spoke together in whispers as the emperor led Peary to a seat. There was a loud scurrying noise from the hallway and then a knock on the door. The emperor called "Enter!" and the door swung open to reveal a host of servants with trays of food and tea. They bustled around the room, setting a table for four amidst the oversized and ornate furniture and trappings that seemed to cover the room.

The four sat while the servants placed food and drink on the table and the emperor pestered his mage about something obscure. The mage wasn't Montrade, which Amerlie found hopeful. The emperor kept stealing glances at Peary. He was tall, with burnished-copper hair and a strong nose. There were lines in his forehead and on his cheeks, undoubtedly caused by the difficulties he faced as the ruler of such a diverse and vast empire.

"Tell me, Periwinkle, what are these papers of which you spoke?"

He saw her wince at the use of her formal name so he added, "And what *would* you like to be called?"

"Sire, I've been called Peary all my life, and I am not yet accustomed to my formal name."

Amerlie tried to interject something but one glance from the emperor silenced her.

"And what have you come to tell me?"

"Initially it was just to tell you about the conspiracy but it seems much more has happened on our way here, my liege."

Alcorn looked at the emperor and raised his eyebrows. The emperor looked at Alcorn with amusement. "It always comes to those who wait." He chuckled softly. Turning toward Peary, he said, "I am willing to hear all you have to say."

She told him about the papers first, and Amerlie produced them for him. He indicated for Peary to pause while he read them. When done, he handed them to Alcorn, and turned back to Peary. "Are the whereabouts of your brother and Briaint known at this point?"

"It comes up later in my tale. Would you like it now?"

"No, please go on."

Peary told about the demon's attack and his capture and imprisonment. When she mentioned Montrade's name in association with the demon, she saw the emperor and wizard exchange glances. Continuing, she recounted the problems in Markerburg with strange men, and the attempt to catch them in the market. The story of the ring seemed to make them thoughtful once more.

She spoke briefly of the goings-on in the palace, along with what they had seen and heard of the attack. There was no mention of the similarity between Nenory and Peary. The emperor followed closely her tale of the departure from Markerburg and was particularly interested in the incident with Briaint and Henry with the black fog.

"I'm skeptical Briaint was killed by whatever that was. Alcorn, does that sound like a demon to you?"

"It sounds much more like a construct, sire. An artifact made by a magician to stun the uninformed."

Peary asked, "Would the construct be able to transfer the caught one away? Because when I reached into the cloud, there was only one body in there, although there were faces of other men floating in the fog."

"You reached in? Are you crazy?" Alcorn said.

"Manners, Alcorn," said the emperor. "Remember whom you're addressing!"

"My liege, I apologize."

"To her, idiot!"

"My lady, please forgive my rudeness," Alcorn said. "Please, why did you reach into the fog?"

"There was something in there struggling. I was careful not to let my face or head come in contact with the fog."

"It could have taken you, my lady, even with just your arms exposed."

Amerlie laughed and said, "I think not. You should know Peary has already acquired her full inheritance."

"Ah," said the emperor, smiling. "Are you in control yet, or are you still learning?"

"I'm still learning, sire. I generally only need to see something once or twice before I get the way of it." Peary looked very young as she said this, a small amount of pride fighting with intense shyness.

His smile grew broader. "I'm pleased to have another strong duchess among my loyal citizens. Can you tell me anything about your cousin Nenory? Will she also be strong, do you think?"

"Nenory hasn't had the experiences I've had, but she will in time grow out of the protected child her mother made her, my liege. She shows signs of it all ready."

"Such diplomacy in one so young is very impressive. Perhaps I should ask of your companion for *her* opinion," he said.

Amerlie said, in response, "That isn't necessary, my liege. Peary is my duchess, and I concur with her always in public." Peary stared at Amerlie, eyebrows raised and mouth in a small O.

"I believe your response has surprised your duchess, and I wouldn't say you're exactly in public here, yes?" the emperor said.

Fidgeting, Amerlie said, "I'm not a political animal as such, sire. I believe it would be impolitic in the extreme to contradict my duchess. If you order me to answer, I will, but otherwise, I'd prefer to hold my peace."

"I must insist. Your greater experience and your magical abilities may have seen something someone younger and less trained could have missed."

Amerlie looked to Peary, who nodded. "I wasn't impressed with Nenory. She's young, spoiled, and not well educated. However, Peary is right that she rose well to the occasion after the sudden loss of her mother. She handled the problem of an abusive, if incompetent, regent with surprising skill. Although she had help from both Peary and me, she was able to take what we gave her and improve upon it in a way I didn't expect. I must also point out: we discovered on this trip that Nenory is the heir to the Duchy of Winthrop should Peary not produce an heir."

Alcorn made an involuntary exclamation at this news. "How, may I ask, did you discover that?" he demanded.

"Alcorn! You may not ask this of either Amerlie or the young duchess. Had you been by my side for a slightly longer time, you would have learned that nature of a magical duchy's inheritance is not subject to public knowledge. And in this case, you qualify as public."

"My liege," he responded, "I beg your pardon. And that of the ladies too."

43

After a light tap at the door, Festino entered the room. "Excuse me, sire, the chef wants to know when you'd like dinner, and where you will be taking it. Also, Lady Oghamry requests the honor of your presence at her dining table. She said that your visitors should be leaving soon anyway."

"Lady Oghamry takes much upon herself, don't you agree, Festino? We four will dine here tonight, and the lady may dine wherever she pleases. I won't be joining her. You might tell her we need candles for the large chandelier in this room. Also, you could offer to fetch them for her so as not to put her out, but I doubt she'll allow it. Oh, and tell her my guests will be spending the night and perhaps several days, so rooms near mine are required."

Festino nodded and said, "I'll do my best, your excellence, but I suspect the rest of your staff and I will find the candles and beds necessary."

Alcorn smiled. "I can provide the light if all else fails, my emperor. I'm not so handy with beds."

After an hour's wait, imperial soldiers brought in a table for four. They were followed by others carrying food. The smell was off-putting, and the emperor walked over to see what had been brought. He stepped back from the table in disgust, and ordered the soldiers to take it away.

"Festino! Find Rognard. Tell him the duchess is to be brought here immediately and in chains. I don't care what she's wearing or who she's with. If anyone questions my order, arrest them too."

He turned to Peary and Amerlie. "The food was slop for the pigs. I've seen it used in my time here. It generally isn't tasty or nutritious, which is surprising in light of where we are."

Moments later, there was the sound of fighting down the hall, near the main stairwell. Alcorn left immediately to investigate while the emperor steered the two women into an inner room.

Festino returned. "Rognard's leading the men against the duchess's men. It appears to be evenly matched. There's something going on down where Montrade is being kept, like there's a jailbreak in process. One of my sources just informed me that this is the beginning of an assault by three principalities against you, sire. We must find a way to get you out of here before our enemies arrive."

Pietro entered, carrying homespun clothing and common footwear with him. The emperor didn't appear to be surprised. He vanished into another room and came out wearing the disguise. Amerlie changed his face slightly and his hair color completely. He now had gray-white hair, and lines under his still-clear hazel eyes.

Peary was already turning into a lanky boy of about fourteen, with skinny wrists and a cowlick in place of her shoulder length hair. She pulled out of her bag a pair of old skinny pants and the rough shirt she'd worn leaving the valley. The emperor watched her in consternation as her face and body changed before his eyes.

Alcorn returned, and his scowl warned that the news wasn't good. "Montrade has been released and he's teaming up with Oghamry and the rebels. I can perform a holding action, but you must escape soon. Alistair's fetching the five nags we have in hiding and will meet you at the gate into the woods. Sire, you know the servants' way out through the back room. Take it, and let one woman go before you and the other behind. They both have enough magic to get you to safety. You must go!'

Pietro grabbed up many of the valuables and tied them in a pillowcase. He handed them to the emperor and sank to his knees before him.

"You must come with us, Pietro. We need another man, and there are five horses."

"No, my liege, you must take Festino. His spying has been found out and he can do nothing for you here. His life is in danger too, and you would forever regret leaving him here, sire. Please."

Festino ran in with a bag full of food. "I took it from the duchess's table after they all ran out. I got it out through the servants' way. Sire, you must go now!"

"You're coming with us, Festino, and that's an order!"

"But—"

"No arguments!" The emperor led the way to the farthest room at the back of the suite, and reached to push the third carved lily on a bookcase against the back wall. Before he could touch it, Peary pushed in front of him and ran her hand over the lily at a distance of about an inch. She paused, muttered under her breath, made the same movement over the lily again, and opened the door.

On the floor on the other side of the door lay three unconscious servants with knives on the floor next to their outstretched arms. Peary nodded to herself, grabbed the three knives, and looked both ways before heading to the right.

They moved as silently as possible, Amerlie again old and near the old appearing emperor. Peary's boyish figure seemed agile and light-footed as she quickly descended the stairs, stopping just short of the bottom. She paused with a hand sign to those behind her. With her right hand held up before her, she moved it back and forth in something akin to a caress. She poked her head around the corner at the bottom of the staircase and signaled the others to follow her softly.

They had arrived in an area that was laid out for the servants' relaxation, with a few comfortable chairs and a distressed sofa. The lounge was empty, and the disarray on the dining table at the end of the room spoke of a speedy withdrawal.

Peary approached the table, reached a hand over every plate and the two unopened bottles of wine. Very quietly, she said, "We should grab a few bites to tide us over to the forest. Grab what you can bring with you comfortably, and don't worry if you have to drop it."

Festino slid forward to put what he could in his provisions bag, which he secured through his belt, leaving his hands free. He took one of the knives from Peary for himself, and handed the other to Amerlie. When the emperor started to protest, he was met with three steely glares.

The back door was only a hallway away. They hurried to the door, slipped it open, and escaped into the cool night air. The sounds of fighting were farther away here, toward the front of the complex. They slid through the small formal garden, sadly gone to seed, and headed toward the forest gate, with Festino now taking the lead. To the emperor's dismay, Peary took the back position.

44

As they moved through the grounds, they frequently heard others in the surrounding area. At each close noise, they stood still while Peary and Amerlie investigated in some way. Sometimes they moved toward the sound, while other times, they pulled the emperor and Festino into the cover of the shadows. When they finally made it to the gate to the forest, although they were stressed, they maintained their silence.

The gate was opened from the other side, and the emperor went through before the others could stop him. He looked around but could see nothing.

They all stopped when a craggy voice came from behind a tree. "Keep moving, grandfer, there's a more important man than you coming through tonight."

"Stow it," said Festino. "This is your liege lord, Alistair, notwithstanding what the Duchess Peary and her witch did for him."

Alistair came out from behind the tree, his sword drawn in a most dangerous arc that stopped when he saw Festino, though it was still held at the ready.

"Alistair, you old stickler, this is why I wanted you here."

"What've you done with the emperor? He's unrecognizable, as if that damned turtle bit him."

"The turtle didn't bite me," the emperor said. "Two witches have saved me. And I expect you to be responsible in your dealing with them."

Peary asked weakly, "What turtle are you talking about?" She hadn't altered her voice, but it was an acceptable voice for a boy whose voice hadn't yet changed.

The emperor laughed and said, "It's an old phrase in Arthur's Seat. When one hasn't seen someone in a long time, and they've aged substantially, we say the turtle's bit them, to explain the aging, the lines, and the wrinkled neck. Let's get out of here."

Alistair led them about a hundred feet into the woods, to an area by a game trail where five unimpressive horses were tied to tree branches. As Alistair untied them, Festino passed around chunks of bread so they could fend off hunger. Peary asked for the saddle to be removed from her horse, as she didn't know how to ride with one. The emperor, not accepting her excuse, said she could learn.

Alistair showed her how to sit in the saddle, and briefly gave pointers on how to ride with it. He planned to lead the small party along the game trail, but he wanted Peary to ride with him so he could teach her. The group was quickly on its way, taking a route that would allow them to cut through most of the Oghamry property, putting them that much closer to Winthrop.

They had gone about three leagues when Peary drew her horse to a sudden stop. Alistair pivoted around her but saw nothing out of the ordinary. Her chin fell to her chest, as if she was contemplating something deep. Suddenly her head rose, along with her right arm, which pointed in the direction from which they had come. Amerlie slipped from her horse and moved into deeper shadow behind a broad tree. The others heard a noise like a cat's cough. Alcorn strode into view, sneezing. Peary didn't release her arm. Amerlie came around the tree behind Alcorn and struck him across the back of his head with a shank of wood.

Alcorn's aura changed as he fell to the ground. Peary was upon him in a leap, trussing him with magic that was purely Winthrop based. With the closing of the Winthrop loop, the individual changed again and turned into Briaint. His face was mottled with bruises and he whimpered in distress.

Festino stepped forward and demanded, "How did you find me? What are you doing here?"

"I need to find the emperor. Montrade has betrayed him and us. He's played us all for fools."

"If you think I'm going to tell you where the emperor is, you've got another think coming. We set up this foray to attract what was after us, and you were the first to fall into the web. You're seriously on the wrong path." Festino said angrily. "And we know you tried to kill Lord Robert in Winthrop. You'll be taken there and put on trial for the attempted assassination of Lord Robert."

"The demon shot that arrow. He compelled me to run to attract the guards while he escaped down the pipe."

"That doesn't explain how you disappeared." Amerlie spoke in an elderly woman's voice.

"Who the hell are you? And where is your respect, old woman? I'm a prince of the realm of Wallameer!"

Festino reached out with his foot, and tapped Briaint's damaged face. He howled. "You'll learn to respect your elders on the trip to

Winthrop, young man. And when the emperor hears of your involvement with the attempt on Lord Robert's life, you'll be a prince no longer!"

Peary came forward as a gawky boy, and asked in her boyish voice, "Did you really disappear into thin air? I wish I'd seen it!"

"When a demon pulls you from one place to another, you won't like it, kid. Burns as hot as the sun. And if the demon doesn't like you, you end up with a face bashed into a stone wall three times in quick succession."

"Wow, a demon! What did it look like?"

"This is what I'm trying to tell you," Briaint whined. "That demon replaced Montrade after the Duchess of Middleland was killed. Montrade's dead, and that demon's taking his place."

Festino asked, "Did you see Montrade dead?"

"Yeah, and I saw the demon sucking out his brains, so he now knows everything Montrade knew."

Amerlie approached him, and put a hand on either side of his head. He tried to resist, but he was enervated by the Winthrop binding.

"We must take him to Derona. It's the only way we'll know if he's telling what he thinks is the truth."

Festino agreed, and after the young man was tied to a pony, the party moved away from where they'd been found.

45

Lady Oghamry was with the one who called himself Montrade. Lady Oghamry believed she could sense demons in her state with her magic, but she wasn't aware that some distance away was a man who claimed Montrade had been replaced by a demon. She saw nothing in him that would suggest this was so. Instead, she saw a typically arrogant wizard who thought he had the right to tell her what to do.

"I wouldn't take such language from the emperor, Montrade, and I have no intentions of taking it from you!" she said.

"Don't be an idiot. Do you think your petty revolt against the emperor went unnoticed? Do you think he didn't notice that you fed him swill and deprived his rooms of proper lighting? Your little games were readily apparent, and he would've left sooner had he not committed to your people that he would remain for a full twenty days to hear what they had to say."

"I won't listen to any more of your impertinence," she said, turning on her heel and heading for the staircase. She felt an icy slithering sensation roll over her body, and was instantly immobilized.

"You didn't think I was that easy to get rid of, did you?" The man laughed and twisted his hand in the air. She screamed in agony. The look on her face, eyes clenched, lips in a rictus, thrilled him, inciting more violence. As Oghamry emitted a shrieking scream several notes higher than her prior cry, blood flowed from her nose, eyes and ears.

He strode away leaving her hanging in the air in the hallway. When he was three hallways away, the spell attenuated and fell, as did she. Slowly, she crawled into the small sitting room on the north side of the hall. There, she found the rope pull to bring a servant and she pulled it as hard as she could before falling back to the floor, pain echoing her every movement.

When a kitchen boy responded to the bell, he found his lady unconscious. He ran to a settee and pulled off a blanket for his lady's comfort. He covered her and ran for her primary valet who was still dining in the servants' hall. As he gabbled about the emergency, four of the men at the table responded to his urgency and were out of the room before he drew another breath.

Her valet Antonos reached her first, uncovered her and picked her up in his arms. A fellow servant arrived and awaited orders.

"We must get her to her salon. Her maid'll know what to do and who to call. Perhaps we should call for the physician in the village."

"He won't come," said the other man, named Flitus. "She's told him his inadequacies too often." They hurried along the hallways, Flitus opening doors as they came to them. Up one final staircase, they entered the lady's rooms.

The maid, Marinia, sauntered out but changed her demeanor when she saw whom Antonos carried. Marinia ran to Antonos and led him to their lady's bedchamber, where he laid Oghamry on her bed. The blood had stopped but there was still a great amount of it visible.

"Go find Tobias!" Marinia ordered. "Tell him to bring his satchel!" She then went to the table holding the water ewer and carried the water to the bedside table. From under the bed, she pulled out a covered bowl into which she poured some water. Antonos helped her hold the heavy bowl while it began to steam of its own accord. Marinia dampened a cloth in the steaming bowl, wrung it clear of fluid, and started washing the lady's face, removing the dried blood. She then cleaned her ears and neck where the blood had flowed. With a fresh cloth, she again wiped the lady's face and then loosened her bodice a little. She was rewarded with movement in the lady's face and hands.

"Wha-what happened?" the lady whispered.

"I don't know, milady," Marinia replied. "You were brought in looking like you'd been struck many times. Do you not recall who did this to you?" She noticed the lady's mouth seemed to be dry and she gave her water to drink. The lady drank thirstily and asked for more.

"Is my wizard available?" she asked. Antonos left to find out.

"Would you like to dress for bed, milady? Or shall I brew you some tea and let you rest until it's ready?"

"That would be good, Marinia. Is the emperor still here?"

"Oh, no, milady, we had that raid today and I believe they must have taken him away as there was no one in his rooms after those men left."

"Raid? I have no recollection of the raid. I must be suffering from some sort of shock, I guess."

Marinia returned to brewing the tea, humming gently under her breath—it was a tune she knew pleased her ladyship. When she carried the tea to the bed, her ladyship was lying with mouth agape and she was breathing heavily. Marinia quickly put the tea on the table and reached out to sooth her lady's brow. She rushed to dampen another cloth and tried to wipe her lady's forehead, but was brushed aside by an iron hand as the lady rose to her feet and walked stiffly toward the door. When the lady reached the door, she uttered an appalling scream that echoed through the building. She then ran to the stairs, as if she'd never been injured, and went down hastily, stumbling and falling the last several stairs. She arose from the floor, limping, and ran for the front door.

A manservant intercepted her and she turned on him with an angry glare; he pulled up. Marinia yelled at him to grab her and he made a dive to stop the apparently crazed woman.

"I have to see, I have to see, is it him or me?" she cried.

The servant again assayed to grab her with no new success. In fact with her arms swinging wildly, she clipped him over his ear and he went down like a sack of flour. With her staff on her trail, she ran outside but soon came to an abrupt stop in the middle of the grass concourse leading to the front gate. A gibbet had been raised, and hanging from it was the body of her wizard Heramino. Sobbing, she fell to the ground at his feet.

Marinia knelt beside her and held her tightly. They were still as a tableau until a wild laugh brought them to their feet. Coming down the concourse toward them was Montrade, his black hair flying from his face, which was pulled into a hideous smile that mirrored her earlier one. He let out another peal of laughter, and his face split open. The wiry figure of a demon stepped out of the sinking body, his four arms waving as his feet did a subtle soft shoe.

46

When they found a safe place for the night, Amerlie, Peary and the emperor stepped away from the others so they could discuss their options distant from the prisoner. Alistair cared for the horses and Briaint, while Festino hunted game for dinner.

"We can't go all the way back to Winthrop," Peary said. "There's too much going on here." She turned to the emperor. "Where are your guards?"

"They were fighting back at the manor. The bulk of them are out exploring the countryside to ensure there's no trouble brewing. We have a rendezvous set, should anything go wrong. By now, the word should be out something has gone very wrong. We're about eight leagues from the meet-up, and it's in a different direction than we've been taking."

"We can confuse Briaint over the course of the night so he won't know about any change in direction we've made. His skills in the woods are limited if I can believe what I hear." Peary sounded confident.

"How many men do you expect to find?" asked Amerlie.

"We should have in excess of two hundred at the muster. I came to Pocari with a presumed guard of fifty, but they are part of a larger group. Most have taken round-about routes, using their time to get a sense of the empire. I'm anxious to hear their reports."

"Will there be enough to spare a few for Briaint? If we can send him back, we are freer in our movements," Peary said.

"I was thinking of sending you back with him, if you must know. The battlefield is no place for an underage duchess. I would ask Amerlie to stay as I'm without wizardly help until Alcorn catches up."

"I'm much stronger than Amerlie, and I can do a number of things she cannot. I'm the better magical guard for you until your wizard returns, and possibly stronger even than he." Peary pushed as hard as she felt proper, recognizing that her valley ways weren't as far from her as they had all thought.

The emperor laughed, an old man's croaking so unlike his hearty laugh which Peary had come to enjoy.

Amerlie fussed a little. "We'll both stay because you're far too important to be left without sufficient magical company, sire."

"You ought not to call me that while we're disguised. Although I admit it feels strange to be treated as a commoner, it's undoubtedly good for me. And you give me the respect you'd give the aged, Peary, for which I'm grateful." He chuckled, a sound much closer to his true laugh. "I am, after all, the age of your father."

"Do you know Da? It's been so amazing meeting my real father and my brother Chres! Henry was another matter, but the other two make that worth it!"

"Your father and I spent a lot of time together when we were much younger than you. He and his brother were regular guests at Arthur's Seat when their father came to meet my father. When there was unrest in the capital, I'd travel to Middleland to spend time with them. That happened more than my father would have liked, but it was great fun for all of us."

"What happened to his brother, who must have been Nenory's father?"

"He died saving Madory's life in a rock fall that was clearly aimed at her. Nenory couldn't have been more than eight years old when it happened. The rock fall had been set deliberately, and Madory did everything in her power to find the culprit. Now I know it was Montrade in his early attempts to unsettle me. When I accepted Madory's decision to investigate on her own, he was stunned. It seemed Reymond was only a consort and not of royal blood. To investigate it myself as an imperial matter would have given him too much stature, no matter what I felt in losing him. I never wondered about Montrade then."

Alistair approached with the news that two of the horses had slipped a shoe during the strained run. The emperor's aged eyebrow rose high at the comment. Peary watched with her head cocked to one side, eyes slightly closed. Amerlie watched alertly, head up, face serene.

"Do they need to be shod now, or can we walk a ways into the wood?" the emperor asked.

"I don't know how long it'll take. The mistress can sit by the fire and not be distressed by the walk in the dark."

At that Amerlie raised an eyebrow to the emperor, who nodded.

"I do fear the woods are more than I can handle after this day," she said.

"Well, the boy and I will take a short stroll, and you won't even miss us."

Alistair and Amerlie retreated toward the camp, while the

emperor and Peary walked farther into the woods. After going about a hundred yards, the emperor swung Peary around a tree and whispered to her. "That was code from Alistair. There's some sort of danger back at the camp and he wanted me and you away from it."

"So he knows I'm your magical protection?"

"Alistair did what he did for my protection and for you, because of your noble blood, for your protection."

27

"You know, we don't have any supplies," Peary said after they had traveled perhaps a mile from the camp. "I don't want to be difficult, but my knife is with my pack, and you aren't carrying yours."

"Alistair will have arranged something, be sure. I'm getting a little peckish and could use a little food myself. When we're a ways from camp, you might even be able to remove my disguise."

"I don't think that's prudent, do you? You're extremely recognizable from your silhouette on coins and the posters put up for your progression. Your disguise is made with Winthrop magic and it should fool any demon that may be on the loose. If it's the one we captured back in Springfield, I have control over him. If it's a new one, all bets are off since we're not in the Duchy of Winthrop where my magic is nearly unlimited as far as demons are concerned."

"How do we know if it's the same one?"

"I should be able to recognize it," she muttered, looking away.

"You're unsure of yourself, aren't you?"

"This is important, more important than anything I've ever faced in my life, and the people who have helped me before aren't here. I don't mean this as a slight to you, but I'm used to having backup if my magic goes out of control."

"Has it ever?"

"Twice. Both times Amerlie was there to pick up the pieces. What if I do it again?"

"You've grown a lot in the last few days, and you've come to an equilibrium, I can see. I'm not worried you'll lose control." He stopped walking. "Now, we wait here for whatever Alistair has sent our way."

"How do you know it's here?"

"I'm not giving away *all* my secrets. You'll just have to wait and find out."

They settled against a large tree, and within minutes Peary was asleep. The emperor realized it and turned, watching her face as she leaned against his shoulder. He was surprised how right it felt, having been a confirmed loner since his wife had died ten years earlier. He chastised himself for even thinking about a relationship with a seventeen-year-old girl, the daughter of an old and valued friend. He heard a noise very close by, and sat up, letting the girl slide away.

"It is only I, sire, Festino. I have two new horses, your packs, and maps to get you where you need to go. There is fresh food as well as trail food for you, too. You have the duchess with you?"

"I do, Festino, and —"

"Yes, I'm here," Peary said, scowling and tapping her foot.

Festino bowed gracefully, "It's a delight to see you both in such fine fettle. I'll leave you to your refreshments and report back to the others that all is well. By your leave, sire?"

"You're free to go, Festino, and please make sure that Amerlie is aware and comfortable. These damned disguises are no fun."

They were alone again, and the emperor opened the still-warm package that was to be this evening's food. The heavenly smell wafted over Peary, reminding her of the stews Mam had made back in the valley, so fragrant and filling they were better than desserts.

She smiled at the emperor. "Do we have utensils with which to eat, my liege?"

"No formality. I'm Max for the foreseeable future and all honorifics are out. Or you could call me Uncle Max, if it suits your pleasure." He grinned back at her. Then he handed her the bundle of warm food, and began to rummage through one of the packs. When he produced trenchers and wooden spoons, she pulled out a blanket and spread it at their feet.

After he had evenly divided the food, they sat and ate in friendly quiet. Their appetites had been thoroughly satisfied once they finished.

Peary realized she was exhausted and said as much.

"We have bedrolls and we ought to find a more shaded place; we're too much in the light of the moon here."

She closed her eyes, concentrating. Then she opened them. "There's a small unoccupied cave about a hundred feet that way," she said, pointing in the direction they'd been heading. At his nod, she led the way through the undergrowth to the site of the cave.

She signaled for him to stay outside as she entered slowly. She sniffed but found nothing untoward. She lit a small light in her hand and gazed at the walls and the floor to make sure all was as it appeared. Then she looked up at the ceiling and fell back as quickly as possible.

"Peary, what is it?"

"There are dead bats hanging from the roof. Something must

have done it to them." The emperor moved to look but Peary blocked his way. "If something killed them, it might work on a non-magical person too."

He softly chuckled and said, "It's a well-kept secret that I have magical powers. They're not as great as yours, since they span the breadth of the entire continent, and they're somewhat thin in places. This cave doesn't have anything in it inimical to me. If it worries you, we'll find somewhere else."

"It feels safe. I was only worried it might take you like it took the bats. But if you have magic...."

"We can discuss my magic after we set up camp, and we should split the watches. You're dead on your feet. I'll explain until you're out and then I'll wake you halfway through what's left in the night."

They unsaddled the horses, and set them to graze after currying them. They moved the packs, saddles, and bedrolls into the cave, and rolled out the sleeping material side by side. Peary sat down to take off her boots and then slipped into her bedroll.

The emperor lit his pipe, puffing away as she settled. "I found out I had magic on the day my father officially made me his heir. It almost settled over me like a cloud. My father laughed at the look on my face and whispered that he would explain before dinner. He came to my dressing room, and said that his grandfather had felt the same thing descend on him when he was about ninety percent done uniting the continent, and it helped him get through the last few difficult principalities. He found he could listen to the thoughts of those who sought to co-opt him as well as those who wished him well. He used this knowledge to bind both groups to him more strongly than he otherwise could have. That was his only magical experience in the field of magic.

"My father had felt the same feeling of magic washing over him when he was named the dauphin of my grandfather. After some experimentation, my father noticed that his magic was stronger than his father's and grandfather's and he could do more things with it.

"Mine was the strongest yet, and I couldn't allow anyone to know of it, not even Montrade. I'm grateful for that at least. The demon can't know I have magic. It's our best chance to defeat it."

"What can you do?"

"Mainly I can find routes that are safe, and I can determine if there is an inimical force against me. It was how I knew the one who approached us wasn't Alcorn, though I couldn't reveal it, for fear someone opposed to us could see through Briaint's eyes and discover my abilities. What worries me is that my senses didn't warn me of Montrade's scheme against me with my own son. That worries me."

"You said you'd been doubting Montrade before he moved against you. Couldn't that have been your sense trying to overcome whatever compulsion Montrade could have put on you?"

"You're too generous. But you may have a point. If he'd put a concealment charm on me, would I have known?"

"We can try. I won't tell you when I try, it could be tonight or tomorrow. We'll see if you sense the intrusion. But now I'm fading quickly. Remember to wake me."

48

Peary awoke to light entering the cave, the bright aura of the sun rising through the trees. Sitting up, she saw the emperor snoring gently by the cave's opening. She cast her senses out and found nothing of concern, just local woodland creatures going about their morning routine. She reached out with a compulsion toward the sleeping man, ordering him to forget he was the emperor and to believe he was her servant Toby.

She rose from her bedroll, and sauntered toward the sleeping man. She cleared her throat loudly. When that produced no response, she pretended to sneeze. Finally, she paced from the cave, ignoring him, and wandering toward the sound of running water. She kept her senses alert for inimical forces, and finding none, she went to the water and bathed quickly.

Drying her hair on the blanket she had brought with her, she heard the emperor stirring in the cave. She smiled and waited to see what would happen. Suddenly a frantic voice called out, "Madam, where are you?"

She laughed and turned back toward the cave, where she was greeted by an unhappy servant.

"Why didn't you wake me? You should never walk out alone, my lady. You should let me go first to assess danger. I haven't been with your family these many years without knowing how to care for headstrong youth!"

"Why, you're shaking. Were you that afraid for me?"

"My lady, I know you have powers I don't, but at least let me be a shield for you. Your Toby adores you and wants to return you safely to Springfield."

Peary paused, having sensed inner amusement from Max. She tested her compulsion, and found it had only imprinted on the surface of his mind, not penetrating past the first tiny bit. His shield had held, and she felt her face heat up as she clenched her hands. His laughter did not in any way ease her discomfort.

"Why didn't you just tell me it didn't work? I've never tried anything like that before and had no idea how to do it." She glared at him before turning and striding to the cave. She heard his footsteps behind her, and his light chuckle. It only increased her sense of being wronged.

"Wait, Peary," he said. "You have to see it differently if we're to work together. You didn't have any training in this and you got me to think, at least for a few moments, that my name was Toby. And where'd you get that name anyway?"

She stopped and turned. He was smiling at her; she pulled her arms around herself, and gazed at the ground. She felt his hand on her arm and lifted her eyes when he pulled her into his arms. Holding her gently, he kissed the top of her head.

"I forget sometimes how young you are. My daughters are your age, and they would never hold themselves with the confidence and poise you generally have. Part of it's your magic, but most of it is you coming into your own. The women of your line have old souls. You might not yet be eighteen, but you're older than I in so many ways. Can we be friends?"

Peary sighed and leaned into his shoulder, her head fitting into the hollow right above his collarbone. She just let it flow over her, knowing he spoke the truth. She didn't understand what she had become. She knew she could never again be comfortable in her hidden valley. She felt a strange connection with this man, knowing it to be part of the magic that allowed her to be a ruler as well as his subject.

"We ought to get our stuff together and get moving," she said as she pulled away, smiling up at the emperor. "If we're to meet the muster, time is short…. And Toby was my best friend in the village. He died a few years back."

"I'm sorry. You're right of course though I'm finding it sufficiently comfortable here to stay for a while." Nevertheless he turned with her back to the cave and the horses waiting.

It took them about fifteen minutes to gather their things, feed the horses, curry them lightly, and then mount them, ready to move out. It turned out to be fifteen minutes they couldn't afford. They hadn't gone more than a quarter of a league before Peary grabbed Max's arm, pulling them both to a stop. When he looked at her, she shook her head and slid from her horse, signaling him to stay in the saddle.

Max felt a feather-light touch in his mind. He heard:

<Be ready to flee. They're very close now. I can try to hold them. And don't say anything!>

He stood in his stirrups to see what he could between the trees, and felt a sharp rap against his calf. He sat again, looking sheepishly at Peary.

She moved like a shadow through the trees, not making a sound. She came within twenty feet of the party she'd sensed, and saw ruffians, worse than the rabble they had seen in Middleland afoot. They were led by a man who looked vaguely like Montrade; it was as if his features had been smeared. She *hid* her presence just as the creature turned in her direction; his gaze went by her without pausing. She felt the darkness in him, but she was unable to find out if he was a demon without piercing her protective shield. He didn't show any knowledge of the emperor behind her. He yelled a guttural command and he and his troop pushed on, leaving the area. Sensing their continued movement away from them, Peary didn't move for more than five minutes.

She returned to the emperor, who hadn't moved from his saddle since she had stopped him. He was rubbing his neck, brow furrowed, though he smiled at her return. She put her finger to her lips and took the reins of both horses, quietly leading them away from where the ruffians had been. When they had covered about half a league, she mounted her horse and they began to move with more speed. Then she told him what she'd seen and sensed.

"Was it Montrade?" he asked.

"The being in that body wasn't human, but I couldn't discover more than that while maintaining my shield. Oh, if only we were in Winthrop! I'd know so much more!"

"Do you think it might be a myth that your powers are limited outside of Winthrop? You've done quite a bit, you know."

"No, I know with certainty that my demon sense is tied to Winthrop. If Nenory were here, she'd know."

"Did you get none of her skills given your close relationship?"

"I'm stronger in this duchy now that Nenory is duchess. Demon skills are tied to the land, because it would be watered down if it were available everywhere. Sensing a demon truly is a defensive skill. There are other demon spells but I haven't learned them yet. There's a lot I haven't learned yet."

They rode on in silence for a time until she again sat up, turning her head in all directions.

"What do you sense?"

"We seem to be surrounded. I can't tell who's surrounding us or even if they're all the same group. Give me a moment to see what I can find out!"

After a few moments, she looked at him and said, "A group of your soldiers are involved in a skirmish off to our right, while others seek you in the woods. Not everyone who is here looking for you is on your side, including one or two of your men. We should be very careful. Have you noticed any place we might hide?"

"I think there's a thick copse of trees a little bit behind us and to the right. If we can fit ourselves and the horses in there, we should be fine, as long as the horses stay quiet. This way." He pointed back toward the ruffians' trail.

They moved swiftly, if quietly, to the thicket. When they reached their destination, Peary held the emperor back while she scanned the area. Then she nodded, and they pushed through the trees and heavy underbrush. There was a clearing in the center that looked untouched by human hands. A little grass grew in the middle of the glade, and the horses contentedly settled down to a feed while Peary and Max took off the animals' saddles and packs. Peary settled onto the ground and was soon in a meditative state. Max stalked the area, gritting his teeth and stretching his shoulders to release tension. He looked repeatedly in Peary's direction and occasionally sighed upon seeing that she hadn't moved.

Finally, she stirred and said, "The news isn't good. Your men are fighting the enemy in several small groups. They seem unable to come together to present a united front, and I feel there's magic at work there. The Montrade look-alike is now in the mix and he may be the reason for the confusion. We should stay here until the situation clears up some."

"This copse isn't much protection! How can you say that?" His voice rose as he spoke.

Peary glared at him. "Do you think I would count on a few trees and bushes to protect us? We are guarded by a spell wall running along the perimeter of the copse. To the common eye, it's not a copse at all, but a gnarly briar patch. To the magical eye, it's a pile of windfall, with wild roses and other thorny vegetation in and around the downed wood. No one would be able to penetrate it. The shield also disguises our magic as nothing more than the energy of the planet and its denizens. Amerlie will recognize it as she taught me the trick. But we'd better be quiet. This spell doesn't disguise noises as well as I'd like."

She went to the other side of the clearing and placed her bedroll under a tree. She lay down on it and turned her back to him.

49

Amerlie and Alistair stood still as they looked through the trees to examine the newcomers.

When he saw the man on the first horse, Alistair cried out, "Gregorio!"

The troop of soldiers came to a stuttering halt at Gregorio's signal. They alit and began to set up a camp around the one the emperor and Peary had just left.

Amerlie approached Gregorio with Alistair. "Tell me your news and how you came to be here. I'm a representative of the Duchess of Winthrop."

Alistair confirmed Amerlie's statement and urged Gregorio to tell all he could.

"We were with a troop of seventy-five, and we split up about four hours ago when the trail we were following split in two. There are bands of local folk out and we've fought a number of skirmishes with them. We were following one of those bands and were concerned when they broke up. Have you seen anyone near here?"

"We caught one person who came here under a spell of misdirection. It turns out he's Briaint, one of those whom seek. We can tell you the whole story at dinner tonight." Amerlie motioned them to the fire.

Later, after Festino had slipped back into their camp, Amerlie approached him, hoping to hear news. He looked to her and very slowly shook his head. Continuing to walk, as if she had somewhere to be, she passed Festino with a murmured mention of the soldiers. She went to where the privies had been dug, tarried there for a few minutes, and then headed back. She stopped to pick a stone out of her shoe, hiding the fact that she'd heard the slight scuffling of a shoe not lifted enough to clear the layer of leaves and pine needles on the forest floor.

She probed with her general seeker sense, and felt a man standing not ten feet from her. She sensed his position, and calmly walked a little closer to him on the path back to camp. She didn't sense any danger from the figure, but was surprised at the soft voice that hailed her.

"Robin! What are you doing here?"

"Amerlie? I hardly recognize you. Is this the way you looked to Peary in the valley? Anyway, I left Chres in charge and came as soon as I sensed that Max, Peary and you were in danger."

"You used your skill?"

"I did."

"You haven't done that in decades! You know how dangerous it is!"

"My life is worthless if you all die. I wouldn't want to live in a world run by the dauphin and Montrade with my own son under their thrall."

"It's much worse than that." Amerlie filled him in on the latest, including Briaint's capture, and the plan to bring the captive to Springfield. He stepped back when she told him that Montrade was likely dead and a demon walked in his stead.

"Should I make myself known? Or should I shadow you as you go?"

"I can make you look like the old man we changed the emperor into, and nobody would be surprised to see him return. I could explain to Festino and Alistair who you are and the need for discretion. No one else in our group would wonder. You might need to joke a little about being treated as a commoner."

Robin laughed. "I've been a commoner most of my life! It's only in the regency I've been treated as something other than Isobel's unnoticed appendage. I best not let it show."

Amerlie worked her magic on him, and found difficulty in getting the disguise to stay on. Within a few moments, anything she did was changed back to his normal countenance. When he saw the frown on her face, Robin asked if there was a problem.

"It just won't stay. I get your face right, and start to work on your ears. When they're right, I look back—at Robin's face. What's going on? Is it part of your magic?"

"I completely forgot," he said, shaking his head, "though I didn't think it would apply outside of Winthrop. Part of the magic that makes me regent prevents anyone from tampering with my appearance. It's supposed to prevent brigands from kidnapping me and then changing my looks so I can ride openly among them. It would also make it difficult for disgruntled lords to exchange me for someone more to their way of thinking. I always thought those and other plots were the result of too much storytelling when I was young, but there you have it."

"Who do you know in our group? Do you know Festino and

Alistair?"

"Those are the only two I know. I certainly don't know any of the soldiers, except perhaps their commander, whoever he is."

"His name is Gregorio." When Robin didn't react to the name, she went on. "I'm thinking we could present you as a courtier from Winthrop who has come to support your duchess. You'd know the right things to say, and the right way to say them."

"If they aren't likely to know Winthrop nobility, you could say I'm Lord MacAlpine of Sutherland. He'd enjoy knowing his name was used to bamboozle a plot against Max and Peary!"

"Fine, let's go do the introductions."

They walked toward the encampment, past the campfire where the wounded were being cared for, and the soldiers were preparing a stew under Festino's stern eye. He glanced up and saw Amerlie walk over with a middle-aged man who looked vaguely familiar. Before he could say anything, Amerlie spoke.

"This is Lord MacAlpine of Sutherland. He heard there was a threat to his duchy out here and came out to investigate."

"Another good hand can always be of use," Festino said, "and I should tell you we have caught one of the assailants against your regent." Amerlie caught a slight emphasis on the word regent and realized Festino did know the stranger.

"Oh really? I have nothing to do with that investigation and I don't know the boy. This fine lady was telling me it was a prince of Wallameer who shot that arrow at the regent. When I left home, this wasn't known. I have some skills at swordplay I'd like to offer and I have a horse with me, which I've left in the woods."

Festino called Alistair over, and told him to find the lord's horse. He then cocked an eyebrow at Robin.

"He shouldn't be too far from your privies," Robin said. "As I walked toward your light, the privies were about ten yards to my right. If you call his name when you're close to him, he'll whicker. He's called Golden Boy. He's just proud because we named him after a precious metal!"

Alistair nodded, eyebrow cocked and a faint smile on his lips as he bowed to the "lord."

Festino then drew Robin toward the fire, asking him pressing questions about the new duchess and the royal family. Robin ducked most of them but had to confirm the duchess had been returned, fully educated as promised, and was scheduled to ascend to the throne in about six weeks. It was enough to satisfy Festino, who invited Robin to join them at dinner. When Alistair returned with the horse, Festino passed "the lord" off to Alistair and went off in search of Amerlie.

Once Alistair found Amerlie, they talked while walking around the perimeter of the camp, which was larger than expected due to the new arrivals. Much of their conversation concerned the use of magic in warfare and what, if anything, Amerlie could accomplish as a spy.

Festino and Robin joined them and Festino indicated his concern about the rumors of a demon.

"I heard a rumor that a demon escaped from an impossible prison in Winthrop," Robin said.

"Surely not!" Amerlie exclaimed.

50

Max looked at the sulking Duchess and decided it wasn't his job to comfort her. He would, instead, try to use his magic for something worthwhile. He reached out for the thoughts of any who supported him in the surrounding areas He expected to find Amerlie and Alistair, Festino and a few of his commanders. He jumped when he realized he heard Robert. He almost ran to Peary to tell her the news, but thought better of it. He'd wait until he had real news to tell. Settling against a tree, he "listened" to the conversation.

He quickly realized Robert was going by the name of a Winthrop lord, and Amerlie and Festino were aware of the pseudonym. When he heard the news of the escaped demon, Max became concerned, since it meant they possibly had two demons to deal with, and only one was under any constraints. He had no doubt Peary had cowed the one demon before and hoped the hold on him was still strong, although his knowledge of demonology was slight.

He then reached out and tried to sense any enemies within his range. He was cautious since he wasn't sure if anyone would be able to sense his magic. Max had just begun to send his thoughts out of the copse when Peary sprung up and ran to him.

"Stop it!"

He turned toward her, eyes wide open, mouth hanging flaccid.

"I could sense your intentions and yes, they're out there. Two demons are scheming together and fighting. If we can get them to turn on each other, it may solve at least one of our problems."

"Why aren't you talking more quietly?" Max whispered.

"They're at least five leagues away, but I stopped you because your thoughts could travel that distance so quickly they could have you before you knew it. Demons are ridiculously powerful, and they can fly down your thought waves to reach you before you could retract."

"How do you know all this?"

"I touched the one we had captive, and I saw the one that possessed Montrade. They're threatening to you, me, and Nenory, and that lends a power to my ability to sense them. It also attunes them to the three of us. They would recognize you immediately because your magical identity is so clearly emperor. Mine is my duchy, as Nenory's is hers. It makes us all easy to identify. The one good thing about that is it substantially reduces my da's identity, which is why they don't know he's with Amerlie."

"Now how do you know that?"

"They both contacted me and filled me in on what's going on with the muster."

Max's lips pressed together and his eyes failed to meet hers. "How can you do all these things? All I can do is sense their conversations, but you have so much more information. What's the purpose of my magic if I can't use it?" His face turned red, and he began to sweat.

"You haven't had any training in how to improve. It'll have to wait until we're all settled somewhere safe. Amerlie can certainly help, and if we go back to Springfield, Derona can help. She teaches at the Collegium and can teach anybody anything."

She patted him on the shoulder and gestured to the horses in their corner of the copse. "We have to look out for them, and then take a reading on where we should go next. I don't know if it's yet safe to rejoin them, since I don't know what if anything they've learned about the conspiracy."

As they walked toward the horses, Max murmured, "You are very wise for one so young. I believe you *do* have an old soul."

"I believe I'm what my duchy has made me. When I left the valley just a couple of months ago, I was silly and naïve, knowing nothing about the world. Amerlie lived as an old lady in my village for as long as I can remember, and I never sensed anything strange about her. I was happy there although my desire to wander grew stronger with each passing day. I now know it was the sign of my awakening."

"You know, your father misled me about your whereabouts and activities. He told me you were in a neighboring land where you could be disguised while being educated, staying with an unsuspecting family. Why would he lie to *me*? His friend?"

"Surely you know how letters can be mislaid or stolen. He couldn't be sure his letter would reach you without being read by your enemies—or ours. It had to be a fiction no one could disprove, and it had to protect where I was hiding. I had no idea about anything until we were out of the valley and on the way to the train. I'm afraid I was a bit of a gawker at first." She chuckled at the memory. "I wish I could give up on the clothing though. I've worn britches as long as I can remember. With all the men dead, we had to do all the manual work along with our homework. So we dressed like farmers."

"That's why you look so comfortable in them! I thought it was an act.... I hope you dress up well too!" He laughed then.

Peary grinned at him and ran toward the horses, Max not far behind. She pulled out the curry brushes and tossed one to the emperor. Oh, he looked funny trying to groom his own horse.

When the horses were ready, they pulled together the saddles, bags and other tack and led the horses to the center of the copse. Once there, Peary began to gaze, first toward the east, then the south and the rest of the way in the circle. She paused with a frown on her face, and then slowly turned in a circle again. The second time seemed to work better and she addressed Max.

"It's very confusing out there. Our people are in three groups and they aren't in touch with each other. Some of them are dealing with enemies groups. The folks we left are in the best position, having fortified themselves behind a breakwall established on the shore of the lake, which they seem to be fighting around. It's huge! Do you know of such a lake?"

"I don't believe I do; I'm somewhat lost without Festino."

"The mountains come down to the water in two places, behind a bowl like area. I don't see how we can get around the first troop sitting there, arguing. They're having a field day with your absence and what to do about it."

"Can you find my largest group of men?"

"About how many men are in the group?"

"They could be as many as two hundred fifty, and as low as one hundred. I would think and hope it's closer to the larger number."

"Give me a minute," she said as she lowered her head to her chest, her hands fluttering briefly at her side. Max took hold of her horse's reins to free her up for the search. He began to shift his weight back and forth on his feet as the time lengthened, his brow furrowing.

Finally Peary lifted her head. "The highest number of your people I can find is about seventy. There are three groups around that size, but one is a mixture of your folk and ruffians. I can't tell if they're fighting or if one side has been captured. They're in fact the closest group. We could go check it out and see if we can help in any way. The leader of your folks seems to be called something like Bormahilt."

"Oh that's Bromahildy! We should go help!"

They got on their horses and rode where they had entered the copse.

Peary stopped suddenly and signaled to Max. "There's someone just outside!" she whispered.

51

They were awakened in the morning by Amerlie, who warned them that there was a band of rebels nearby. The soldiers arose and packed with speed while Alistair and Festino managed to get their group ready in nearly the same amount of time. Two soldiers took over watching Briaint, allowing Festino and Alistair more room to maneuver.

Within minutes they could hear the rebels, and they positioned themselves to meet them. A few soldiers moved into the trees on either side of the trail; Amerlie went with one of these groups. The first rebels appeared on foot, swords drawn and pikes ready. The terrain funneled the mutineers down the path—and to the soldiers awaiting them. The trees were dense on either side of the trail, and the remains of rock walls on both sides made an easy exit impossible.

The battle was quickly joined and the soldiers found themselves equally challenged by the topography. Amerlie fired a few bolts of magic that made the rebels try to retreat. They fled up the trail with the soldiers in hot pursuit. After they entered an open field above a lake, the fight began in earnest.

The skirmish was chaotic and confused and the frustrated soldiers drove their horses through the rebel troop. Gregorio noticed that some of the enemy's dead seemed to self-heal and arise from grievous wounds. He ordered his men to decapitate the rebels, if possible; this ensured that the dead rebels wouldn't rise. Amerlie added her magic to the beheadings causing the heads to shrink once separated from the body.

The fight was ugly as the soldiers were outnumbered. Amerlie guessed there were three or four rebels for each soldier, and couldn't figure how to help with her magic. She turned to the wounded, hoping to aid them—especially those she could help out of the battlefield. Those she could cure returned to the battle and were very effective in freeing soldiers from encircling rebels. With the more seriously wounded she levitated them to the forest for safety while she began the healing process. The day drew on, as first one side and then the other prevailed. Amerlie was exhausted when the rebels finally quit the field.

The battle had ended better than it had started and they'd emerged nearly intact. They had settled to sleep by the side of the lake when a sentry's broken cry from the perimeter sounded. Riding into their midst on top of a strange four legged animal that none of the group could identify was the Montrade-demon, bearing the remains of the sentry on the end of his pike.

"Where is the emperor?" it hissed. "Where is the Duchess of Winthrop?"

"Who are you?" Amerlie demanded, rising to her fullest ancient height, and staring into the demon's eyes.

The fiend cackled and pointed at her.... Nothing happened. "What is this magic? How can you block me?"

"You're using the last of your strength, demon. When you absorbed Montrade, you became partly human. I'm guessing you got more than you bargained for—his mortality on top of the knowledge you wanted." She laughed harshly. "You came uninvited, and you left yourself open to this." She reached out with both hands and twisted them. The demon howled in pain. She twisted her hands again and the demon turned into a cloud of smoke, which dissipated slowly.

Amerlie swayed with the exertion and was grabbed by Robin, who held her tightly. Festino ran over to help and they led her to the fire, helping her down onto a blanket.

"Are you well enough to explain?" Festino asked. "Do you need a tot of brandy?"

Amerlie laughed softly. "Oh, that felt good! I haven't felt such strength in a long time." She looked at Robin and Festino. "He was here without anything to tie him down. He was always at risk of dissipating. It's something the demons have forgotten but *we* haven't. It's one of the benefits of community. We shared and passed down this knowledge through the ages, since the banishment of the demons. I wasn't sure I had it right until his magic barely tickled me. Then I knew. W could beat these creatures all those years ago, because we could break their ties to the earth. When they realized this, they accepted banishment with the understanding that they could only come forth if someone who had the ability to anchor a demon summoned it.

"As was bound to happen over the eons, the demons seem to have forgotten what it was all about. It looks as if they thought they were tied by our greater strength, forgetting that they had initially sought banishment to preserve what they call life. This one, who came through when Montrade was sloppy, was one of the nastier demons. He forgot another important fact. A demon that comes over and never uses his magic is at very little danger of being destroyed. Earth is repelled by the demon's magic. Because we broke their ties to Earth, every time a demon uses his magic, he's pushed a little farther from Earth. He requires more magic to stay, which leads to another push from Earth. In the end he's subconsciously using so much magic to stay here he's greatly weakened."

"So we know he did something—and probably something very bad—to fall so spectacularly by your hand," Robin said.

Amerlie's smile was weak, trembling. The brandy arrived and was warmed briefly at the fire, before being handed to Amerlie. She held the mug in her hands for a moment before sipping at the fiery liquid. Alistair sat down by her and began to murmur to her. Amerlie's eyes began to droop.

Festino drew Robin aside. "What are we now facing with Montrade and one demon gone? Briaint and Henry have been captured, so that leaves only the demon you previously caught and the dauphin among the main conspirators."

"If what Amerlie said is correct, the remaining demon is no longer anchored to the earth. Montrade was his anchor and he's gone. Now our biggest problem is getting everyone together again, because we have quite a few minor uprisings to deal with, even if the ringleaders are no longer in charge."

"We ought to go get Peary and the emperor then," said Festino. "If they haven't moved too far from where I left them...."

"Knowing my daughter, anything is possible. Perhaps we should try to find the other troops first."

Festino agreed and called for some of his better scouts to look for the other bands of imperial soldiers. Then they all tried to sleep. Amerlie was the most successful.

Robin took a sentry shift he wasn't scheduled for, and Festino didn't find out for another half hour. When he learned through another lookout, they both went running towards Robin's post, which was empty. There was no sign that Robin had been there. Festino sounded the alarm and was quickly joined by Gregorio and a number of others. Under Alistair's command, a few soldiers were left behind to stand guard over the remaining sleepers.

Festino led the group in the direction of where he had left the emperor. He hoped Robert was on the same route, and that they'd run into each other. Finding his way in the dark wasn't as easy as Festino had imagined. He twice had to stop the soldiers and hide after hearing the approaching gallop of horses moving, not knowing if they were allies or foes. He had nearly called out to the first group when he heard the unmistakable Abenathian accent. Abenathis hadn't produced any horsemen for the emperor or the duchess in an act of rebellion, and their presence in these woods was troublesome at best. He couldn't decipher their dialogue, and thought they might be speaking in code.

The second group, which they encounter mere minutes after the first, was more difficult to identify, as no one spoke. The sound of their horses and their equipment was unfamiliar to Festino, even though he'd been a political spy until recently. His knowledge of and experience with troops had evolved over the many months of the progression, and there was no assurance that he had heard the voice patterns of all of them. His caution was strong, as he felt he was protecting his emperor and the duchess. Gregorio on the other hand intended to follow this strange group; he took his men with him.

Only when the second group and Gregorio were out of hearing did Festino spur his horse on. He kicked out at a shadowy figure that jumped at him, trying to grab his reins; the individual used Festino's foot against him, dragging him from the horse. When the man tried to mount the horse, Festino rose up and grabbed him from behind. The struggle only lasted a few moments when the man spoke.

"Damn it, Festino, I need the horse more than you do!"

"Lord Regent," Faustino said in surprise. "I would have given it to you if you had asked."

"I can feel her and I have to go to her. She needs me." Robin's voice had a frantic note to it.

Assuming the regent spoke of the duchess, Faustino asked, "Is the emperor with her?"

"How would I know? She's the one I feel. She feels so much like my wife, and I never realized it until today."

"Stop, sir, you must explain. And we can't go further tonight. There are too many forces on the move. Even if I let you take the horse, there's a high possibility that you'd be taken." He paused before asking, "Is she afraid, can you tell?"

"No, I believe she's asleep. She seems to be quite peaceful. I need to be with her, much the way I needed to be with her mother. I believe it's the binding of the magic, at least as long as I'm regent. I didn't notice it until I was away from Amerlie while Peary wasn't with Amerlie. I thought I simply yearned for my Izzy, that Amerlie reminded me of the days we had together before Izzy died. I didn't realize the feeling was my own daughter. When I sent them both away, my thoughts went with them. When I went out to sit watch, I could feel the pull again, and it wasn't pulling me toward Amerlie. I just started running toward it. It was so far away...."

"How far is it now? We're quite a way from the lake."

"Oh, we're not even half way there. And I'm too tired to go on, even with the horse."

"You stay here and keep the horse quiet. I should be able to quickly find a safe place to sleep. I've been in this area before when we escaped from Lady Oghamry. I believe we've returned to Pocari. I'm a little worried if the emperor is back in this awful place." Festino headed off in search of shelter, and Robin sat against a tree, his head nodding.

When Festino returned, he found the regent asleep and the horse missing. Shaking his head, he tried to follow the horse's trail and was relieved that it was only at a nearby stream, slaking its thirst. As he pulled on the horse's reins to return to the regent he heard the leaves being moved, as if by a walker, with a steady beat between him and the regent. He moved quickly to protect the regent, and arrived to a strange scene. A distraught woman was shaking the regent, apparently trying to wake him. Her hair was a rat's nest, her clothing ripped in a number of places, bare feet peeking out under the ragged hem of her dress.

Festino dropped the reins and lunged for the woman as Robin was awakening. Robin jerked away; the woman grabbed at him; and Festino lifted the woman, screaming, from her place next to the regent. Festino put his hand over the woman's mouth to silence her, and she tried to bite him, succeeding briefly by getting her teeth around a finger. Festino tore his hand away and struck the back of her head, knocking her out. He lowered her carefully to the ground, all the while listening for any sound indicating an attempted rescue of the lady.

Robin, mouth agape, eyes wide open, looked over at his assailant. "What.....?"

Festino stared at the woman, saying, "I believe it's the Lady Oghamry, who was so uncouth to the emperor. I have no idea what's happened to her. Her scream was so chilling that I have to believe she's gone mad." After laying her on a blanket, he covered her with a second one. Robin folded his coat to act as a pillow.

52

Peary signaled to Max with her finger to her lips. She slipped through the undergrowth until she reached the edge of her illusion. She was surprised to see Marinia, moaning and occasionally calling out, "My lady? Where are you?"

Peary suppressed a snicker as she returned to the emperor. "You won't believe who's out there! It's Lady Oghamry's maid, and she's looking for her mistress. She's all sad and weepy."

"I wonder what's happened. Can you grab her and pull her in, keeping her quiet? We might get useful information."

"She won't recognize either of us."

"No, but you can say we want to help her."

Peary grumbled but went back to do as the emperor asked. Using a tiny bit of magic, she confused the poor woman and drew her down a path that wasn't nearly as dry and neat as she thought it to be. She lifted the glamor from the servant's eyes as she entered the clearing.

"Oh, where am I? Have you seen my lady? She's out of her wits, poor dear, and who can blame her? I must find her. That idiot Antonos is no good for anything."

"Who is your lady? Perhaps we've seen her," Max said.

"Oh, I don't go telling stories to just anybody, you know. How do I know I can trust you?"

"Well, I have a little magic, and I might be able to find her for you," he responded.

With a little more chivvying, the maid gave forth the whole tale of the wizard's abuse and the murder, being especially detailed when she described how the demon had come out of the body of Montrade. She suggested that her lady's wizard had probably gotten what was coming to him, even though it was a demon that killed and partially ate him. By the time she was finished with her tale even Peary looked a little green and loose kneed.

They offered her refreshments for it seemed she'd come a long way without eating. Peary put a slight spell on the woman's food inducing her to fall into a restful slumber after her appetite had been appeased. Max and Peary moved a short distance away so they could converse comfortably without stirring the woman's sleep.

"I think I can probably find Lady Oghamry, if you want me to. I have a few ideas on how to isolate her spirit if there aren't too many other evil folk in the area. If she's hooked up with the villains, I won't be able to winkle her out." Max nodded his approval and Peary settled against a tree and slowly closed her eyes. Her forehead wrinkled a few times; then she let out a very small "whoop."

"She's with my father and Festino. Apparently, they're out looking for us and were attacked by the lady. She's rather the worse for wear, which I suppose is to be expected if she was thrown around and tortured by a demon." After a moment, Peary added, "Which she deserved."

"While I agree with you, I suggest it might be time to learn diplomacy."

"Do I have to be diplomatic with you? After what we've been through?"

"Not in private, but in public, I'll be your emperor again." He thought for a moment how much he'd enjoyed this interlude with her, but the needs of his people were more immediate than any dallying with this young lady. She smiled at him and he was reassured.

When the maid awoke, the emperor told her they knew where her mistress was and it was their intention to join that party.

She became quite bouncy at the news. "Can we go right now? How far away is she? Do we have to wait for that idiot, Antonos?"

"Antonos is looking for you outside this copse. We can pick him up as we go along," said Max.

They gathered their things and saddled the horses. Max was prepared to let the maid ride his horse, but she declined.

"I'm afraid of the big brutes, sir, and with your advanced age, you should take it."

Peary chuckled. She mounted her horse and led the way down the path, stopping at the edge of the illusion. She muttered something under her breath and a fog appeared. Peary rode her horse through the vapor. Marinia halted before the fog, but was pressed on by Max's horse. When she came out of the copse, she made a slight cry at what she saw. Peary dropped the illusion as soon as Max exited, and Marinia looked around fearfully, eyes wide and mouth stretched in a fear.

At Marinia's cries, Antonos came running, but pulled up short upon seeing the two on horses. "Who are you and what are you doing to Marinia?" he demanded.

"Be still, idiot," Marinia replied. Before she could say more, Max added the news that the lady's whereabouts were known.

"Take us there immediately," Antonos said.

"Don't talk to us like that," Peary said. "We aren't your servants. In fact, *you're* a servant and should listen to us."

Max shushed her and turned to Antonos. "I know you're anxious, and we'll get you there as soon as we can. On foot, it will take the rest of the day, so we should get started."

"Old man, get off that horse, and I will ride there to my lady."

Peary subtly waved a finger and Antonos fell over. Then she laughed. Antonos raged to his feet, face red and hands clenched.

"My good man, if you continue to be this belligerent, we'll have no choice other than to bind you," Max said. "If you will calm down, we will make it as quickly as possible to rescue your mistress."

Antonos didn't take this advice, instead advancing on Max. Peary rose up in her saddle and pointed at the man, who was suddenly lying on the ground, trussed completely in ropes.

"Do you get it now?" Peary asked. She released his legs from the ropes and took the end of the rope into her hand. "I won't pull you if you behave properly, but if you continue to act like an idiot, I'll drag you the whole way."

Max cleared his throat and said, "This really isn't necessary, is it? You understand now, right, Antonos?"

The man was cursing and swearing, paying the emperor no mind. Peary kicked her horse gently and began a slow walk away from where he stood. As Antonos realized his position, he tried to dig in his heels, but found himself being dragged across the forest on his face. Peary stopped her horse, sighed, and lifted him onto his feet with a wave of her finger. After a few more starts and falls, he finally seemed to understand his fate and accept it.

The party moved off in the direction of Robin, Festino and the lady.

53

Festino had found enough wood to start a small fire to warm up the lady, who was shivering and sobbing at Robin's feet. Her words, when audible, dealt with demons, wizards, and assaults, but none of it made sense. Robin's forehead was lined and his mouth downturned, his eyes mere slits. He shook his head, and the woman wailed even louder when he did.

"Maybe this fire will comfort her," said Festino doubtfully. He then looked up, eyes alert and scanning. "There's someone coming. It sounds like our horses."

"You mean Max's?" Robin asked, keeping to their decision to avoid mentioning the emperor by title as long as the lady was in their company.

Festino nodded in reply.

The fire was beginning to burn brightly when the first soldiers arrived.

"Gregorio, well met! What did you discover about those riders?"

"Festino, where is he? We thought to find him with you! You haven't got him yet?"

"No, but we have an idea where he may be. This is Lady Oghamry, and she has apparently fallen on desperate times."

"Oh, the Lady of Pocari, eh?" Gregorio turned to Festino. "We took care of that group we followed and headed back to find you, expecting that you would have found the emperor." Then he called for his medic to come take a look at the lady.

A wizened old man walked toward Lady Oghamry. He made himself known as Alferb, something of a hedge wizard with a few skills in healing. He undertook to at least calm the lady.

Alferb spoke first. "There's a demon involved in this! How can this be?"

"Heramino, Heramino," the lady cried. Alferb looked on, not understanding. "My wizard, he killed my wizard, my love."

As the lady cried out, Amerlie, Alistair and the rest of their party joined the group.

Amerlie put her hands on either side of Lady Oghamry's head and closed her eyes. Her brow furrowed and her lips tightened. The lady began to calm down in spite of Amerlie's reaction. When she was finally asleep, Amerlie turned on Robin and Festino.

"Where did you two go? We were looking all over for you! Talk to us!"

Festino dipped his head and said, "The lord had a sense of the duchess and thought he could follow it to find her. You were exhausted from your bout with the demon, and we didn't want to wake you. We're nearly halfway to them now, but his lordship needs to be away from you to feel the duchess's magic."

"Not anymore," said Robin, walking to join them. "She's coming this way. I can feel her getting closer."

Festino turned to Gregorio who was busy with his horse. "Do you hear that, Gregorio? We can find the duchess and she's with the emperor! Do you want to ride out with a small troop? You should take Lord Robert with you. He's the one who knows which way to go!"

"Are you sure the emperor's with her?" Gregorio asked. "How do you know?"

"The duchess was sent as his magical protection. She wouldn't desert him. She's helping him," Festino protested. Gregorio glared at him and began to resaddle his horse.

"I want the second patrol with me now!" he shouted as he swung up onto his mount.

Festino found horses for himself and Robin, and they joined the group mustering around Gregorio, who saw them and yelled, "Where the hell do you think you two are going?"

"I'm the only one who knows the way," said Robin, "and I hope you will keep a more civil tongue in your head when we meet the emperor!"

Festino chuckled and said, "He has you there, Gregorio. He's the leader, a regent, and he outranks you by quite a bit."

"Enough," said Robin. "We take the path that way," gesturing toward the direction he sought.

He and Gregorio rode side by side, speaking occasionally about the trail they followed and the direction in which Robin felt the duchess. They had only been on the road about fifteen minutes when an advance scout rode back to warn of an oncoming, large group of armed men.

Gregorio quickly dispatched orders that had all the men concealed within the woods on either side of the path. He was disconcerted to see an old man and a young boy riding into view, the old man with a woman behind him on his horse, and the boy pulling a man on a rope. A short ways behind them was a troop of soldiers led by one known to Gregorio, Bromahildy.

As the riders advanced, the glamor fell from the old man and the boy and the emperor and duchess were revealed to the cheers of the hidden men. Robin and Festino ran out to greet the pair. Peary slid from her horse and ran to her father, leaping into his arms.

The emperor slid from his horse and advanced toward the two. "Robert, well met! I've crossed paths with your marvelous daughter and am looking forward to her ascension!" He put his arms around the father and daughter, while the men continued to cheer.

Bromahildy moved over to Gregorio and they put their heads together to whisper.

"I didn't know it was the emperor! I thought I was delivering these folk to the Lady of Pocari, from what they told me. Can you explain?"

"You'll have to ask Festino. He's been in on it from the first. Something to do with demons and Pocari. That's as much as I've figured out."

"Demons? Lordy, we don't want demons!" Bromahildy's face paled at the thought.

"They've killed a few and sent one back I think; I'm lost on it too. But I've seen one!" They continued their conversation while wandering off to see to the settling of the troops into one force.

Upon their return to the camp, Festino drew the nobility and Amerlie back toward the fire that was built near the Lady of Pocari. The wind had picked up and there was a chill in the air. Antonos and Marinia tried to save the Lady's place and to push away the others to no avail. Festino and Alastair made appropriate seating arrangements for their emperor and the duchess, ignoring Lady Oghamry's servants.

"The first thing I want to do," said the emperor, "is find all my troops and bring them back together. Then we're going to find out where the demon is, and go after it. Finally we'll go to Winthrop and see an ascension."

His speech was greeted with a cheerful roar from the soldiers. Bromahildy and Gregorio offered to investigate which soldiers were present to determine who was missing from the muster. They departed together, talking amiably.

54

A short while later, Amerlie and Peary wandered a short distance from the fire to consult. When Peary had told all that had occurred to her and the emperor, she and Amerlie agreed to search for the remaining demon.

Peary reached out with what she thought of as her "demon sense" in the direction of Markerburg and then the rebellious area of Abenathis. She felt nothing inimical in either direction, so she sent her attention in a more global way around the area.

Meanwhile Amerlie searched for any stray clusters of people who might be looking for them, whether friend or foe. She was more immediately successful than Peary, having felt a ragtag group that seemed to be traveling from the vicinity of the Pocari estate. She reached out to Peary, nodding her head in the direction of the newcomers. "Is that Alcorn, do you think? Who's with him?"

Peary looked and tilted her head to one side with furrowed eyebrows. "There's someone magical in the group, but it doesn't look like Alcorn, unless he's injured."

The two witches slid through the trees, hiding in shadows and behind bushes, moving slowly toward the group they'd sensed. A querulous voice murmured ahead as they sighted between two trees to a small clearing not a quarter league from the camp they had just left.

"I've gone as far as I can. Go on without me," the voice said.

"Nonsense, Alcorn. We've brought you this far, and I'm sure help is nearby. We must be catching up to the emperor by now!" Pietro's voice was not as firm as the words suggested.

Peary moved as if to join the party and was held back by Amerlie, who nodded toward first one and then the other side of the clearing. Peary reached out her senses and felt two other men hiding, but from whom wasn't clear. She focused on one for a sheer moment before reaching out and twisting. A scream echoed through the forest, prompting action on a number of fronts.

Amerlie ran toward the screamer, while shouts arose back at the fireside they had recently left. Pietro jumped up and whirled around, trying to locate the scream's source. With the thunder of hoof beats, a troop of Max's soldiers rushed to the scene.

Peary walked into the clearing, calling to the other hiding man. "You can come out now, it's safe."

Amerlie entered from the other side of the clearing, pushing a very bedraggled Henry in front of her, while a weary looking soldier came from the other side.

"My lady, have we found you at last?" Pietro was grinning at Peary.

"You have indeed, and what is my brother Henry doing in your company?"

"We came upon him at the scene of a battle where many had been injured, and he was bound for trial somewhere. We released him and brought him with us, thinking a mistake had been made."

Peary noticed Alcorn wink at her while she listened to Pietro. She turned to Henry and smiled. "Well, brother, you have a habit of showing up where you're least expected." She reached out and twisted again, and the entity that appeared to be Henry flickered a few times and turned into a demon.

"That's better! Now can I tell who you are?" Peary laughed. "Why, you're our old friend from Springfield, but quite a bit weaker now. Do you miss your tether? Of course you do. You know Montrade is dead, killed by one of your brethren. Now you have no link to the world and every time you try to grab on, it pushes you farther away. Maybe this time you will tell me which one you are, Iblis, Shaitan, Devil." As she was speaking, the demon lost shreds of its substance to the breeze.

An audience arrived: a portion of the royal party and a group of Max's soldiers. Upon seeing the demon, someone who cried out was quickly shushed by the emperor and the regent.

"You won't win, human!" The demon attempted a swagger, but began to disperse and stopped to pull itself together.

"I'll give you a choice. You can stay here as I am now holding you until you evaporate, or I can send you back to your home, where you will be able to live at least for a while. You won't wander free on this world again." She cocked her head to one side and looked at him. "You're beginning to dissipate. Want to go home?"

"I will * cough * own you!"

"Goodbye, Iblis," Amerlie called.

As the crowd watched, the demon shredded and disappeared into the wind.

Amerlie went to Alcorn, and began to perform a healing on him, although he was resistant. As she worked more on him, she began to feel uncomfortable, not understanding why. The wizard pushed her away with strong hands, and the contact was broken.

Alcorn rose to his feet, laughing. Montrade's voice came from his mouth. "I am reborn. This coward's body will have to contain me, but I live! And the witch saved me," he said, his laughter filling the clearing.

Max and Robin confronted him. Neither was strong enough to hold him, and Amerlie was crumpled at his feet. Soldiers dashed toward the laughing man, and were struck down by bolts of fire.

"Stop!" Peary's voice contained an imperative that made everyone and everything in the clearing freeze, even the Alcorn figure. It was as if she'd stopped time. Peary stalked over to the wizard and, hands hovering about an inch above his clothes, she scanned his body. Both her hands shot forward and repeated the twisting movement she'd used before. Black tendrils of smoke drifted from Montrade-Alcorn's head and chest. She did not release her hands until the smoke stopped.

"Who are you?" she snapped.

"I'm...I'm Alcorn. What happened?"

"You were possessed by the remnants of Montrade's soul. You must have been near by when the demon took him." Peary drooped with exhaustion.

"Here, sit down, my lady. And release the others." As everyone stirred and awoke, he led her to the log on which he'd been sitting.

A babble of voices rose as soon as the spell was completely gone. Max's voice was loudest and he finally got everyone to be quiet. "What just happened?"

"I froze the clearing and everyone in it," Peary said slowly, looking up at the emperor. "I evicted the remnants of Montrade's soul from Alcorn. He's okay now."

Pietro was stunned, eyes wide and mouth open. "You mean I traveled all the way here with Montrade?"

Peary laughed wearily. "He and Alcorn struggled mightily the whole time you were trying to find us. It was only in the last few minutes that Montrade gained the upper hand, and that only happened because Amerlie was using healing magic. He grabbed enough of it to tip the scales. But he's gone now, and Alcorn is safe and free." She leaned back against the tree and closed her eyes.

Max approached her, leaned down, and picked her up. He straightened and began walking back to the camp. Robin and Amerlie followed, as did the others, slowly, with Pietro in the rear, helping Alcorn along.

55

It had been a long but productive day. There was a sense of festivity among the guards who had split up, fought a rebellion, rescued people and generally had a better time than any had expected during a boring progression. The emperor's personal servants were also delighted to have come through the incidents of the past few weeks relatively unharmed. Alcorn himself was recovering nicely and felt a little jubilation at being rid of Montrade forever now.

Max, Robin and Amerlie sat quietly around the fire while the others enjoyed themselves. With concern, they watched Peary sleep.

"It must be just a terrible letdown to have finished off all the magical enemies, and be left with nothing to fight for the time being." Amerlie pursed her lips and nodded to herself.

"She's so much like her mother," Robin sighed. "I didn't think I'd feel this pull ever again. I'm so proud of her and all she's accomplished. Max, ought you to let the dauphin continue to sit in your absence? Can anything be done about it?"

"I'll send for him to join me. Alcorn can immediately deliver the message that he's expected at the Duchess Periwinkle's ceremony. That'll make him think a little. I don't know if he expects to hear from the conspirators, but I hope it gets him thinking he has to marry soon."

"Not to Peary!" Robin blurted.

Max blushed, a fact not lost on Amerlie.

"Of course not!" he replied. "It could be Nenory, couldn't it? Shall I command her appearance at Peary's ascension?"

Amerlie laughed. "I'm not sure that's needed. I expect she's already planning her traveling clothes to get there in time!"

"Then we'll all just have to go to Markerburg and get Nenory crowned after Peary is taken care of. I hate to think that my progression was responsible for Madory's death. I bet Peary's nonappearance had a lot to do with it, too. Your son was easy to rope in, I'm afraid, Robert."

"I'd say from my early exposure to Henry that he was on his

way toward patriarchy well before his mother died and his sister disappeared. It's his plotting at regicide that bothers me the most." Amerlie sniffed.

"I've had difficulty with him ever since Chres was born, and it got even worse when Peary was born and his mother died. His magic, such as it is, came in early, and he was a bully from the first, but able to hide it behind impeccable manners. He thought Peary wouldn't come back, and when she did, he figured he could control her. The only reason he could have thought that was if he knew the way his mother was murdered. And I forbade anyone to tell him."

"He knew, and he told Chres that Chres had killed them both. He told Chres he was evil, and they'd put this innocent façade about the evil, but the innocent façade wasn't him. But that innocence was always Chres. The evil was always Henry." Amerlie bit her lip.

Both Max and Robin stared at Amerlie. "How do you know all this?" the emperor said before turning to Robin. "How does she know all she does?" He was pale and obviously tired.

"I know because I've worked hard at knowing as much as I possibly can. Peary knows because every great duchess of Windsor has been reborn in her, available for her consultation. The magic has never done this before, but it has found this vessel worthy and given her a heavier load than it has to any of her predecessors. Because she's bound and determined to understand what she is, she pushes herself as hard as she can. She's been running with no rest for these last several weeks, and it finally caught up with her. Let her sleep through the night, and be prepared to feed her a full horse tomorrow. She'll need it." Amerlie turned and went to her bedroll, next to Peary's. She lay down and patted Peary's hand before rolling over to sleep.

PART 3

Duchesses Rising

56

I awoke with a hunger I'd never felt before, so intense I nearly cramped. Looking around, I saw the camp stirring with the rising sun. The fire was growing, and cooks surrounded it with pots and pans and *FOOD!* I crawled out of my bedroll and rushed to their side.

One or two flinched at my rush but others welcomed me with bread and butter, and fresh fruit. I barely thanked them before consuming with vigor everything they brought me. I heard laughter behind me and turned to see Amerlie and Da watching me.

"What? Why is it funny that I'm hungry?"

"Oh darling, it's just Amerlie said last night that you would eat a horse today, and you're starting small with what you have!"

I had finished eating what they'd given me, and was about to turn for more, when a soldier handed me a plate piled with eggs and potatoes fried together. He then gave me a fork, a wink, and a smile before returning to the fire. I nearly inhaled the food. Another plate appeared as I finished the first, but by that pint, I was slowing down a little.

"So explain why I need all this food. If you knew last night, it must have been obvious to you."

"Come sit with us under this nice tree, and I'll tell you what I know while you fortify yourself." Once I settled, Amerlie continued, "You've been running a very high-energy magical campaign since before we reached Markerburg. You were involved with the stranger on the train and that began a non-stop usage of your growing magic. Since we met the emperor, you have been operating at a level I didn't reach until I'd been working magic for ten years. You'll have to learn to eat more often if you continue operating at this intensity. You've lost weight you couldn't afford to lose because of your activities. You cannot perform magic at this rate and be a calm, level-headed ruler of your people."

"You're both going to box me in, aren't you? I've loved this life; it's all the adventure I ever wanted in the valley, and it came as my birthright. I know I have to go back and be a ruler, and I'm grateful I'll have both of you to help me, but I want to live, too!"

"And you will!!" said Max as he came up behind me. "This progression will continue, and I want you to join me as my hostess. I want you to come to Arthur's Seat to see the capitol of my empire. I want to introduce you to the people who help me run this system, the ones who give me the opportunity to get out and meet my people." He swung his arms wide and roared with laughter.

"Oh, Max, don't put stars in her eyes. She has a job to do and she's still just a young girl. Please don't do this." Robin begged his friend with damp eyes.

"It'll all work out, Robert. You'll see. I've had a brainstorm!' Max pulled Robin to his feet, threw his arm around his shoulder, and calmly walked off whispering into his ear.

"Close your mouth, Peary, you're not trying to catch insects. I know, it sounds a good game, doesn't it? But he's had his eyes on you since we met, and this is the first chance I've had to clue you in. He's going to make a play for you, and you have to resist. You're way too inexperienced to be an empress, and he'll still want you in five years. Tell him you're happy to be his hostess during his next progression, but you have work to do before you can take time off from your duchy."

I was surprised, but convinced by the concern in Amerlie's eyes. I'd had a slight interest in Max, but I suspected it was more because I'd never met an emperor before and he was fun to be with. He was a real person, which I didn't expect.

"I think I could love him, but he's as old as Da," I confessed. "And he already has all the kids he needs. And he'll die when I'm still quite young, and that won't be good. But wouldn't it be wonderful to be the empress?"

"It might grow as tiring as being a duchess will grow. Your parents loved each other very much, but politics separated them at an early age. Isobel was only twenty-five when she died. Robin has been unhappy both because you were absent and because he lost his true love. Look what happened to Madory. Your uncle sacrificed himself for her, and she had to go on alone without him. You see how she didn't give Nenory the freedom you had to learn and to grow into yourself. Nenory was all Madory had left of her husband." Amerlie sighed. "Life is never as much of a fairytale as we'd like it to be. Max lost his wife in childbirth many years ago. You look like hope to him. But he can only serve to take you away from the duchy that calls to your blood." Amerlie laid her hand on mine, and squeezed.

She was right. I was as much drawn to him because he was my

superior and could raise me as because of his character. I liked him, but I didn't love him, and I wasn't willing to be compromised by traveling with him at this time. I smiled at Amerlie, and squeezed her hand back. I didn't have to say anything.

We both got up to gather our belongings, which had been spread about the campground. We talked a little about how we would return to Springfield and whether it made sense to go ahead of the emperor and his train. There was much to be arranged at home in terms of the upcoming event's plan and formality.

We found Alistair and talked with him about breaking us free to head home.

"Aye, you have to be away, don't you? You have much to do before we get there. Will the regent go with you or stay with my liege?"

"We don't know that yet. They went off talking and I haven't seen them since. Can you send someone for them while we work out how to do this?" I looked as wide-eyed as I could at him.

He called for a runner and sent him off to find Da. Then he turned to Amerlie. "You'll take an honor guard of hand picked fighters. I won't be having any more fighting involving the two of you. And the duchess really ought to go as a lady, although that isn't her wanting. It's time to be a little more formal, out of respect to the emperor, who has come this long way to see you invested."

"I don't have any fancy clothes with me. I came on this adventure posing as a man. Won't we make less of a target if we just go back as the husband and wife we've been playing?"

But he wouldn't be swayed, and he called for reinforcements.

"Faustino, Pietro! Come talk sense into this headstrong young woman. She wants to go back to Springfield as the newlywed husband she appeared to be when she came to us. But our sire is going to visit her and will be present for her installation as the duchess. She cannot go back in anything other than in style!"

Pietro agreed immediately. "It would be a disgrace to the emperor to go back in disguise when you've saved his life and helped him so much. He'll send you with such an honor guard as you've never seen!"

As I had never seen an honor guard, to the best of my knowledge, it would indeed be such.

Amerlie and I agreed, and asked them to begin preparations, as time was getting short. We were just finishing as Da and the emperor hurried our way.

"What's going on?" Da looked concerned.

"Amerlie and I decided we should get back to Winthrop now that this problem has been resolved. There's a lot to do for the ceremony. Would you like to stay with your friend and make a triumphal entry with him? I'm sure he'd be glad of the company." I pushed lightly for him to agree.

"That would be great fun, wouldn't it, Max? Think of all the times we played at it as children and now we can do it for my child!"

Max caught my eye and nodded slightly. "A very good idea indeed, my friend," he said, smiling at my da.

Things moved quickly with the emperor's blessing, and Alcorn and Amerlie adjusted one of her dresses to fit me. As I changed clothes, the honor guard assembled and two horses with sidesaddles were brought for Amerlie and me. Within a half an hour, we were leaving the camp, having said our farewells to all our new friends.

We were out of the forest within an hour and easily found the road into Winthrop. I could feel the call of my land grow more intense the closer we came. I was concentrating on the comforting feeling and so missed whatever precipitated the sudden alertness of Amerlie and the guard. But, having been alerted, I spread my consciousness through the surrounding area. I laughed.

"The group is centered in the copse of trees about a quarter league away," I said. "What they don't seem to realize is they are within the bounds of Winthrop. They're now disarmed. Men, go get them!"

Amerlie and I followed slowly, with the two men left behind to protect us. We exchanged glances, Amerlie and I, acknowledging that we would be the ones doing the protecting, if any was needed. Hiding our amusement, we rode up to the ragtag group the guards had herded from the trees.

I was shocked by what I saw. There were five men and three women, and not a complete set of clothes on any of them. Another guard stood at the edge of the wood with a group of five children who looked defeated and starving.

"Get out provisions and prepare a meal for these people," I ordered. I motioned to a guard to bring the donkey carrying our packs of clothing. I pulled out the two pairs of pants and the three shirts I had brought, and shared them out among the men, while Amerlie found clothes for the women and children. The guards built a fire and we pulled the folks into the warmth, passing out food as it became ready. After they had eaten their fill, I asked for their story.

"Marm, we was jus' farmers doin' our work when a band of evil come through. Horses and men wif swords, and a 'orrible black man that no horse wud carry. They burned our fiel's and our homes, and took my Sadie wif 'em. Haven't seed her since. Nuffink to eat and our chil'ren went wiv'out. We wasn't gonna hurt you. Jus' wanted hep."

"Tell me, are you from Pocari or from Winthrop?"

One of the women looked up in fear, but the man continued, "We doesn't know, but them Pocari allus said we was theirs and took what they cud. Winfrop never bothered us."

"May I touch each of you? I'll know where you belong, and the answer won't matter too much." When the man nodded, I laid my hand gently on the shoulder or back of every one in the group. "In spite of what you were told, you're all from Winthrop. Do you want to stay here, or would you like to move closer to the city?"

"I wuz bornd here, lady," said one of the women. "My mama's in the ground here."

"Then here you will stay. We'll build you new homes. We'll get you fresh seed. Is there still time to grow a crop this year? Yes? Then we'll also supplement your stores since you won't get a full year's growth." I turned to the guards to ask for their help, but they were already taking off their armor and pulling out axes and hatchets. They headed off to do what needed to be done.

Amerlie and I sat with the people, listening to their stories, and discussing where they wanted to build and grow.

One of the little girls pulled on my sleeve, and I knelt to talk with her.

"Please, miss," she whispered. "They broke my doll." She held up the most woebegone stick doll with both arms dangling by a thread. I nearly cried. I felt into my good earth and found a fairly well-to-do manor only a few leagues away.

"Amerlie, who would live in a special little house about two leagues that way?" I pointed.

"That, milady, is one of yours."

I grinned. "You and I are riding there at haste, to return with goods for these fine people."

58

The lead guard, a man named Logonio, joined us on the expedition, wary of what we might find. It wasn't a difficult road, and we trotted into the yard not more than fifteen minutes after we left our group.

A sour looking woman walked out of the house, dusting her hands on her apron. She squinted up at me, and screamed, "Oh, my lady! Oh, my lady! You've come home to us at last!" She was alternately clapping her hands and bowing, so overcome was she.

I slid from my horse and took her hands in mine. There were tears in her eyes. "Please, tell me your name. I am—"

"The Duchess Periwinkle, home at last!"

"Yes, your name please?"

"I'm Bertha, and I was your nurse for all of a day or two before they took you away, my lady. Oh, I am that happy."

I hugged her and turned back to my need. "Bertha, a group of farmers near the border were hurt by the rebels, and I need clothes and toys for their children. I need food to help them get started again and I need seeds they can plant."

"Hush, hush. Tom! Larro! Hop to it!" She turned back to me. "I'll take care of this, my lady, they are undoubtedly kin." One man had come around the house, but one was still missing. "Tom!" Bertha rushed to him and asked him to prepare a wagon and gather firewood to take.

The second man, Larro, came down the lane. "I was in the pasture. What do you need?"

"We've got a mission of mercy for the duchess!"

He turned, and a big smile broke out over his face. "Why so it is, my lady, to be sure."

We all went into the house and raided the linen cupboards and the nursery, which was chock-full of toys. I took a doll for each girl, all of them beautifully dressed and a little ragged. I found a box full of little metal soldiers and I packed it for the boys to share. Additionally, I found a few balls and a jack-in-the-box, which Amerlie said had belonged to my grandmother. They all went into the cart.

Then we raided the kitchen, and Bertha was prepared to take everything to the refugees. I cautioned her to slow down and consider perishability as well as the need to keep enough to feed her farm hands. When the cart was full, Larro brought out a feisty colt to put between the shafts. The animal calmed down as soon as the harness touched his neck.

Bertha, Tom and Larro all climbed aboard and rode the wagon behind Amerlie and me, and our guard followed in the rear. We returned to find the area for three houses marked out as well as for two barns, and near the construction site lay an increasingly larger pile of wood being built up by the soldiers' and farmers' industriousness. The children were playing near the women who had started establishing an outdoor kitchen area, including a fire pit, in hopes we'd bring them supplies.

Amerlie and I examined the three dolls and found that each was meant for a different-aged child. We looked at the three girls from across the meadow, and determined which dolls were appropriate for which child. I took the one meant for the tiny girl who'd wept at the destruction of her stick doll, while Amerlie took the other two. Before we could move, a soldier came over with the girl's stick doll, now repaired, and wearing a small dress made from a soldier's handkerchief. I nearly cried at the sight, but took the doll from him and joined it with the one already in my hand. Then I kissed the soldier on the cheek, to his and Amerlie's horror.

We turned to the children, advancing toward them. One whispered to the other two and the trio looked our way. They slowly stood, the little one bouncing up and down in excitement.

I went to the little one, while Amerlie motioned to the other two. The small girl squeaked as I approached and knelt; and she ran to me. I handed her the doll, a girl with curly brown hair nearly the color of her new owner's. Then I gave her the stick doll. She shrieked when she saw it and pulled it into her grasp, along with the new doll. Then she pulled away a little, so I wouldn't see her cry. But I reached for her and held her, until she calmed down. I heard her calling the stick doll Tuppy.

"What will you name the new girl?"

"Doesn't she already have a name?"

"When you adopt a child from another place, you must give her a name that will be comfortable for her where you are."

"What's your name?" she asked, her curls bouncing with her energetic movements.

"I'm Peary. What's yours?"

"I'm Bethana. They call me Bethy." Her shyness was gone.

"What's your favorite girl's name?"

Bethy stood stock-still for a moment, clinging to her precious cargo. Then her face split into a grin. "Peary!"

We both laughed, and I took Bethy and her dolls into my arms.

The other two girls sounded thrilled as they examined their new dolls, as Amerlie showed them the way the clothes worked, and the arms and legs moved.

One woman approached to see what the excitement was about and started protesting. "Oh, no, milady, these are too nice for our kind. They'll only get broken and torn. You shouldn't..."

"No, I won't have it. These girls deserve the very best! And they shall have it. Bertha has brought clothes for all of you, and you must take them too. If I am to start as I want to go on, I must be allowed to help my people, my friends, when they're in trouble. I'm going to make sure you have as safe and happy a life here as those living farther from the borders, and it starts now! So, where are the boys? We brought things for them, too."

The three houses would take another week or two to finish, so Amerlie and I decided only to stay until the next morning. When Bertha returned from distributing clothes, I spoke with her about lending these families some of her farm workers so they'd get crops in the ground quickly.

"Don't worry, milady, there's a village not much farther on, and we'll get the young ones out to start the work. They're on their break from school because of the progression, and they'll be idle hands if we don't give them something to do."

A festive atmosphere developed as the children enjoyed their new toys and their parents enjoyed their new clothes. The cooking proceeded apace, and soon savory smells wafted over the area. We all ate together, although there were protests at my sitting on a log like the rest of them.

The next day, construction had progressed enough that Amerlie and I determined to go to the village to find workers. We also had several lists: the items the farmers absolutely needed immediately as well as the wives' shopping lists, and the soldiers' requests for building supplies.

When we walked into the small store in the center of town, all eyes were on us. The whispering was animated and occasionally hushed by neighbors. Amerlie asked for the proprietor, and an elderly couple stepped forward, with two young men and a girl behind them.

"Excuse me, ma'am, but isn't that our duchess?" The shopkeeper turned red at his own temerity.

"I will be in a few weeks, but right now, I'm just a lady. And I have a few orders for goods from you as well as a request of the town." That brought everybody a little closer, and people were gathering on the steps outside.

"There are three farming families near the border with Pocari. Do you know them?" The many nodding heads indicated they did, but there was a slight negative mumbling under the nods.

One of the townspeople spoke up. "They been consorting with the enemy, they have."

"Let me explain what they told me, and then you can tell me if it makes sense. They've always believed they're part of Winthrop, but a wizard from Pocari told them that they were in Pocari where they farmed."

That caused an outcry. A number of them claimed that Pocari had, indeed, lied while others said the folks were ensorcelled. But they all agreed the farmers were Winthrop, no doubt.

"You see, I tested them, and they *are* Winthrop. But they told me they were afraid of the wizard, so they did what he said. And that was giving Pocari half of what they grew. When they protested, their crops were destroyed and their houses and barns put to fire. We found them hiding in the woods, starving and barely clothed."

Now the cries were "That's not right!" and "Damn Pocaris, we'll fix our farmers up again!"

The storekeeper declared, "We can have a building party out there tomorrow. I'll outfit them and...."

"That will be great. We left our soldiers there, and the construction is getting started, but there are three houses and two barns to build. And they need workers to help them get crops in the ground so they'll have something to harvest this year. They mentioned that the students might be available." At that, a roar of youthful voices came from the street. "The soldiers belong to the emperor and the workers will surely have the chance to meet them." Shouts of approval from the crowd, and the only thing left was to get a team ready to send out to our new friends.

59

Amerlie and I took our leave of the village, which was called Straythorn for the many prickly bushes and trees around it, and headed off for Springfield on a route the locals had pointed out. It wasn't much more than a game path, but they assured me it would get us to the road in just an hour or two.

We rode through thickets of thorns, but the path was kept clear. There was a bog that made horrible sucking noises to our left. The air smelled of rotting vegetation, with a sweet overlay from the water lilies off to the side where fresh water ran into the swamp. We took advantage of the fresh water both for ourselves and the horses, and then moved a little farther away to avoid the noxious fumes to take our lunch.

We climbed a hill on the other side of the bog, and found a huge shade tree at the crest. From the height, we could see great distances, and thought we could pick out the smoke from the fires at Straythorn. In the other direction, a train of wagons traveled toward us, though still far away. The wagons were brightly colored with words on the sides, which we couldn't make out from this distance.

After finishing our lunch, we rode toward the wagons, which were very slowly climbing up the hill. As we got closer, I saw there were families on the wagons, and the women and children seemed upset, crying and holding each other tightly.

Amerlie humphed when she saw the wagons more clearly. "It's only the gypsies, milady. Pay them no mind."

"Why should I pay them no mind? They're in my duchy and I'll deal with them as I see fit."

"They're thieves. They're deceitful, and cannot be believed, milady. They'll spin you a tale of woe because you're young and tender. They'll throw themselves on your goodness."

"I'm not without tools to read them, you know, Amerlie. While they are in my duchy, I can detect any lies from them. You know I can do this with all noncitizens."

Amerlie sighed. "I suppose there's a reason all the great duchesses are available to you. Do what you think is right."

By then the gypsies had stopped their wagons, and the men

came out front, pulling their forelocks. I rode a little ahead of Amerlie and stopped about ten feet from the men.

"Where are you going, my good people?" I didn't to accuse them of absconding, as Amerlie would have me do.

"May it please you, my gracious lady, do I have the honor of addressing my duchess?" the oldest man asked.

"I will be the Duchess of Winthrop within a few weeks. What brings all of you traveling now? Ought you not to be performing and telling fortunes at fairs at this time of year?"

"My dear lady, we have been banished from this duchy by one who styles himself the regent, though he certainly doesn't look like your father." This man appeared to be of an age with my da, and he was darkly handsome if a little pudgier than the fit young men around him.

"When and where did this happen?"

The girl on the first truck, a pretty dark-eyed teenager, cried out, "It was when I was going to perform for the first time, and it's not fair." She stamped her foot on the front board of the wagon.

My raised eyebrow elicited a response. "It's true, your grace, we were to perform in Willoughby as a major part of their fair, when a man approached and told us to get out. He has harried us all the way since we left the town. We should be hearing from him in a few minutes, as he won't be happy we've stopped for so long."

I nodded at Amerlie, and we both got down from our horses. We walked over and stood behind the men as a young man came riding up the hill.

"Why are you stopping, you evil people? Get on, I say, get on. Or do you want me to whip you again?" By then he was up parallel with us, confronting the men. Pulling out his crop, he began to strike downward but was suddenly frozen in place. His momentum carried him off his horse and onto the ground in front of the gypsy men.

Amerlie and I moved forward.

"Do you know who this fine fellow is, Amerlie? Or should I put him to the test?"

"No, milady, it is only the younger son of a particularly litigious man of your duchy. He's even tried to sue you in absentia to prove your existence because he has a weak claim to the throne through a third or fourth cousin, should you vacate it. I can't remember his name, but perhaps if you unfreeze him just a bit, we can get it from him."

He was very good-looking except for the sneer on his face. I walked over to him and stood as close to him as I could.

"Do you know who I am?" I released him enough so he could answer.

"You're that fake pretender to the throne. I know you're a fake because I *know* my cousin Periwinkle and you're not a bit like her."

"And where's this cousin of yours? I'd like to speak with her."

"As if I'd tell a fraud that!"

"Oh, but you will even if I have to force it out of you."

"You can't torture me! I'm of royal blood!"

"So am I, as it happens, and have been accepted by my father as the true heir. I gather your candidate has not. And I don't need to torture you to get you to talk. All I need to do is this," and I expanded a little, making all of my features as benevolent as possible, while exuding my particular brand of majesty, looking almost matronly. He was begging to kiss my feet within seconds.

"What is your name, child?"

"I'm Jothro, my lady, of the lesser branch of Winthrop known as the Winters."

Amerlie laughed. "The Winters have been trying to prove a connection for more than a hundred years, and your mother and grandmother were never convinced."

"Tell me, Jothro, why are you hounding the gypsies?"

"Because my girlfriend wanted to perform and the folks liked those gypsies better than my girl."

The young girl who had spoken earlier sent a raspberry his way, and he became upset.

"Jes' because you're prettier doesn't mean you're better," he wailed at her.

"Does your father"—I looked to Amerlie to confirm, and she nodded—"know you've done this?"

"I dunno," he answered a little sullenly.

"What do you suppose he would say?"

"I dunno. I guess he'll be mad at me."

"Why is that?"

"'Cuz I got caught."

"Ah ha! So that's the way the wind lies, is it? I'm afraid, Amerlie, we have yet another detour. And we'll be bringing the gypsies with us back to where they belong."

"Nooo," cried the boy.

Two gypsy men came forward, picked him up and placed him in the first wagon, with the young girl to watch over him. Then they began the laborious process of reversing their course.

Amerlie and I spoke a distance from the gypsies while they

sorted themselves out.

"Is there discrimination against the gypsies in Winthrop?"

"Oh, I suspect so. There certainly was when we took you away, and I see no reason for it to have changed in the last seventeen years. The prejudice is because they're different and refuse to formally join the duchy and adopt its culture."

"But they've had their own culture for ages. We wouldn't like it if the emperor came and told us how to run things, would we? We're just as bad if we expect them to kowtow to the ways of our duchy. They can stay in Winthrop, and I'll make it my first edict if I have to."

"What if they want to go? Will you let them?"

"Of course. Why would I want to keep an artist against his will? Could I expect a happy performance if he were forced to perform? No, it's best to give them their freedom to go where they choose. But they will have my protection as long as they're in Winthrop."

I dismounted and walked among the gypsies. The young girl called me over, very excited.

"Can you arrange for us to perform before the emperor? That would be the best! I want him to pick us to travel with him on his progression. We'll get to perform everywhere—and get rich too."

"Hush up, Aishe! You are too proud by half." The older gypsy woman was bent over by the curvature of her spine, and she had to cock her head to one side and approach diagonally to talk to the girl.

As Amerlie watched, the woman stood a little straighter. And then more and more, until she was almost fully upright, her head still leaning forward away from her shoulders. The woman wiggled her back a little, then her hips and then she raised her arms over her head, shouting the while her delight.

Amerlie looked at me, her mouth agape. "How did you do that?"

"It was like using building blocks. I pulled her spine straight, or at least as the edges said they line up, and then I tightened the muscles and the rest so her body will stay that way. After all, she was in pain and feeling terribly old, when it's quite clear she's still young at heart. Why let a mechanical thing like that stay when it's easy to fix?"

Amerlie's voice was suddenly quite weak. "I suppose it's just because it's never been done before. At least I don't think so."

"Oh. We'll ask Derona when we get back. I'm sure it's a teachable skill and it could help a lot of people. There's something to be said for not having been 'properly' educated. I might not have tried that if I'd known it hadn't been done. We'll have to look into this theory, won't we?"

I wandered about the train of caravans, looking at people in a new way. If I could help at that basic level, improving lives, all my people would benefit.

60

We reached Willoughby well before suppertime, having attained the road not more than half a league from where we had met the gypsies. After releasing the young man, we had him take us to his father, having already sent the gypsies off to set up their show for the evening performance.

Jothro led us to the most ostentatious building around the main square.

"Well, the little lordling has returned," the guard at the front door joked, "and with a brace of dames, no less!" He roared at his own wit, but stopped when he noticed no one shared his delight. "Hey, you little ladies aren't...." His voice faltered at the look in my eyes.

"Shall we try this again, officer? But with a little more respect this time, please. Show the proper honor to a son of this house. Even if he is a bit of a fool. It shouldn't be bandied about in public that he's not as honored as he could be. You may announce my arrival."

"Excuse me but I don't know who you are."

"If you think about it for a minute rather than going with the first thought that comes into your very disordered mind, I'm sure you can figure it out. If you're to be any use to this family, you should be able to deduce the rank of anyone who appears before you. Shall we try this again?" Although I desperately felt like giggling, I maintained my stern expression.

"My lady, my mind is befuddled. It's clear you're a great lady, but I don't know of.... Wait, you must be our duchess!" He bowed repeatedly, if somewhat foolishly, and required a further push to enter and announce us.

The house was over-ornamented and showed distinct signs of a general lack of taste. I realized for the first time how comfortable my castle was in Springfield, with fine taste and decorum used in selecting furnishings, hangings, and vases and such things. Nothing I'd seen thus far had prepared me for such awesome gaucherie. Lamps had gilt on top of gilt, with jewels—of paste probably— randomly affixed around the bases. The furniture was also gilded, and the upholstery was cloth of gold or silver, or a pale imitation of each. A large man sat by the fire, which was stifling given the weather outside. His foot was raised and wrapped as if injured.

"The Duchess of Winthrop, milord," announced the guard, who appeared to have returned to his senses.

The large man drew sharp breath. He then rather ponderously tried to raise himself from his chair. I knew he expected me to allow him to stay seated, but I wasn't in a charitable mood. I waited patiently at first, but found my foot tapping in irritation the longer he took. Finally throwing himself out of the deep chair, he tottered to a standing position. I waited. He looked stunned at my behavior, but he knelt and reached for my hand.

"Isn't this enough? I'm an old man and I should give myself credit for getting this far."

"Sir! You *will* show proper respect or I shall oust you from this comfy home and make you work on a farm. We'll start with cleaning the stables. Then we'll help the physician with the pigs. I'm sure there are a hundred other ugly tasks we can find for you." My foot was tapping loudly now as I barely controlled my anger. I'd been willing to be diplomatic in dealing with him, but his sense of entitlement lit me up. Amerlie tried to get my attention, but I ignored her. I had resources that told me how to deal with this fat prig.

"Please accept my humble obeisance, my duchess. I will stay on my knees for the next quarter hour to show how I honor you."

"You will stay on your knees until I give you permission to rise. You do not dictate to me. Am I clear? Now I want you to tell me how your son Jothro came to believe he had the right to drive gypsies from my duchy."

"They are thieves and malcontents, and they refuse to adopt our pastimes and manners. They are not sociable, or allowed in polite society."

"The apple doesn't fall far from the tree, does it?" I said to Amerlie. She laughed and indicated she wished to ask a question. I nodded.

"Tell me, sir, where the witch Mesericordia is. We've tried to reach her for a long time to no avail, although we know she lives. The last time she contacted one of our sisterhood, she was here in your presence."

"Don't know what you're talking about. Never had a witch here. Don't believe in them." He scrutinized Amerlie. "And who the hell are you?"

"My dear sir, I can leave you kneeling there for a day or more. I won't have you be rude to my companion. Do you wish to reconsider your answer?"

The boy spoke up. "I know where she is and I can show you. Just don't hurt my father. Please." His voice caught as he slid to his knees, eyes wide and looking at me.

"Jothro, your feelings for your father are a good sign. I'll go with you, and ask Amerlie to stay here and keep your father on his knees until I return." She nodded as I pulled the boy to his feet.

He led me out of the drawing room and down a long corridor toward a large, wooden, barred door. A single guard stood by the door, looking at us curiously but not with any apparent ill will.

"This lady is the Duchess Periwinkle and she wants to see the witch. Open the door."

The guard went to one knee and brought his hand up to his forehead. "Milady, I'm sorry, if I had known, I—"

"Don't worry, there was no reason for you to assume I'd be here. But I do want to see Mesericordia as soon as possible."

"Milady, I had nothing to do with it, I promise you."

"To do with what?" I asked as innocently as I could.

"She's in terrible shape, and she hasn't been fed properly."

"Then get a move on!" I waved my hands in the door's direction and he hastened to open it.

Behind the door was a long stone staircase that twisted to the left. To the right was a torch in a holder with a pile of replacements on the floor. The guard picked up one and lit it before starting down the stairs. Jothro followed me, having picked up another torch, so the stairwell would be well lit.

We went down enough stairs to take us to the depth of my castle's third or fourth level. As we went lower, the walls became damp and a fetid smell assaulted my nose. When we finally reached the bottom, we faced a door similar to the one at the top of the stairs, although this one had a heavy bar across it. The guard handed me his torch and lifted the bar. From the look on his face and the sweat on his brow, I concluded it wasn't a task he was used to doing regularly, which worried me no little bit.

A sconce on the wall held an unlit torch. I lit it with the guard's torch. I could then see the walls were weeping and the floor was wet; I muttered to myself about the horrid smell. The guard recovered his composure and the torch, while Jothro pulled the door open.

Looking through, I could see vertical bars along either side of the room; a door was set into each row of bars. Behind the bars were sodden mounds of hay and the air was filled with the stench of human waste. Behind the bars to the left a few men were chained to the wall; all were in ragged clothes and having difficulty standing. I swung my eyes to the right, and peered into the gloom.

The guard and Jothro brought their torches closer to the bars on that side. There was a slight stirring in the hay halfway down the wall, and then a face appeared, eyes crusty, lips chapped and bleeding, lesions on her cheeks, hair lank and stringy.

"Mesericordia? I've come to help you." I couldn't bear to see the pain and hope in those eyes, but she stumbled to her swollen and bleeding feet. Her dress had never been fine, but the remnants that clung to her body bore no resemblance to a garment at all, especially not one worn by a woman.

I turned to the guard but he was already moving. He had the door unlocked by the time I realized what he was doing. He swung it wide as he offered his arm to the woman. She could barely reach him without falling, so he swept her up in his arms, dropping his torch, which sputtered out in the damp. He turned and walked out the door, causing the hanging men to cry out weakly.

Jothro took my arm and led me out. He reached up and pulled the torch from its socket in the wall, handing it to me. "Would you like me to go first, milady, to light your way, or behind to catch you if you slip?"

I had to keep myself from laughing. "Run after the guard, I want his way lit. I'll follow as fast as I can." I nodded at him and waved an arm up the stairs. He paused and then went.

I walked slowly up the stairs, my skirt wet at the bottom, heavy and pulling at me. I watched as Jothro's light disappeared around the bend and felt surprisingly little panic. Putting one foot after the other took all my concentration; it was a slow ascent. I was stunned when the guard came back and swept me up too.

Twenty minutes later, Amerlie, Mesericordia and I were bathed and in fresh clothes, waiting for tea and food to arrive for the starved woman. A knock on the door and a servant entered with a magnificent tea on a tray, which she placed on the table between the three of us. Following the tea was Jothro, looking very young and more than a little scared.

"If you let my father go, please don't tell him I released those men from the dungeon. They're in the kitchen now, getting fed and our housekeeper is preparing beds and clothes for them. They'll stay until they're healthy, and if they want jobs they can have them."

"Tell me something, Jothro. Do you know why they were held captive here or who they are? What was your father thinking?"

He sighed before answering. "He put the witch there for telling him to straighten up. I thought that was what people did to witches. I thought what I did to the gypsies was the normal and right thing. I'm sorry. I haven't been down there for six months; it's horrible." He seemed to have trouble saying this. "Two of the men were farmers who didn't bow fast enough to Father. The third man was already down there when I found out about the place. I don't know if he'll get any better."

I wasn't alone in my sorrow and disgust at this news. Mesericordia wept again and Amerlie put her arm around her friend's shoulders. I asked Jothro to do what he could for the men and he could come back in an hour or so when I would be ready to deal with his father.

61

Jothro, Amerlie and I returned to Lord Willoughby. He was kneeling where I had left him, although he now had a brocade pillow under his knees. I looked at my companions and saw Amerlie blush slightly. I smiled at her and then walked to my vassal, whose eyes were closed, his cheeks wet, his breathing strained.

I leaned down and offered my hand to help him rise. It became apparent my hand alone wouldn't raise him from his perch. His son came to his father's other side, and together we got Willoughby to his feet and then into his chair. Amerlie brought over a small footstool, and we raised his swollen foot to rest on it. I looked with curiosity at the awkward wrapping, and then probed more deeply.

I discovered he had a piece of wood, larger than a splinter, but smaller than a pencil, embedded in his heel. The wound was raw and ugly, showing signs of prior attempts to remove the shard of wood. With a little more exploration, I found I could push from within his foot against the sharp end of the shard. Willoughby gasped and tried to pull his foot away. Applying even pressure to the shard, I managed to push it partly out of his foot. I knelt beside the footstool, removing the bandage from around his foot. That elicited a soft cry from the poor man. With the bandaging removed, I could see and grab the piece of wood, and pulled it free.

The foot bled rather thoroughly, and I kept my senses on the interior wound as it did. A few small shards came out with the blood before I started to close up the wound and heal it. With magic, I examined the area as thoroughly as possible and found no sign of further damage. As my magic flowed through the foot, the redness and swelling subsided, and fresh pink skin covered the wound.

The man's body stayed tense for a moment or two, and then slowly relaxed as the tears began flowing down his cheeks. "Why would you do this for me, after what I've done, what I've become?"

"Tell me, Sir Willoughby, how long have you had this wound? There is something peculiar about it."

"It must be more than a year."

"And when did you start imprisoning people?"

"About ten months ago," Jothro spoke up.

It wasn't difficult to come to the conclusion there had been considerable changes in the lord's behavior in the days and weeks following the receipt of this wound. Wounds like this were usually fatal in a period much less than a year and I wondered what made this one different.

"I suggest you call for help and put your father to bed. He may not want to put much weight on that foot, but come morning, he must—or he will lose function and limp for the rest of his life. Will you help, Jothro?"

"Of course, milady. How can I ever thank you for healing my father? I thought he would surely die from this injury." He bowed deeply before running off to get assistance.

Amerlie and I looked at each other and shrugged. We both knew people without access to magic stood a much lower chance of survival after an injury of this nature.

"My dear, your mother would be so proud of you. You are everything she aspired to be and more. The fact that the other great duchesses are awake in you—you know what I mean by that, don't you?—gives you great wisdom for one so young. All that has transpired since you beat the poison has served only to strengthen you and to allow these consciousnesses to join you on your journey. Integrate what you can from them, and let go what is of no use, concentrating down to the very essence that which will stay with you. It may be a bit rocky, but I have faith in you." She stopped and smiled at me warmly. "You delight me and I know you delight your father."

I blushed. I didn't feel as if I'd done anything to deserve this praise if that's what it was. Part of me felt that I was my duchy, every bit of it, but much of the time I was just a scared seventeen-year-old.

Amerlie patted my hand. "Shall we see if we can get a real meal here? Mesericordia can undoubtedly eat a little more if she's awake, and if she isn't, the smell of good food may rouse her."

"That sounds wonderful."

We rose together to seek sustenance when Jothro returned and asked for me to speak with his father one more time. I agreed, of course, and we went to his sleeping quarters on the next level.

Halfway down the hall, a guard at the door pulled himself to attention as we approached and I recognized the young man from the dungeon.

"I'm afraid I didn't get your name, but I would like to tell the lord what a help you were."

He pulled at his forelock, a very countrified motion, and whispered, "Markham, milady, Enos Markham. I'm from the farmland closer to the border. I came here to make my way."

I touched him gently on the arm, and then moved past him into the lord's chamber. The windows were open and fresh air replaced the sickroom smells well with the help of the late afternoon breeze. The lord of the place was propped up in bed, his foot raised on a number of pillows. His color was much improved from earlier, and the pain lines in his forehead had eased considerably. They twitched a little at the end of every sentence, but when no accusation was forthcoming, they smoothed away.

"I was going to ask a favor of you, my duchess, although I know I have no right to expect any favors after all you've done for me."

"Why don't you tell me what it is you'd like? Maybe we can make a bargain somehow."

"I was hoping you would take my son Jothro with you to Springfield for the ceremony? He is so inexperienced in the way of higher folk, and he could learn much from just observing the rite. I haven't been fair to him in regard to his education, spending all my time with my older son who has gone off with the rebels and we may never see him again." The man's breath hitched and he lowered his head.

"I would be happy to take Jothro with me to Springfield. He's shown he has a level head on his shoulders. But I would ask something from you in return. Will you come this evening to the gypsies' performance to show you countenance their appearance here?"

"I'll try if I can have help walking there. It's the least I can do, milady." He didn't look entirely sincere as he said this, but I decided to give him the benefit of the doubt.

"I'll make sure you travel there safely and return in good time to get a good night's sleep. Agreed?"

He nodded and fell back against the pillow as if exhausted, although he appeared to be watching me out of the slit of his eyes. I smiled, turned, and left.

62

We arrived at the festival as the gypsies finished setting up their show after the act before them had left the scene. Servants had preceded us to arrange seating for the royal party. There was snickering at them among the bystanders who didn't expect their lord to appear, his antipathy for the gypsies being well known.

Enos made a ringing announcement: "The Duchess Periwinkle and Lord Willoughby! All rise!"

Sounds of surprise and disbelief could be heard from the crowd as it rustled to its feet. A staircase was cleared, allowing my party to ascend to the central box, which had been hastily vacated by a few scamps. We settled into our seats and Enos indicated that the crowd could be seated. Amerlie, Mesericordia and Jothro sat on either side of us, while the servants stood behind us, occasionally handing out drinks or snacks. We looked down on a large circular area, dusty from many days of shows, but well lit by torches spaced evenly around the perimeter.

Lord Willoughby leaned forward and dropped a handkerchief. A group of gypsies ran out and performed tumbling runs and acrobatic feats of near impossible formations. Every time I thought they'd reached their limits, the performers topped it with something even more daring. They finally ended with forming a shape that looked like an arch.

Under their arch came the young girl, Aishe, from earlier in the day. She swished in a black skirt with sequins that shone in the torchlight and glanced slyly at the top box and scanned for other more interesting young men. Then she broke into song in a voice that was stunning, coming from such a tiny girl. The sound filled the area, and the crowd grew silent as she sang of her love who had left her for another gypsy family. The pain in her voice sent chills up my spine, and I saw tears welling in the lord's eyes. I was going to make a remark to Amerlie, but she too was caught up in the voice with tears on her cheeks. When the song came to its glorious conclusion, the crowd erupted, screaming and stomping their approval and delight. Aishe bowed to the audience and left the stage in a silky way that swept her skirt from side to side.

The tumblers made another run through the area, followed by the entry of a sword-swallower and his assistant. The assistant, a pretty woman quite a bit older than the singer, probably in her thirties, carried a number of swords. The performer pretended to survey the swords seriously before picking one to his liking. He then arched his back so his neck was fully extended and his head fell back to his shoulders. Holding his head steady, he lifted the chosen sword above his head and aimed the point down his throat. A light drumroll sounded from the tent area. As he lowered the sword's tip close, he opened his mouth so wide he appeared to have dislocated his jaw. But all must have been well as the tip of the sword descended directly into his mouth and kept going until only the hilt was visible. The crowd gasped as one. After a moment, during which he turned in a circle so all could see, he pulled the sword from his throat and mouth, with a quick flick of his wrist.

The second sword he chose was a large two-handed broad-bladed piece with a handle more ornate than any I'd seen. I gasped along with the rest of the audience as the display began. Both he and his assistant showed signs this weapon was much heavier than the first.

His show went on with the use of three more swords and then it changed into a knife-throwing exhibition. His assistant stood a distance from the man, against a wall. Once she assumed her position, he threw twelve knives in quick succession, outlining his assistant, never nicking her or her clothes. The audience roared with appreciation. He held a hand out to lead his assistant to the center of the circle; they bowed, and hurried out of the area with a flourish.

Music filled the area, sprightly and lively, while a group of men in black baggy pants, brilliant red and green sashes, and white voluminous shirts pranced out and performed interesting kicks and squats at breakneck speed. We all clapped in time to the music as they leapt around the performance space. I took a moment to glance at Lord Willoughby and found him clapping and cheering with the others, a broad smile on his face.

Women joined the men as they danced, and they paired off into couples, with the men whirling the women through the area and occasionally throwing them several feet into the air. Then they broke apart and came to grab partners out of the audience. The young singer ran lightly up the steps and dragged Jothro out to dance. Lord Willoughby roared with laughter at his son's predicament.

Amerlie cautioned him to calm down but he chuckled at her

admonishment. "I haven't felt this good in years! I believe our duchess healed more than my foot!"

I smiled at him. "The healing touch picks up small problems and clears them while doing its main task. But I have no control over what it does. I merely put the healing into motion and hope it hits the right target. Magic may have helped you, that's all."

The music died away and the audience members who'd been participating wearily found their ways to seats. Jothro bounded up the stairs to us, grinning from ear to ear. "I'm so excited! They say they're headed toward Springfield, too!"

I beamed. "It's not surprising since I've asked them to perform in the celebrations following the ceremony. We can travel with them for a day or so, but then we'll have to move more quickly toward Springfield. They'll have plenty of time to get there."

Lord Willoughby was speaking with Mesericordia and didn't pay any attention to his son. I couldn't hear what they were saying, but the look on her face was priceless. She blushed, giggled, and looked with wide eyes at the lord as he spoke.

Jothro whispered to Amerlie and me, "She was thrown into the dungeon for turning down my father's proposal. But he was so sick by then he couldn't see how terrible the entire situation was. A number of the guards are said to have mistreated her, but he didn't know. And now he's back to himself, he's trying again."

Amerlie's brow furrowed as she stroked her chin. "She's in no shape to make a decision that important now. We can't let this happen."

"Don't you think it's her choice?" I asked. "She hasn't said a word against him since we recovered her. And she's protested every time we tried to blame him for that awful dungeon."

"We can't let her decide *now*. Think of the condition she was in when you found her in that cell. She was days away from dying. It was and is abuse, pure and simple."

We continued our discussion while heading back to our rooms but we found we couldn't come to agreement. Jothro had accompanied us on our walk, his concern clear on his face. Enos had guarded us, but remained silent during the walk.

As we arrived at our rooms, Enos cleared his throat. "My lady, I feel I have to tell you of something I saw one night while on guard at the top of the stairs. Lord Willoughby was sleepwalking, and looked terrible because he couldn't really walk on his injured foot. But he was crying out for her, wondering why she'd left him. I went to him, and said I could find her for him, if only he would go back to bed. I thought I'd let her free and get help. But then that blackguard Rafe came and told me to get back to my post, and leave the witch where she was."

Jothro cried out, "Not Rafe! Dad threw him out a year ago. How...?"

I pulled them all into our sitting room, and asked about this Rafe. It seemed he was something of a rake who'd enjoyed playing with all the pretty women in Willoughby's court. He made a play for Mesericordia, even though he knew the lord was wooing her. When the lord protested against Rafe's infamous behavior, they struggled and Lord Willoughby sustained the wound that crippled him until that very day. Rafe had been banished but the lord had questioned Mesericordia's fidelity afterward. Soon thereafter she'd been imprisoned as the lord's illness had progressed. What Rafe was doing back in the manor was open to question.

I inquired for more detailed information involving Rafe. As the two men painted the picture with their words, I wondered if they were describing Montrade. I turned to Amerlie and saw the same realization dawning on her.

"How long has Rafe been coming to this place? Do you know when he first appeared?" I watched them closely for their reply.

"He'd already been coming here when I was a little kid, and he acted like he was an uncle or something. I never really liked him, but my father viewed him as an important advisor and took him pretty seriously, so I kept quiet. Rafe was sent away when they fought over Mesericordia. But if he came back, what does it mean?"

"It means he won't be coming back again." Amerlie's voice was harsh. "He's dead. Thoroughly dead."

"And he may have had something to do with your father's change in character and injury. I'm fairly sure his name wasn't Rafe. He was a powerful wizard in his own right. If he was who we think he was, he may have been trying to separate your father from Mesericordia. His feeling of wellness after I healed him was likely due to a spell being lifted. I'll have to think about whether I felt such a thing during the healing process."

63

The next morning found us all at breakfast in the lord's private dining room. Amerlie and I had explored my memory of the healing and found evidence of a taint in the lord that was no longer present. It was Amerlie's desire to converse with him about his old friend Rafe.

"How did you meet Rafe and how long have you known him?"

"I really don't want to talk about that man. I never guessed how evil he was." Willoughby refused to look at us, and grumbled under his breath.

"It might be vital, if we're to understand any of the political mess we're in," Amerlie coaxed him.

"He was a traveler from the south who came through shortly before my wife died, so it must have been nearly twenty years ago." Willoughby seemed to relax once he started talking. "After saying he'd been to Arthur's Seat, which was a marvel to us, we asked to hear his tales. He was a natural storyteller, and we were beguiled. I told him he would always be welcome with such wonderful tales, and asked if it was his calling. He laughed, and it was a laugh that would warm you like a tot of good brandy. He said he was an historian, and then had to explain that to us. If I had known then what I know now, I would've thrown him out or drawn and quartered him."

"What do you know now?" Amerlie sounded very innocent.

"I've put two and two together finally, now that my mind's clear. Ten days after he left, that first time, my wife sickened and it took her two long years to die. He didn't come back until after she was gone, but I suspect he killed her. She raved at times when she had the strength, and her words were echoes of some of Rafe's stories, the nasty ones that were meant to scare us."

"But you continued to see him over the years?"

"It wasn't as clear then as it is now that I've put things together. He's the one who drew my older son away, the one who should be my heir and whom we haven't heard from in five years. Now it appears he may have been part of that uprising in Middleland and he might be dead." Tears that had only welled up while discussing his wife's demise now flowed down his cheeks.

"When did you find this out?"

"One of Rafe's associates came through about five weeks ago and told me he was there."

"Who was this?"

"That brat from Wallameer. He's been Rafe's toady for at least a few years."

"You mean Briaint?"

"That's the one. He was here not five weeks ago boasting about the army he was building and he said Tomas was there. And as good a rabble-rouser as Briaint could've asked for. I asked him to send Tomas home, but the little brat laughed at me. Said he wasn't mine anymore, but it made no sense. If I'd been stronger, I would have taken him on, and I had to hold Jothro back."

Jothro had been eating steadily throughout this history, but he spoke up at this. "He's a little snot-faced liar, and I don't believe Tomas was there at all."

I felt the time was right to tell Willoughby what I'd found. "You know how you said you felt so much better after I healed you?" At his nod, I continued, "I removed something else from you during that healing. There was a slight taint to your blood that felt magical. I tidied it up without recognizing what it was, but I now know it was a spell that had been cast on you, one that's been there for a long time. There was also a spell on the wound so it would never heal but also never kill you. If you feel lighter and more awake now, it's because that taint that has been poisoning you for years is gone."

Willoughby looked wide-eyed at me; I noticed small tremors throughout his body. "You mean that bastard poisoned me? I'm going to find him and kill him!"

"No need," said Amerlie. "He's been hoisted on his own petard! He welcomed a demon to this world, and the demon ate him. We killed that demon and the little bit of 'Rafe's' soul that was clinging to Earth. He was telling the truth when he said he had been to Arthur's Seat. He used to be the master wizard to the emperor, whom he treated no better than you. His name was Gabrille Montrade, and he was the most arrogant, amoral man I've ever known."

Mesericordia had been watching this discussion with astonishment, but now joined in. "I knew there was something wrong with you other than your foot injury, and I was trying to find it when Rafe came that last time. Or I guess I should say Montrade. He seemed to know what I was doing, and he did something to me. That's when we had our falling out and you put me in the dungeon.

It was his way to prevent me from finding out what he 'd done to you." Tears flowed down her cheeks as she tried to bite back her sobs.

Willoughby went to her, pulling her into his arms. She laid her head against his shoulder and allowed the tears to pour. I decided the time had come to leave them alone, and pulled Amerlie and Jothro with me as I went. Amerlie protested mightily, feeling there was much more information to glean from this source.

I laughed. "We leave for Springfield in two hours. When are you going to *get* this information? Be still. I've invited them to the ceremony. By then, they'll have worked through their heartbreak, and will be able to face us without the pain they feel today. Better all around."

64

When we exited the manor with the servants carrying our baggage, we found our horses ready and the gypsy caravans lined up to follow us. One of the gypsies offered to carry our baggage in his cart to lighten the load of the donkey until we parted, which we gratefully accepted.

The gypsy leader came to speak with us. We learned his name was Djordji and the little singer, Aishe, was his daughter. We agreed to ride alongside their caravan and talk for the first part of the trip.

We set out only half an hour late, and that was mostly because the lord and Mesericordia wanted to hug and kiss everyone before we left. We managed to break away and settle into a slow pace consistent with the needs of the gypsy wagons.

Djordji called out a wailing refrain that was echoed by the leaders of each family group to indicate readiness, and then the enormous group began to move as one. We were now lucky enough to be on the main road to Springfield, and knew there was a safe way home.

"I appreciate the chance to talk with you at a more settled time than when we first met," Djordji said. "We're quite impressed with the changes we see in old Willoughby and young Jothro. Your magic is indeed powerful."

I laughed. "Willoughby, surprisingly enough, is a good fellow if slightly concerned about status. He'd been tainted by a wizard, though that's been cleared up. Now he just wants to win the heart of someone who already loves him, so he's a happy man. I hope I've opened up his eyes a little to the spice variety can give to his life. He greatly enjoyed your performance last night."

"That's the first time we've tried dancing with an audience in this area. It went very well, don't you think?"

"Ask Jothro. He was exhilarated when he returned to the stands."

Our conversation continued thus for quite some time. I observed his dark eyes and full lashes, his darker skin, the joy in his smile and the love he clearly felt for his people. I finally asked, "What's your greatest wish to maintain your peace and prosperity in

Winthrop?"

I was a little surprised by his answer.

"We need a haven that's ours alone that we can retreat to when we're tired or assailed by enemies. I don't know what such a sanctuary would look like, but I'd rather it not be in a city or town. They're too easy to overrun."

I offered to think on it and left to commune with Amerlie. I thought I might own a forest or hunting preserve along the road to Springfield and wanted to ask.

"There's a rather nice forest about a day away that has a few clearings in it where they could set up their circle of wagons. But do you have to *give* it to them?"

"In light of the prejudice against them, they need a place to call home, not a permitted place where people could argue about their rights. We might have to put up signs around it indicating I've given it to them and they're the sole owners. If the signs have my seal, there can be no question, can there?"

"There will be poachers when they're not in residence, unless there's a group that would stay during odd enough times that the locals would be unable to figure out the schedule."

"It might be a place that those too old for the road would want to retire. And they have their own magic to protect what's theirs. This could work. Do any of the locals make their livelihood from this forest?"

"I don't think anyone lives near enough to do so, though there are farms in the area, and they may use it as midsummer cover for their beasts. I can inquire if you give me a few minutes."

I nodded and watched as she slipped into trance to contact those she knew in the area. I wondered if I'd ever know my people well enough to be able to call on them this way. I was seeing parts of my duchy for the first time, and feeling my connection with the land deepen with each new sight.

Amerlie awoke, so to speak, and turned with a smile. "There's no one using the forest now because there's a rumor that gypsies have taken it over. That's certainly a sign this is meant to be. Shall we go talk to Djordji?"

"Oh, yes! This is wonderful." We laughed together as we turned our horses toward the head of the caravan once again.

"Djordji, I have good news," I called out.

He poked his head out of the wagon's body and pushed Aishe to one side so he could step out, smiling at us. "I will listen closely, I assure you."

"Would you be interested in owning a forest of about ninety acres? It has a number of clearings in it, as well. We'll reach it tomorrow and you can inspect it at your leisure." I grinned.

"Oh, my duchess! Can it be? We only spoke moments ago, and you have answered my prayers. You're a true friend to the Roma. You've welcomed us as we have never been welcomed before by a ruler, and you have asked us to perform at a major event in your life. How can we possibly repay you?"

"But there's no need. You add to the various arts available in my duchy and therefore benefit my people and me. You can still travel wherever you'd like, though now you'll have a place to call home when you need a rest, or for your older folks who can no longer travel to stay in safety. It's my job to make sure the people in my land are cared for. You are such people even if you have a different culture. You should be allowed to live as your history requires and without discrimination. That's all I'm arranging."

He laughed. "It'll be a cause for great celebration when we stop for the evening. There'll be singing and dancing, I suspect. Don't tire yourselves riding horses. Take a ride in the wagon for a nap if you wish. We will dance you to Heaven this evening!"

We made good progress that day in spite of the slowness of the gypsies' caravans, and came to a comfortable field by a rolling brook to settle for the night. With the wagons all set up, and the fires burning brightly, a community of lively and vibrant people was formed.

Djordji brought an older woman over to meet Amerlie and me. She was one of the elders and was quite proficient in telling fortunes. He introduced her as Esmeralda.

"I wouldn't dare, my lady, tell your real fortune at a town fair. You're of too high a rank to be told in public. Here, we are quiet, at home, under the beautiful sky with no one to overhear or interrupt. I don't know what I'll see when we start, but I'll do all in my power to help you understand the reading. Sometimes the meaning doesn't become clear until later in time."

"I understand. What do you want me to do?"

"I want you both to come into my wagon. We'll have more privacy, and you can sit more comfortably."

I confess I felt both a little excited and a little worried. I didn't know what to expect, knowing I had a few inexplicable powers and believing she did too. Amerlie looked surprised at my willingness to try. I figured I'd bring her to my way of thinking about the gypsies, one way or another.

Esmeralda's caravan was colored mainly blues, reds, and yellows on the outside, and to my mind one of the prettiest. We climbed in through the back door and were met with a tidy small room with neat cupboards on the walls and benches with scattered pillows.

Esmeralda indicated we should sit on one side while she placed a pillow for herself to sit on. "My old bones need a little protection from the hard wooden seats when I need to listen to the future. Please, make yourselves comfortable."

I selected a beautiful silky pillow with a paisley design in deep purples and reds, and settled myself as well as I could on the bench. I looked expectantly at Esmeralda who was breathing deeply with her eyes closed, a placid look on her face.

Then she spoke. "A long life, with pain and pleasure. A family, an heir. I see madness, both close to you, and in the people. You will have great power, not always used for the best. But you will remain whole and as you are. When the man with the lost eye and mind comes, you must believe him even though he frightens you. The arrogant one will try to stop you in this as in other things." She paused. "There's more, but I must rest. Would you like some tea?"

I was dazzled by the thought of a long life, and with children. The negative words had slid away with that news. Henry had taught me madness could lay close without hurting me, and I hoped that was what she meant. The specifics eluded me; I recalled the need to believe someone and not someone else. Keeping track of the details was what I thought Amerlie was here for.

Esmeralda continued to give me minor warnings about when to do something and when not. The closeness of the air in the enclosed space began to put me to sleep. Esmeralda's voice wove in and out of my consciousness, and I picked up little disjointed bits of information that I could feel worming their way into my awareness. I felt no need to become fully alert.

Esmeralda turned her attention to Amerlie. I heard none of what she said to her; the friction between the two of them was evident. I felt Amerlie's resistance to the power Esmeralda was using and wanted to laugh. Amerlie was rather set in her ways and seemed loath to recognize the validity of a foreign use of the power we all accessed.

I left the caravan a little groggy and out of sorts. Amerlie seemed confused, as if she wanted to believe what she'd heard, doubting it could be true. A few minutes in the cooler nighttime air sufficed to awaken me to the activities around the fire.

Some of the gypsies had brought out instruments and were playing softly by the main fire. People had not yet settled in to listen, instead walking around in small groups conversing or putting away items they had brought out of their wagons as if preparing for the finale of a show.

Jothro and Aishe met us and took us to a seating area near the musicians but far enough away from the fire to be comfortable in the gentle summer air. They prattled away about the evening's entertainment: how Aishe would get to sing and how the day would end with dancing. Listening to them, I wondered if such simple friendship would ever be available to me. I had been involved in politically significant activities, not this carefree and youthful playfulness, and found I wanted it back. I had it in the valley...and then I knew what I was missing. Would it be possible with the heavy load about to be placed on my shoulders?

The music began in earnest, and a few tumblers tried some new routines. Catcalls and teasing came from the audience when combinations went terribly wrong. Scattered applause greeted success while lively conversation continued among the audience.

The music changed, Aishe humming along and standing up. Within moments, her amazing voice rose with a vivacious song involving the speedy listing of a lover's flaws. The music sped up and the list got longer until I couldn't believe how quickly she was singing. The song ended on a high note, and Aishe nearly fell back to her seat, breathing heavily.

"I've got to get better at that one if we're going to put it in the show!" she said.

"It's nearly there," her father said as he joined us. Looking at me, he said, "I wanted to talk to you about something we'd like to offer you. I don't know if it's something you can accept as a ruler, so I thought we could discuss it now and perform the ceremony tomorrow if you agree."

"You've intrigued me. Please go on."

"In our traditions we have a way to make a *gage*, which is a non-gypsy, a special gypsy friend, called a *didkai*, which means one is a formal member of the clan. The friend can then come for shelter or aid in the way any gypsy can, and will be in all respects a gypsy, just without our powers. You don't need our powers as you have your own, but we would like to make you a *didkai*."

"Goodness, that's a great honor! And I admit it could be very helpful in times of trouble, to have an outlet if I needed to escape for any reason. This wouldn't be talked about outside the clan, would it?

Your people wouldn't brag about it, for example?"

"Oh, no. It's between us and the *didkai* only." He turned to Jothro. "You won't talk about it, will you?"

"No, certain people in the population wouldn't understand, and might take it the wrong way." Jothro blushed.

"Ah, you *do* understand." Djordji winked at the young man.

"Yeah, I've changed my attitude about you guys completely. You're great!"

We laughed and I turned to Djordji. "You'll let me think about this overnight?"

"Of course. We thought we'd do the ceremony tomorrow at the forest if that's satisfactory to you."

I smiled my reply, while feeling Amerlie's caution and calculating thoughts regarding the politics of it all.

We danced for a while and then headed off for bed.

65

Amerlie wanted to discuss the proposed honor that night, even though I told her I was tired and needed sleep. When she became insistent, I ordered her to stop. At this, she stormed away from where we'd planned to sleep. I let her go and tucked myself into my bedroll, pulling the blanket over my head.

It worked because when I was next aware, the sun was rising. I looked toward Amerlie's bedroll to see that it hadn't been slept in. I pulled myself up and out, looking around for any evidence of wrongdoing, but found nothing. The camp was still quiet with only a few of the women pulling the fire alive again in preparation for breakfast. Recognizing one of them, I approached to see if they had any news of Amerlie. They didn't but one of them moved to check the caravans.

I helped them magically with the fire, and they laughed while thanking me.

"My husband will be surprised when I wake him with tea so quickly," one woman said. Then they competed with tales of how surprised their husbands and children would be. It may have been an attempt to distract me from worrying about Amerlie.

Aishe arrived and gestured for me to follow her. I went, wondering what the summons could be about. When we were far enough from the fire, she told me she knew where Amerlie was.

"Tell me, Aishe, I need to find her."

"She's with Esmeralda, trying to convince her to say something to you about respecting your elders. She already tried with my father and he declined her suggestion. She's been in Esmeralda's caravan most of the night and hasn't made any progress."

"How do you know she hasn't gotten anywhere?"

"If she had, Esmeralda would have come to you in the middle of the night, and scared you."

"That's not a pleasant thought. Well, I guess I ought to go confront her now."

"I hope you straighten her out. My dad says she picked the wrong person to bother about you. Esmeralda likes you and thinks you'll be great for this world."

We hurried to Esmeralda's caravan and I couldn't help noticing that the women were watching for the explosion. I was determined there wouldn't be a public display. Before we reached the caravan, the back door opened, and Esmeralda waved me in. Aishe was sent on her way.

When I climbed the stairs, I saw that Amerlie had her back to me and her shoulders were shaking.

Esmeralda followed me and closed the door. "My duchess, I told this person part of what I saw that involved you and I told her the potential consequences if she defied you. You can imagine my surprise when she came last night, begging me to convince you not to accept the honor my people have offered you. I suppose an honor such as this from us is suspect, but that is is being made to harm you? It's laughable. She's been in this state for hours, and I cannot tolerate it. If you take her advice, you will leave now and fail to give us the forest you have so graciously offered. If you don't take her advice, we look forward to welcoming you into our family. I will say no more."

I pondered this for only a moment, and then said, "Amerlie, get a hold of yourself. Leave this caravan and wait for me at our bedrolls. I'll tell you my decision there."

She shook harder, and her sobs became loud enough to hear. She didn't move. I looked at Esmeralda, and she shrugged.

I *reached* to Amerlie and shook her. "I will not tolerate this behavior from a grown woman. You've taken too much liberty with me in this case. I'll deal with you later. Leave." I put a small compulsion in the last word, and was surprised when she tried to resist it.

After a moment, she swept by us and ran down the steps, refusing to look at me as she went.

"I'll tell you, Esmeralda, I'm very disappointed in Amerlie. It bothers me she would seek out your people to withdraw the honor you've offered me. I know she harbors some of the standard prejudices against your people, but I had hoped traveling with you would change her mind."

"My duchess, don't be sure that your own people will agree with you. You may put your rule in jeopardy by accepting our offer."

"Hush. I'm young and aware of the danger as ruler of this duchy. I should tell you I intend to rule here for more than fifty years. Even if at the end of that time, I'm still suffering consequences from this decision today, I won't regret accepting this honor. You're a noble people with a rich history, and I'll do everything in my power to educate my people as to the worth you bring our community. I intend to leave her with you. I won't give her any more opportunities to question me and destroy her life in the process. Jothro and I will continue on. My soldier guard should be through here in about three or four days. They'll catch you on the road. If she's intolerable to you, feel free to have the soldiers take her on."

"You cannot go alone with that young man. We'll send a few of our young men with you. They and Jothro will all behave properly for fear of being deprived of your company."

I agreed, laughing.

I went to Djordji before confronting Amerlie. I wanted him to know before the whole camp that I had agreed to join them as a *didkai*. He was joyful at the news though worried about Amerlie's objections. I was adamant.

I found Amerlie in her bedroll with the blanket pulled over her head, much as I had been an hour earlier. I stood over her, willing her to look at me and rise. It took a little longer than I would have liked, but it was faster than I expected. She stood before me with her head down, her hair falling around and over her face.

"I don't know why you've chosen *this* to rebel over. You've known my feeling about this group of people for almost a week. You're in no condition now to discuss this matter in an intelligent and unemotional way. I'll go through with the ceremony this evening, and then Jothro, a few gypsies, and I will ride on to Springfield. You can stay with the gypsies until the soldiers overtake you and come along with them, or you can wait until the progression reaches you and try to convince Max and my father of my unfitness to rule. You have a multitude of choices. Pick one and you don't have to tell me which."

I turned and walked away.

Esmeralda offered me breakfast, which was welcome after the emotions of the dawn. She led me to her steps at the back of the wagon, and we ate side by side.

"You know you have the right to make your own decision, yes?" she asked.

I nodded. "But this is going to be my first separation from Amerlie since I left the valley in which I lived. I'm a little scared I was too forceful and without enough thought."

"Tell me, if anyone else had gone behind your back to undermine you, how would you have reacted?"

That gave me pause. I remembered how quickly I'd charged a maid with treason for being rude. What Amerlie had done was significantly worse. We'd never discussed or resolved her unwillingness to teach me in Markerburg. As I added up the times when Amerlie had pressured me against my instinct, or casually took charge when I should have been consulted, I realized she'd been pushing me into a role that would make me dependent on her for guidance.

"Do you think she wanted to control me?" It seemed a possible conclusion.

"There is a phrase that's often found in the skits we see at town fairs. The ones that are political often talk about a person who is a 'power behind the throne.' You should ask questions about this." Esmeralda bit her lip and raised her eyebrows.

"I guess I have to figure it out for myself and a time away from Amerlie may be good for me. I have to learn to take care of myself for soon no one in Winthrop will be taking care of me."

"You have family and friends. Don't give up on them so quickly."

That cheered me up considerably. I believed in my da, and Chres was supposed to be doing better. I just had to get home to Springfield and that could be accomplished quickly. I smiled at Esmeralda, and she perked up at my expression.

"Shall we get on the road to the forest?" I asked, winking at the wise old woman whom I had come to cherish.

She chuckled and called out, "Djordji, time to go home!"

I̲t took less time to get on the road this morning as word had apparently spread there was a home at the end of today's journey. I could hear snippets of song from around the camp as items were packed away and horses were placed in the traces.

Jothro brought my horse, already curried and saddled, and helped me load up the few things I carried with me on the horse. Aishe came by to make sure all was in readiness, and then hopped up onto her father's caravan. I hadn't seen Amerlie since we had parted earlier, and mentioned it to Jothro.

"She's riding in Esmeralda's caravan. She was given something to help her sleep, though she doesn't know it. It was in her tea."

"Don't count on it working. If she sensed anything odd, she could destroy it in her stomach, or so she's told me." I must have look worried because he responded quickly.

"Don't worry, it wasn't just what was in her tea. Esmeralda also said a spell over her when she wasn't paying attention. You could see her eyes droop when the spell hit her. It was actually kind of funny."

"Well, it might work, and it's better than her crying or complaining. I don't want any of the gypsies to feel they have to take care of her. She's a competent woman and should get over this problem with a fair amount of ease. The only issue is if she continues to undermine me. But once this day is over, it's done."

Jothro nodded but said nothing. It occurred to me he probably wasn't the best confidante I could have. Neither his training nor his character gave him the resources to deal with intrigue at this high level of government.

I smiled at him and pointed toward the moving caravans. "It's time to go. Do you know who the others are who will be coming with us to Springfield?"

"Esmeralda said they would introduce themselves over the course of today's journey to the forest." He wet his lips and rubbed the back of his neck.

"Don't worry. I suspect she hasn't agreed with Djordji on which ones to send yet. We'll meet them as they're chosen."

We laughed and rode off to join the lead caravan, with Aishe driving and Djordji nodding off on the bench seat at the front. We spoke a little about the plans for later that day, but then settled into the slow pace of the wagons.

The travel was uneventful, and the stop for food midday was brief. We came over a rise and spotted the dark green blur of the forest in the distance. As each caravan came over the rise and saw the distant trees, the number of voices chattering and exclaiming increased until it sounded like a marketplace on a busy Saturday. The energy rising in the gypsies was palpable, filling me with warmth and joy. It took Djordji's substantial leadership skills to prevent any of his people from dashing at breakneck speed to get there sooner.

When we first saw the forest, we were still almost four leagues from it. Time stretched as we continued, but the forest didn't seem to grow closer or fill more of the sky. A small amount of complaining began among several of the younger gypsies, and their elders laughed at them. They spoke to the complainers in a language I didn't know and Djordji translated as he could.

"Let's see. That one was 'it is worth waiting for the big thing,' and earlier I heard 'when you have earned it, you can have it.' My people have a number of these sayings that don't translate well. I'm sorry."

Jothro laughed. "We have a similar one: 'it always come to one who waits.'"

"That may actually be better than ours. Maybe someone who specializes in languages would know if we're saying the same thing."

This conversation led to a discussion of the scholars in Springfield, and then changed, as such conversations often do, through a number of topics, useful mainly for the passing of time.

We came around a small hillock and the forest expanded before out eyes. There was a slight increase in our speed as even the horses seemed to sense the imminence of our arrival.

67

As we traveled closer, we noticed a small group of people standing in the road at the entry to the forest. They appeared to be local people from their clothing, and I couldn't see any weapons. I reached out with my senses and felt there was a clumsy shield around them, likely spelled by an inexpert.

I turned to Jothro. "Go back to Esmeralda's caravan and ask if Amerlie is awake. See if she sent a message ahead, but let Esmeralda do the asking. Get back as quickly as possible. This is important."

When he had left, I told Djordji what I sensed. "Since Amerlie is the one who checked the availability of the forest, I wonder if she's tampered with the people here to raise trouble. Any advice you can offer would be gratefully accepted."

"Let's wait and see what Jothro finds out. It was good to get him away before you told me about the shield. We should continue on as if nothing has changed. No reason to give them any suspicions about us that they don't already have."

We laughed and tried to chat about something else. Tension was clear in his shoulders and eyes, and I suspect mine showed the same.

In a matter of moments, Jothro returned. "Esmeralda says to tell you this is your first test. It has been created by Amerlie not so much to fight you as to see if you can handle it. She says she knows you can do it, and so do I!"

"I guess I ought to move forward and talk to them. I know I'm safe from whoever made their shield. I wonder if I can shield you too, Jothro. Give me a minute."

I searched through the memories and thoughts sitting in the background, the other duchesses Amerlie had spoken of. I hadn't really had an opportunity to do this earlier, and I was a little worried that now wasn't the best time to start. When I *reached* for the memories, it was like talking with other witches who were far away. I could hear them, and when I asked a question, I could feel them adjust so the correct duchess would answer.

I received instructions to set up a field of protection that expanded around me to include people within a certain area nearby. It was a straightforward spell, and I prepared to cast it when one of the other duchesses suggested I should envelop the people who awaited when I reached them. I thought on that for a moment, and then reached out with the field of protection around Jothro.

We trotted toward the group of people with no hint of aggression or worry. We talked casually to each other while covering the short distance, but I have no recollection of what was said. My mind was concentrated on my citizens who were standing in a way in opposition to me. When I came within twenty feet of them, I slid off my horse and walked toward them, mindful of keeping the protection over Jothro.

"Hello, I'm your new duchess, Periwinkle von Winthrop-Ransom. To what do I owe this wonderful greeting party? This is one of Lord Willoughby's sons, Jothro, who is coming to Springfield with me for my ceremony. Please, tell me who you are and what I can do for you." I smiled as graciously as I could given the tension I felt.

The group included no more than ten people, and most were men of middle years in farmers' clothing. There were two women who stood to the back, both dressed in dresses common in farmhouses. I could feel that the shield covering them had been created by the older of the two women, and she was getting no magical support from the others.

One of the men, red in the face and his cap clutched against his chest, stepped forward and did a deep bow. Echoing him, the men bowed and the women curtsied. He cleared his throat twice, and said, "My lady, it is so good of you to come to our neighborhood on your way to your ascension. We hoped to see you and wish you well, for we're simple country folk and have no place in the halls of the mighty." He bowed again and looked around at his companions.

"Why, thank you so much. It's an honor for me to meet the people of this duchy who I will try to help and care for in the coming years."

The woman maintaining the shield, blurted out, "Then why are you taking our forest? It has stood for many generations and is part of our home."

"Where do you live, my dear? Do you live in the forest?" I wasn't going to reveal more about my intentions until I figured out what she was trying to get me to say.

"I and my family live on the other side of the forest, not two leagues beyond its end. Our farm stretches another hundred acres along the road."

"Do you use the forest and its products in your farming?"

"Oh, no ma'am—my lady, I mean—it's too far to bring the animals here, and we have plenty of fire and building wood in a small woods closer to our home."

"I see, then your concern is for the taking down of the forest or its change from what you are familiar with. Have I got that right?"

I was surprised to see smiles grow on a few of the faces, as others nodded.

"We just don't want our forest burned or torn down!" said one of the men.

"I've found the right people to care for the forest, to keep it healthy, and to live within it in peace with nature. They'll cherish and find it a sacred space. They'll be good custodians of the trees and streams, the animals and the growing flowers. Would you like to meet them? They're very good friends of mine."

The people moved around and shuffled their feet. The first speaker said, "Aren't they foreigners?"

"If you mean they aren't citizens of Winthrop, you're right. They're honored guests of Winthrop because they are from a very old culture that has much to offer us. They're not used to our ways and find life in the city a bit too much for them. They need a safe place to retreat. I thought if they would care for this forest and keep it healthy, they might live here forever or for as short a time as they want. You won't see them unless you want to. And you won't know that until you meet them. Look, here they come." I pointed up the road where the caravan had stopped perhaps twenty feet beyond our horses.

Djordji and Aishe stepped down from their caravan and walked toward us. I sensed tension in the farmers, though several of them also seemed interested. I introduced the two gypsies, and asked the others for their names.

"Well, I'm Georgie too!" said the man who first spoke.

The laughter we shared seemed to loosen everyone up a little. The others gave their names, and the woman who'd been maintaining the shield gave hers as Alicia. We all mingled and talked as others of the gypsies came forward. I strengthened my field of protection to cover as many as I could, sending out gentling thoughts to prevent any unnecessary conflict.

Finally Esmeralda appeared with Amerlie in tow. My old mentor looked weary and sapped of energy though Esmeralda was as warm and happy to see these new people as one could ask. In no time, she and the two farmwomen were exchanging recipes of lotions and medicaments for various aliments they all treated. The men, after looking once or twice at Aishe's lithe body, talked with Djordji and others. Only Amerlie looked apart, not one of the community.

Alicia walked over and spoke with Amerlie. Both Esmeralda and I watched the exchange as well as we could without being obvious. They stood awkwardly; neither seemed comfortable in the other's presence. After a few minutes Alicia threw up her hands and rejoined the group. Before I could move, Esmeralda had grabbed Amerlie and was talking animatedly as she pulled her away from the group.

Djordji and Georgie came to discuss the two ceremonies. I was surprised at how far they had gotten in their discussions, for they had planned the granting of the forest to happen before dinner, and my induction into the clan to take place during the evening entertainment. They had already figured that two of the open wagons would take our new friends back to their homes to gather up their families to come for the festivities.

I smiled. "I hope my arrangements in Springfield come together as well and as easily as this!"

The two wagons trundled off with most of the ten. Two stayed because others in their families would gather the needed folks. The rest of the caravans moved a short way down the road to the first track into the woods. From what I understood this path led to one of the smaller clearings. From there we'd be able to wend our way into the biggest clearing, with one of the farmers showing us the way. Our guide had been very quiet during early conversations but had appeared to have finally made friends with two of the tumblers.

The large clearing was all we could have hoped. At the north side was a spring that came bubbling out of the ground and then ran into a small stream flowing west. The trees around the clearing were large and taller than my castle, to my surprise. They were a mix of hardwood and evergreens, laying a soft carpet of needles and decayed leaves underfoot.

68

By the time the two wagons returned with all of the guests, the camp had been established and the fire pit built, lined with rocks, and with a fire laid but not lit. Jothro helped wherever needed and twice came with a young gypsy man who would accompany us. Luka was a buoyant man, bubbling with good cheer and humor. Gueril on the other hand was the silent type, a little brooding and perhaps too conscious of his very fine hair. Luka I had noticed before. He was obviously well liked and helpful to his elders. He flirted outrageously with the girls, and teased Aishe, who gazed at him with mooncalf eyes. Gueril was so quiet that he could have passed me several times and I would not have noticed.

I had some time to get to know a little of them both, but Gueril was a mystery. Compared to him Luka was an open book of joy, laughter and swagger. He teased me and then apologized. He pretended to treat me as a fragile flower, and then would twirl me around as a dancer might. He made me feel normal again, as I had seen Aishe and Jothro, and I confess my heart soared.

Aishe came to fetch me because I was to be clothed properly for the granting of the forest. In their various wardrobes they had a number of fine dresses, and the only question was if there was one that fit me that I dared to wear. Most were built for someone more well-endowed than I am. That's the reason I have passed so easily for a boy. But finally they found one made for an ingénue, not too revealing and less outrageously laced and beribboned.

When we emerged from the caravan, the whole community was gathered around the fire, Djordji and Georgie sitting on a stage off to one side. Aishe led me to the steps up to the stage, wished me luck, and pushed me up the first step.

When I came to the top of the stairs, I was greeted with applause. I blushed, for I had not had public acclaim of this nature on my own before. I smiled at my people and waved once, then walked to the two men.

Djordji asked in a low voice if I'd figured out how to do it. I nodded, but found I couldn't speak. My nerves were making themselves known for the first time in a long time, and this would be my first really big solo spell. I had no one I could talk to about it except the duchesses in my head, and they weren't helpful this time. I steeled myself, ordered the collywobbles down, and walked to the front of the stage.

Raising my arms wide over my head, my hands and fingers splayed as broadly as possible, I *pulled* from somewhere outside me an envelope that began on the outskirts of the forest, came over the trees, and joined in a dome above us and the forest. I *summoned* from every gypsy in the clearing the essence of their membership in this clan. I took only the smallest amount from each, and I joined that essence to the energy field I had built around the forest. Bringing my hands together in a sharp clap over my head, I felt as if a mist settled over me, blurring my vision of this little piece of my duchy. I was still powerful here, but the power was weaker, less available, as if I were trying to reach it through a body of water.

Lowering my arms, I looked out over the crowd. The gypsies were reaching out to each other and touching themselves as if they had changed in some way. The citizens looked a little lost as if they too missed a connection with the earth of the duchy. Jothro and Aishe were nearby, holding each other as if to touch was to hold tight to the earth. I stepped back from the edge of the stage, bumping into the two men who looked to see if I was all right.

"My duchess, are you well?" Georgie asked.

"My lady, you've given us too much," said Djordji.

"Then it's done. I have given you what I promised you, your own place in my duchy. I still have power here that is veiled by your ownership of this land. Because you aren't part of my magical grant, there's none of the blending that would occur with a true child of Winthrop. I admit it feels strange, like when everything is hazy when you're very ill, and everything occurs beyond the fog surrounding you. But the feeling is right and so it shall be."

The two men stepped to the front of the stage and called for attention. The crowd calmed, still marveling at the change that had flowed over them.

Georgie spoke first. "It is done. This land is of mixed ownership now, the primary owners being the members of Djordji's clan. The duchess is now the lesser owner of this part of her duchy. I suspect, much as it has affected the gypsies, my fellows can feel the change also, so different from when we walk on our land at home. It's a marvelous piece of magic our lady has done, not only to change the land, but also to bring us such wonderful neighbors."

A cheer went up from the people, universal approval for the act

I'd completed. I felt depleted, with emptiness similar to what I felt when I wasn't in my duchy. I hadn't realized until now how rejuvenated I felt when in my land. I looked up and smiled at my people, both native and gypsy, and their cheers increased. Esmeralda stood off to one side, tears streaming down her smiling face, and Luka at her side with his arm around her shoulders.

My male companions helped me down from the stage. Men and women hurried to oversee the cooking for the big meal to be had in an hour. The younger folks were energetic so they were sent to feed the animals. It gave them more scope for play away from their elders.

Jothro joined us as we meandered through the crowd toward Esmeralda and Luka. Georgie came with us while Djordji went to finish the arrangements for the later ceremony.

Luka came to me first, his eyes glowing, and he again played the fool, but with a difference. Underlying his goofy grin was an element of awe, and I feared it had broken what he had given me. But he swept me into a hug and twirled me again until I laughed.

When he put me down, I faced Esmeralda who threw her arms around me. "I have never felt so safe in my life! This is amazing, you've given us so much, and nothing we can do will ever repay you."

"I don't *want* to be repaid. I want you to have a safe haven you can call your own. One where even I am somewhat limited to act." I smiled at her.

"You're limited? Tell me how. This shouldn't be!"

I explained to her about the source of my magic and the way it worked. Once she understood I had severed my special connection to the land, she became upset, and wanted me to reverse it.

"I've spoken with Djordji about it," I said. "We think I may get some, if not all, of it back with the ceremony later tonight. If I become a *didkai,* I might get the same link you now have. So we'll wait and see. Don't worry yet."

"Is this why Amerlie was so upset?"

"She's a little bit prejudiced, and uncomfortable with my independence. It grates on her."

"Ah, I thought it might be something like that. She just needs a cooling-off period. We'll try to keep her with us for at least a day or two after you leave. Don't you worry about her." She smiled back at me.

We sat on the steps of her caravan until dinner was ready, talking about magic, and the things she could do, while Luka watched and made the occasional funny comment. We compared spells that had similar outcomes, and found that Esmeralda's and my spells were nearly identical, given the language differences. We talked about herbs that were common in the forest and what they could be used for. Alicia joined us toward the end of the conversation and our comparisons ran further along.

"I may ask the Collegium to study different forms of magic among different people to see if we can find the common grounds, and more importantly, those things some of us can do that others can't. Maybe we could figure out a way to standardize it so students from all communities can come to the Collegium to learn."

Alicia thought it would be unaffordable and Esmeralda thought gypsies wouldn't be allowed, but I shushed them both.

"It will continue to be free, with entry by examination, and all will be welcome. I know a student at the Collegium who would be delighted to learn with Luka or Jothro, or a boy from your community, Alicia."

The bells clanged, telling us the festivities were about to begin.

69

Dinner was raucous with loud conversations, singing, and frequent consumption of wine. I drank very little though I quite enjoyed the food. I was protected from the others by Jothro, Luka and Gueril. The third gypsy hadn't yet been chosen though I was enjoying myself with the two I'd met. We were all of similar ages, though the gypsies seemed older than Jothro or I, probably because of their life on the road. Luka was particularly attentive.

Djordji approached with another young man, and I noticed Luka bristled when he saw the other young man.

"This is your third member Niku, and he would have been here earlier but his mother has been sick."

"Is she all right now? Because I don't want to take him from her if she needs him."

"My father has rejoined us and he will take care of her. It's only for a few weeks after all." Niku's smile was the most beautiful I'd seen among the gypsies, and they all had beautiful smiles. I giggled a little, returning his smile.

Luka stepped up beside me and said, "We don't need Niku. We're three without him. That's plenty given the duchess's power."

Djordji stared Luka down. "If you two can't be friends, you can at least be polite to each other. This is a test as you should've realized."

"I'll knock their heads together if they upset the duchess," Gueril said.

"Djordji, do you really want this to be a test now? Can't you wait until I'm safely home to push them together?" I pretend pouted.

"Gueril, it'll be your job to make sure any misbehavior doesn't reach the duchess. You and Jothro must be the peacekeepers on this trip." Djordji nodded and walked away. He turned back to admonish me to be ready in about half an hour.

Esmeralda joined us, shaking her head. She glared at Niku and Luka, and then said, "This is *not* the time to be making a test of this issue. I'm unhappy Djordji thought that you could fix this problem when it's the boys themselves who have to figure it out. For brothers to act this way in this clan is inexcusable."

The boys said at the same time, "He's *not* my brother."

Esmeralda sighed. "They share a father who shares their mothers. It's completely against our rules but he claims to love both women, and they claim to love him. The boys were born within a month of each other and their mothers have gone far in poisoning their sons against the other. It was one thing when they were young for the fights seemed to be more for bragging rights. To carry it into adulthood is unacceptable. One or both will be excluded from the clan if they cannot learn to be civil."

"You don't want to set me any *easy* tasks, do you?" I said with a laugh. "A lifetime of warfare to be resolved in a few weeks? I'm not a miracle worker."

Jothro smiled. "Yes, you are."

After a little more back and forth, I was summoned by Djordji. As I walked toward him, I noticed that my fellow Winthropians seemed to have separated themselves from the other revelers. I pulled at Djordji's sleeve and pointed in their direction.

"This ceremony is for the gypsies, the Roma—not your people."

"They're entitled to know what their duchess is doing. They're entitled to witness it to ensure I'm not harmed by the process. Why would you exclude them?"

"It is a part of our culture the *gaje* have no need to know. You wouldn't have known of this process if I hadn't told you, and I only told you after a full discussion among our elders in which we agreed to make you the offer. You have said we're entitled to maintain our own culture and this is one of our undisclosed rites."

I stared at him. Hard. "I don't agree to the ceremony if my subjects cannot attend. They're my family in this context and they have the right to know what I do in adopting another family. So it's up to you. They attend and we go forward, or they don't, and we don't. This won't change my gift to you in any way. It's simply what must be."

"Esmeralda said you would say that. You are as difficult to work with as that old woman, and you're a mere slip of a girl. You win. It means too much to my people for you to become one of us." He turned away for a moment, looking for someone in the area of my people. He made hand signals that were practiced and easy, and I learned of another skill of my new family.

Several men and women walked among the locals, and led them into the main body of the group, laughing and joking with them. I didn't know whether to be impressed with the preparedness of the gypsies or angry at the trick Djordji had tried to pull on me.

I was again led onto the stage with Djordji, Esmeralda, and three other older gypsies I hadn't yet met. Esmeralda stepped to the front and chanted in a language I didn't know. The others on the stage hummed harmonically to augment the chant. The audience was motionless and quiet. Slowly Esmeralda's arms rose in the air, spread apart and came back to her sides making a full circle. After a few minutes, she performed the movement again and was accompanied by those on the stage and many in the audience. The third time she created the circle, the participation was greater and I was beginning to recognize the parts of the chant during which the arm movements were made.

Esmeralda's voice grew louder and her body moved to the beat of the chant. She turned, continuing her song, and with the others encircled me. They moved in toward me as their arms came down, and retreated as their arms went up. I couldn't help moving a little to the rhythm they'd set as it echoed through my very being.

Esmeralda changed the chant to words in my language; she was saying they were of the Ruthenian Clan of musicians, performers and singers, of the family of Herne. They were an open and loving people, and they were asking the universe's permission to make a *gaje* one of them. This would continue until there was sign of acceptance, but no one knew what that sign would be. Djordji whispered that the energies they roused in their people would produce a sign. Esmeralda, in spite of her age, showed no sign of wanting to slow or stop the process.

We heard cries from the audience, and I saw a smile spread across Djordji's face. The circle around me opened so we could all watch the audience. The people who had cried out were leading groups of gypsies and *gaje* into lines that snaked through the audience. I could see five lines had formed by the time my vision was unobstructed. As they moved, they accumulated all the audience as followers until there were only five chains traveling in an intricate pattern, dancing and chanting. Aishe headed one line, but I didn't recognize the other leaders. It took perhaps half an hour for the lines to become orderly and to move into rows before the stage, dancing in place and no longer circling the clearing. I was surprised to see Amerlie in one line, between Gueril and Niku.

Esmeralda sang out, "Who has come, who has come?" over and over in a lilting voice. The first line responded, "We have come, we have come!" and each next line picked up the chant, one by one.

"Why did you come, why did you come?" Esmeralda changed her words, and again the words changed from the first line to the fifth, "To meet our sister, to meet our sister."

"Who is our sister, who is our sister?" drew the response "Peary Herne, Peary Herne!"

Then Esmeralda called out once, "She is Ruthenian, she is Ruthenian!" and stopped. The audience swayed back and forth, murmuring softly, "Ya, ya, ya hey, ya, ya, ya hey," over and over. As the murmurs faded, someone brought a tray of tea mugs to the stage while others circled the audience with great urns of tea and mugs for those celebrating.

Djordji moved forward and spoke loudly. "Let us now sit for tea with our new sister, and bind her to us with the ritual sharing of this great blessing." We all held up our mugs in salute, and then lowered them to drink.

A strange feeling washed through me as I swallowed my first sip of tea. It felt as if the tea had been poured over my head, drenching me in water of love, holding me forever. I felt my connection to the land return in full measure with all those in the clearing, equally and lovingly. I cried from the strength of the emotion, tears of joy, of welcome to my new clan.

Esmeralda came over when she saw my tears. I smiled through them and whispered my connection to the land was once again whole. We embraced each other, and then each of the elders hugged me, the last being Djordji.

He turned me to face the crowd and shouted, "Behold our new sister! Behold our duchess!"

The crowd roared its approval, and rose to celebrate once again. Over the course of the next hour, I was hugged and kissed by, it must have been, everybody in the clearing. The last one was Georgie, who drew me aside to speak with me.

"I don't think it was intended, but we of your ordinary citizens acquired a small measure of connection with these people during the ceremony. As if it rubbed off on us. I can't speak for the others but I feel as if my soul has expanded to twice its normal size with the hopes and dreams of all these people. I remember feeling something similar when your mother blessed us and our fields over twenty years ago. This seemed more powerful, more universal." He stopped and shrugged, smiling. "It's hard to speak of it."

I felt a glow of warmth from him, of inclusion in this mixed family. He looked into my eyes and smiled broadly at what he saw. I could almost hear his thoughts, he was so open to my mind.

This time, the party was short lived. We'd all been through much this day, including two ceremonies that changed our relationships with each other. The local people asked if they could stay, rather than taking the ride home, and they were welcomed with open arms and richly accommodated. I slept in Esmeralda's caravan, a haven for me from all my well-wishers whom I loved but was too tired to greet.

10

The sun woke me a little earlier than I would have liked, but it was the day to head for Springfield, and the underlying excitement of home pushed me out of bed. Esmeralda was already awake and looking through the back door at the clearing and forest, humming and smiling.

"You know, I woke and thought yesterday was a dream. It *was* a dream, but one that came true. It seems strange my heart's desire could be granted by a young girl like you, but I see you have a great soul. You'll be an immense boon to your duchy, and I hope you never change. I think you'll find our wandering will now be primarily in your duchy, close to home."

"Not if Aishe gets her wish to travel with the progression!" I laughed.

Esmeralda smiled and said, "There's breakfast in the making. Shall we go?"

When we reached the center of the clearing, women from both groups were gathered, sharing recipes and tips, laughing and tasting each other's work. They looked up as we approached and performed a tiny cheer. I'm sure I blushed, but it was meant to be a kindness.

I was eager to be on my way, but the women laughed again. One said, "Those young lads will still be sleeping after all the 'celebrating' they did last night!"

We sat on the logs surrounding the fire pit. The conversation was lazy as we drank tea and ate fresh biscuits. Occasionally one of the women would get up to stir a pot or push a pan further into the coals—a mystery, as I'd never cooked for more than two in my prior life.

People slowly emerged from their caravans in twos and threes, coming to get tea and browse the potential food offerings. A few looked to be suffering from the prior night's excesses, but most were cheerful and relaxed in their new home. There was talk of creating order in the clearing and making it more like a small town, and the arguments started up, generally good-natured.

Jothro made his way out of a small caravan I hadn't noticed

before, stretched, ran his fingers through his hair, and looked around at the people beginning to stir. He saw me and, like a happy child, hurried to my side. I was a little concerned about the look in his eyes, which was something approaching awe.

"You were magnificent last night! I thought you were great with my father, but that was small compared to this!"

Esmeralda shushed him. "Oh, ridiculous boy, don't you know this is what a magical duchess does? Hero worship doesn't help anyone. Calm down."

I was thankful for her intervention. This was one area my prior education had not addressed, the adulation of young men. I'd thought of Jothro as a friend, and now I knew I would have to keep my distance from him and the others. This had been only a pleasant interlude before I began to take on my formal duties as duchess.

In due time, all of my escorts arrived and ate breakfast. Two of the animal handlers had already saddled our horses and loaded up our supplies, so by the time we finished, they could bring the horses over for all to see.

I thanked them, running my hands over my horse, checking for any swelling or any other indication of injury.

"Of course you would know how to take care of your horse," one of them said.

"It's simple care to know what may or may not be hurting the horse. I knew this from before, though I never had a horse where I was. It was considered too dangerous."

We talked on in this manner until the four young men, Jothro leading, joined us. We exchanged greetings and mounted our horses, then slowly wended our way through the groups of people who stood to send us off. I waved to my new friends and family as we rode onto the path that led to the road. There was shuffling among the young men as if all were trying to push in next to me. I told them to stop. as we had plenty of time for them all to ride next to me.

The beginning of the ride was beautiful, a brilliant sun shining over my rolling green hills. We went at a healthy trot to warm the horses up and then alternated paces to keep them comfortable. We were moving more than twice the speed we'd gone with the gypsies, and it felt wonderful to have the wind flowing across my face and through my hair.

Then the discord between Niku and Luka began to rear its ugly head. It started with comments under the breath, then occasional digs at each other until it blossomed into a full-scale argument involving mainly insults and curses. I couldn't see that one was guiltier than the other; their participation seemed equal and voluntary.

Gueril and Jothro took the fighters in hand and separated them. We ended up riding five across the road with the dueling half-brothers on the outside and my two saviors next to me. This calmed the situation long enough for me to try to think of a solution for their difficulties.

We stayed in relative harmony until we stopped to eat and to water and rest the horses. Then the bickering resumed, and I turned on them.

"Look at the two of you! You're acting like children. You're so wrapped up in your little drama you're failing to appreciate the beauty around you, or the good company you're with. If you can't grow up a little, one of you is going back." I turned my back on them and walked away because I was afraid I'd do something I would regret if I stayed any longer.

Luka approached Gueril and spoke to him in a low voice. Gueril walked away shaking his head. Luka glared at him, then looked around and saw I was watching. He spat on the ground and then walked to his horse. I called him over.

I *compelled* him to tell me what he'd said to Gueril, and he resisted mightily, to no avail. "I said, 'We'll get him if we work together.'"

I was shocked. I'm inexperienced in dealing with people on a worldly level; I never expected such malice in an otherwise charming young man, who had given me such a lift. I *held* him where he was and turned to look for Niku. He was standing by the edge of the road, his head lowered, his arms crossed over his chest. I tried to read him but could only sense a small frustration and rigid control.

Jothro approached us. "Gueril's upset and wants to take Luka back. He says Luka is the problem and has always been. Niku gives as good as he gets, but he never starts it."

"Thank you. We're all going back. I can't solve Luka, but I can absolve Niku."

I sent him to get Gueril and Niku working toward a return. Then I looked at Luka, who was struggling to get free from my compulsion. I thought for a moment and then remembered something I'd seen Amerlie do. With a small effort, I tied Luka's torso thoroughly with Winthrop rope.

I called to Jothro and Gueril to put Luka on his horse and

secure him there. I kept a light compulsion on him that prevented him from struggling or trying to kick his horse into a sudden bolt.

We took longer to return than our trip out because of Luka's inability to move quickly. It was after dark when we returned to the clearing; the folks were gathering around the fire for entertainment. Someone cried out when we rode in.

The elders approached us first. Djordji asked, "Why is Luka tied up and not talking?"

"Luka is the reason these two are fighting. Niku responds because he must, as your culture demands. Niku couldn't tell you what was going on because it's against your ethic. I discovered it when Luka didn't respond well to my instruction to stop the bickering. His immediate thought was to seek assistance in 'getting' Niku while they were away from your community. I cannot go on with Luka, but Niku is welcome in my company."

Esmeralda nodded. "It's what we expected. We hoped your abilities would make Luka see the light. It is not so. We'll deal with him. Come to the fire, and we'll get you all dinner. You must stay the night and set out again in the morning. Thank you again for your service to our family."

I wanted to talk with Esmeralda about my confusion with regard to Luka. How could he be so delightful with me, yet so irrational with Niku? She was unable to help, only saying it had been a longstanding problem. The entire group knew that Luka was a fine man in everything except the relationship with his brother.

ℤ

"Before we settle for the night, could I see Niku's mother? I'm wondering about her illness."

Esmeralda choked up. "Are you willing to help? None of us can find what's wrong, but she's wasting away."

We hurried to the caravan that I'd earlier noticed as looking a little shabby compared to the others. Esmeralda knocked softly at the back door, and it was slowly opened by a very handsome middle-aged man.

"Borak, the duchess has come to see if she can help Luminista. May we come in?"

The momentary flash of hope across his face was unmistakable. I shared his hope that I'd be able to fix whatever was wrong. I walked into the caravan to the cot where the ravaged figure of a once beautiful woman lay. I buried my shock at her condition as well as I could, and reached down to hold one of the frail hands lying outside the covers. The absolute sense of wrongness I felt in her raised my hackles.

"Is there a something on which I might sit? This could take time."

A stool was pulled from its hiding place in the rafters and I settled in for serious work. I took her hand again and followed the angry lines of evil into her body. As I felt the wickedness fray, I somehow pulled it up and expelled it both from her body and the caravan rather than let it fester inside. I came to a node that was unknown to me; it was angry and filled with toxins. I again extracted and deposited the mess outside.

It was a slow but steady process as I followed the malevolent trails, removing all I could. I felt the pain trickling from her body as I delved further. At some point, Esmeralda placed a hand on my shoulder and new energy flowed through me. With that assistance, the process quickened, and I noticed another presence in Luminista's body: Esmeralda was following me, sweeping out anything I might have missed. After what seemed an eternity, we were done. A final scan of her body showed no remnant of the wicked energy I'd sensed. I knew one thing: that evil was not natural.

"I threw what I removed into a pail outside. Shall we go look at it?"

Borak had gone to his knees at Luminista's side and was crying in relief, for she was sleeping peacefully with a rosy glow in her cheeks.

Esmeralda and I went out to find the bucket, which was wooden with metal bands around it at various heights, holding the thing together. As we neared, we saw it smoking, and it burst into flames, the metal having melted from the heat. I rushed over, sending my senses into it, and somehow by *twisting* it, I pulled out a bundle of the evil, which hung suspended in air a foot or so in front of me. Flames and sparks flickered around it.

"I know what it is." Esmeralda's voice was low and ominous. "It's a spell known to all gypsy women. It's used rarely, when there is pain in our female parts. It is used to expel a fibrous mass from our wombs. It is *never* used lightly or on someone without the mass."

"Horrible! Can you tell who cast the spell? Is there a signature of any kind on it?" I couldn't see the magic and realized it wasn't available to me, as it was gypsy magic.

"I know who did it."

"Who?" demanded a male voice. I looked up; Borak was standing on the top step.

"It's a matter for the elders. It's out of your hands, Borak. Don't interfere."

By this time, people were gathered around the caravan as word had spread of what I was attempting. Djordji pushed his way through the crowd, but stopped short when he saw Borak's and Esmeralda's faces.

Borak's expression was an odd mixture of anger and grief. I realized who the culprit must be, and it told me the acorn didn't fall far from the tree.

"She will be given a fair trial, Borak. You can't ask for more." Djordji's eyes were wet and close to overflowing.

A group of men advanced on a particularly nice caravan. Well painted and well maintained, it stood out from the group. One of the men pounded on the door, and Luka opened it.

"Quiet, my mother is sleeping. What the hell do you all want?"

An elder said, "Come out, Luka, and don't make a fuss. We have business here."

When Luka tried to close the door, two of the larger men

forcibly removed him from the caravan.

A reedy voice came from inside: "What's all that noise? Can't you be quiet for a minute, you awful boy?"

The elder spoke again. "In the name of the Rutheni, I command you to come out, Gitana."

The ritualistic words drove Luka berserk. He struggled wildly against the men holding him, kicking out and hitting both the men and other bystanders. Someone from behind coshed him on the head, and he ceased, hanging limply from the two men's hands.

The caravan rocked a little as someone moved within. Appearing in the doorway was a scrawny woman who had once been attractive. She now wore excessive make-up and too much jewelry in an attempt to compensate for what she'd lost.

"What right have you to call me out, Clan of the Rutheni?"

"You are called by the Rutheni to answer to your wrongful use of magic to harm another. It is by the grace of our duchess that we discovered your crime before your victim died."

"I deny the charges. You will have to prove them. Name the witnesses against me."

"The duchess and Esmeralda."

The audience cheered. I could hear excited voices saying we were the best witnesses in the clan.

"What? The so-called victim won't come forward? Is that one afraid of me?"

Borak came racing across the field, intent on reaching his target. Several men had to wrestle him to the ground before he could reach Gitana.

"Aren't you going to call Borak as a witness? He knows everything about it!" Her peals of laughter had a madness that made me shiver.

I walked toward the beautiful caravan. "If I'm to be a witness, then the trial must be held in Springfield, as I am going there in the morning. Do you have a way to prevent her from doing any more harm while you make your way to Springfield for the ascension?"

Esmeralda said, "We do, and we'll keep her and her son in custody until we get there."

Djordji then ruled, "They will be placed in the barred caravan; the supplies can be moved elsewhere. We'll need guards on it at all times. Her magic is not as strong as it once was, but she can take from Luka."

As all the arrangements were being made, I asked Esmeralda about what Gitana could take from her son.

"My dear, it's an awful thing, and if it's been going on for a time, it explains why you couldn't reach him. We have the ability to share our powers. Did you feel it when I joined you to help poor Luminista?"

"Yes, I did, and I couldn't have finished without you."

"Aside from sharing, we can also take magic from one another. In the old days, the strongest Rom was the one who could keep his people alive while stripping them of their magic to increase his. This has been outlawed for many years. There are always stories of two close friends doing it innocently or diabolical people doing it in a way that can't be seen. We know, however, when it's done over a long period, persistently, there are personality changes in the 'donor' of the magic. Unfortunately, those symptoms are surprisingly like a short-tempered young man might act, easily angered, occasionally irrational. We wondered with Luka, now and then. Now I suspect we know."

"What will happen to him?"

"He can't be cured."

I was shocked. The implications were awful, he had been turned into what he was by an unlawful act, and he would be punished for it. When he had so much to offer.

"Nothing will be done to him before he gets to Springfield, is that right?"

Esmeralda nodded.

"Then the Collegium will search for a cure."

My word was final. I knew Esmeralda would share my promise with the community. I still went to sleep that night with a heavy heart.

12

We started out again the next morning, a group of four who had been shaken by the events of the night before, but relieved to be away from it all. Niku participated more in our discussions and helped more when we camped.

We moved more quickly than we had the day before, I suspect as much to distance us from the forest as to get to Springfield faster. Within a few days, we came upon villages more frequently where we were usually greeted with delight. The tale had gone before us of the doings in Middleland, and people were eager to meet me and hear my story. I had prepared a clean and brief narrative I'd say quickly and then remind the folks of my need to get home. We were assisted with anything we needed, and occasionally got to sleep in real beds.

When the soldiers caught up with us, we were in the outskirts of Springfield. Amerlie was with them and she remained quiet. I rode with the leader of the group, Logonio, to catch up on what they'd experienced during our separation.

"My lady, it took most of the time just finishing up the barns and getting the youngsters started working . Then we rode as fast as we could to catch up. We heard tales of you along the way, so we knew we were still behind you. Then we reached a few farmhouses, and they sent us back to the gypsies in the forest. An old lady told us Amerlie was still there and in disgrace, and told us to bring her along."

"How has she behaved?"

"She's been very quiet. She has helped with the fire at night, getting it hot faster, and healed up a blister one of the men got. But she won't tell us anything about why she was left behind. She has said you've done marvelous things, but we knew we could count on you for that."

He didn't seem concerned about what Amerlie hadn't told him, and I had no intention of enlightening him. I was glad they had caught up though before I headed into my city. It would look much better to be accompanied by imperial guards than two young gypsies and an inexperienced younger son of an earl.

We reached the city on the hill at mid-afternoon, and began the climb to the castle. I had magically freshened my dress so I looked more authentic and styled my hair in a way that would not offend my maids, I hoped. People came out of their homes and shops to see what was going on and got into the spirit of celebration easily. The imperial guards had polished their armor to shining and we must have looked more impressive than when I'd arrived in a hired carriage.

I waved at my people who responded loudly with cheers, questions, and exclamations. When we reached where the nobility lived, higher on the hill, there were people watching from windows and roofs; a few had raised the duchy flag above their own, and I marked those houses.

It was with a sigh of relief that I entered the gates of my home. My brother Chres stood on the steps waiting for me, and I was amused to see Mikal standing next to him. The guard who came over to hand me down from my horse was Wilfie, and I grinned at him in delight.

"Welcome home, my lady. We've missed you," he said. I strode as quickly as my dress would allow up the steps to Chres and hugged him as hard as I've hugged anyone. I then turned and waved to all those in the courtyard; the guards, the workers, several merchants, and a few of the nobility who were trying to get in to see me first.

I whispered to Mikal, "Do you see the two gypsies and the young man off to the side who look so awkward? Well, your job is to bring them into the castle. Find Sylvester or Willery and get them rooms close to mine. Got it?"

He nodded and smiled at me. "Welcome back!" Then he ran down the steps toward my friends.

I took Chres's hand and we turned to enter into the castle. I wasn't more than five steps inside when he asked me where Amerlie was.

"What! No welcome home from my brother? Instead a question about someone else? Amerlie got a little out of hand and pushy and didn't take 'stop' for an answer. She's in mild disgrace and will have to apologize and swear not to do it again before she's allowed to come before me again."

"Wow, you're a lot stronger since you left. It's like you grew up! Did you see Dad?"

We spent the next hour talking about all we'd discovered, and all we had done in ridding the world of the demons let loose by

Montrade's misbehavior. Henry was apparently already in a cell deep within the castle and Briaint was in one next door. I checked to ensure our cells were cleaner than Willoughby's and then forgot them.

We had tea in the drawing room and I invited my three young men. Chres was fascinated by the gypsies and greeted Jothro like a long lost friend. They had apparently played together as children when Willoughby still traveled to Springfield for the season.

I was delighted to see Sylvester, but he remained proper of course. I thought I caught a wink from him during the tea, but was sufficiently unsure I didn't return it. He would have to accept my smiles as a response.

Rooms had been prepared for my companions and I sent them off before asking Sylvester to ensure they were not embarrassed by their clothing at dinner, which was to be held in my dining room. He took my hint with his usual aplomb, so I walked back to my bedroom.

Upon returning to my room, I was delighted to find Daisy placing a fresh bouquet on the central table. She turned when I entered and I was heartened by the broad smile on her face. Once the door was closed, I ran to her and hugged her. After a brief pause, she returned my embrace.

"Oh, my lady, I've been so afraid for you with all the news we've gotten. Demons and mad wizards! Murder! The emperor!"

"Calm down, Daisy, the really scary part was the murder, and I wasn't even in the room. We had just arrived there and I had expressed our concerns but I don't think she took me seriously."

"It's a horrible way to find out you were right, for sure. Let me help you change your clothes. What an ugly dress, my lady. Wherever did you find it? It looks like an old bedspread from a second-class inn. I'm sure we can find you something much better for your dinner."

"Thanks, Daisy. I won't mind losing this thing. And Amerlie and a wizard made it out of stray fabric. I'm ready to get thoroughly cleaned up and have a sit-down meal."

Dinner was a simple affair, with the four young men paying court. Chres was anxious for news; Niku and Gueril were amazed by the many forks and spoons in their table settings when they weren't worrying about their clothes; Jothro was stunned by the subtlety of the decorations. We had a great time informally, this odd mixture of country girl/duchess, noble sons and gypsy boys. The rich food after days on the trail was enough to put us to yawning and fatigue so we had an early night.

73

After breakfast, I met with Sylvester and Willery to discuss what was left to be arranged about the ascension ceremony. I was pleased to discover all the announcements and invitations had been sent, and the food had been ordered. Rooms that hadn't been used in nearly twenty years were being aired, as was the bedding. Additional housemaids had been brought in, several on loan from other noble houses, a few relatives of current maids who had substituted during illness or other absence.

Sylvester had been a young footman when my mother ascended the throne, but he remembered every moment of it. He explained the ceremony, and it was quite simple. The participants were the ascending duchess, the emperor, two pages, and those chosen to give oaths. He told us where everybody stood and sat, what everybody said and did, and it was short and sweet.

We agreed this was a good plan and were just beginning to discuss who the pages would be when a knock came at the door and a footman poked his head in.

"There's a huge party in the courtyard, and a woman who says to tell you her name is Nenory. And she looks just like you." He was breathless, and amazed.

I whooped and ran out the door. Wilfie was by my side as I dashed down the hall, the stairs, and out the front door. Nenory was on the bottom step and I launched myself at her. She caught me and we whirled around as the rest of the courtyard looked on in amazement. We were wearing almost identical dresses and only the color of our hair gave away which was which.

When we stopped to catch our breath, I saw she had Samony with her with no sign of Rosamund. I whispered a question, and her one-word response was "Uppity." I laughed. We walked arm-in-arm up the stairs and into the hall where Sylvester stood to greet our guest.

"My lady, we are delighted to have you come so early for this celebration when your own will come so quickly after it."

"Oh, tush, Sylvester. Mine is all arranged, I just need the guests, and I mean to bring them all back with me after we finish partying here!"

She began as she meant to go on, and she was the wild card in my last week and a half of freedom. I brought her up to my drawing room, and we fell onto the couches, exchanging news of our mentors. Rosamund had taken a page from Amerlie's book, fighting too hard against a matter of belief. In Nenory's case, the question was whether to keep Samony in her employ. Rosamund wasn't as strong a witch as Amerlie, and Samony was quite a talented wizard. The decision was a wise one especially since Rosamund's objection might have been one of self-interest.

I was about to explain the gypsies when Sylvester knocked and told me Niku wished to talk. I asked him in and introduced him to Nenory. He looked as surprised as everyone else at our similarities.

"Niku, if you wish to have a private conversation, I'm sure we can arrange a convenient time. But my cousin Nenory is very much like me and will, I assure you, be as understanding as I am."

'My duchess, I only wanted to explain a little about the difficulty when we were last in the forest."

Nenory sat up. "What's this? Difficulty in a forest?" Her eyebrows shot up and she wiggled them.

"Oh, shush, Nenory, this isn't a laughing matter. It may actually be a matter of life or death. Niku, please, tell me what you know of this sorry history."

"Borak, my father, was in love with my mother, Luminista, and they planned to marry. As often happens, they were a little ahead of the ceremony, and I was conceived. But Gitana, who was quite a strong magic user, set a spell on Borak, and he lay with her a few days later. She arranged for them to be discovered, and my grandfather called off the wedding between Borak and Luminista. Although she begged her father, he would not relent, and so my parents ran away. With the help of Gitana and her magic, they were brought back, and Borak was whipped. Luminista wanted to heal him but her father again stepped in. By then it was clear that both women were pregnant." He shifted a little in his seat, and asked for water.

When I gave him some from the sideboard, he continued. "Borak was hurt and confused. Both of us were his sons, and he wanted to be a father to both. When we were little, Luka and I played regularly under the eyes of our father. We were, I thought, good friends, until the day Luka brought grapes with him, and gave them to me. I ate a handful, and began to cramp immediately. I was little and didn't know what it meant. He laughed and said he would be the first son now, and then ran off. Our father found me, and the grapes, and was able to get me to the healers in time. The grapes had been dusted with a powder none of the witches seemed to recognize. There was no evidence, and my father chose to believe I was mistaken in what Luka had said. There were many other incidents after that, and my father finally began to believe me." That memory cheered him enough to provoke a smile.

"Five years ago, my grandfather died. Borak and Luminista married within the week. We had a month or two as a happy family and then my mother became sick. Luka brought a message to our father, laughed, and left. Borak never told me what was in that message, but the following week he was repairing and painting Gitana's wagon. He'd work for her for a few weeks, and then come back to my mother. Every time he stayed with us for more than a few days, my mother got worse.

"For the last two years he has lived with Gitana. The first time he visited my mother was when I told him that I'd been asked to accompany you but couldn't leave my mother alone that long. When he came to see her, he threw me out, and I heard them inside talking and crying for over an hour." He looked as if he would cry.

So I spoke. "And then I cured her. We found out what Gitana had been doing. We now know she forced your father to stay with her by threatening to finish off your mother if he did not. You and your father had no reason to believe anyone would to be able to cure her, since everyone had tried without success. So you did what was necessary to keep her alive. You're both heroes." I heard a soft noise and looked at Nenory. She was crying.

"That's just a terrible story. What was wrong with that woman?" she wailed.

Niku sat back, eyes wide. "She loved him too. Love makes you do crazy things, and she was more powerful than my mother. She thought that meant she should win. There are many people in this world that feel that way."

Nenory sat up. "I never thought of it as a power thing."

I laughed. "It's all about power. Anything you want—love, money, authority—the powerful think they should have. We just need to change the discussion about what power actually is. But no one's talking about it now because the good guys have won again for a short while. I guarantee when the emperor gets here, he'll be all jolly because we came to his rescue and now he's safe again. He won't want to talk about right and wrong, power and what should replace it."

"Whoa, you've been thinking about this, haven't you?" Nenory asked.

"Niku can tell you some of it. The emperor won't be a good reporter of what happened but a couple of his servants will be." I reached for more tea and decided it was time to move on to other subjects. "Did your lovely regent make it home safely?"

"He arrived a day or two before we left. I was ready to go the moment he arrived. I'd set up a Council of Lords and Ladies while he was away to supposedly help me in his absence, and they had removed him as regent. The grounds were dereliction of duty based on reports we had from the field, which were confirmed when the soldiers brought the prisoners in. The Council is ruling in my absence, with magical advice from Rosamund. They've all been warned of her tendency to overstep bounds, and have their own magicians monitoring."

Niku asked if he could be excused.

"Well, you have two choices. You can fetch Gueril and Jothro and tell Sylvester to bring lunch here, or you can stay and I'll ring the bell."

"You mean we're eating lunch together?"

"Yes, I promised Jothro's father I would introduce him to the court and its processes. I assumed you'd want to join your friend rather than leave him alone in our clutches."

"Oh, of course," he said, hurriedly. "I should clean up first, so why don't I go make the arrangements?" He rose, bowed to us both, and scurried from the room. We giggled rather a lot at his manner of leaving.

Sticking my head out the door, I motioned to Wilfie. "Could you ensure the young men come to lunch here? Arrange for Sylvester to set a table for the five of us to dine. I gave Niku that task but I doubt he's reliable."

Just then a horn sounded from the courtyard.

Nenory ran to the window to look out. "It's the progression!"

I turned to Wilfie, wondering if I could take another big arrival. "Cancel that last order. I guess I have to go down. Am I presentable?"

He blushed a little. "To my mind you're always presentable. But yes, you look fine, as does Lady Nenory. Did you set up your identical dresses, my ladies?"

"You get to escort us both down. Aren't you lucky?" I grinned at him and grabbed Nenory's hand.

We walked a little faster than was probably appropriate, but we wanted to get there before they started up the steps. We made it although Da and Max were quite close when we stepped out the door and curtsied together.

When we rose and put out arms around each other's waist, with our heads leaning together, I suspect we made quite a picture. Da sputtered a little, but Max was struck dumb. He just stared at us.

"Welcome to Winthrop, my liege. Please come in out of the heat and we will refresh you with a luncheon in a bit after you've had time to wipe the road dust off your faces. You must be longing for a good sit-down meal by now." I tried very hard to sound serious though Nenory was doing her best to make me laugh. Tickling me was *not* her only trick.

"My liege, may I introduce my cousin, Lady Nenory, soon to be Duchess of Middleland?" She curtsied again. That got him moving, and he walked up the steps to greet me with a kiss on my forehead, and Nenory received one on her hand.

Festino and Pietro climbed the steps with the luggage necessary to make their master presentable, and they pulled Da, who was still stunned, up with them. He hugged me, and then bowed to Nenory, who pulled him up and hugged him.

"You look just like my da did!"

"We were twins. I'm so sorry for that loss and for your recent loss. You'll always be welcome here with your family. I guess I can still say that until your birthday."

Sylvester arrived and helped Festino and Pietro move the party indoors. Footmen were running everywhere, showing people where to go. The castle was bustling more than I'd ever seen it. Max was spirited off by his servants and three footmen, and Da was corralled by Sylvester and two more footman. Nenory and I, accompanied by Wilfie, returned to my drawing room and awaited the inevitable summons to a major luncheon.

Da arrived to escort us, putting each of us on one of his arms. He was smiling happily when Chres appeared to wrestle me away.

"You can't have both, Dad, and I haven't seen enough of my sister. You ran off to be with her and left me in charge. You get all the fun. Now it's my turn."

I took Chres's arm but kept hold of Da's since the hall was wide enough for us to walk four across. We were enjoying ourselves, a small family reunion, when Max stepped out of the dining room.

"There are my favorite people in the world!" He strode up to Nenory and pulled her away from Da. "You're one I haven't had the chance to talk with yet; come sit with me and tell me of your home."

Sylvester appeared behind Max and shook his head at Da.

"Well, Max, we have to go by the seating chart in terms of precedence you know," Da intervened.

"Nonsense, it's only a few of us for lunch, isn't it? Nothing formal. Why can't I have fun?"

"Sire," I said, "we have our funny ways in this place, and we'd like to be consistent with those ways if you'd allow it. After our luncheon, there will be time in the drawing room for you to mingle with those you'd like to speak with in a more casual setting." I smiled as sweetly as I could.

"You weren't nearly so formal in the woods." He wiggled his eyebrows at me.

"My liege, you may recall I was by appearances at that time a fourteen-year-old boy, and you were an old man."

"Oh, good grief. I give in." He stepped behind to follow us in, but pulled Da back to walk beside him. "My son should be here shortly. One of my assistant wizards has figured how to sail the river very quickly. I won't be able to have *any* fun when he gets here."

Chres moved between Nenory and me, escorting us into the dining room. Sylvester sat us all by the appropriate seating plan, and I was delighted to see my friend Lord MacAlpine among those dining with us. In fact Sylvester had managed to gather a party of about twenty local nobles to join us though I also noticed two gypsies and a minor lordling were among the guests.

I didn't sit at the head of the table as it was given to the emperor. I sat at his right hand. Da, as usual, sat at the other end of the table with Nenory on his right hand. My three young men were sitting near enough to each other to be able to look at each other but not to talk. I wondered whose idea that had been.

As the meal progressed, the emperor and I spoke stiffly as if we'd parted on bad terms. I wondered a little about the awkwardness, and watched with interest as he kept looking at Nenory. Suddenly there was an outcry near Gueril. One of the women I didn't know was pointing at Gueril and stumbling over her words as she tried to say something. I rose though Max put his hand on my arm to stop me.

I strode down to the lady. "Is there anything wrong? Please do tell me if I can be of assistance."

"There's a...there's a...gypsy at this table!"

"Why yes, he's one of my personal guests. In a way he's part of my adoptive family." I smiled at Gueril, whose wide eyes were unblinking. "Have you been introduced? I'm afraid I don't know your name, I'm still learning."

She looked at me with wide eyes; her mouth hung open. "What on earth do you mean 'your adoptive family'? You have no gypsies in your lineage. I should know, I'm the court historian. I don't mean to be rude but there is no reason for gypsies to be in this castle. Your mother would be appalled!"

Da and Max both stood at this last cruel statement.

"Madam," said the emperor, "you will apologize to her ladyship, and you will do it now."

"But we don't stand on formality in this family," she protested. "I really don't understand the problem."

Da exploded, "Melia, you will address the emperor properly or you will leave this house."

She muttered, "But...but..." and fainted.

Niku, who was sitting next to her, caught her before her face could fall into her food. Sylvester arrived with two footmen and carried her from the dining room. I returned to my seat after patting Niku on the shoulder and smiling at Gueril.

"Would you mind explaining what that's about?" Max growled at me.

"Fairly simple, actually. As I was traveling home, I came upon a clan of gypsies being driven out of my duchy by a fairly wild young man. I put a stop to it and gave the gypsies land of their own, a safe place they can reside while in Winthrop. They thanked me by making me a member of their clan. Then they sent two of their young men to escort me on my way home. Who are both sitting at this table."

"Where were my soldiers who were supposed to be escorting you? Why did you need gypsies?"

"The soldiers were rebuilding several houses and two barns that had been burned out by soldiers from Pocari; they were needed to help three families. But they caught up as soon as they could."

"How could Amerlie let you do this? Where is she? Why isn't she here?" He was beginning to sound exasperated.

"Amerlie disobeyed me rather seriously. She's currently not allowed in my presence until she apologizes and admits her error." I would avoid telling him or Da the reason for Amerlie's disobedience for as long as I could.

Chres, who sat to my right, hung onto every word I said. "I'm glad to hear you got tough on her. She was pushing you around a lot from what I saw."

I was pleased that he stood by me but it wasn't quite the right thing to say at that time.

Da and Max both blew up. Da shouted, "You are not of age, and you have no authority to dismiss Amerlie. I placed you in her custody for this 'adventure' but it appears you've overstepped the permission given you."

"I did not dismiss her, but I hardly think this is time to discuss this, a formal luncheon for the Emperor of Andirony who has come for a very formal ceremony that will make all of this irrelevant."

Max hissed at me, "Maybe I'll cancel the ceremony. I have that right!"

"It's not the ceremony that makes me the ruler of this duchy. It's the magic of the land, and I doubt you have the ability to stop it. In fact, by opening me to my full magic two months early, it granted me all the authority I need to rule this land."

Da announced rather coldly, "I'm afraid we must declare this luncheon finished. Thank you all for coming. I apologize that a family argument has caused me to terminate it now."

The guests slowly rose, bowed to the emperor and Da, looked askance at me, and left. The only remaining diners were Nenory, Chres, Jothro, Gueril, and Niku. Da started to say something to them when I raised my hand.

I turned to my backers. "I appreciate your support, but this is my fight."

Gueril replied, "We are family. We'll stay."

Max threw his arms above his head. "What do you mean you're family? How has all this happened?"

"I was adopted into the clan Ruthenian. When I made the forest the gypsies', I partially severed my connection with the land there. When they adopted me, the connection was fully restored."

"Tell me again why you gave land to the gypsies?" Max was growling again.

"I believe you heard me the first time. They were being chased out of my duchy, and they had no safe place to go. I won't stand for discrimination against these people in my duchy, but since I can't be everywhere, I provided them with a safe haven."

"They don't have a good reputation, you know," Max said.

"Have you ever met any?" Chres asked. "I've been with these men for the last few days and they're fine people."

Jothro added, "I was the one chasing them out of the duchy but my duchess has taught me how wrong that was and now I count them among my friends. She also saved my father's life, helping him to return to his old self. The woman he loves will now marry him because of what the duchess did."

"My, you have been busy, haven't you?" Max said snarkily.

Nenory stood from her seat. "She's been doing what a duchess should be doing and she's helped me enormously. Don't treat her like a child!"

"Thanks, everybody, but I still think this is among the emperor, the regent and me."

"I'm proud of what you've been doing, Peary," Da said. "To rebuild farms, to save innocent people, to heal one of your subjects; these are signs of greatness especially for it all to have happened within a few weeks. However, I wish you could've had more time to think about the consequences of your actions."

"Having traveled with the gypsies for several days, and having spent time with them, I made the decision that they were people I should protect when they were within my duchy. I saw the sneering and heard the lies told about them. I watched others spit upon them. That is not the behavior I will accept from my citizens. If I must lead by example, I will. And I will accept the repercussions, come what may. I did it because it was right. That will be the compelling force in my reign here; I will always choose rightness over politics. I gave something up to protect them, and they promptly gave it back. I'm whole, and I now have a very large family. I am who I am, and I won't apologize for it."

"What thrills me the most is you've won over your own supporters here," my da said gesturing around the table. "Jothro, you're Willoughby's son aren't you? It sounds as if you've grown up on this trip, and I'm inclined to agree that the ascension is now a mere formality." He stopped and turned to Max. "My liege, what do you think?"

"It appears I'm outnumbered here. The worst part is I owe both Robert and Peary a great debt of gratitude for their efforts in saving me from attack. What I see here is a family that is sticking together, due, in large measure, to your devotion to this young woman. She's extraordinary as I have reason to know myself. I was present during a part of her maturing, but it appears her time alone in her duchy has completed the process." He put his hands up in surrender. "I give in. Can we at least sit down and finish our meal, all at the same end of the table?"

Two footmen came forward and cleared several spaces around the head of the table, to make room for the five from farther down. Within moments we were all seated comfortably as a group of seven, Da sat next to Niku, who had been fairly silent throughout the luncheon. Max insisted he be flanked by the two new duchesses.

The remainder of the meal was spent with Da and Max getting a sense of this younger generation that would be taking over in due time. I was relieved it had settled down, and without being compelled to disclose the nature of my falling out with Amerlie. I was amused when Nenory told the whole table that she had demoted her mentor, too, but that she had the advantage of a wizard who could assist her as needed.

The next few days moved quickly as guests arrived, I was fitted for a special gown, and arguments ensued over which families got the plums of providing the pages. I decided to be difficult and told them I'd already chosen my pages and that they'd be available for the rehearsal the day before the ceremony.

I took my people to the Collegium one day, explaining as we walked that the issue was of great importance and could mean life or death for a young man. This was said for Chres's sake since he hadn't been aware of Niku's family tragedy.

Tom the gatekeeper was at the gate when we walked up. He looked at us suspiciously until Chres presented the letter, signed by the regent, authorizing us to meet with Professor Belvedere. Da had mentioned no titles when I told him how difficult it had been in the past to communicate with Tom. The letter didn't stop Tom from trying to figure out the purpose of our meeting. He finally let us go, after providing the worst instructions I'd heard for finding someone.

I remembered the route Belvedere and Mikal had taken the last time we'd been here and headed in that direction. We saw a few of the landmarks Tom had mentioned in his instructions. We came around a corner a little too quickly and ran into a group of students, including Mikal. He was happy to escort us to Professor Belvedere's office where he was sure the professor would be waiting.

"How can you be so sure?" I asked.

"Because I was supposed to be there about five minutes ago," he replied happily.

He knocked at the door, and we heard Belvedere call out, "You're late, Mikal, and you know what I think about—" He pulled the door open and saw me with Mikal and a group behind me.

"My lady, it's good to see you again. To what do I owe the honor of this visit? Not some demon problem again I hope?"

"No but it does involve a person as close to a demon as I ever hope to meet. At this point we just hope you can point us in the right direction, to someone who can help us."

"Come in, come in, I'm sure I can fit you all."

A large table with many chairs around it was in the center of the room and we all took a seat as I made the introductions. He commented on Nenory's resemblance to me, and Chres being my brother, but the gypsies fascinated him the most.

I explained the story regarding Luka, and those who didn't already know it were horrified. When I said we hoped to save Luka, Belvedere's brows knitted.

"I'm actually the one most interested in different forms of magic," he began, "so I would be one of those called to help. Marjoram might be interested, too—don't you think, Mikal? Could you go see if she can step in for a few minutes?"

Mikal was gone only a short time when he came back with a small older woman who was awkwardly bent due to bone disease. She was clearly in pain though being stoic about it. I watched her for a few moments and then *reached* out to straighten several pieces of connective tissue in her back that seemed to have been twisted in an injury sustained some time ago. It took only a few seconds to repair the damage, but I was sure to block the pain briefly while I manipulated parts of her body. As the ligaments settled into their proper channels, she sighed.

"Which of you is the one who just did something to my back? Whatever you did, thank you. Even if the relief is only temporary, I'm so grateful."

Belvedere introduced each of us to Marjoram, and I admitted attempting to fix what I could in her back. "I wouldn't want to give hope before confirming that I can help in some way, and once I'm in there, I just do what I can."

"Well, this will be a boon to the Collegium, a duchess who can heal!"

After I'd once more explained Luka's predicament, Marjoram exclaimed at the nature of the injury. "I'm most interested in the childhood cruelty that occurred as that piece of evidence that can support either side unless we find markers." At my questioning look, she explained, "Either his magic was being stolen before he could understand what was happening to him, or he is an inherently cruel young man and may have voluntarily provided his mother with his magic."

Niku spoke up. "My father is coming with the performing troupe because Luka is his son, and he wants to be here for the trial. He'll do anything he can for Luka. He'll know if there were other problems. I certainly don't remember them, but I was quite young."

Belvedere interjected, "There is a third possibility which is that he is naturally a little cruel but it was twisted and intensified by a lifetime of theft. Does he have much magic?"

I hadn't felt anything more that a sultry charisma from him, and Niku's contribution was not much better.

Gueril lifted his hand, indicating that he had something to add. "There were times when he tried to convince me to do something against my better judgment, and I'd feel him pushing against me, but not physically. There were times when he turned me because I wasn't expecting it, but after once or twice, I stayed on my guard around him. He could push people with something inside him."

"So he can coerce. That's helpful," Marjoram said. "One of the senses that is activated by the forced taking of magic is the ability to coerce another. It seems to be the sensitization process for coercion." She looked around at our puzzled faces and smiled. "Sorry, that was probably too professorial, using jargon without explaining my terms. The ability to coerce is an innate trait, which means you're born with it. It can't develop on its own. It needs to be triggered by a brutal attack of coercion, or a persistent source of regular coercion."

Jothro added, "The boy is subject to gypsy justice since it was gypsy law that was broken. They're being generous in letting us try for a cure. They should be here any day now, and I can try to get you both in to see Luka within a day or two."

After another few comments, we said our goodbyes, ready to head out. Before we went, I took Mikal aside to ask if he would be willing to be one of the pages in my ceremony. He was thrilled at the possibility.

We walked out of the Collegium and wandered the streets leading home. Occasionally I was recognized, and Nenory got a few false alarms, but we managed to easily slip away and it didn't hurt that Nenory and I were just two of a large party. We were also helped by Wilfie and his comrades who carefully watched over us.

When we returned to the castle, the watchtowers had reported that, late in the afternoon, a large group of gypsy caravans had settled about two leagues out of the city. We had time to ride out to them and be back for the formal dinner at nine o'clock. We'd raid the kitchens for cheese and bread to get us through until then.

Niku, Gueril, and Jothro were eager to go. I knew they'd all want to stay the night there, but Jothro at least had to come to the dinner, and it would be prudent to bring the gypsies too. Chres and Nenory seemed keen on the idea, so we headed directly to the stables. Wilfie and three of his cohorts insisted on coming along and the other two guards were prepared to brave the lions' den to inform Da and the emperor where we'd gone.

We were mounted in no time with all the grooms there to help us. We departed at a slow canter down the hill and reached the encampment in half an hour. We were surprised to see Da and Max had arrived before us and were sitting at the fire having tea with the elders.

Da smiled as we ran over to the fire having left our horses with Wilfie and his men. "Good, you got our message!"

"What message? We got back, heard the gypsies were here, and rode out immediately figuring we'd have time to get back for the dinner." I looked at Esmeralda and Djordji, trying to read their faces, but they showed nothing.

Max laughed, saying "The dinner has been canceled at my request so we could come out to meet the new family. They have kindly offered to feed us. We thought it an excellent idea. Come one and all, join the party!"

I slipped around to sit next to Esmeralda, who squeezed my hand and winked. The others found their own seats on the logs and log chairs that were placed around the fire. It was clear this wasn't the full clan, rather the performing members plus the elders. I looked around and saw the barred caravan, which held the two prisoners. It was rocking and a shrieking noise came from it but was muffled by the wind in the trees and the river flowing by the edge of the field.

Max peered at me and Esmeralda, then asked if there was a problem. I indicated the barred caravan to him, and he tilted his head to one side. I moved over to him and told him the story. I was careful not to disclose my theory of power versus justice although the role of strength in this tale caused him concern due to Montrade's misuse of magic.

"I gather you have a plan to try to help Luka, if not his mother," he said.

"We spent most of the day at the Collegium with two professors who are studying issues involving the victims of magical coercion. They say it depends on whether he showed signs of aggression before the coercion could have started, in which case he might just be a person without compassion or empathy. But if Luka's abuse of Niku started after his magic had awoken then his mother could have already been stealing it from him. The professors have tests that they can run they hope will help them though they still aren't sure of a treatment. They're working on it now."

We discussed the misuse of magic a little before dinner was announced. The meal was not as fancy as the dinner we'd eaten during the trading of our gifts, but it was tasty and satisfying until the disturbance.

As we sat down to relax after dinner with tea, we saw a bright light exploding in the direction of Springfield. It was followed several seconds later by a loud boom. Two more lights exploded, again followed by the booms. My father had stood up when the second set of explosions happened, and I heard Wilfie calling for the horses to be saddled.

"That's the sign of a problem at the castle. We must get back. There are too many important people in residence now," he said. The urgency of the situation was obvious and I quickly began gathering our possessions for departure.

Djordji and Esmeralda arose and said they'd accompany us; since gypsy magic was sufficiently different from mine and Nenory's they might be able to fill a gap. In a matter of moments we were riding toward Springfield with three imperial guards and five Winthrop guards. We galloped and then slowed to a trot, then galloped again, pushing the horses as hard as we dared.

It was a much shorter journey back to the castle than out to the gypsies, but it felt longer. I was desperate to reach my city; I could feel turmoil running through the earth. I got a sense it was something to do with Max, and then suddenly I knew exactly what was going on.

"The dauphin's arrived. In our absence he's trying to take over. Sylvester is fighting back, with Pietro, Alistair and Festino and most of the house and imperial guard. He brought soldiers. I can feel them on my land."

"Your mother could reach her enemies through the land." Da said. "Can you try?"

I tossed my reins to Gueril and settled deeper into my saddle. With my eyes closed I felt the enemy, and I realized I could send energy pulses into one foot and have it come back through the other, allowing me to identify the people whose hearts were with us and to *protect* them. I attacked the others. Many of those I attacked fell and didn't get up. Then I felt a strange magic, and immediately knew it was an enemy magician. I blocked his earth magic, then his air magic, and I got him. I burned the magic out of him with my Winthrop magic.

I heard my father calling, so I pulled out of my trance. We were at the base of the hill and about to start climbing toward the castle. Thanking Gueril for his help I took my reins back. Then I forced my horse to run faster up the road to the castle, the others streaming behind me. I fed the horse energy through his hooves, and he met my demands, climbing valiantly. I came around the last corner and saw men fighting at the gate. I jumped down, anchored my feet to the ground, feeling the power flow into me, and I roared as loudly as I could. It was percussive, knocking down only my land's enemies. My stalwart fighters took advantage of what I'd given them and defeated their foes.

As soon as the gates were clear, I strode through them, feeling as if I were expanding to ten or twenty feet high. I sent energy at any foe that stirred, loaned energy to my fighters who needed help, and cleared a path for my companions. I ordered them to stay behind me. I could now sense and focus on the various individuals battling, and there were two wizards fighting in my throne room. Examining the room more closely, I found the dauphin sitting on the monstrosity. Stupid man. I had a direct channel to that seat. I sent a flood of power through it to lift him twenty feet into the air, and I held him there as I walked as quickly as I could to the room.

I threw open the doors and stopped time. Samony was one of the wizards engaged in battle and he was taking a bit of a beating. I filled him with energy. The other wizard I didn't know and I slammed him with hostile energy. I then allowed time to run again and caught the dauphin as he fell. I swung him around, depositing him at Max's feet. I then walked to the monstrosity and sat.

This was my center of operation. From here, the situation throughout the castle became clear in my head. I felt Amerlie fighting in the dungeons, and yelled to Samony, who immediately ran to me.

"Amerlie is fighting in the dungeon. They are trying to release Henry and Briaint. Go help! I'll do what I can from here."

I reached out to the cell in which Henry was housed. Several of his allies were trying to break through the door. I sent strengthening power into the door's metal and wood, and it was whole again. I did the same for Briaint's door. I watched Amerlie who was rapidly weakening. I sent a surge of power into her, leaving a trickle flowing while I turned my attention elsewhere. My four young men had run farther into the castle and I followed them until I saw them join with Sylvester in protecting the kitchens where all the help were hiding from the fight.

Samony reached the dungeon and fought at Amerlie's side. The two of them had no difficulty in squelching that part of the assault. I stretched my senses throughout the castle and could find no active fighting. Then I settled down to find all the foreign individuals in the place. I found Alcorn lying on the ground about twenty yards from the throne room and sent Nenory to locate him.

Lowering my guard a little, I looked at the scene of the emperor, my father and the dauphin, who was sniveling. Then I heard Max say the words he'd hoped never to say.

"You have committed treason, as I'm sure you know. There is only one punishment for treason. I have no choice. Nor do I want one. I don't want to hear your silly excuses. I want you to take it like a man—like the man I thought you were. I will never understand why you thought you were ready to be emperor at just twenty years old."

The dauphin screamed, pointing at me, "She's old enough! If she is, so am I!"

"You little fool. Did you learn nothing from all the schooling I gave you? She has an incredible amount of magic, which she just used to defeat you *nearly* single-handedly. She pulled the land into the fight against you. She can rule because she has a level of magic you could never acquire. Compared to her, you're a two-year-old. She is the most ethical and honest person I know, and she allows herself to be driven, not by a desire for power, but by a desire to do the right thing. And her moral fiber is strong enough to show her what is right and just. Virtually every time I speak with her, she teaches me something new. And there you are, a disgrace. One of your sisters will be my heir after we're done with you and I'll make sure they compare favorably with this duchess."

A pair of soldiers entered to take the dauphin away. I heard him screaming "Father!" for a time after, though I came to realize that it had been burned into my head. My da looked at me but I motioned for him to comfort Max. The man was in serious pain, and understandably so. Nenory returned with a seriously shaken Alcorn. By that time, I was too tired to heal him any further. We all sat in the throne room, emotionally and physically exhausted.

Djordji and Esmeralda were the first to find us. Esmeralda tended to the emperor as Djordji came to me.

"You burned with fire and grace tonight, my duchess. Now you must rest. You will be recovered in the morning, and this will feel like a bad dream."

"Why did none of us suspect this? Why were we so naïve to believe the dauphin would come peacefully?"

"You see and recognize evil before you. You can't imagine it because it's so foreign to the way you think. You assume people approach you with good intent. This is the innocence in you we all love. We fear for you. Do you realize you didn't kill a single person tonight? The others did the killing for you. You provided the power and strength so they could. They already had the desire because their loyalty to you is intense. It is a great power you have." He laid his hands on my shoulders, and I felt warmth and love flow through me. I was in the arms of my family and it felt good. "Use it wisely."

Esmeralda brought everyone to sit near me. Her slight touch on my hand made me whole again. My da sat in the regent's chair next to the monstrosity and massaged my legs, which hung over the arms of our chairs.

I didn't notice when Samony and Amerlie walked into the room though the air suddenly felt thicker. I heard others whispering, so I opened my eyes.

Kneeling in front of me was Amerlie.

"I was wrong. I am so sorry. I knew you were destined for greatness but didn't recognize it when it appeared. Please forgive me. You saved my life tonight, and it gave me hope I could be by your side again. If you say no, I accept that. If you say yes, I will help you in any way I can, because I know whose moral compass we'll be following."

"You're welcome at my side, but never above me. And don't you dare start crying again. I've had enough of that for a lifetime." I must have sounded grumpy.

Esmeralda's laugh was a delight to hear.

The next day dawned clear and bright, and proved that Djordji had been right. The prior night felt like a bad dream.

Daisy entered with a pot of tea and muffins for me. As expected, I was ravenously hungry.

"Sylvester told me breakfast will be served in the large dining room on the second floor. He says it's cozier than the banquet hall, and will hold all those who became intimate friends last night. I guess you've added five and they're all magical."

She continued to chatter away and I found it comforting. The horror of the night before had become the subject of gossip, and that was a good way to deal with it, for the time being.

Alyssa had already chosen my dress for the day and the two women fussed over me as if I were a doll they liked to dress up. My hair was washed and flyaway, but they got it to cooperate using a clip. The dress was a little loose, and Alyssa proclaimed her shock at the weight I'd lost. They clucked like mother hens, but finally had me in acceptable shape. I kissed them each on the cheek and went out to Wilfie who was to lead me to breakfast. He looked a bit sore and stiff, so I placed my hand on his sleeve and pulled the aches from him. He smiled with relief, and off we went.

The early risers were in the dining room, which meant all the gypsies were there, as were Amerlie and Samony. Da came in moments after me, and kissed me on the forehead.

"You're sitting with me this morning. I won't have anyone bothering you about anything unimportant. And everything is unimportant until at least lunch today. We have cleaning up to do."

"I do have one thing I want to clear up this morning. I've asked Mikal to be one of my pages, and I want to ask Aishe to be the other one."

Djordji looked up. "What does a page have to do?"

"They carry in the coronet and the stole." Da's voice was mild.

"As I understand it, the emperor comes in first and goes up to stand next to the monstrosity, excuse me, the throne." They all laughed. "The pages follow, and I follow the pages. Max takes the coronet and puts it on me, then does the same with the stole. The pages step back a little and watch with all due solemnity. I state an oath to my people and my duchy, based on the furtherance of the goals of our empire. Then I sit and a few representatives of the nobility, the professions, and the tradespeople come up to take an oath for all in their class. Finally I rise and walk out followed by the pages, followed by the emperor, followed by those who took the oath, and then the general audience."

"It doesn't take too long, less than half an hour, and then we party for the rest of the day." Da smiled around the room.

"Aishe will love it. She loves to be on stage. I'll warn her not to break into song." Djordji laughed.

"They're great choices, darling, and it will really irritate the nobility, especially those with their snoots in the air. They won't support you anyway, so it's just as well." Da grinned.

Amerlie commented, "Peary will need to be politic with them for the first year or two, don't you think?"

"Not once word of what happened last night gets out!" Da laughed at that.

Then a teasing session began, with them all trying to outdo themselves with comments regarding my excessive response to a small rebellion. Everyone remarked on my manifesting myself as a twenty-foot-tall woman though my memory was hazy on that part.

Our light mood was interrupted when Sylvester arrived with a message for me from the Collegium. The professors were ready to meet Luka. We discussed the possibility of bringing Luka into the Collegium for the testing as it was unlikely Marjoram would be physically comfortable going to the encampment.

I asked Djordji if the camp planned on moving closer if we could find them a suitable place on the hill. Because the castle grounds were still being cleaned, and the various carriages taking up much space, Da called on Willery for assistance in finding a large enough area for the caravans somewhere on the hill.

"I know a place!" the young man pronounced before disappearing.

I drafted a reply to the Collegium, saying we planned to Luka to the city and we would let them know as soon as he was available.

"You're being so helpful with this problem," Djordji said.

"It'd be nice if we only lost one person in this mess," I replied.

When Max came in a little later, he looked as if he hadn't slept at all. The burden of his son's treason was weighing on him, and his greetings were subdued. He was not heartened when I told him an additional thought I'd had on the matter. "You realize Henry is in the same position as your son."

The dining room went quiet. Da's face drained of blood. Chres dropped his head and shook. Amerlie's face closed down, and she gave me a quick nod. The others shifted uncomfortably in their seats, refusing to look at me.

"You would kill your own brother?" Max asked.

"You would kill your own son," I replied. "I know all the arguments for and against this decision. If we add Briaint to the group, will we not cut off what remains of this monster? We don't have to rush this decision. Do a show trial, probably in Markerburg, and avenge the Duchess Madory at the same time."

That was enough to spark discussions of the politics of the decision, avoiding the treacherous waters of emotion. I realized we might not like having to do something; if we could make something useful out of it, such as avenging Madory, it wouldn't be a wholly bad thing.

After the meal finished, I spoke with Djordji and Esmeralda about heading back to the camp and packing up. I assured them Willery would have a space for them by the time they made it back to the hill. I arranged for them to have a guard because I wasn't convinced that my people had yet come to the same conclusion as I about the worthiness of gypsies.

Then I had to talk with Chres and Da. "I know you both have many years invested in Henry. To you he's a real person with some good moments, some bad moments—a history. You, like Max, have emotions entangled in your thoughts about him. I don't. I didn't even know he existed until a month or two ago. I can see him as a movable piece in a game, but I doubt if either of you can do the same, and I wouldn't you to. He's your son, your brother. He's *Henry*. But sooner or later, it would have occurred to someone trying to make waves that Henry was in the same position as the dauphin. Isn't it better to handle it now and not hold on to hope or expectation? Isn't it better to handle it in a way that leaves us untainted by his treason? Isn't it better to have it resolved now and get it behind us?" I begged them to understand what I had done though I suspected it would take them time to come to it.

Chres surprised me. "I thought it, too. I didn't dare mention it so close to your ascension. I do have good memories but they've been buried by the bad. We were happy together as kids. I don't like what he grew into, and you're a much better sister than he is a brother." We hugged, and Da joined us.

Max had been watching us and came over to speak. "I wish I

had my daughters here to console me as you have each other. That was a brilliant idea, Peary, and it solves so many issues. How are we going to get them to Markerburg?"

"The gypsies have a barred caravan that can be strengthened with magic. I'm sure they'll loan it to us. They have Luka and Gitana to deal with now. Once they're taken care of, the caravan will be empty and it can carry the three men, properly guarded. I'll have to speak with Amerlie and Samony to see if they can block Henry's magic for the trip. The dauphin has magic too. Does anyone know about Briaint?

Amerlie and Samony were called into the conference to discuss various ways to protect the prisoners. When it became clear they were able to handle this, I moved on.

Most of us were out of sorts the rest of that day. Between the decision about the conspirators and the upcoming examination of Luka, everyone was testy. I went to the throne room and, staring at the monstrosity, I wondered if I could alter it at all. I walked around it, examining each side to see what was needed to keep it stable. I removed pieces of it that offended me. Apparently I just needed to point at the offending piece, define it in my mind, and it disappeared.

I worked on changing the monstrosity quite happily for about an hour until it began to look like a regular chair. Of course, I left part of the design since it had to look like a throne. Sitting in it I realized it needed to be higher. I replaced some material in the base to lift it up. I puttered around it until it was comfortable and not an eyesore.

I heard someone laugh behind me. Da and Amerlie were watching me and whispering to each other.

"Why is it funny?" I was curious, not nasty.

"It always turns into that monstrosity when a duchess dies," Da said, walking toward me. "When the new duchess sits on it to receive the oaths of her people, it turns into the appropriate throne for her. It will be much fancier than what you've just designed." He pointed to various parts of the throne.

"You mean all this work I've put in this morning is for nothing."

"Yes, it'll return to the monstrosity the moment you leave the room. It will be the monstrosity through the ceremony, until you have the coronet and stole and are firmly seated. Then it will mold itself into the *right* throne for you." Da's eyes shone with unshed tears.

"I'm mad I wasted the time, but you've just made me so happy. The thought of this ugly thing for the rest of my life was scaring me! When I first came, the people were talking about how wonderful the throne was, and I thought they had to be crazy."

"We actually came looking for you for a reason," Da said. "Willery has found a place just a few hundred feet down the hill for the gypsies. Your friend Lord MacAlpine has an old field behind his house that he's kept open because he swears he'll have horses again at some point. They've started up the hill and should be in the field by midafternoon." Da went to sit in his seat.

Amerlie came farther into the room and took a chair near the front. The chairs were already in place for the ceremony, which was still two days away. I sat on the monstrosity that was, currently, a quite comfortable chair.

Amerlie cleared her throat. "We've been talking¬¬—"

"Who's we?"

"Samony, Nenory, your father, and I have been talking. Your father brought up something you said before we went on our adventure, that you were uncomfortable when he sent people out to do something you believed he could do. When we came home through Winthrop, you got the excitement of doing everything for yourself. You were able to do very important things, like saving the gypsies, curing a deathly ill man, and helping those wretched farmers to rebuild. This has helped your growth immeasurably and you have announced a wonderful way to rule your duchy."

"What Amerlie's getting at is you have to allow others to do part of the work. Last night you were magnificent and you shortened what looked to be a long and deadly battle. By taking over, you quickly brought it to a successful conclusion. You supported those acting for you by supplying energy to replenish their stores. You gave Amerlie a lifesaving boost. You were like a general moving his army around. That's your role. You can't help the doctors evaluating Luka. You can't manage the lives of those three young men. You can't keep the gypsies here forever. You have to delegate, and to let people live their lives."

Amerlie picked it up again. "People want to do things for you. They want to look for evidence you need, they want to help heal a young man, they want to be by your side when things get interesting. And they won't always be the ones you *want* by your side. You can't have favorites, and you can't snub people you don't like, unless they've done something wrong to you. There will be resistance to your desire to do what is right and just. Be prepared to be nice to these people. Many of them are well-intentioned if not very bright. These are your people and you must treat them all fairly."

"I can have favorites, I just can't show it." I wasn't going to let them tell me how to feel. The rest of what they'd said made sense, and the old duchesses in my head nodded in agreement.

"What happened last night was the end of my freedom of movement, wasn't it? I don't get to go on any more of those outings, do I?" I paused. "We'll see about that. There's still that seeing

Melalee had of the two of us in the woods when I have longer hair in the fall."

"Trust you to remember that!" Da laughed heartily.

"And I have a prophecy from Esmeralda, too."

"It's true, as do I." Amerlie looked at me closely. "What is yours?"

"I only know part of it consciously. She fed a lot of information into my subconscious. I expect I'll know what to do when the situation she saw come to pass. But the prophecy was for me, not my people, and I will keep it to myself for now."

Sylvester arrived to report lunch was ready in the small dining room. It was a small group today. We ate in harmony and then moved to the drawing room; small talk, if any, was the rule. We knew we were waiting for word from Luka's testing, and there was nothing we could do. The emperor hadn't joined us. He was out for a ride with Pietro and Alistair, as well as a small group of soldiers riding as guards.

As the light changed we got word, but it was inconclusive. Jothro brought it as the gypsies had returned to the camp with their families. He told us the work would continue in the morning.

"Was it just the two of them working?" I asked.

"It started that way but others came throughout the course of the afternoon as they seemed to learn something unexpected. Professor Belvedere sent a note."

I reached out eagerly for it. "He says he'll come by around 9 o'clock to tell us how far he got. Let's have a light supper here, so we can be ready for him."

The chatter at dinner was a little livelier than earlier, but only because we knew we would get real information shortly. All of us were clock-watching.

The appointed time arrived, and Sylvester brought the professor into the salon. He bowed to me, Nenory and Da. He shook everyone's hand and kissed Amerlie on the cheek. Then he sighed.

"He doesn't understand that there were witnesses. His reality is skewed. He thinks he will be believed over Niku because of his conviction that Niku is bad. Our only hope is if this break from reality is a construct his mind has created to deal with the trauma of coercion. If this is the real Luka, he can't be healed.

"Tomorrow, we'll bring in specialists on this level of trauma. They have ways to show if Luka's behavior is voluntary or learned. After that, we determine, if a learned behavior, how learned. There is another expert on whether a learned behavior is defensive or offensive. It could take all day. Only then will we know if he can be treated."

Nenory said, "The day after tomorrow is Peary's ascension. It would be terrible to learn he can't be cured before then."

"You will need Mikal for the rehearsal tomorrow? At what time?"

Da replied, "After lunch, probably around two or two thirty. Is he needed for your work?"

"No, but he learns more quickly by seeing rather than hearing or reading, and so it is a great learning experience for him. He's provided two comments that showed us a different way to try something and they were successful. I don't expect that to happen tomorrow as it's beyond his theoretical level."

"He told me he wanted to do history; has he changed his goal?" I recalled wanting him to learn history.

"I hope that's a passing fancy, as his skills are much more analytical than that."

"Ah, but he told me what he wanted to do was to use historical texts to find evidence of spells we've lost that might be useful. That's plenty analytical."

"My lady, he's told you more in the few days he's spent with you than in the years I've known him."

Everyone in the room laughed at that. Amerlie and Da were nodding at each other, and Nenory grinned at me.

"I gather this is one of my lady's better-known traits!" He got many nods of agreement.

80

The next morning was busy with food making, dress alterations, flower choices, seating preferences, and hundreds of other little details that I had to approve before lunchtime. Most of the time I sat in my drawing room with Da, Amerlie, Chres, Nenory and Samony. Every so often messengers from every group working on the ceremony would come by with a question. They all helped when I had no idea what a messenger was talking about. The silly knowledge spell Amerlie had cast on me back near the valley hadn't yet proven to be useful in preparing for the ascension ceremony. Somewhere in the last few days, it appeared the word "ascension" had acquired a capital letter in everyone's speech. The slight emphasis turned it into an event.

When we weren't answering messengers' questions, we played a word game Chres and our father had developed when my brother was young. It had been created to improve Chres's vocabulary but quickly changed into a game of skill and patience. The first player said a single word in everyday usage. The next player would have to say a single word that began with the last letter of the prior word, and it had to be related in subject matter to the prior word. Because words can have many meanings and usages, the subject matter could change very quickly with one player, so all players had to stay alert.

Chres started with lily.

Da said yarrow.

Nenory said willow.

Samony said watermelon.

Amerlie said nettles.

I said sting.

I have no idea how long we played, probably ten times through, and we covered so many subjects that we ended back at flowers. Apparently the rule was returning to the original subject was the end of the game. We started again and played until Mikal arrived.

We all walked downstairs to the throne room where Max had already settled in. Aishe came moments later, accompanied by Djordji. I introduced the two pages and hugged them both.

Da took on the role of director of our pageant as he and Max had both been present at the last ascension but Max had been an actor in the play. Da had a difficult time calling us to order as I was talking with Djordji, and Max was flirting with Nenory and Aishe. Mikal was examining the monstrosity. Finally he got us to settle down.

"The first issue is how slowly to walk. It's supposed to be slow and formal. Last time, Max, you brought the moving foot beside the standing foot and paused before you took the next step. Can you show them?"

That was the overly detailed level at which he was directing. I ignored the first part because he was trying to get the pages to walk at the same pace as Max, but they were quite a bit shorter than he was. They argued over it for a quarter of an hour before they did the second attempt. I had to go on that attempt because they finally got it right. I had no difficulty getting my speed right.

Then Max stage-managed again, and Da humored him for a few minutes before the emperor backed down. While they were talking, Mikal wandered off and was again looking at my throne. I excused myself from Djordji and went to see what was so interesting to Mikal.

"This is an ancient piece of magic," he told me.

"Yeah, it was made for one of my very far-back-ancestors." Who at the time was telling me all about it in my head. "She was the first to be magically placed on the throne here."

"Is that just a myth?"

"Not exactly. I can't tell you how I know but I do know."

"Because this magic attunes itself to the rightful heir."

"Yeah, it will change when I sit on it tomorrow with the coronet and the stole, and become the throne that's right for me. It's supposedly when I come into my magic, but I did that a month or two ago."

"We have no idea how to do this magic now. This is the sort of thing I want to study."

"I can cut off a piece and give it to you, but it's supposed to go back to this shape when I walk out the door. You'll have to go out before me, and then we'll see if it stays magic or disappears back inside or what. We can try now, if you want. They won't stop arguing for a while."

He agreed, and I went to the monstrosity and pulled off a piece that fit the palm of my hand. I handed it to Mikal, and it disappeared. He raised an eyebrow at that. I took another piece and walked out the door with Mikal beside me. It sat in my hand until I tried to pass it to Mikal when it disappeared again.

Da yelled for us to get back inside. "What are you two up to? Get back in here!"

"I'm trying to give Mikal a piece of the throne so he can figure out how they did this so many years ago."

"And I bet it disappeared as soon as he touched it. You think you're the first to try it? Your grandmother told us all about it. She learned about it from her grandmother."

There were three more run-throughs of the ceremony before we got it right. We were getting ready to stop and go find tea, when Belvedere appeared in the door, followed by Luka. The room became so quiet I could hear the clock ticking forty feet away.

Then Luka stepped forward, "Hi, everybody. My duchess, and you must be the regent, sir. Oh, and the emperor." He knelt to Max.

I watched and wondered if he was faking.

His face was strangely blank, and there was little energy in anything he did. What little speech I heard was arrhythmic, unmelodic, halting. There was none of the fire in him that was present in most gypsies. I looked at Aishe and the look of horror on her face jolted me.

"Belvedere, what's happened to him?" I was breathless.

"We pushed the healing too far. There was so much aggression in him. We found him innocent of initial bad intent, and tried to bring the aggression down. His language was foul, and his affect was so brutal. Marjoram and I took it down so slowly, and we had to go so deep. We would stop and test him. He'd lash out physically. We went a little further and it was too far. We've damaged him and we don't know how to fix him." Belvedere sounded desperate.

Aishe went to Luka and put her arms around him. He looked down at her, and the most childlike smile appeared on his face.

"Aishe, you're so pretty now. Why are you here? Will you sing for me?"

She nodded and began to sing a lullaby I'd heard in the encampment a week and more earlier. Luka lay down on the floor, curled up, and fell asleep. Tears were pouring down my cheeks, and Aishe's too, when the song died out.

Belvedere spoke again, "If you will leave him with us, we'll try to rebuild a little of what we took out. It may not be possible but—"

"No! I'll take him to my people and we'll heal him in our own way. You will not touch him again. Peary, can we get him home somehow?" She was sobbing now, and all I could do was hold her. I looked up at my da. He nodded and pulled the rope.

Sylvester came, looked, and said, "The carriage, sir?"

"I think so."

I rode with them to Lord MacAlpine's field. We were greeted by Borak, Djordji, and Esmeralda. She had sensed us coming and had gathered the others. The footmen helped us get poor Luka out of the carriage, and Borak grabbed him. Aishe ran to her father and I stood there trying not to cry.

"What have you done to my boy?" Borak wailed.

Niku had seen his father coming and he'd arrived in time to hear his father. He joined him in holding Luka, running his hand over Luka's curls, whispering in his ear.

"Niku? You're my big brother, aren't you?"

"And you're my little brother, Luka. I'll take care of you."

Esmeralda and I held each other, grief pouring from us both. I muttered, "He was innocent when it started, but it was too deep."

"He was three years old when she started." Esmeralda said. "She will pay. They returned him to us innocent once again. He grew up once. He'll do so again."

"I'm so sorry. I wanted to save him. I thought they could help."

Borak looked at me. "You are my sister. You did what you could. I still have my son. You've given me enough to work with. You've saved my older son for me too. My two sons will figure this out and my wife will help."

"If I can do anything. Please let me know." I couldn't help the sob that punctuated the sentence.

Esmeralda nudged me toward the carriage and climbed in with me. "You have a big day tomorrow. We must go and make sure you don't have crying eyes in the morning."

Djordji smiled a little crookedly and waved.

81

It was still light when we got back to the castle. Esmeralda got out first and then helped me out. I had cried the whole way back. Wilfie came down to help me up the stairs to the door, and another guard offered his arm to Esmeralda. Da ran to meet me. He held me. The tears didn't stop.

He led me to my suite. My family waited inside, as did Amerlie. Samony wasn't there. Esmeralda and I sat side by side on the couch, clasping each other's hand. We were given tea, that all-healing drink. Nenory came and sat on my other side, putting her arm around my shoulder.

"You could be sisters," Esmeralda said.

Nenory explained our complicated family background and the multiple ways in which we were closely related. She turned it into an absurd story, and I found myself laughing a little through my tears.

Esmeralda told funny gypsy stories about unknown relationships that were made when two traveling groups came together for a period. When the third group arrived and saw the liaisons that occurred, it was a time for merriment as they sorted out who was related to whom.

Chres suddenly stated, "You wanted to help him so much because you couldn't help Henry."

It made us all wonder, but I'm not sure we were all wondering the same thing. Da was shocked. Amerlie was sure I knew Luka much better than Henry, and I had a crush on him. Nenory was sure I felt guilty because I thought we knew everything and could fix anything. Esmeralda stopped them all by saying, "He was her brother."

"Thank you everybody, and it might have been a little of all of that. I liked him when he wasn't playing his games with Niku. He was funny, full of himself, and charming. He seemed to go through a complete transformation when he saw Niku. I didn't like that person. I had just really hoped they could take out the part that hated Niku and leave the rest. And Niku is so good he will now care for his tormentor. That makes me cry." I began to cry again.

"Niku still remembers how close they were before the damage

was done. He has always hoped that Luka would come back to him. Now he has." Esmeralda smiled at me. "It may be the only way the two of them can live with each other."

"But think of poor Luminista. She'll care for the boy who hurt her son, the son of the woman who nearly killed her and certainly deprived her of the one she loves for so many years." I know I sounded bitter.

"I suspect Niku and Luka will move into the fancy caravan, and Borak will rebuild Luminista's to be even prettier. Niku will bring his brother over for an occasional meal or social hour, and Luminista won't be put out by it at all. She'll have Borak as she should have all these years."

Da asked, "Will you try to heal Luka?"

"We'll care for him as we have for other damaged children. Sometimes they can learn, sometimes they can't. It doesn't matter. They're ours and we love them. Maybe that's enough for them. It certainly is for us."

82

The morning of the ascension is sunny and warm. Daisy rouses me for a bath and a hair washing. New unmentionables are laid out for me. Sitting in my robe, I eat the light breakfast they have sent up. Tradition says I am not to be seen by any but my servants and guards before I enter the throne room at ten in the morning. It's supposed to be a time of quiet reflection, putting away my youth and coming into my power.

I put away my youth last night after experiencing the tremendous loss of the Luka I knew. I came into my power two months earlier during a time of great conspiracy. This is not in any way a normal ascension. I was not raised traditionally, nor was I awakened as I should have been by sitting on the throne. My ideas of how to govern were learned in the middle of a war and on the long trek home.

Some of this might have happened without the battles. I was chosen in a way by being given access to the great women who went before me; I have within me greater teachers than any who have gone before, and I will accept whatever help they can provide. It will be a shame if the only reason for giving me these great gifts was to save the emperor. To have had my shining moment before I ever ascended would be a sorry epitaph. I must accept what Esmeralda told me. I have great power and will not always use it well.

I cannot imagine a few of her other predictions; to be married and have children seems so far beyond me now. She said much that I did not consciously understand, with signposts I will know. And it'll be interesting to know if I'll recognize the man with a lost eye and mind.

I know a man with a lost mind. Will he lose an eye?

Now Daisy and Alyssa come and get me for it's time to dress. They pull out the magnificent gown, layers of lace, silk and cotton so I feel I'm floating. It weighs almost nothing and the heat of the day will not stifle me. Once I'm in the dress, they do my hair and light make-up. My hair, now long, is piled in swooping curls on top of my head. I don't know how they make them stay. I believe it's a magic

I'm not meant to know. The final bit of face powder is brushed, and I am swirled around to see the wonder they've made of me.

I'm no longer the wild girl who came out of a valley less than three months ago. I have lived a lifetime and more in those three months. Mam, sweet Mam, would not recognize her Peary in this confection.

Daisy and Alyssa lead me to the door, awestruck by their work. They open the door to reveal Wilfie, who bows as he has never bowed before. I raise him and put my hand on his arm. He leads me down the hall to the stairs that will end across the hall from the throne room. The sound of many people talking softly wafts up through the stairwell. As we reach the final landing, Aishe enters the throne room. Mikal stands at the door, counting on his fingers. Then he, too, moves.

Wilfie lets go of my arm, and gently pushes me to the door. I enter, oblivious now to any noises the audience may make. I slowly pace toward the monstrosity, and turn before it to face my people. I am there, but not there, until I feel the coronet being nestled into my curls, and the stole placed over my shoulders. I turn, making my curtsey to the emperor. I raise my hands and he takes them within his. I speak the oath that was spoken by my mother and grandmother before me, and he helps me onto my throne, which I find to be quite comfortable.

From my throne, I tell my people that my sole concern now is to help them live comfortable and meaningful lives free of want and care. That I devote myself to my land and people as my role commands. That I will rule and judge as fairly as I may and that they can bring disputes before me on days and times to be established in due course. That they have the right to petition me, if my attention seems to wander, or there is a problem I don't see.

I lean back in my lovely throne and await my people.

The lords and ladies come first. They must personally swear, I've decided. It's a break with tradition, but I trust my professionals and tradespeople more than I trust people of privilege. First Da, then Chres, and then the Lord of Sutherland, my friend MacAlpine. After him, I do not know them, but I study their faces as they swear. It seems I can read those who are dishonest in their oaths. I make a small sign with each dishonest one, and note Sylvester making a list. The ceremony is longer and drearier for my insistence, but it may be of use in the future. Finally they're done. They return to their seats scrupulously silent.

A lone man comes forward. He is, I've been told, a doctor from the city. He has been chosen to give the oath for all the professionals. He's nervous, with sweat on his upper lip and a compulsive licking of his lips. I give him a small smile and he smiles back. He gives his oath in a strong and lyrical voice as if he means every word. I smile again; he rises and returns to his seat.

The next to come before me must be a blacksmith. He's huge, and his muscles seem likely to tear his jacket off his back. When he kneels before me we are eye-to-eye even though I'm considered tall. I take his rough hands in mine and he says the words for all the tradespeople in town in a gruff and scratchy voice that's more used to a smoky hot room than the rarefied heights of the hill and castle. I kiss his hands and let him go.

I believe it's time to rise, but there is one more delegation in front of me; Djordji comes to stand before me. He does not kneel to the audience's horror. Instead he speaks.

"As the representative of the independent nation of Rom, I swear my people will live in peace with your people, that we will honor all transactions between us, that we will not take what is not ours, nor harm the goods and property of your people. We are here to dance and sing and otherwise amuse you, and we will stay as long as you allow." He bows and walks out.

I look around briefly to ensure there is no further interruption in the schedule. Sylvester winks at me. I rise, take one look at my glorious throne, a golden chair with a high, fan-like back and lions carved in the arms, and walk from the room. Wilfie greets me and takes me back to the landing. Mikal is next, followed by Aishe who is swooped up by her father, laughing.

Max, Da, and Chres come out next, and come up the stairs to stand with me. Nenory is next and she too joins me. The others are drawn away to the great ballroom where the festivities are about to start. MacAlpine waves at me and says loudly, "Best throne I've seen!" I giggle. So does Nenory. And Chres. With two throat clearings that become giggles, we all laugh.

About the Author

bh alsop is a retired lawyer who started writing fiction in retirement. Following the advice of many famous authors who have given their thoughts about how much to write before one considers oneself an author, she wrote a book and two sequels, which are not available to anyone (though they may be rewritten). This is her first story for publication, although she is working on two more that take place in Andirony.

You can find her blog at www.bhalsop.com
You can find her on Facebook at
https://www.facebook.com/bhalsopauthor
Her twitter handle is @barbals